FORGOTTEN: LUCA

THE FOUR, BOOK 1

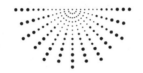

SLOANE KENNEDY

CONTENTS

Cover Image: © innervision

Cover Design: © Cate Ashwood Designs

Copyediting by Courtney Bassett

ISBN:
9781086247800

AUTHOR NOTE

While Forgotten is the start of a new series, it is closely related to my Protectors series, so for those who would like to read them in order, you can start with book 1 in The Protectors.

However, it is not necessary to read that series in order to enjoy this one.

TRIGGER WARNING

Includes references to sexual assault of a minor and drug use

PROLOGUE

LUCA

+4

"Yeah, he's fine, Aleks. We'll probably be talking long into the night, but I'll have Remy check in with you tomorrow for sure."

I didn't know what to make of the fact that the young man who stepped into the darkened apartment was talking about himself in the third person, but part of me didn't care as I drank in the sight of him. There was a light on just above him, but it was only enough to make out a few of his features.

But it didn't matter because everything about him was stamped into the deepest recesses of my brain.

Billy.

No, not *Billy*.

Remy.

I'd known him only as Billy the first time I'd met him when he'd been a kid. That moment was also etched into my mind, but for very different reasons. And it seemed like it wasn't just my brain that couldn't rid itself of every second of that dark day when I'd done something, *become somebody*, I never would have dreamed possible.

Every cell in my body remembered that day.

The smells.

The sounds.

The feel of the terrified, crying boy who'd had to have the strength of an adult to deal with what I'd had to do to him to keep us both breathing.

They would have left him *alone, you cowardly piece of shit.*

The voice in my head was ugly and cold, but I knew it was true.

Billy... no, Remy, wouldn't have been punished for what had happened. He'd been too valuable to them.

I would've been the one who wouldn't have walked out of that house alive.

The kid had saved my ass by playing along with everything I'd told him to do.

And I'd fucking left him there.

"Yeah, Aleks, here's Remy. It was nice to meet you, finally, even if it was just over the phone," Remy said. He had a messenger bag strapped across his midsection and sitting on one hip. I could see his left hand fisted on top of the cheap-looking material. His right hand was holding the phone against his ear. He pulled the phone away from his face for a moment as if he were actually going to hand it to someone. I watched as he drew in a deep breath, then put the phone back to his ear.

"Satisfied?" he asked with what probably was supposed to have been a humorous drawl, but he didn't smile. The voice he used was the same one I'd heard earlier in the day right before he'd slammed his fist into my jaw.

His *natural* voice.

"Yeah, Joe's great," Remy said.

I knew he was talking to Aleks Silva, my brother's boyfriend. What I didn't understand was why he had pretended to be someone else... *Joe.*

Who the fuck was Joe?

I actually felt jealousy curl through my belly, and that made me want to throw up.

Because no way in hell could I or should I be attracted to this young man.

Not after what I'd done to him.

"Yeah, I'm just going to stay with Joe for a few days... until he's sure I'll be okay on my own," Remy said, his voice a strange mix of confidence and certainty that, again, didn't match his body language. I willed him to turn completely around so I could see his face full-on.

I knew I should probably say something to make my presence known, but I needed these moments to take in everything about him. I'd already been through his apartment... *after* I'd broken into it.

And breaking in was exactly what I'd done—and it had taken a hell of a long time, considering the young man had four different locks on his door. Thankfully, he lived in a small building that didn't have a lot going on so late in the evening.

"I'll call you when I'm back in town," Remy said, clearly lying, since we *were* in town... downtown Seattle, to be exact.

I leaned back in the chair I was sitting in. It wasn't particularly comfortable, but from looking around Remy's apartment when I'd first managed to get into it, I'd already determined Remy seemed to prefer function to fashion or comfort. His furniture was the kind you could get from any cheap furniture store, and while not exactly new, it hadn't seemed like thrift-store used, either. His bedroom had just a mattress and a dresser in it, and his small kitchen sported only the basic appliances and a few pots and pans. His refrigerator was mostly empty.

Which might explain why Remy was so skinny.

"Yeah, I'll tell him," Remy remarked as he said his goodbyes to Aleks. From the expression on Remy's face, I could tell it pained him to lie to his friend.

So why was he doing it?

You know why.

I actually shook my head before I caught myself.

No, I refused to believe that. From the information I'd managed to pull together in the last few hours, Remy had been living a quiet, comfortable existence in the two years since he'd moved to Seattle from Chicago. He had a good job at a local security firm and from what I'd seen this afternoon, he was part of a large group of men and women who considered themselves family, despite so few of them actually sharing any blood.

I dismissed the fear that seeing me had somehow set him back. It was just another layer of guilt I wasn't prepared to deal with.

But I also knew why I was really here.

It wasn't to apologize to him for what I'd done, because there was no way to apologize for something like that.

I'd destroyed his life.

My brother, Vaughn, had tried to convince me otherwise, but I knew the truth. I'd promised to save him, and I hadn't done it. I'd chosen another child to save instead of him.

And I'd ended up destroying them both.

I refused to let my mind shift to my son, Gio, because I just wasn't capable of dealing with that right now.

I couldn't even deal with the fact that Remy was Billy and that the boy I'd thought I'd never see again was standing right in front of me.

He'd been around thirteen or fourteen when I'd last seen him. The information I'd managed to have my private investigator pull together on Remy in the last few hours had been sketchy at best, but one thing was clear.

He'd never gotten to go home.

I only knew that because Remy's identity on paper had begun only two years ago. He'd been issued a new Social Security number and there'd been no mention of any kind of previous history in his records. His credit and employment history were only two years old, and there was nothing about parents or family in any of the little bit of a paper trail my investigator had managed to find. Normally, I'd have any one of my brothers do that kind of research, but I definitely hadn't wanted to explain to King, Con, or Lex anything about Remy and why I was trying to dig up information on him.

Vaughn was the only one who knew what I'd done to Remy, aka Billy, eight years earlier when I'd entered a world I hadn't fully understood… one in which kids were sold and traded for sex.

Remy had been one of those kids.

My son, Gio, had been too.

I'd been trying to find Gio when I'd met Remy. I'd thought myself so lucky to have managed to get access to the sex trafficking ring that had stolen my child from me, but when I'd been led into an old farmhouse several hours west of Chicago, I'd known it wouldn't be so simple to find my son and bring him home.

But I'd been desperate, and I'd understood that my only chance of finding Gio had meant playing the game. Only, I hadn't understood the price I'd have to pay until I'd walked into a dirty, dark, nearly empty room with a single bed in it.

I also hadn't understood that *I* wasn't the only one who'd have to pay a price.

After hanging up, Remy merely dropped the phone to the floor. The entryway to the apartment was carpeted, so it barely made a sound. I could see the young man was agitated.

Really agitated.

He was shaking with whatever emotion he was dealing with.

I almost laughed at that... like it was a question or something. Like I didn't know *exactly* what the fuck he was dealing with.

He was dealing with having run into the man who'd promised to save him but had left him to his fate.

Do you know how long I fucking waited for you to come back for me?

I must have made a sound as I remembered the pain in his voice when he'd asked me that very question this afternoon because Remy froze, then turned to look in my general direction. The section of the apartment I was sitting in was dark, but his eyes landed right on me.

I expected him to say something or at least turn on the lights for the rest of the apartment so he could see me, but he didn't. Instead, he looked at the wall in front of him, then slowly eased the messenger bag off and dropped it to the floor next to his phone.

"You're late," he said softly. "By about eight years." He leaned against the door so he was still facing the wall. His voice sounded resigned and all the agitation just fell away until there was nothing. He pulled in a breath and said, "Actually, eight years, four months—"

"—three days, six hours, and thirteen minutes," I finished for him.

He glanced at me in surprise for the briefest of moments, then the emotion slipped away.

"Who's Joe?" I asked.

Remy let out a soft laugh, then turned so he was facing me. He reached out with his right hand to flip on the lights. "What?" he asked dryly, his lips pulling into something of an amused grin. But it wasn't a natural one. "You worried I'm not quite right up here?" he asked as he pointed to his head.

The reference to his mental health hit a little too close to home considering what my son was currently going through, but I managed not to react. Although Gio had been rescued from the man who'd hurt him for so many years, my child wasn't okay.

Not physically.

And most certainly not mentally.

In fact, he was so far gone I couldn't even conceive of the fact that he was now even further out of my reach than he'd been when he was missing.

"Don't worry yourself about it," Remy said, the smile fading away. "They turned me into a junkie, not a psycho."

I knew who "they" were.

The men who'd taken him and forced him into a life no child should ever have to even know about, let alone face.

The confirmation that he was indeed an addict made something seize in my chest. My PI had found evidence that Remy had been enrolled in a methadone program when he'd arrived in Seattle two years earlier, but I'd wanted to believe that meant his life had gotten...

What, Luca? Better? How the fuck does life get better after something like that?

I didn't have an answer for the question.

"So Joe is your sponsor," I said as I stood. I saw Remy tense up slightly, but otherwise he didn't react.

"Was," Remy corrected. "He OD'd six months ago." Remy crossed his arms. "He'd been sober twelve years. Then his wife left him and he went in search of his old friend... they say it doesn't take much to have you wanting to reach for that needle," he added casually.

Like it was all some foregone conclusion.

"Could be something as simple as a smell that reminds you of the room you used to get high in... or someone who looks like your dealer... or something from your past shows up to remind you how fucked up the world really is."

I ignored the not-so-subtle message.

"And the voice?" I asked. "*Joe's* voice?"

Remy actually looked guilty for a moment. "Aleks would come over here if he knew I was by myself."

"They were already here," I said as I motioned to the door behind him. "I was half expecting my brother to break the damn thing down, with the way Aleks was calling your name."

I didn't tell him that I also figured the hotel I was staying at probably would have been Aleks and Vaughn's next stop after Remy's apartment. My brother had messaged and called me multiple times, but I'd ignored his efforts to reach out to me.

I began walking toward Remy. With every step I took, he got more tense.

Other than being a little too thin, he was a beautiful man, and I didn't recognize any of the child he'd been when I'd first met him. His hair was a lush brown that had lighter streaks running through it. It was haphazardly styled, like he was the kind of person who ran his fingers through the silky-looking locks a lot and didn't realize it. His eyes were a deep blue color and he had full eyebrows, a straight nose, and a square jaw with just a hint of stubble on it. But it was his mouth that I was having the hardest time keeping my gaze off of.

His lips were a soft shade of pink and there was no other way to describe them than totally kissable.

I lifted my eyes and saw that Remy was watching me with what could only be called caution.

He'd undoubtedly noticed me checking him out.

"Nice trick with the voice," I said. "If I hadn't been looking at you, I definitely would have been fooled."

"I'm good at tricks," Remy said, his hard eyes pinning mine. My

7

confusion must have shown because he tilted his head at me. "Oh, so he didn't tell you," Remy said softly.

I'd closed the distance between Remy and myself by at least half, but something in the way he said those last words had me coming to a stop. None of this encounter was happening how I'd envisioned it. I'd just wanted the chance to make sure Remy was okay and try to explain why I'd done what I'd done eight years earlier. Maybe we could…

What?

I didn't have an answer for myself. Well, I did, but they were all selfish ones.

Maybe he'll forgive me and I can stop hearing his sobs in my head every time I close my eyes.

Maybe he'll say he's okay and there was nothing I could have done differently.

Maybe he'll tell me he's happy and I can finally fucking breathe again.

Remy kept moving toward me, his eyes never leaving my face. I expected him to stop long before he reached me, but he didn't. He didn't stop until his body was practically brushing mine. His right hand came up to stroke down my chest and my cock instantly responded. I'd already felt like the lowest form of life on the planet for the fact that I'd been half-hard since he'd walked into the apartment, but now I just wanted to curl up into a ball of shame because I couldn't control my reaction to his nearness.

And my entire life was about control.

"Do you know what they do to you when you don't play by the rules, Luca?" Remy asked softly, almost seductively as he skimmed his hand down my chest. I told myself to step back, but I couldn't move. I knew how fucked up all this really was, but I just couldn't move. My body was homed in on his touch, but my mind was focused on his voice and his words, and I knew whatever was coming would just make everything worse.

But fuck if I didn't deserve worse.

So much worse.

My suffering was a drop in the bucket compared to his.

"They let the pimps have you because you're too much trouble for the high-paying clients," Remy said quietly. His fingers touched my dick through my dress pants, but my body was thankfully catching up to my mind and my flesh wasn't responding. But unfortunately, my cock wasn't deflating fast enough, so to Remy it probably looked like the whole thing was turning me on.

Which just made me more of a sick fuck in his eyes than I already was.

I let his words wrap around my mind as I accepted the truth of what he was telling me.

"I'm sor—"

The fingers of Remy's left hand quickly closed over my mouth to silence me. His touch was gentle, but his eyes were full of bitter, brittle anger.

"You owe me this," he whispered. I nodded because I understood what he was saying, and he was right.

The least I could do was listen to what my actions had done to him.

"They first took me when I was eleven. I lost track of how many guys fucked me, but I never forgot the one who *didn't*," Remy said softly. "Even after they sold me to a pimp who shot me up with heroin right before he 'tested the merchandise' for himself, I couldn't stop thinking about the promise that help was coming... that *someone* was finally going to come for me. All I could think about was the gentle voice that had told me about the beach and dolphins and the promise that he'd take me to see them someday."

Remy dropped his hand from my mouth. My heart was pounding against my chest and my throat felt so tight I was sure I wouldn't be able to take even one more breath. I remembered all those things I'd said to him as if it'd been days ago, not years.

"I wish you really *had* fucked me in that room that day, Luca," he said, his voice husky with unshed tears. "It would have been kinder."

I nodded because I knew he was right. I dropped my gaze. When Remy reached for my hand and pulled it to him, I let him. His fingers nudged mine open. Then he was putting something in my palm before he covered my hand with his.

"It's my turn to forget about you," Remy bit out, his voice incredibly even. "Take this with you when you go." He pulled his hand back slightly to reveal a plastic baggie sitting in the middle of my palm. The bag had a small, black rock in it.

But I knew it was no rock.

"You're not worth losing two years of sobriety," he whispered as he closed my hand so it was fisted around the baggie. Then he was walking past me and I heard a door snick closed from somewhere behind me.

His bedroom door, probably.

Or bathroom.

It didn't matter.

It also didn't matter that he was wrong about one thing.

I'd never forgotten him.

And I knew now, more than ever, I probably never would.

I deserved no less.

CHAPTER ONE

REMY

†4

The whole thing was so ridiculous I just wanted to laugh.

Or cry.

Well, okay, maybe not the crying thing because I'd learned a long time ago that tears never got you anywhere. If anything, they just gave people more power over you. The *really* sick fucks knew how to use your tears against you. They were in it more for the mind fuck than the actual fucking. The *regular* sick fucks usually liked a little bit of fight… enough to get them more worked up and nothing more. But they didn't really want to work for it, especially not having paid top dollar for what was supposed to be a sure thing. You had to walk a thin line with those guys because they tended to react to too much fight with their fists, and if there wasn't someone around to stop them from beating on their valuable property, said property might not walk away from the encounter at all.

I'd learned that the hard way.

I'd learned a lot of things the hard way.

So crying was out.

Okay, yeah, laughing was out too because I only did that when I had to fool someone into believing I was the *well-on-the-path-to-recovery* Remy.

And the dick who was probably still standing in my living room didn't really count as someone. He was nothing more than a ghost from my former life... he was one of those hard-learned lessons that'd left a deeper scar than the ones I carried over much of my body.

I'll come back for you, Billy. I promise, I'll come back.

Cold sweat broke out over my skin as one violent tremor after another ripped through me. I wanted to believe it was my body's endless craving for that fleeting high I'd gone seeking earlier tonight, but I knew better. The reality was that what the man in the next room had given me had been more all-consuming than any substance my captors and my pimp—and later myself—had used to extinguish the burning need to fight back.

My encounter with him today had been the ultimate mind fuck, just like it'd been eight years ago. Only I was no longer the stupid kid who believed in shit like hope.

I closed my eyes and tried to slow my breathing as I let my back slide down the smooth wood of my bedroom door. I knew I needed to reach up and flip the lock above the knob, but I was afraid to release the hold I had on myself. Besides, Luca had already proven that what I'd considered decent quality tumbler pin locks weren't going to keep him out. The only weapon against mind-fucking was mind-fucking. I might not have understood that when I'd been fourteen and he'd promised me things he'd had no intention of delivering on, but I'd had plenty of time to practice the concept.

Too bad I hadn't remembered that fact when I'd needed it most.

Like when Luca had eyed me up and down like I was some kind of tasty treat. While I'd been drowning in recognition even before Aleks had introduced me to the man, Luca hadn't suffered from the same problem. At most, he'd seen something in me that might have been vaguely familiar but nothing more.

It'd been the perfect opportunity for me to escape the entire encounter with no one being the wiser. If I'd just brushed off any kind of attempt at polite conversation after the introductions, my best friend and his boyfriend would have briefly wondered about my odd reaction before forgetting about it entirely, and Luca might have passed the whole thing off as me being shy or quirky.

But instead of swallowing the realization that the man who'd changed the trajectory of my life had had no clue who I was, I'd let the white-hot anger inside me off its leash and I'd punched the son of a bitch as hard as I could.

If that hadn't been bad enough, I'd actually forgotten how the game was played and I'd let the fucker *see* what he'd done to me... what his empty promises had done to me.

Game.

Set.

Match.

I might have gotten my say after finding Luca in my apartment, but it was a hollow victory. I'd won the battle but lost the war.

Though, admittedly, I hadn't really won the battle. I'd just walked away from it, declaring myself the victor before he could.

Some victor I was.

I reached up to run my hand through my hair but caught myself at the last second. Instead, I dropped it and ran my fingers over the bruised knuckles that were now a dark, ugly-looking purple color. I hadn't thought to see if Luca wore any kind of matching mark on his face and I was kind of glad about that.

I wasn't sure why that was, though.

Probably because I didn't really know if I wanted there to be a bruise there or not.

I knew what I *should* want, but what if what I *should* want and what I *did* want weren't the same?

I dropped my hands so I could wrap my arms around my legs as I drew them up to my chest. I was actually grateful for the painful sensations that began firing beneath my skin as my body's physical needs began to show themselves again. My stomach cramped at the same time that saliva flooded my mouth. I could practically feel the heroin at the back of my throat and the pinch of the needle as it pierced my skin.

That was something I knew I could do battle with and win.

Heroin or meth or whatever drug I chose to pump into my bloodstream was just another guy trying to pin me down so he could use me like I was nothing. And maybe that guy was right... maybe I *was* nothing, but that wasn't something he or anyone got to decide for me ever again. I'd paid for my freedom a hundred times over and when I was ready to give it up for good, it would be my decision.

Not some drug's.

And not some slick asshole's who dressed the part.

I shuddered as I tried to wipe the memory of Luca from my mind. But just like the stubborn bastard who'd actually had the balls to try and save face with a worthless apology, the image of him in even the furthest recesses of my mind ignored my silent command to leave me alone.

He hadn't changed much in the past eight years. I hated to admit that I'd even noticed such a thing, but I couldn't pretend I hadn't memorized everything about my would-be rescuer's features in the few brief moments we'd spent together. I hadn't even really seen his face until after he'd finished...

I swallowed hard as I quickly dismissed *that* particular scene from my mind. No way in hell did I want to go there.

I won't hurt you, Billy. I just have to pretend, okay?

He'd kept *that* promise. He hadn't hurt me. I'd known what was supposed to happen when my captors had led him into the dingy room I'd been pushed into just minutes before he'd been brought in. It'd happened often enough. After all, I'd been *The Sample*.

That's what the men and two women who'd moved me from place to place had always called me, though never in front of the customers. In front of them, I'd been Billy. Since that hadn't been my real name, I hadn't really cared either way. And truth be told, Luca had been thrust into my orbit when I'd been at my weakest. I'd been with my captors for what I'd figured to be around two years and every single day had been pure agony. I'd been violated in more ways than I even knew were possible. So when the tall, dark, well-dressed man had been shown into the dimly lit room and eyed the dirty mattress with no emotion whatsoever, I'd given up and I'd done what I'd promised myself I wouldn't.

I'd broken.

And I'd begged.

Not for my life… I hadn't even cared about them killing me.

No, I'd begged the dangerous-looking man not to touch me. The tears I'd never let myself shed in front of the people who'd taken me and decided I wasn't even worth auctioning off to the highest bidder had fallen freely. There'd been no fight left in even a single cell of my body.

With every step the man had taken as he'd approached me, the panic and desperation had grown.

But I hadn't tried to fight back, and the only words that'd fallen from my lips were the same pleas over and over again.

I just want to go home.

I felt my breath catch in my throat as I realized I was doing exactly what I'd promised myself I wouldn't.

Remembering.

I lurched to my feet and began rubbing my arms as my skin felt both hot and cold at the same time. The itching sensation beneath my skin made my heart beat faster in my chest until I was sure I was going to have a heart attack. I automatically started scratching at my skin, but the second my fingertips came into contact with the raised flesh on the inside of my elbow, I let out a rough curse and spun around.

Part of me was hoping Luca would still be in the living room so I could demand he give me my drugs back, but by the time I reached the small space, that thought was already gone.

The drug wasn't going to fucking win this one.

Not again.

And certainly not because of that son of a bitch.

I forced myself to walk slowly past the living room in case Luca was still around. But I knew he was gone before I could even check it.

I hated that I knew.

I hated that I could sense his absence.

I hated that I was actually disappointed.

It's only because I wanted to lay into him some more... fuck with his head, I told myself.

I ignored the sarcastic denial that seared through my brain and quickened my pace. It took just seconds to reach the bathroom, but it felt like hours. I got the shower going even as my skin burned in protest.

"Not fucking happening," I muttered.

I was beyond grateful that I could afford to live in my own place because all too often I had this same argument with myself and it wasn't conducive to having a nosy roommate, especially when the taste of heroin was so prominent on my tongue. I hadn't used in two years, but times like these made it feel like I'd given up the drug only hours earlier.

Ask for help.

"No," I practically snarled as I ripped my shirt off, not caring that the buttons on the moderately priced dress shirt went flying. My wrists got hung up on the rolled-up sleeves but the discomfort of dragging it over my shaking hands helped me focus. I turned the water on its coldest setting at the same time I kicked off my shoes. My blood felt like it was boiling and my stomach started to roll violently.

It was like my body knew what was coming.

And what *wasn't.*

I fumbled with my belt and somehow managed to get it undone, but when the zipper and button proved to be too much for me, I stepped into the shower with the pants still on. The shock of the cold water stole my breath, and I stifled the cry of relief as my body's natural defenses kicked in. It was like robbing from Peter to pay Paul. As the heat inside me dissipated and was replaced with bitter cold, I sighed in relief and began working my pants open. But just as quickly as the adrenaline had kicked in, it started to fade as my body adjusted to the new onslaught of sensation and exhaustion quickly overtook me. I felt the coil inside of me threatening to unfurl much like it had this afternoon when I'd laid eyes on Luca again, but this time I managed to quell the need to do anything but stand there silently as the water rained down on my wrecked body.

Fuck the pants.

Fuck my body's endless hunger.

But most of all, fuck the man who thought I was still some stupid kid waiting to be saved.

Luca wasn't the only one who'd gotten good at forgetting.

CHAPTER TWO

LUCA

✝4

He moved like someone who was in trouble.

Looking over his shoulder all the time, doing his best not to get too close to anyone, which wasn't always an easy task while walking along the tourist-infested sidewalks of downtown Seattle. And he did his best to stay unnoticed.

But a guy like Remy Valentino was anything but unnoticeable.

Or at least, I thought so.

The people around him didn't seem to suffer the same affliction because few even noticed when he dodged their steps.

With the way Remy kept looking over his shoulder and taking in his surroundings, I was amazed that he hadn't noticed me. Sure, I was being careful to try and stay out of view, but for someone who was clearly expecting to be followed, Remy was pretty shitty at identifying when it was actually happening.

Of course, the more important question was why the hell was I following him in the first place? The young man had made his wishes pretty well known when he'd left me standing in the middle of his apartment with a handful of heroin, but here I was, a week later, still seeking him out.

Yeah, okay, not exactly seeking him out because I was too much of a fucking coward for that. The kid had basically stuck a knife in my gut when he'd so easily confirmed that I had, indeed, ruined his life. A better man would have just taken that wound and accepted it... lived with it.

But here I was, seven days later, on his trail again, making sure he didn't...

What, Luca?

Do more drugs?

Sell himself for cash to pay for those drugs?

I pulled in a breath and forced the image of Remy on his knees for some faceless asshole out of my brain.

It didn't work, of course. My hands fisted like they usually did when I thought of the degrading things Remy had been forced to do to survive. My gut twisted painfully around itself so many times that it was all I could do to keep putting one foot in front of the other.

Fortunately, I was forced to focus on keeping out of Remy's sight as the sidewalks started to clear out a bit. Remy had left the touristy part of the waterfront and was headed south.

While I'd been following Remy for the better part of a week, I still couldn't figure out what he was up to. I'd lost him in the crowds twice, while the times I'd managed to stick with him, he'd merely walked down side streets, alleys, and even into a few buildings, but he'd never stayed long. I didn't want to admit that his behavior smacked of someone looking to score his next fix, but it was getting harder and harder to deny. Not only had Remy not been to work at all in the last seven days, he'd stopped going back to his apartment.

The latter could have been because of me, but I had a feeling I wasn't the only one he was trying to hide from. My brother, Vaughn, and his boyfriend, Aleks, who also happened to be Remy's friend, had shown up at Remy's apartment a couple of times. I'd known that because I'd been sitting on the place after I'd lost Remy those first times when I hadn't been able to keep up with him. The only reason I'd even managed to find Remy at the motel was because I'd asked my brother, Lex, to hack into Remy's phone records. Lex had done it, no questions asked, but I knew my younger brother was dealing with his own issues. He hadn't said as much, but the fact that he hadn't flown to Seattle when we'd found my son spoke volumes. I'd tried to talk to Lex, but he hadn't answered any of my calls or texts beyond the stuff about Remy.

I pushed thoughts of my brother aside as I stepped into a doorway while Remy stopped to talk to some guy wearing a dirty hoodie. I couldn't hear what they were saying, but it was all I could do not to stride across the street when the man reached for Remy. Remy stepped out of his grasp, but that was it. When the man motioned to a nearby alley, I was silently yelling at Remy to turn and walk away. Remy seemed to hesitate for a minute, then he was following the guy.

White-hot rage replaced all the anxiety and guilt I'd been feeling, and I was moving before I could even consider what I was doing. I wasn't sure what I'd find when I rounded the corner, but it didn't matter to me. Remy on his knees or Remy accepting a handful of drugs were equally abhorrent to me, and no way in hell was I going to let it happen.

I found the pair about halfway down the alley standing near a side exit door for one of the buildings.

Thankfully, Remy wasn't on his knees, but that didn't do much to take away from my fury.

Because the guy had Remy pressed up against the wall and was grinding his crotch against Remy's. He was speaking softly to Remy so I couldn't hear, but one look at Remy's face and I instinctively knew what those words included. Remy's hands were pressed against his sides, his hands fisted. He looked pale and shaky, but when the much bigger guy reached for one of his hands and pulled it toward his own crotch, Remy didn't resist.

I used every ounce of rage and guilt I'd been feeling for the past seven days to grab the man's hand before he could force Remy to touch him. I wrenched the beefy arm hard, causing the man to scream in pain and drop to his knees.

"What the fu—" was all the guy managed to get out as I twisted his wrist, causing it to snap. He screamed in agony, but his cry was muffled when I slammed my knee up into his face. Blood spurted from his broken nose.

"Luca, what the hell?" Remy called from somewhere behind me, but I ignored him. I punched the asshole at my feet repeatedly until pain from my knuckles began to finally permeate the agony that ate at my insides.

"Jesus, Luca, stop!" Remy yelled. I was dimly aware of him hanging on to my left arm, but all that meant was that I needed to be more creative in how I made the fucker pay for every hurt that had ever been inflicted on Remy's innocent mind and body.

It wasn't until Remy pushed himself between me and the man and shoved me hard that I finally was forced to stop. Released from the grip I'd had on his hair, the moaning, bloody man fell to the ground. Remy walked me backward with surprising strength. My back hit the wall behind me.

"What the fuck?" Remy shouted as he looked over his shoulder at the guy writhing on the dirty ground.

"No one touches you like that ever again, do you hear me?" I yelled right back before I could consider my words. My body was still itching for a fight because the pain that made my chest feel tight was starting to come back. All I could see was that man's hand on Remy's and then the image shifted to eight years earlier when it'd been *my* hand on Remy. When it'd been my fingers closing around his slim arm and pulling him to his feet even as he'd cried and begged me not to hurt him.

I pulled free of Remy's hold so I could go after the guy again, but Remy practically got into my face.

"I need him, you asshole!" he bit out.

"No, you don't! I'll help you, Remy. I swear it. Money, rehab, whatever you need—"

"Information!" Remy cut in. "I need fucking information, you dick!"

His words cut off mine. "Wh-what?" I stammered.

At some point Remy's fingers had closed around the front of my dress shirt. I'd left the top button open and during the melee, probably when he'd grabbed me, the next button had torn off. So Remy's closed fist was actually pressing against my skin rather than the expensive fabric. He and I seemed to become aware of that fact at the same time because we both ended up looking down like we were trying to figure out what was happening.

I had no clue what Remy was feeling, but electricity was firing beneath my own skin and heat pooled throughout my entire body... and settled in my groin. It took everything in me not to make a sound or even take a breath as Remy stared at where we were momentarily connected. I swore I felt his hand soften so he could rub his knuckles up and down, but the moment was so fleeting I couldn't be sure.

Remy yanked his hand away and took a few steps back.

His eyes lifted to meet mine. His breaths came in sharp, harsh pants. He looked as confused as I felt. Before I could say or do anything, he turned on his heel and moved to crouch next to the man I'd beaten the crap out of.

"Where is she, Taz?" he asked.

The man on the ground moaned, then muttered, "Fuck you, you little bitch," before spitting a mouthful of blood in Remy's direction.

"Taz, she's just a—"

The man lunged for Remy with his good arm, grabbing his elbow. Remy winced as the bloody fingers bit down on his flesh. I was moving almost instantly, but by the time I reached the pair, Remy had twisted the man's thumb back until he was yelping with pain.

"Where is she?" Remy screamed, the distress in his voice clear. It was exactly the ammunition the guy on the ground needed. He rolled onto his back and in between moans, he let out a wet-sounding chuckle.

"Probably sucking some guy's—" The guy began coughing, then started laughing again.

Remy lurched to his feet. The expression on his face tore at my insides.

I knew that expression.

I'd carried it for eight years.

Remy took several steps back from the man. All the fight he'd shown a moment earlier drained out of him.

No.

That was the only thing going through my mind over and over. That single word.

No.

I reached down and grabbed the man by his hair and pulled my Glock from my back where it was covered by the long jacket I was wearing. The man, who'd initially cried out when I'd snagged him by the hair, began whimpering when I pressed the gun to his forehead. He closed his eyes and put out his good hand. "No, please, no, no."

"Tell him what he wants to know," I said coldly.

I was in my element now. *This* was what I knew how to do. Granted, these days I didn't have to use a gun to get what I wanted out of an opponent, but admittedly, the cool, sleek metal felt good in my hand.

It was easy… and honest.

I didn't need to pretend or bluff or bullshit. There was no wheeling and dealing.

I didn't look at Remy, but I could sense his tension… or maybe it was shock. I wasn't sure. But he didn't say anything or try to stop me.

When all the man did was continue to whimper and whine, I pressed the gun harder against his temple.

It was Remy who said, "Where is she, Taz?"

"I don't know!"

The second I shifted my weight just a little, he yelled, "That crazy bitch took her. Said she was gonna take care of her."

"Carla?" Remy asked as he stepped closer. "Are you talking about Carla?"

Taz nodded emphatically. "Bitch didn't even last an hour before she was try'n to sell her."

"Oh God," Remy breathed. His knees actually began to buckle. I released my hold on the man and reached for Remy and put my arm around his waist. I was stunned when he grabbed onto me to stay upright. I kept my gun pointed at Taz who was once again lying flat on the ground.

"Where is this woman?" I asked. I had no clue what Remy and Taz were talking about, but Remy clearly needed to find this Carla person.

"Don't know," Taz muttered tiredly.

When I took a step toward him, he quickly added, "Last I heard, she was hanging out at The Palace."

"The Palace?" I asked in confusion.

It was Remy who answered me. "It's an abandoned warehouse down by the water."

I was actually disappointed when Remy pushed away from me. He still seemed wobbly, but that was clearly preferable to him than having any kind of physical contact with me.

I couldn't really blame him.

Remy began striding out of the alley.

I ignored the man on the ground and turned to follow him. I tucked my gun at my back and picked up my pace so I could catch up to Remy. Not surprisingly, he didn't acknowledge my presence.

"Who's Carla?"

Remy ignored me. I fell silent as I walked next to him. I expected him to eventually respond to my presence, but it was like I wasn't even there.

I almost laughed when I finally got his silent message.

He'd forgotten about me.

Or at least, he was trying to.

We walked for a good two minutes before I noticed Remy's agitation building. He was no longer looking around like he had when I'd been following him. No, this time his eyes were straight ahead and he kept reaching one hand up to rub his opposite arm in what seemed like some kind of self-soothing motion.

"Remy," I said as I reached for him. My intent had been to offer comfort, but when he quickly stepped out of my reach, I felt my stomach drop out. I knew it was what I deserved, but it still hurt like a son of a bitch. I dropped my hand and kept pace with him, but I did so silently.

His distress seemed to grow with each hurried step, but it wasn't until he let out a little sniffle and wrapped his arms around his upper body that I reached for my phone. I doubted he even heard the quick conversation I had with the person on the other end because when the black Jaguar passed us and pulled up to the curb ahead of us, Remy didn't even seem to notice.

It was proof that he was somewhere deep inside his own head.

This time when I grabbed his arm, Remy wasn't quick enough to side-step the move. I led him to the car.

"What are you doing?" he asked, his voice going high and panic-filled within seconds.

"This is my car—" I began as I motioned to the car and the two stern men who'd gotten out of it. One was holding the back door open while the other was monitoring our surroundings.

"What? No!" Remy cried as he began struggling in my hold. "Let me go!"

"Remy—"

As small as Remy was, he was surprisingly strong and it was all I could do to hang on to him when he completely flipped his lid. Thankfully, there was no one around to interfere.

"Let me go!" Remy screamed. "I have to find her!"

My bodyguards both took steps toward me when Remy's fist managed to clip my jaw, but I quickly shook my head at both of them and motioned them back to the car. I tightened my hold on Remy's flailing hands and pulled him closer to me so he wouldn't be able to strike me as easily.

"Remy, listen," I entreated.

The fact that our bodies were flush against one another set off a whole new round of anger and panic for Remy because he shouted, "Don't touch me! I hate you!"

I already knew that, but hearing the words were like a knife to the gut.

"Remy—"

"Do you hear me? I fucking hate you, Luca!" Remy snarled. But his struggles had started to wane and there was a choking quality to his voice as he once again said, "I hate you."

He wasn't crying but he should have been. His pain was that obvious.

"I know you do," I yelled back in the hopes that he'd actually hear me above his own grunts as he fought me. "I just want to help you find whoever you're looking for."

"No," Remy snapped. "Just stay away from me!"

"Think about whoever it is who needs your help, Remy," I urged. "Just think about them. This place you're going... just..." I almost said "let me help you," but I suspected that would set him off all over again. It wasn't necessarily that he didn't want help, he just didn't want *my* help.

"You can get there faster in a car and if you need to get somewhere else quickly..." I used my chin to motion to my car. It was a lame argument, but it was the best I could come up with that I didn't think he'd refuse just out of spite. I was used to having people automatically do what I wanted either out of fear or respect, but Remy was the last person who was going to follow my orders. I was in completely unchartered territory here.

Remy stilled in my arms and looked at the car.

"Who are they?" he finally asked as he eyed the two men by the car.

"Bodyguards," I responded, figuring he deserved the truth.

He didn't ask why I had them. Instead, he looked at the car, then down the sidewalk. I had no doubt he was doing a risk-benefit analysis of sorts in his head.

We stood there for a few long seconds, then Remy tugged on my hold a little. I forced myself to release him, silently praying he wouldn't take off on me. As soon as I let him go, he turned and strode to the car. The driver quickly opened the door for him. I followed. When I got into the back seat with him, Remy pressed his body against his door.

More silent messages that I understood just as easily as if he'd yelled them. He was practically vibrating with emotion, but I couldn't be sure if it was just anger or if it was fear for whoever he was looking for.

"Where to, sir?" the driver, Terrence, asked.

I looked at Remy. He was looking straight ahead but before I could say anything, he answered Terrence himself. "The ferry terminal."

Terrence didn't respond other than to pull the car into traffic. My men hadn't been in Seattle long, but Terrence expertly navigated his way back the way Remy and I had walked. It didn't surprise me that he knew his way around the city already. It was exactly what I paid him to know.

Among other things.

Remy was practically hugging his door as we drove. I had a million questions, but I knew he wouldn't answer any of them, so I remained silent. I didn't even look at him. I was hoping the more I ignored him, the more he'd relax. But I could see in my periphery that his frame remained tense. The only thing he did do was start rubbing his forearm again with the opposite hand. He was also passing his finger over the button that controlled the power window.

I risked looking at him fully.

He looked physically ill and it was all I could do not to reach out and touch him. I had this weird feeling that I'd somehow lost him.

Which made no sense because he and I had no connection whatsoever.

"You can open it," I said softly when Remy continued to play with the power button. He actually jumped a little at the sound of my voice. His head turned tiredly and our eyes met for the briefest of moments.

But I didn't see Remy in those big, beautiful blue eyes anymore.

I saw Billy.

"Remy," I whispered, and this time I did reach for him.

Predictably, he jerked away from me. He pressed his head against the window for a moment, then lowered it. I watched him suck in a deep breath. His eyes drifted closed as the breeze fluttered through his hair.

My limbs felt heavy as I focused my attention on the scenery passing by my own window. But I didn't see any of it.

27

Please, Luca, I just want to go home.

I'll come back for you, Billy. I promise, I'll come back.

By the time the car came to a stop in a small parking lot across from the busy Seattle waterfront ferry terminal, I felt like I was going to throw up. I almost didn't notice when Remy practically jumped out of the car before it came to a full stop.

"Stay here," I said to the two men in the front seat. I could tell neither man was happy about the order, but I wasn't particularly concerned about my own safety. In the mood I was in, I'd probably be more than happy to run across any of my own enemies.

I hurried after Remy as he ran toward an old warehouse with more broken windows than unbroken ones. There was garbage and debris all around the hideous-looking building, and multiple warning signs about trespassing and the building being condemned were all over the place. I managed to catch up to Remy along the side of the building where there were several loading docks. A side door was half-open. I followed Remy inside. He glanced over his shoulder at me, but surprisingly, he didn't tell me to leave.

He just continued to pretend I wasn't there.

It was clear what the warehouse was used for the second I stepped into the darkened interior. The smell of rotting garbage mixed with various bodily odors had me trying to hold my breath. I didn't even want to know what it was that was squishing beneath my shoes as I sidestepped piles of garbage and debris. As Remy and I worked our way farther into the interior of the building, we began encountering people in various states of incapacitation. Some were passed out where they'd fallen, others were asleep. But most were huddled over a lighter or some other heat source or trying desperately to find a usable vein in their arm. The few that looked up at us did so only for a split second before going back to what they were doing.

Remy would occasionally ask one of the more lucid individuals where Carla was, but most didn't answer him. The ones who did just shook their heads.

There was more light on the second floor since many of the windows were broken. Unlike the first floor, there seemed to be more individualized living units made out of tents or boxes and scraps of weathered and torn fabric. But the state of the people were the same. However, the search for the mysterious Carla proved more fruitful because a woman wearing nothing but a T-shirt and underwear pointed up in response to Remy's question.

Right before she went back to inhaling something from a piece of tin foil.

The third floor was different from the first two in that there was considerably more activity.

Of the fucking kind.

The floor had rooms that had probably been offices at one point but which had been converted into bedrooms… well, rooms with beds in them. Men and women were fucking and getting fucked in the rooms. Several were doing drugs while fucking. It was a sickening sight.

Remy seemed unsurprised by the scene as he glanced into each room. His moves were once again frantic like before we'd gotten in my car. He asked several of the johns and their tricks about Carla, but most told him to fuck off. It was about halfway down the row of offices that we encountered a young man who couldn't have been more than eighteen. He was wiping at his nose while an older guy was snorting lines off a small mirror with a rolled-up dollar bill.

"Have you seen Carla?" Remy asked.

The kid looked Remy up and down, then turned his attention to me. "You guys looking to play?" he asked suggestively.

"We're looking for Carla," Remy repeated.

The kid's interest evaporated instantly.

Until I handed him a fifty-dollar bill.

"Get in here, you little faggot. I'm ready," the john blurted drunkenly. He was undoing his pants.

The kid's dead eyes didn't even flicker. He took the money from me, then waved his finger across the open space that overlooked the main floor of the warehouse. The opposite side also had a row of offices on it.

As the kid turned to go back into the room, I snagged his arm. I handed him a wad of hundred-dollar bills. "Go home, kid," I said.

I expected him to react in some kind of meaningful way, but all he did was take the money and then shut the door in my face.

Remy, who'd seen the exchange, shook his head and then turned on his heel.

"What?" I asked because my gut was telling me the action had been directed at me, not the kid.

"Nothing," he muttered. He sounded disappointed.

"No, what?" I asked because if anything, I'd expected him to be pissed since I hadn't helped him get home. I grabbed his arm to stop his forward trajectory. Not surprisingly, he pulled it free and kept right on walking.

"You're assuming he's even got a home to go back to," Remy said dispassionately. "Even if he's one of the lucky ones and does have a family who gives two shits about him, do you really think it's lack of cash that's keeping him here?" He shook his head again. "You have a lot of money, Luca, so clearly you're a smart man, but you don't know shit."

"Money will give him a chance, at least."

Remy snorted. "If he's gutsy enough to hide it from his pimp, he'll put most of it up his nose. It's just a question of whether he'll do it all at once or try and make it last."

I felt my heart constrict at his comment and I actually stopped in my tracks. Would the kid really use the cash I'd given him to buy enough drugs to end his suffering?

"You got out," I murmured, more to myself than anything else.

Except he hadn't. A week ago he'd been handing me a baggie of drugs that he'd bought after two years of sobriety. His hate for me had driven him to do that, but I had no idea if he'd bought more that night or in the days that had followed. And of course, I'd assumed he was turning tricks a mere twenty minutes ago.

Jesus, what kind of arrogant asshole was I that I thought I could save some kid just by giving him some money? I'd spent years trying to save kids like Remy and my own son, but what did I truly know

30

about their lives? I was the bank account. My brothers were the ones who did the real work. They got the kids out, they took them home or found them new lives... I'd known those kids had suffered, but I'd never let myself think about it. It would have meant having to confront the reality of what my own child had been enduring.

I hadn't been able to save him, either. Yes, he was alive, which I would be eternally grateful for, but the torture he'd experienced...

"Hey."

I was surprised when Remy touched my hand. He seemed surprised too because as soon as he looked down at where our hands were connected, he pulled his away.

"A dozen guys have probably offered to save him just this week," Remy murmured as he motioned in the direction of the room with the kid. "Doesn't matter how he got here... he's the only one who can get himself out now. Maybe you'll be the one who makes him want to try."

He didn't sound particularly hopeful. As he turned away, I found myself grabbing his hand, but I wasn't sure why. Amazingly, he didn't pull his hand free right away. I ended up staring at his long, slim fingers as I considered all he'd been through in his young life and how badly I'd really failed him. I wanted to tell him I was sorry again, but I knew he didn't want to hear it and it didn't really matter. There were no words, no actions that could undo what I'd done.

At least he was here. At least he'd been strong enough to survive it all. I remembered what his friend, Aleks, had told me a few weeks back. I hadn't realized he'd been talking about the young man I'd known as Billy, but he'd said his friend was a fighter... that Remy was the reason Aleks had escaped the same brutal life.

"I didn't know," I heard myself whisper. "I didn't *want* to know..."

I expected him to berate me. I wanted him to because I deserved it. But he surprised me once again by softly saying, "Who would?"

Remy gave my hand a gentle squeeze before he released it and turned away. I hurried after him. I kept my hand beneath my long jacket so I'd have quick access to the gun at my back, especially when a few men eyed Remy as he passed them.

It took just minutes to get to the opposite side of the warehouse. Remy finally found what he was looking for in the third room he checked.

"Hey!" a man's voice grunted when Remy threw open the door.

"Where is she?" Remy yelled just as I stepped into the room and took in the chaotic scene. There was a woman lying naked on the bed, her eyes glazed over. Her legs were splayed open and there were several discarded needles on the floor next to the bed. The man with her was mostly dressed. He was fumbling to get his condom-covered dick into his pants.

Remy ignored him and went to shake the woman. "Carla, where is she?" he repeated.

The woman awoke from her stupor and looked around in confusion, then muttered, "Fuck off!" before reaching for one of the discarded needles on the floor.

"Hey, get the fuck out of here," the man snapped. "I ain't finished yet!" When he reached for Remy, I grabbed his arm and twisted it. The man cried out and stumbled backward. As soon as I released him, he yelled, "Next one's free, bitch!"

Carla waved the angry man off. As he left the room, she sat up and began rifling through the little table next to the dirty mattress that was probably supposed to pass as a bed.

"Carla, where is she?" Remy demanded. He snagged a little baggie off the table before Carla could grab it.

"Hey!" she whined. Not caring about her state of undress, she tried to stand, but her knees wouldn't hold her. She collapsed on the floor.

"You want this?" Remy said, holding the drugs in front of her face. "You tell me where she is first."

Carla put her head in her hand and waved her free fingers at nothing in particular.

"Carla," Remy began, but I grabbed his arm when a strange sound caught my attention.

A sound that didn't belong in that terrible place.

"Luca, what—"

"Shhh, listen," I said.

32

We both fell silent. Sure enough, about fifteen seconds later, I heard it again. I was moving instantly because I knew in my heart of hearts that the sound was the reason we were there.

I hurried out of the room and began throwing open doors.

My suspicions were confirmed when Remy frantically called out, "Violet!"

She was behind the third door I opened, and I was equally horrified and relieved. "Here!" I called to Remy even as I stepped into the room and slowly approached the wide-eyed toddler who was standing barefoot in a trash-filled room, holding on to the edge of a table covered in drug paraphernalia. But I had eyes only for the uncapped syringe she was holding in her hand, the needle dangerously close to her eye.

CHAPTER THREE

REMY

†4

The rush from Carla's nausea-inducing room to the room Luca disappeared into felt like the longest seconds of my life. A million things went through my mind at what I'd see when I entered that room. But seeing the beautiful little girl clad only in a diaper standing among discarded needles, rotting food, and used condoms made me both want to throw up and cry in relief at the same time.

Then I saw the needle in her hand.

When Violet saw me, the two-year-old's scrunched-up face relaxed and she let out a little toothy grin as she began waving her arms. Luca used that moment to scoop her up and take the needle from her hand at the same time. The second Luca picked her up, Violet began screaming like a she-devil and holding her arms out for me.

"It's okay, sweetie," I crooned as I moved into the room. Luca quickly handed her off to me. A strange half-sob, half-laugh escaped my throat as I hugged the baby against my chest. She began patting my cheeks.

"Me-me," Violet repeated over and over again.

I ignored the need to collapse right there on the floor and just cuddle the little girl. But as it was, I couldn't make myself move. It was like my body was racked with one tremor after another and I was afraid even the smallest move would have me exploding.

Exploding with what, though?

"Remy..."

I heard my name repeated a couple more times, but I didn't actually react until I felt something warm touching the back of my hand.

And it wasn't Violet's squirmy little body, either.

"Remy, baby, look at me."

The endearment had me looking at Luca in surprise. He'd moved closer to me at some point... close enough that Violet had gone silent and was watching him with her big, wary eyes.

"Remy, is she the one you were looking for?" Luca asked. I heard the words but was having trouble making sense of them.

What the hell was happening to me? Why did I suddenly feel cold all over?

Heat sparked along my cheek. The stark contrast to how the rest of me felt had me whimpering.

What the fuck? I didn't whimper. I didn't respond to cheesy terms of endearment like *baby*.

And I sure as hell didn't freeze up.

I acted.

I moved.

Those reminders had me opening my mouth to tell Luca to get his hand off my cheek, but all that came out was this weak little whisper that sounded a lot like his name.

"It's okay, Remy, she's safe," Luca responded. I watched in a daze as he pulled his gun from his back and stuck it in his waistband, then shrugged off his long jacket and folded it in half and began wrapping it around Violet. I knew I should help him tuck it around the child, but it felt like I was drowning and I was afraid to open my mouth.

After all, I'd already said his name... what the fuck would I say next?

It was Violet who managed to tear me from my daze because she scrunched up her face as fat, heavy tears began to collect on her thick lashes.

"You're okay, Violet," I somehow managed to choke out as I began bouncing her.

"Here, Princess," Luca said as he suddenly handed Violet a small keychain with a soccer ball on it. The squishy toy quickly caught Violet's interest and although a few tears slipped down her face, she didn't make a sound as she examined the keychain. "Remy, is she who we came here for?" Luca asked again.

I nodded. "Y-Yes," I whispered.

Luca's hand was suddenly at my lower back as he began maneuvering me out of the room. I knew I should tell him not to touch me, but I kept my mouth shut. I told myself it was because I needed the physical support in case I stumbled over something with Violet in my arms.

I ignored my brain calling bullshit on me.

Violet gurgled happily as she played with the keychain. She showed it to me a few times. Her bubbly baby sounds helped ease the mysterious tension in my body and I was able to move more quickly.

"Meet us on the third floor," I heard Luca say. I glanced at him and saw him hanging his phone up.

"Who was that?" I asked.

"My men," Luca said. His eyes were darting all around us. His free hand was still at my back, but he quickly replaced his phone with the gun.

"Your men?" I asked dumbly until I remembered the guys from his car.

Bodyguards.

Why the hell did he need bodyguards?

"Most of these people are too fucked up to try and rob us," I murmured.

"That asshole in the alley said Carla was trying to sell 'her.'" Luca looked at Violet. "Not taking any chances that she didn't find a buyer already."

36

I nearly stopped walking, but Luca's hand on my back kept me moving forward.

Luca was worried about the baby? He'd called his bodyguards for *her*? He was a selfish prick, so what did he care about a little girl he didn't know?

No, he was lying. He was worried about getting his own ass out of there in one piece.

My throat felt tight and I suddenly found it hard to swallow. For the second time, I wondered what was going on with me. I'd found Violet. She was safe and I'd make sure she stayed that way.

Case closed.

So why was I so fucking shaky?

I stayed silent as Luca led me down the stairs. His bodyguards met us on the stairwell, and even though I knew they were there to protect Luca and not me and Violet, I still felt relieved.

Which just pissed me off even more because I didn't need any of these guys to get me and Violet out of there. I would have been just fine on my own.

Once we were outside the building, I commanded my brain to step away from Luca so Violet and I could be on our way. I hadn't come up with an exact plan of what to do next, but I would.

I always did.

But once again, my mind or my body—or both—refused the demand and I ended up letting Luca lead me to his car, then settling me and Violet in the back seat.

"Remy, where's Violet's mother?" I heard Luca ask.

The image of Jackie's lifeless body flashed in my mind, stealing any promise of speech away. So I just shook my head and kept my eyes on Violet as she played with the keychain.

There were a few beats of silence before Luca gently asked, "Is she your child?"

I shook my head again and silently begged Luca not to ask me any more questions. I didn't like that I was having so much fucking trouble answering them. I was glad when I managed to pull away when Luca touched my shoulder in what was probably supposed to have been a reassuring pat.

Good, at least *something* in my brain was working.

I could feel Luca's eyes on me, and it took every ounce of self-awareness I had not to look at him. I didn't give a shit if my distance bothered him.

I *didn't*.

Luca made a phone call, but I tuned him out and tried to get my own thoughts in order. Violet kept thrusting the keychain at me, so I settled her on my lap and took it. There wasn't anything particularly special about it, but the ball was odd. It looked like any cheap novelty you could get at any kind of toy or sports store, but while most of the soccer ball was a spongy material, there was one part of it that was hard and shiny, almost like it was laminated.

I took a closer look at that part and noticed what looked like scribbles on the ball. It wasn't until I turned it a certain way that I realized the scribbles were actually letters.

One of the letters was a G. The other looked like an I. I couldn't tell what the last letter was because it was smudged with some dirt.

It was an odd thing for a grown man to be carrying, especially a man like Luca. Even if he was a fan of soccer, he was clearly a very rich man, so it made no sense for him to be carrying around a trinket that wasn't worth more than a few quarters.

I glanced at him and saw that his eyes were on me.

Well, not me, but the keychain.

And he looked... fuck, I didn't know what he looked like.

The only word I could come up with was... *haunted*.

No.

No way.

A guy like him didn't understand that concept. He was the type who took what he wanted, did what he wanted and said "fuck" to the consequences. Hell, for someone like him, there *weren't* any consequences.

Luca's eyes slid up to mine and I actually wondered if I'd said any of my thoughts out loud, because the way he was looking at me was unnerving. This time, I couldn't read him.

He looked away first. I couldn't help but glance at him every now and then as he balanced his elbow against the window so he could rub his lower lip with the ends of his fingers.

"Me-me," Violet called loudly as she grabbed for the keychain. I returned it to her and then studied the passing scenery from my own window. The tension was leaching from my system hard and fast and I hated how shaky I felt.

I also hated how the tiniest part of me was envious of that kid Luca and I had encountered in the warehouse. The amount of shit he could get with the cash Luca had given him would buy him nonstop bliss for days.

Assuming he was brave enough to hide the money from his pimp.

If he did shove it up his nose or shoot it into his arms, he wouldn't have to feel for a while... well, that wasn't entirely true. He'd feel, but it would be only good things. And only when all the cash was gone would he get on his knees for the next guy who wanted to use him. Then the hunt for bliss would start all over again.

"We're here," Luca said softly, but I still jumped because I'd forgotten his presence. I'd forgotten everything for a while.

"Where?" I murmured as I looked around. Holy hell, we weren't even in the city anymore. I'd just assumed Luca would take me back to my place. How long had I been daydreaming?

I glanced down and saw that Violet had actually fallen asleep against my chest, the keychain clutched between her grimy fingers. The very strong stench of a dirty diaper assaulted my nose.

"A friend's," was all Luca said.

We were in a quiet neighborhood of upper-middle-class houses. I actually knew the neighborhood because Aleks had lived a few streets over with his older brother, Dante, and Dante's husband, Magnus.

"Why are we here?" I asked. Violet woke up and looked around for a brief moment before she started crying. "Shhh, honey, it's okay," I cooed as I began bouncing her up and down. I tried to keep my voice calm as I said, "Why didn't you take me home?"

Luca glanced at me. "Which home, Remy? Your apartment or that piece of shit motel room that isn't fit for you, let alone her?" he asked calmly as he nodded at Violet.

I opened my mouth to tell him to fuck off, even if he was right. But I snapped it shut when he got out of the car. My door was opened from the outside by one of the bodyguards. Violet cried harder.

"It's okay, sweet girl," I said as I pressed a kiss to the top of her head. I snuggled her closer as I got out of the car. Luckily, by the time we reached the walkway that led up to the large house, she'd nodded off again. Luca was several steps ahead of me and when the front door opened, he extended his hand to the large man who came walking out of the house. There was a large German shepherd along with a smaller mixed-breed dog with him. I automatically stopped in my tracks at the sight of the larger animal. Every instinct in my body told me to run, but I knew it wouldn't do me any good.

"Bullet," I heard the man call to the dog, which was staring at me, but hadn't made a move toward me. The shepherd quickly returned to the man's side and dropped down to the ground. The mixed-breed dog began jumping all over the shepherd, but the larger dog stayed where it was.

I managed to pull in a breath. Luca appeared at my side, though admittedly, I hadn't seen him move in my direction.

My only focus had been the dog.

"You okay?" he asked, his hand once again going to the small of my back. Odd that the need to move away from his touch wasn't as profound as it normally was.

"Not a fan," I said softly as I kept my eyes on the pair of dogs. The shepherd wasn't even looking my way anymore, but it was still all I could do to quell the fear that was clawing at my insides trying to get out. My fear of dogs was something I'd battled with for a long time, especially since the family I worked for had so many of them. The Barretti brothers who employed me often invited me to family gatherings that included loads of kids, dogs, and other animals. I'd gotten out of most of the events, but there'd been a few that I'd attended, and it'd been all I could do to hide my stark fear of the four-legged attendees.

I trembled when Luca's fingers began rubbing my lower back.

"Jamie," the other man called out. His eyes were on me and Luca. I finally realized I knew him.

A little boy of about five or six came running out of the house. He was wearing a Spider-Man costume that included little red tights.

"Yeah?" he said.

"Why don't you and Daddy Seth take Bullet and Bella with you to Uncle Hawke's house, okay?"

"Okay!" The boy, Jamie, threw his arms around his father and then took off, calling the dogs. Both jumped up to follow him. When they reached the end of the block, Jamie stopped and began pretending to shoot webs from his wrists. I found myself smiling at his antics as he acted like the stop sign was some kind of foe he'd caught up in his webs.

"Ronan, do you know where Jamie is?" a voice from inside the house called.

"Out here," the man responded.

"Please tell me he's wearing pants," the exasperated voice returned.

"Yes and no," the man, Ronan, said with a smile as he watched his son.

A second man appeared at the door. He had a bag slung over his shoulder. Ronan's arm immediately went around the slimmer man's waist when he stopped at his side. I remembered the younger man being introduced to me as Seth, Ronan's husband.

Seth leaned into his husband's side as they watched their child battle the evil stop sign. I wasn't sure I'd ever seen anyone look so content. I was envious, but when I looked down at Violet, my heart felt like it shattered into a million pieces. Would the little girl ever know what it was like to have someone who loved her that much? So unconditionally? Or would she end up like her mother or Carla or the kid at the warehouse?

Lost?

Forgotten?

Would she even be either of those two things if there wasn't anyone left to miss her? To want her back? To always be searching for her, or, at the very least, be wondering about her?

"Remy, let's go inside, okay?" I heard Luca say gently. "The dogs are gone."

I looked up from where I'd been staring at Violet's innocent, sleeping face and saw that Jamie, Seth, and the two dogs were nowhere in sight. Ronan was gone too and the front door to the house was wide open.

Fear for Violet overruled my brain and I heard myself whispering, "What are we doing here, Luca?"

It was a moment of weakness that I wasn't proud of, and I swore to myself there wouldn't be another around this man, but I needed...

What?

What was it that I even needed?

I shook my head because I didn't even know the answer to that.

I just *needed*.

And as much as I hated to admit it, I knew I wouldn't be able to take another step forward until Luca gave it to me... whatever *it* was.

CHAPTER FOUR

LUCA

†4

"Have you met Ronan before?" I asked as I stepped around Remy so I was between him and the house. He was staring at the ground and I could see the distress in his eyes that had been in his voice only moments before. I felt like shit for not having given him a heads-up about why we were coming here while still in the car, but he'd been so preoccupied with his thoughts, I hadn't wanted to pull him from them.

Not to mention I'd been dealing with my own issues.

Remy nodded. "He's a friend of the Barrettis. And Aleks's brother works for him."

"Dante." I nodded in agreement. "Did you know he's a surgeon? Ronan, I mean."

That had Remy lifting his eyes. "Dante doesn't work in medicine."

The way Remy said the words almost had me smiling. He was almost daring me to contradict him. It seemed to be a game of "how much do you know?"

"No, he doesn't. The 'group' he works for is run by Ronan, but Ronan still practices medicine. I thought we could have him take a look at Violet to make sure she's okay. I wasn't sure you wanted to take her to the hospital."

"Oh," Remy murmured as he looked down at the baby. "Right."

For once, he looked clueless and I saw his pale cheeks stain with color.

"I, um… I don't know much about kids," he whispered. "Does she… does she look okay to you?" he asked, his voice trembling just a bit as his eyes met mine.

"She looks good," I reassured him.

"All that shit she was standing on in the room… she didn't have shoes on. What if she got stuck by a needle or something?"

Remy got so agitated so fast that I nearly got whiplash.

"I knew I had to find her after I heard about Jackie, but I didn't even think about what to do when I did—"

Remy started trying to examine the toddler even though she was still wrapped up in my jacket. His jostling started to wake her up, but he seemed oblivious.

"Remy, sweetheart," I said as I reached out to grab his chin.

"What if I missed something, Luca? What if I didn't get to her quick enough? Can Ronan give her something if she got stuck or if she touched something?" He paused and choked out, "What if Carla let some guy—"

"Remy," I said more firmly. I gripped his chin just a bit harder, enough to get his attention. "I think she's okay, but Ronan can tell us for sure, okay? Let's just deal with that first." I gentled my hold, but for the life of me, I couldn't release him. Not when he was looking at me with something other than hatred in his eyes.

He finally nodded. "O-Okay."

I meant to release him, I really did. But the fact that he wasn't fighting me or pulling away was like this strange balm that I wanted more of. Every time he usually looked at me, it was like someone was taking a knife to my insides. But this… this was the cure and I drank it down like water.

His skin felt like silk beneath my fingers, and before I could tell myself I was taking advantage of his insecurity, I skimmed my thumb along his cheekbone. I swore he shivered, but I couldn't be sure.

It was Violet shifting in his arms that jolted me back to awareness, and I quickly dropped my hand.

"Are you ready to go inside?" I asked, stumbling over my own words. I hated feeling so off-balance... I couldn't even remember the last time it had actually happened.

Well, that wasn't entirely true. Hearing my son tell me he hated me the very day I'd seen him again after so many years of searching for him had pretty much shattered my entire world.

I forced thoughts of Gio away and focused on the man before me. He nodded in response. I stepped around him and put my hand at his back. He didn't lean into my touch like I was certain he had before, but he didn't pull away either, so I put it in the win column.

Remy stayed by my side as we made our way into the house. I'd only been in the place once, but I remembered my way around the main floor. I instinctively headed for the kitchen. Sure enough, Ronan was there. His back was to us as he prepared a few mugs of what I assumed was coffee.

"You take yours black, right Luca?" Ronan asked. It didn't surprise me in the least that the man knew that about me. I doubted I'd even had coffee around him. He probably knew my shoe size and which side I tucked my dick on too.

"Yes," I responded as I pulled one of the kitchen table chairs out for Remy. He sat stiffly. I saw the hand he wasn't holding Violet with reach up to slide through his hair. I wanted to offer to take the baby from him because I was sure holding her had to be making his arms numb, but I didn't say anything. I figured he needed to hang on to her as much as she needed him at the moment.

Ronan took his time getting my coffee going. There were already some cookies sitting on a plate in the center of the table, along with a bowl of some kind of cereal. I assumed it was for Violet when she woke up.

I didn't think it possible, but Remy stiffened even more when Ronan approached us with the coffee. I was still standing next to Remy's chair and was shocked when he seemed to lean into my body just a bit.

Like he was trying to confirm I was still there.

You're overreaching, Luca.

Ronan slowly set the coffee in front of me, as well as a small ice pack. "For your hand," he murmured. I glanced down at my right hand and saw that the knuckles were black and blue and there was dried blood all over my fingers.

Taz's blood.

I didn't even feel an ounce of guilt for what I'd done to that fucker.

"Remy, do you want some coffee?" Ronan asked Remy gently. He was a big guy with an intimidating presence that spoke of confidence. I'd been the recipient of his cool, calm demeanor, but what he was doing now was very different.

It was definitely his bedside manner.

"No thank you, Dr. Grisham," Remy responded.

"How about some water, then?" Ronan returned. "And please, call me Ronan."

"Okay, yeah, water would be great."

Ronan went to the fridge and got the bottle of water. He set it within Remy's reach but was careful not to get too close to him. A few minutes later he was sitting in the chair kitty-corner from Remy.

"Can you tell me a little bit about Violet, Remy?" Ronan asked as he sipped his coffee.

"Um, okay. Like what?"

"Like how old she is, is she normally pretty healthy, where her mom and dad are," Ronan suggested.

"She turned two a few weeks ago," Remy began. "I, um, guess she's pretty healthy but she's got some... delays, I guess you'd call them."

"What kind of delays?" Ronan asked.

"I'm not sure... Jackie—that's her mom—never took her to the doctor or anything, but I think she doesn't necessarily do all the things kids her age do. I think she's probably supposed to talk more than she does... she only knows a few words. When I'd babysit for Jackie, I tried teaching Violet some words by showing her pictures of things, but she couldn't seem to say any of the words. She can't walk

46

but she can stand if she holds on to something. Jackie only ever gave her milk in bottles, not those sippy cup things..."

"So you think she might have some developmental and physical delays?" Ronan asked.

Remy nodded. "I once googled what happens when a baby is born addicted to drugs and I read some stuff about them having problems as they get older. Long-term effects, I guess."

"Violet was born addicted to drugs?" I asked, unable to hide my surprise.

"Jackie tried to get clean a few times while she was pregnant, but she couldn't stop entirely. Violet spent a couple months in the hospital. CPS wanted to take Violet away from Jackie, but a judge gave her back when Jackie took some parenting classes and joined NA. That's where she and I met."

"Narcotics Anonymous?" Ronan asked.

Remy nodded. I saw a hint of color stain his cheeks and silently hoped Ronan wouldn't dwell on the topic.

"So you and Jackie were friends?" Ronan said as he leaned back in his chair.

Remy shrugged. "Drug addicts don't have friends," he finally said. "I tried to help Jackie out when she didn't have money for diapers and stuff like that, but she wouldn't listen to me when I said she needed to take Violet to the doctor for her shots and stuff. She was afraid they'd take her away again."

"Where is Jackie now?" I asked. I slowly eased around Remy's chair so I could sit down in the one next to him. At one point his eyes shot up and he tracked me for a moment, but I wasn't sure if it was because he was trying to figure out if I was leaving... or staying.

"Gone," Remy whispered. He automatically cuddled Violet closer to him. "She called me last week, but I didn't answer because..."

Remy's eyes momentarily shifted to me before he dropped them. "Because I was busy."

Yeah, busy dealing with all the shit I'd stirred up for him.

"When I finally got her message, I was too late. I went to her place but..."

47

Remy shook his head, then repeated, "I was too late."

"What did you do?" Ronan asked.

"I dialed 911 from her cell phone and left the connection open so they could find her. Violet was nowhere to be found, so I started looking for her. I knew some of the places Jackie hung out when she needed to..."

Remy pulled in a breath. "When she needed to score. But no one had seen her. It took a while to track down this pimp she'd sometimes worked for... and dated."

"Is that what you were doing all week?" I asked.

Remy pinned me with a hard look. "What did you think I was doing?"

The way he asked the question indicated he knew *exactly* what I thought he'd been doing. And he was right. I *had* thought he'd been looking for his next fix.

"Oh wait, we've already established what I need," he added coldly before turning his attention back to Violet.

I flinched as I remembered my own words about offering him anything he needed so he'd never have to get on his knees for money again. *Rehab, cash...*

Fuck.

"Remy, I didn't—" I began, but he waved me off.

"Yes, you did," was all he said. His eyes shifted to Ronan. "Taz, the guy Jackie used to work for, told me Carla—she was Jackie's friend and sometimes dealer—had taken Violet. We found Violet in this room full of used syringes and stuff... she was holding one when Luc —*he*" —Remy jerked his chin in my direction—"got to her." His voice softened considerably when he said, "Do you think she could have poked herself? I didn't see any blood on her, but I didn't think to check... she's already got so much to deal with, Ronan. She can't... she can't get sick. So you have to give her something so she doesn't, okay?"

Remy's voice began to crack. I was in the process of reaching for him when Ronan's hand closed over his shoulder. The contact had me

48

burning with jealousy, even though the logical side of me knew the gesture meant nothing but offering comfort.

But that didn't stop me from wanting to rip Ronan's hand away.

Jesus, what the fuck was wrong with me?

"I'm sure she didn't, Remy. I'll check her over and we can draw some blood and run some tests, but the odds are slim, okay?"

I swore I saw Remy close his eyes and lean in toward the good-looking surgeon. That had my irritation spiking, so I got up and began pacing the space behind Remy's chair. Ronan's eyes latched onto mine, but his expression was unreadable.

Thankfully, though, he did remove his hand.

"I'm going to need to examine her, Remy," Ronan said, but his eyes were still on me. It was like he knew things about me I didn't want to admit to myself.

"Okay."

I forced myself to return to the chair I'd been sitting in, but I couldn't find it in me to sit. My hands felt restless, and since I couldn't exactly light up a cigarette there in the kitchen, I wrapped my fingers around the back of the chair and focused on all the little divots and striations in the wood.

"Ronan," I said to get his attention. When he looked at me, I softly said, "The pimp said Carla mentioned wanting to sell her." I motioned to Violet with my chin. I hadn't meant to look at her, but I ended up doing it anyway. Her head was propped on Remy's shoulder and she still had my keychain clutched between her grubby fingers. She was the picture of innocence and the idea that someone might have touched her had me gripping the chair so hard, it was a miracle it didn't break.

Remy didn't respond to my comment, but he did drop his head so he was staring at the floor. Ronan managed to remain calm, but I didn't miss the way his eyes hardened. He gave me a quick nod, then said to Remy, "I'll go get my things, okay?"

Remy nodded but didn't look up.

I returned to the chair and murmured, "No matter what, we'll make sure no one ever hurts her again." I couldn't stop myself from

SLOANE KENNEDY

reaching out to touch his shoulder. I ended up skimming my fingers over Violet's soft hair too.

Remy remained stiff as Ronan returned to the kitchen and suggested we move to his and Seth's bedroom so the child would be more comfortable during the exam. Violet had awoken and was still playing with my keychain and showing it to Remy repeatedly, but he didn't do anything more than mumble soft words to her that I couldn't understand.

Ronan had Remy sit on the end of the bed with Violet on his lap and as he began his exam, he showed Violet all the instruments he was using. The toddler seemed wary, but Ronan's patience and gentle demeanor won out.

Until the moment Remy had to put her down on the bed so Ronan could examine the little girl more closely. Fire and ice slid through my veins as I considered why all this was necessary in the first place. I wanted to hurt someone.

Bad.

My father had been like that... he'd hurt a lot of people. I'd always pretended I was different... that I could use my brain rather than my fists to outwit an opponent. But once my son had been taken from me, it'd taken every ounce of willpower not to seek answers with my fists. It would have been a satisfying route to take, but I'd known in my gut that it wouldn't have gotten me any closer to rescuing my child.

He was safe now.

Violet too.

But the mere fact that there were men and women out there in the world who preyed on innocent children simply because they *could* made my mind go to places I'd sworn it never would.

"Luca..."

Remy's soft voice tore me from the homicidal thoughts raging through me. I focused my gaze to see that he was watching me with what actually looked like concern.

It took me a moment to figure out why.

Because I was standing at Ronan's back with my hands curled into

50

fists as he leaned over Violet. I could only imagine the picture I made. Hell, I didn't even remember moving from Remy's side.

To Ronan's credit, he stayed focused on Violet, but I had no doubt the man knew I was there... and why. I took several steps back. I could feel Remy's eyes on me, but I was too ashamed to look at him. I turned away from the men when they began working to gently remove Violet's dirty diaper. Violet's tolerance chose that moment to wear out because she began crying and screaming. When I glanced over my shoulder at her, I saw her reaching for Remy. I wanted to grab her myself and get her out of there. It took every ounce of willpower I had to stay where I was.

"Isn't that right, Raggy?" I heard someone say. I recognized the voice, of course. Vaughn and I had watched plenty of Scooby-Doo cartoons when we'd been kids.

As Violet's sobs slowed, I turned and watched in surprise as Remy continued to speak like Scooby. Big fat tears rolled down Violet's chubby cheeks, but her wide eyes were fixated on Remy as he switched from Scooby's voice to Shaggy's. I remembered how he'd changed his voice the night I'd been waiting for him inside his apartment.

Ronan worked quickly as Remy entertained Violet with a Scooby/Shaggy conversation about Scooby Snacks. When Violet held out her hands, Remy dutifully leaned over her so she could pat his face as he spoke. She was completely fascinated with the young man.

The toddler wasn't the only one.

A maelstrom of emotions built inside of me, but fuck if I could figure out what any of them were. No doubt guilt was the main one, but the rest... the rest just left me feeling empty and full at the same time.

I wasn't proud of it, but I turned and left the room.

Just walked out.

No comment that I wasn't going far or that I'd be right back.

I just started walking.

"Where to, sir?"

The voice startled me and I was reaching for my gun before I even realized it. My bodyguard, Stan, tensed up at the move.

"Sorry," I muttered as I dropped my hand.

"No problem, sir," Stan replied warily. "Are you ready to go?"

Go?

Huh?

It was then that I realized in my daze I'd left the house altogether and was standing by the car. What the hell? I had no intention of leaving.

So what the fuck *was* I doing outside?

"Uh, no," I muttered. "I, uh..."

That was all I got out before I turned on my heel and went back to the house. I looked up at the wide-open front door just in time to see Remy turning away, Violet in his arms.

"Fuck," I whispered to myself.

By the time I got back inside, Remy was nowhere to be found. I went to the kitchen but only Ronan was there. He was pouring milk into a baby bottle.

"Is she all right?" I blurted.

Ronan put the cap on the bottle and tightened it before he turned to face me. He leaned back against the counter. Not surprisingly, I couldn't read his expression. That kind of made me glad because the last thing I needed was to be judged by a guy who'd bested me on so many levels. The first time I'd met the man, he'd been like this.

Cool as a cucumber.

Confident.

Powerful.

All the things I'd always considered myself to be.

"He wanted to tell you himself," Ronan finally said after several beats. "She seems to be okay," he added.

The relief that Violet was unharmed warred with confusion over Ronan's first statement.

Remy had wanted to tell me Violet was okay himself? Why?

I managed to keep the string of curse words in my head to myself as I realized what it must have looked like to Remy to see me standing by my car, the door held open by my driver.

"I wasn't leaving," I announced, though I didn't know why. I didn't owe Ronan any kind of explanation. The man didn't fucking know me.

I felt like a bug on a slide as he studied me.

"Here," he finally said as he reached for a small stack of what looked like clothes. "They were Jamie's when he was a little older than her. They'll probably run a little big, but they should be okay until we can get her some new ones. We don't have any diapers but there's a Pull-Up in there. I'll have one of my guys make a run to the store—"

"No," I interjected as I reached for the clothes. "I'll send my guys." Somehow the idea of Ronan buying Violet clothes and diapers irked me, but I wasn't sure why. God, why was I so off balance?

"He's giving her a bath in my daughter's bathroom. Second floor, third door on the left." He put the bottle on top of the pile of clothes. He turned his back on me which, oddly enough, stung.

Fuck him, I didn't owe him anything.

I turned to leave the room, then stopped. "You said she's okay?" I murmured.

Fuck my pride, I needed to know that the beautiful little girl hadn't had her innocence stolen.

Thankfully, Ronan didn't keep me waiting. "I didn't see any physical signs that anyone touched her. No needle marks either. I drew some blood so we can run some tests, but she appears to be okay. I told Remy that we'll want to have her examined by someone who specializes in kids who've undergone trauma, but I don't have any reasons to suspect that anyone laid a hand on her."

I still had my back to Ronan, but he must have seen the breath I released because I sure as hell felt it. It almost made me light-headed. I needed to thank him, but my throat felt too tight at the moment, so I just nodded my head and then went to find Remy so I could explain why I'd left.

Again.

CHAPTER FIVE

REMY

┿4

Violet's antics in the water should have had me smiling, but fuck if I could manage to do anything but stare at her in silence. I'd long ago given up on trying to wash her with the washcloth I'd found in the closet. She was just having way too much fun slapping her hands in the water to deny her that.

Not after everything she'd been through.

"Do you like the water, baby girl?" I murmured. Her answer came in the form of a loud laugh followed by a heavy slap on the water which sent sprays of the warm liquid all over my face and shirt. "I guess so," I mused.

Those few minutes of watching Ronan examine Violet had been the worst of my life, and I still had no idea how I'd managed to keep up the Scooby voice long enough to entertain the toddler. I'd been as close to tears as I'd ever been, and my only comfort had been in knowing Luca was standing behind me, watching... protecting.

Only he hadn't been.

I'd felt that loss keenly and I'd hated myself for it. I'd hated him too. But when Ronan had declared that Violet was unharmed beyond the dirt that caked her small body, I'd practically snatched her off the bed and gone in search of Luca to tell him the news.

Why?

I had no clue.

It'd been that same strange, inevitable need I'd felt when I'd known I needed to enter Ronan's house but hadn't been able to take the first step forward. It'd been exactly like that day so long ago...

"No," I ground out to stop myself from even thinking about that day. Violet stopped splashing and looked at me with what I could only classify as wary eyes.

"Sorry, baby girl," I quickly said as I reached out to stroke her hair. Luckily, she didn't pull away from me. "But where has all the rum gone?" I quickly said in my best Jack Sparrow voice. Despite the toddler having never seen *Pirates of the Caribbean*, she had a thing for my Jack Sparrow voice and it never failed me.

Today was no different.

More water splashed all over me, the bathtub walls, and the floor as Violet began laughing for all she was worth.

I heard the door open behind me and automatically said, "I'm sorry, Ronan, I'll clean up all the water, I promise—"

My voice dropped off abruptly when I saw that it wasn't Ronan standing behind me at all. My belly did this weird flip-flop thing even as anger began to heat my blood. I turned my attention back to Violet. The little girl's eyes stayed trained on the man standing behind me. Her hands were still dabbling in the water, but she was clearly more fascinated with Luca now.

The silence in the small room became a living thing.

"Uh, Ronan has some clothes here for—"

"Me-me!" Violet called, then she was extending her arms. I thought she wanted me to pick her up, but when I reached for her, she shook her head and squirmed away from me. Her eyes were still on Luca.

"Is this what you want, honey?" Luca asked as he crouched next to me. A shiver ran down my spine when his big body brushed mine.

Don't get comfortable. Don't get comfortable. I repeated the phrase over and over, even after he dropped to his knees.

Luca handed Violet a baby bottle that she immediately began

drinking from almost nonstop. It was all I could do to keep my eyes on the child instead of the man beside me.

"I wasn't leaving," Luca murmured after a moment.

"I don't care," I responded before I could think better of it.

Silence. I needed to use silence as my weapon against him. Why couldn't I just remember that?

"When Ronan started examining her like that, I just—"

"I don't care," I repeated firmly. This time I looked at him as I spoke. I swore I saw a hint of some emotion that was just a little off-putting before his face hardened into a cold mask of nothingness.

No, not a mask... *this* was who he really was. All the facades I'd seen up until now... the gentle interactions with Violet, his seemingly protective behavior as he'd been helping me get Violet out of the warehouse... that'd been an act. He'd done a good job of not letting those masks slip... until now.

I waited for him to get up and leave, expected him to. But he didn't move. At least, not at first.

But when he did, it wasn't to leave.

I flinched when he reached for my hand but managed not to pull away. But it wasn't my hand he was going for. I held my breath as he took the washcloth from me and dipped it in the water before wringing it out. "Come here, sweetheart. Looks like Me-me missed a spot," Luca said softly as he reached for Violet. His long arms meant she didn't actually need to move for him to get to her. I waited for her to protest the contact, but instead, she dabbled her fingers in and out of the water. At some point, Luca had rolled his sleeves up, so I could see his bare arms.

Well, not so bare.

His left arm had a tattoo on the forearm. I couldn't make out what the design was, but the contrast of dark ink, tanned skin, and bright white dress shirt did that same unusual thing to my stomach that made me feel too warm inside. The sheer power I could see in his fingers had me wanting to reach for Violet because surely a man as big as him would use too much force on such a small child. I was in the process of taking the washcloth from Luca when he tipped

Violet's chin up just a tiny bit so he could wipe at some dirt near her ear. He stilled when my fingers came into contact with the wet material, but he didn't release it.

Violet didn't seem to notice the strange tug-of-war that was happening between me and Luca. She was too busy drawing some kind of pattern on top of the water.

I was the one who cried uncle and gave up my hold on the washcloth first. Luca continued cleaning Violet's face like nothing had happened.

"Where did you learn to do the voices?" Luca asked after several beats.

"What?" I asked before I could remind myself I was supposed to be using the silence card against him.

Luca's eyes slowly shifted to me and it felt like a gut punch. God, what was wrong with me?

"Scooby, Jack..." he said. *"Joe."*

He said that last one quietly, like he was afraid of what my reaction would be.

Perceptive man.

Because my reaction was the same that it always was when I thought of Joe.

Joe... another betrayal... another person leaving me behind.

"Remy," Luca whispered. The pity in his voice helped me shove the memory of Joe away.

"I don't know, I just learned," I murmured as I returned my gaze to Violet. But my eyes fell on Luca's strong fingers. I remembered how he'd gripped my arm when I'd been a kid. He'd pulled me to my feet but there'd been no real pain behind the move. Then his big body had pressed mine against the wall and he'd started whispering things to me.

Things I'd been silently begging every man before him to say.

I'll come back for you...I promise, I'll come back.

"When they put me in with other kids, they were usually the new ones," I continued.

"New ones?"

57

"Recently taken," I responded. My skin felt chilled as the dozens and dozens of faces ghosted through my mind. "They were always the younger ones. I think they knew."

"Knew what?"

"That I wouldn't leave them. That I wouldn't try to escape... they were too young to try and run with and I couldn't just leave them there by themselves. The people watching us... they didn't like it when the really little kids cried. They weren't allowed to mark the kids up too bad, but a few bruises wouldn't affect the price too much. I used the voices to try and keep the kids calm. They didn't know what was coming, but I did. I figured... I figured they deserved those last moments. The rooms we were kept in usually had a TV and sometimes some DVDs, so after watching a show or movie, I'd start copying the voices." I shrugged. "Maybe I just made things worse—"

"No," Luca interjected. "No, you didn't."

His certainty had me sneaking a peek at his expression. He was watching Violet, but his mind was elsewhere.

I wanted to know where, but I didn't dare ask. I couldn't. This man was not my friend. He was... *nothing*. I mentally nodded my head. Yeah, he was nothing to me.

"I wasn't leaving, Remy."

I opened my mouth to remind him that I didn't give a shit, but Violet used that moment to let out a loud squeal of excitement and then she began paddling her hands in the water so it went everywhere.

Everywhere.

"Violet!" I said loudly, but the little minx knew I wasn't upset. She paused only briefly, then began splashing some more. I swore I heard Luca laugh, but I knew that couldn't be right. I sensed rather than saw him stand. My eyes chose to linger on his backside as he turned away from the tub.

And my stomach started somersaulting all over again as a certain part of my anatomy took notice.

It wasn't the first time that I'd reacted physically to a good-looking man, but it was the first time I allowed my mind to play with certain mental images before locking them in the vault in my head. It'd been hard as fuck to accept I was gay as I'd gotten older. It'd actually only been a couple of years earlier that I'd come to realize that I was attracted to the very same gender who'd only ever caused me pain. It had been a devastating discovery because it had felt like someone had taken away my last chance at some sense of normalcy. I hadn't exactly been clinging to the idea of having a wife and kids someday, but somehow knowing I wouldn't have those things had been like being kidnapped all over again. I'd felt powerless and violated and I'd done what I'd always done... I'd fought it.

It was one fight I'd known early on I wouldn't win.

But fuck if I'd give in to that urge around this particular man, even if it was only in my head. He didn't deserve any real estate in my brain whatsoever.

I turned back to Violet and reached into the water to search out the bar of soap she'd been playing with early on. It was probably the only thing besides getting her out of the tub that would keep her from emptying the thing without the use of the drain. I figured Luca had left the room in a huff because of his wet clothes, so I jumped when his deep voice said, "Here, sweetheart."

I was up to my elbows in soapy water, so when I saw Luca hand Violet the little soccer ball keychain, I made my own mess as I grabbed for his wrist. "No, it might get ruined," I said. "I didn't give it to her in the tub because I didn't want the name to get messed up."

I wasn't sure who was more surprised by my words... him or me. I was supposed to not give a shit about stuff like that. I wasn't supposed to care that the little keychain clearly had sentimental value to him. Luca, for his part, had that haunted look pass over his features for the briefest of moments.

Then his eyes went to where I was still holding on to him. Violet seemed to notice the byplay between us, so she was fixated on that instead of the keychain.

Luca's skin felt hot beneath my fingers. And his wrist was thick... not beefy-thick, but strong-thick. Capable.

I jerked my fingers away.

"It's okay," Luca murmured. I swore he looked as uncomfortable as I felt, but I couldn't be sure. I also wasn't sure if his words were because of the way I'd grabbed him or if he was saying it was okay to give the toddler the keychain.

I made a conscious decision it was the latter, and before I could think about why I was doing it, I reached for his hand and brushed his fingers open. I eased the keychain from his grip and tucked it into my pocket. Violet, of course, noticed the keychain and began repeating my name over and over as she scooted closer to me. I knew we were skirting the edge of a major temper tantrum because I had no intention of giving the keychain to her, so I quickly began searching the tub for the soap again.

"Hey Violet," Luca said as he stood and stepped over to the sink. He returned with the cup that had been holding a toothbrush by the sink as well as the emptied garbage can. He showed Violet the simple act of filling the smaller cup and dumping it into the garbage can. The toddler's eyes went wide and then she was reaching for the cup. Luca held the garbage can so it was floating in the water in front of Violet while she filled it the first time. After that, her "I can do it myself" attitude came out and she held the garbage can herself as she slowly filled it with cup after cup of water. Her coordination wasn't great and she ended up pouring more water back in the tub than the garbage can, but it didn't matter. She was beyond fascinated.

Disaster momentarily averted.

"Thanks," I murmured.

"It's always the simplest things that intrigue them," Luca said softly as his gaze stayed on Violet. "It took me a long time to figure that out. I'd shower Gio with the latest toys and gadgets, but he always gravitated back to the stuff his mother gave him. She knew how to make it more than just a toy, you know?"

I didn't know. I had no clue what he was talking about. I was still stuck on the fact that he was a father.

"How so?" I asked, when he didn't continue.

He was silent for a long beat before saying, "She made it a memory, an experience… something he could keep with him long after the toy was gone. I'll never forget the first time I managed to get it right."

The small smile that graced his mouth made something spark to life inside of me. The sensation was nearly painful and I didn't like it… except that I kind of did.

"What did you get him?" I asked.

"For his eighth birthday I took him to Central Park and kicked a soccer ball back and forth with him. Just us. No bodyguards, cell phone off, used the same soccer ball my brothers and I had kicked around for years when we'd been his age…"

I didn't even know what part of his statement to process first.

Then I remembered the keychain in my pocket.

So the little trinket *did* haunt him. It was his son's.

I opened my mouth to ask him about his son, but snapped it shut just as fast. It wasn't any of my business, and more importantly, I didn't want to know. I didn't give a fuck why he was carrying his kid's keychain around.

"… don't want it to get in your eyes."

Luca's words dragged me back to the present. He was still kneeling next to me, his hand extended. He was holding a hand towel.

"What?" I asked dumbly. He spoke again, but my mind was too muddled to really listen. And when he reached for me with the towel, strangely enough, I didn't move.

Probably because my eyes were still fixated on his mouth and the facial hair that surrounded it. What would it feel like against my skin? It would itch, right? I'd been kissed a couple of times by tricks who wanted to fantasize I was their boyfriend and not just some cheap fuck, but the kisses had been anything but memorable.

It wasn't until the hand towel was softly swiped over my forehead that I crashed back to earth. I jerked backward, but there wasn't any place for me to go. My back hit the wall behind me. Thankfully, Luca didn't move any closer. He held out his hands slightly and said, "You have some soap on your face, Remy. I just don't want it to get in your eyes."

I opened my mouth to tell him that the soap I'd added to the bathwater was actually just a little bit of tearless shampoo, but I found myself unable to speak any actual words. Luca carefully placed the towel in my hand and then motioned to his own face. "Here and here," he said. My arms felt heavy as I swiped at those spots on my face.

"Good," he murmured. Did he actually look a little relieved?

Awkward silence filled the air between us. Violet, fortunately, was oblivious to what was happening and was happily playing with the items Luca had given her. Luca shifted back on the balls of his feet. His eyes lingered on me for a moment, then Violet. Then he rose. His shirt was soaking wet from Violet's earlier splashing around. The material hugged his broad chest and I could see the outline of his nipples.

"Do you need anything before I go?" he asked.

I steeled myself against the stupid disappointment I felt. I shook my head and glanced at Violet. I was clueless and scared shitless about how to deal with whatever came next with the helpless little girl, but I kept that fact to myself. Luca was the absolute wrong person to make that admission to. I could ask Aleks to help me and I knew he would, but he'd just started a relationship that deserved all of his attention. Ronan would likely help me, but the idea of being indebted to the mysterious surgeon scared me.

It wasn't until I heard my name on the softest of whispers that I realized I wasn't alone. I closed my eyes because I didn't want to see him anymore. I didn't want to know that he'd seen even a moment of weakness in me.

Warm, gentle fingers brushed my chin, then tilted my face up.

"Remy."

The pity I heard was like a knife to the gut.

"I'm not leaving," Luca murmured.

Tears stung the backs of my eyes, but I refused to let them fall. It was bad enough that he'd so easily read my emotions. But I'd be damned if I'd react in any kind of way to confirm his suspicions.

The tears didn't come, but neither would any of the biting responses that I knew I should say.

I kept my eyes squeezed shut even as I felt his fingers move and graze the length of my cheek. My traitorous body responded to the contact with a violent shiver. I chose to pretend I was craving a fix and nothing more.

I refused to admit to myself that maybe it wasn't a hit of heroin that my body was demanding at the moment.

He didn't say anything else. He was there one moment and gone the next. I heard the door close and fading footsteps, but I still refused to open my eyes for a good minute afterward. When I forced my lids open, I saw that Violet was still happily playing in the water.

I moved back to the edge of the tub and tested the water. "Only a few more minutes, okay, Violet?" I murmured. Violet's response was to hand me the cup. "You want me to do it?" I asked. She nodded emphatically. Despite all the developmental challenges ahead for the little girl, I still thought she was the most perfect thing I'd ever known in my entire life. I'd fallen in love with the baby from the moment I'd met her, and I'd envied Jackie in so many ways. I'd been foolish enough back then to think that being responsible for an innocent life would be enough to make the lure of drugs fall by the wayside forever, but Jackie had been proof that that wasn't the case. It had been another taste of reality I'd wanted to deny, just like the fact that I was attracted to men instead of women.

I poured the water into Violet's waiting garbage can and she clapped with delight. I felt a smile tugging at the corners of my mouth. I reached out to brush at the wet curls framing her chubby face.

It needed to be about Violet now.

Only Violet.

Of that I was certain.

Problem was, I had no clue how to make it happen.

CHAPTER SIX

LUCA

†4

"How's Gio?"

Those were the first words out of my brother's mouth, even before I spoke. King wasn't big on chit-chat, but since the day we'd received word that my son had been found and rescued from his abuser, none of my brothers had been the same.

And rightly so.

Maybe if Gio had been more of sound mind, we could have all gone back to who we'd been before he'd been stolen from us. But in my heart, I knew that wasn't possible. While King, Vaughn, and I hadn't exactly been saints in our previous lives, we'd done our best to stay on the right side of the law. Con and Lex hadn't had to worry about that fine line as much. But the brutal murder of Gio's mother and his subsequent abduction had changed us all.

And it was a permanent kind of thing.

"The same," I said to King.

There was a beat of silence and then King practically growled, "He's strong, Luca. He's going to come back from this."

His words tugged at something inside of me that already felt like it was only hanging on by a thread, so I didn't respond. Despite him not being able to see me, my brother picked up on my lack of response and said, "What do you need?"

"I'm going to need you to run a name for me."

"Go," King said in a no-nonsense tone.

"I don't have the name yet. Need you to be on standby when I get it. I want *you* to run it, not one of your guys."

To his credit, King didn't ask any questions. It was why I'd reached out to him instead of Con. While Con and Lex did most of the legwork to get an abducted child back to his or her family, King was the muscle. He'd always preferred vengeance to justice. Con had always been the more diplomatic one, though as a professional fighter, he used his skills both in and outside of the ring when needed. And Lex... well, Lex was the youngest and the best of us. He'd been the heart and soul of our group from the time he'd battled his own spindly body as well as the men and women who'd only seen him as a means to an end.

"Any word on Lex?" I asked.

This time King was the silent one. I'd figured King knew where Lex was, or at least what was going on with him, but he'd been keeping Lex's secrets to himself for the past several months. I couldn't blame our youngest brother for confiding in King rather than me... I hadn't exactly been in any kind of position to support the younger man.

"Tell me he's okay," I murmured.

"He's safe, Luca," was all King said. It wasn't exactly the answer I was hoping for, but I knew it was all I was going to get.

"And Con?" I asked. King didn't say anything, and I let out a sigh. King and Con had been fighting about Lex for weeks. All three men had grown up in foster care together, and King and Con had taken Lex under their wing long before Vaughn and I had met the three boys. But whereas King would watch over Lex from a distance, Con was the one who'd be trying to fix Lex's problems for him.

And since Lex had confided in King, it meant whatever he was dealing with probably didn't have a solution. I didn't want to even think about what that meant. But I had no doubt Con was out searching for the younger man. Lex had enough money to stay off the grid for a long time, but Con was as stubborn as they came. The only reason he'd left me behind in Seattle was so he could go find Lex.

"Fix it, King," I muttered. I knew that the men probably weren't even talking at that point, but I was in no position to play mediator and neither was Vaughn.

"Stay strong for our boy, Luca. He's going to need you."

"Us," I responded. Gio was my son but my brothers had all helped raise him. King hadn't been around as much when Gio had been growing up, but he'd fought countless battles to help us bring my child home, along with the hundreds of kids who'd been stolen from their families.

Kids like Aleks.

And Remy.

The reminder of the young man had my fingers itching. "I need to go," I said.

"He's coming home, Luca," King responded, his voice sharp and unyielding.

"Yeah," I said noncommittally, then hung up. I moved to the small bed in the middle of the sunny, yellow room. From all the pictures of horses on the wall, I had to assume the room belonged to Ronan and Seth's younger daughter, Nicole. I'd left my coat and jacket on the bed before entering the bathroom. My gun was still tucked at my back because I wasn't comfortable enough to go without it, even with my bodyguards outside. I'd had the sense to pull my dress shirt out of my pants so I could hide the weapon from Remy's view. But it wasn't my gun that my fingers were itching to feel.

I was in the process of pulling out the pack of cigarettes from my coat pocket when I heard the floorboards creak behind me. I managed not to go for my gun, but the fact that I wanted to was proof of how on edge I was.

Ronan watched me dispassionately as I tried to conceal the pack of cigarettes in my hand. "I wasn't going to smoke in your kid's room," I murmured. I didn't mention that I'd fully intended to smoke on the girl's balcony, though.

It was all I could do to not squirm beneath Ronan's knowing gaze. I could feel my muscles bunch as he moved into the room. Despite the role the man had played in rescuing my son, I wasn't able to let my guard down around him. The only men I trusted in my world were the ones I called brothers.

I kept my free hand loose and by my side as Ronan moved farther into the room. I didn't think the surgeon was armed, but I couldn't be sure. And from the little I knew about him, he didn't need to be armed to take me down. Hell, for all I knew, his men could have already dispatched my bodyguards just like they'd done to Con and King in New York the previous month when they'd come to get Aleks.

I remained still as Ronan approached me. There was no relief as he moved past me. I merely turned so I wouldn't have my back to him. He grabbed a half-empty bottle of water off the nightstand next to the bed and extended it to me. "You can put your ashes in here," he said gruffly at the same time that he motioned to the balcony. "You'll still be able to watch for him."

There was no reason to wonder who *him* was. And it shouldn't have come as a shock that Ronan had figured out that I'd been reluctant to leave the room for the mere fact that I hadn't wanted Remy to think I'd walked away from him again. I snagged the bottle from Ronan and strode to the balcony. I hated the fact that the man was seeing yet another one of my weaknesses, but being on edge around Remy even more than I already was just wasn't going to cut it. The way the young man had jerked away from me when I'd gone to wipe his face with the towel... it stung.

It just fucking stung.

I had the cigarette lit and was already drawing the smoke into my lungs when Ronan stepped onto the balcony and shut the door behind him.

"How many of your guys are out there?" I asked as I studied the backyard between the glances I kept shooting at the bathroom door.

"None."

"Liar," I murmured.

"Ask me why there aren't any, Luca," Ronan responded.

I laughed as I took another drag on the cigarette, then shook my head at the man's naivety. "You think you're untouchable." I glanced at the gorgeous view of Puget Sound and the Olympic mountain range beyond. "You think your money and reputation will protect you. You think it's enough to buy your family a normal life." I took another puff on the cigarette, then dropped the rest of it in the bottle of water. I'd wanted the whole thing but had known after the first inhalation that it would do nothing for me. If anything, I was more jittery than before. But as always, I kept my voice even as I glanced briefly at Ronan. "You want a piece of advice, Ronan?" I asked.

He didn't answer me, of course. I didn't care.

"Power won't protect you from men who can't be bought. Someday the kid or brother or father of some pervert you had offed will come after you with something a thousand times more valuable than cash." I paused and checked the bathroom door through the glass of the balcony door. "It's the same currency you trade in… justice. But the cost won't be *your* life… the return on that isn't high enough."

I handed him the bottle with my discarded cigarette. Unfazed, he took it and leaned back against the balcony. The second my hand touched the door handle he said, "Eight."

I looked over my shoulder at him with a small measure of triumph. So the exalted man wasn't the honest do-gooder he pretended to be.

"You want to know the difference between you and me, Luca?" Ronan asked.

"Please, *enlighten* me," I said dryly.

Not surprisingly, Ronan didn't react to the jab.

"There are four two-man teams covering my husband and children every hour of every day. Eight men and women at any given time who'd be willing to lay down their lives for Seth or Jamie or Willow or Nicole. They give up time away from their own families to protect mine. Do you think they do that because I pay well?" The man took a couple steps toward me. "You're right that the men who come after my family will be seeking justice for some wrong they believe I've committed against them. They'll be looking to make me suffer in the

68

worst way possible… by taking that which is dearest to me. Just like that fucker who took your mother."

I flinched at that. It shouldn't have been a surprise that Ronan knew about my mother's murder. It was public record, after all. But his comment still caught me off guard, and my stomach churned as I remembered watching my mother's blood staining the crisp white snow around her lifeless body.

"The part you haven't figured out yet is that a paid bodyguard, no matter how skilled, can't stop that kind of hatred. But family can. And what you saw in New York was just a glimpse of my family. Those men and women protect my husband and children not because it's their job, but because that's what family does for each other. You stayed away from your son—"

"I had to!" I snarled as I got into Ronan's face. "I had to stay away from him to protect him!" I wanted to kill the man for saying the very words I'd long ago accepted as the truth. If I'd been in Gio's life more, if I'd tried harder to get his mother, Genevieve, to let me put a security detail on both of them, Gio never would have been targeted and he'd still have his mother. But I'd fucked up… I'd failed them both.

"You stayed away from your son to give him a normal life," Ronan continued, seemingly unconcerned by my rage. "What happened wasn't your fault, Luca. It wasn't your enemies who took him, who killed his mother," he reminded me. "There's no normal in our world. Every single man, woman, and child that I get to call a member of my family has had to learn this. We can bury our head in the sand, or we can accept it and deal with it. You've got a second chance with your son, Luca… with Remy. Don't fucking bury your head in the sand."

Ronan didn't give me a chance to respond and, in truth, I didn't have a comeback anyway. He pushed open the balcony door. I watched him go but just before he left the bedroom, I called his name. He stopped and turned to look at me.

"Remy and Violet stay with me," was all I said. It wasn't a request or question. It wasn't an acquiescence of any kind. It was the politest way I could think of to tell him to stay the fuck out of things.

Because I knew if Remy had a choice between my help and Ronan's, he'd pick Ronan each and every time.

And I just wasn't going to let that happen.

I waited for Ronan to say something, but all he did was glance toward the bathroom door... the one Remy was currently standing in with Violet wrapped in a towel in his arms.

A very pissed-looking Remy.

"I'll be downstairs if you need me," was all Ronan said. I had a sneaking suspicion he was talking to me.

And based on Remy's expression, I knew there was a very real possibility that I'd have to take the smug surgeon up on his offer.

CHAPTER SEVEN

REMY

†4

"**R**emy—"

"Don't," I managed to say quietly even as I rocked Violet back and forth. She'd been yawning a few minutes ago, so I knew there was a chance I could put her down for a nap, but if I went off on Luca like I wanted, no way that was going to happen. "Wait for me somewhere else." I didn't wait to see what his reaction would be to my demand because I didn't care.

Okay, okay, so maybe a *tiny* part of me cared. Maybe even *two* tiny parts. There was the part that was a little fearful of how he'd react to the order, but the other part was kind of looking forward to it. Somehow, fighting with Luca was less overwhelming than interacting with him on any other kind of level.

Like when he was touching me.

Or offering me comfort.

Or looking at Violet like he actually gave a shit about the little girl.

Maybe a knock-down, drag-out fight with the man would get rid of all these crazy weird feelings that were zinging through me. Not a literal knock-down fight because he could undoubtedly kick my ass with one blow, but if I could just get in his head…

"Me-me," Violet murmured drowsily in my arms. Her head had

71

dropped to my shoulder and she had her fingers curled around the keychain I'd returned to her after I'd made sure all the water from the tub was drained and her hands were dry.

"Do you want to hear a story, sweet pea?" I asked as I carried her to the bed. I could still feel Luca's presence in the room, but he'd at least moved out of my line of sight. I ignored him as I dressed the little girl and then tucked her into bed. I was dimly aware of the door snicking closed as I began doing some of the voices from the old *Bugs Bunny* cartoons. I strung together a ridiculous tale of Bugs and his friends that didn't make a lick of sense, but Violet didn't care... she always fixated on the voices rather than the story itself. Within five minutes, her eyes were closed. I lowered my voice and continued the story for another few minutes just to make sure she was really out, then I tucked the blanket around her. My heart hurt at how peaceful she looked. Her skin had a healthy glow to it now that it was clean, and instead of that god-awful needle fisted in her hand, she had the little soccer ball keychain instead. My eyes drifted to what I now knew to be Gio's name on the ball.

He laminated his son's name.

I tried not to think too hard on why he'd do such a thing, but I couldn't help but settle on the obvious.

His child was gone.

I didn't want to pity Luca, but the more I stared at Violet, the more I thought about what it would be like for any parent, even an asshole like Luca, to lose their child.

Yours didn't care.

The ugly reminder knifed through me and I pulled in a deep breath to steel myself against the sharp pain. All of that was in the past. Just like the shit that had happened with Luca. I wouldn't... *couldn't* let it affect me.

I leaned down to give Violet a quick kiss on the forehead, then quickly left the room to find Luca and end this shit once and for all. No way in hell was I going to let the son of a bitch rule anything I did. I'd seek Ronan's help first.

I didn't have to go far to find Luca since he was standing right outside the bedroom door. Before I could open my mouth to lay into him, he said, "In here," and opened the door across the hall. I bit back the automatic response that bubbled up in my throat and stepped into the small room that had a couple of comfy-looking couches and a huge TV.

I hadn't even made it all the way into the room when he tugged me into it and shut the door.

The panic was instantaneous and pretty much debilitating. I opened my mouth to scream at the same time that I pushed at him with my hands.

"Remy, wait, I just want to—"

"No!" I shouted, but the sound only came out as a croak. I scrambled to try and escape him. Luca grabbed my upper arms and held me against the door. I saw him open his mouth, but the roaring in my ears prevented me from hearing anything he had to say.

Not that I needed to hear him. I knew what he wanted.

I kicked at him with my legs as I thrashed in his hold. Because of our positions, I couldn't do much good with my feet, but I managed to get my hands free and used them to beat on his back, then his face. His body still held mine against the door as he managed to use his forearms to block some of my blows, but not all of them. I went for his hands next, because I knew he was too strong for me and Ronan was my only hope. I tried calling for the surgeon, but once again, my voice was hoarse and dry. It was like I hadn't used the thing in years.

Luca's hold on me was frighteningly unbreakable, even though he wasn't doing anything more than occasionally grabbing my wrists to try and subdue me. Even though blood began to streak down his wrists from where I was scratching at him, he continued to keep me pinned against the door. I thought I heard him calling my name, but I couldn't be sure.

Though he was right in front of me, I might as well have been blindfolded because I couldn't make out his features. And the more I fought, the more energy I expended, and within a minute, I was hyperventilating and on the verge of a full-blown panic attack.

And the tears.

The goddamn tears started to flow. I wanted to kill him for that alone.

For every fat drop of salty water that slid down my face, it seemed like my last shreds of energy left. I'd stopped clawing at Luca's hands, but held one of them with both of mine. He lifted the other and pressed it against the side of my throat. I accepted the inevitable as his thumb pressed against my jugular.

He'd won.

Yes, I'd still fight him the second he tried to push me to my knees in front of him or turned me around so I was face-first against the door, but I knew in my heart it wouldn't do any good. I couldn't match his strength and help was too far away to be of any use to me.

I'd made a terrible mistake in believing I was somehow safe from this man... that he owed me for what he'd done to me as a kid. I'd actually believed he might harbor enough guilt that I could use to my advantage to keep him away from me.

But he was the monster that, deep down, I hadn't wanted him to be.

I waited for him to make his next move and tried to plan how I'd react, but when he dropped his head to where my neck met my shoulder, I was completely unprepared. He still had his hand at my neck, but it wasn't until that moment that I realized how gentle his touch actually was. No, I hadn't been able to move him, but not once had his fingers pressed cruelly into my skin. And the fingers he currently had at my throat weren't really holding on to me either. That thumb wasn't applying pressure to my pulse point so much as it was... *caressing* it.

"Take a deep breath and call for him again," Luca said softly. "If you want Ronan to kick my ass, then do it, okay? Call for him again." Luca lifted his head. "I won't try and stop him."

Confusion swept through me. What was happening?

The hand at my throat disappeared. When it reappeared in my line of vision a moment later, I saw his gun. I swallowed the whimper that bubbled up in my throat. The game had completely changed now. Would he threaten to harm Violet? Was his plan to kill Ronan so he could take his time doing to me whatever the fuck it was that he wanted?

"I need to hear it all, Remy," Luca whispered. His voice sounded harsh, overused. "Because I get it now."

I shook my head because I was so fucking confused. My throat felt dry from the screams I hadn't actually managed to make any louder than a whimper, and my eyes stung from the hot tears that still coasted down my face. Luca removed his other hand from my grasp, but the gun kept me from making even the slightest sound.

"I thought I knew... I thought my nightmares were close. I thought I'd imagined the worst and that seeing your face night after night, hearing you calling for me... that it somehow made up for what I did to you. I've tried to justify leaving you behind in so many fucking ways, but..."

His voice dropped off and he looked down between us. I could have used the moment to go for the gun or try screaming my head off again, but I was reeling from his words. It was a ruse... this whole thing was some fucked-up game he was playing to mess with my head, to get what he wanted.

But what the fuck was that? What did he want?

I was horrified to hear that very question slip from my mouth in a broken whisper.

"Tell me all of it," was his response. His hand reached for mine and I was too dazed to resist. I felt the strength in his fingers as they brushed mine. God, did he want to hold my hand or something? Was he trying to lure me into some weird sense of security?

I gasped when the warmth of his fingers was replaced with the coolness of metal. I looked down to see Luca holding his gun against my palm. The barrel was pointed at the ground. His free hand came up to wrap around my hand and the weapon. His thick fingers maneuvered mine until I was the one holding the gun. My finger was resting lightly on the trigger. My body was shaking violently as I tried to make sense of what was happening.

But there was no making sense of it.

Either he'd lost his mind... or I had.

Or maybe I was in some drug-induced dream... maybe I'd taken that hit the night he'd broken into my apartment. Maybe I was in my tidy, boringly efficient apartment staring at the ceiling as the sweetness of my high coursed through my blood and flooded all my senses.

I stood there, frozen in a state of confusion and disbelief as Luca raised my arm like I was some rag doll.

"There's no safety on this type of gun, so it will fire every time you pull the trigger until the clip is empty," was all he said when he finally released his hold on me.

After he'd placed the gun against his own chest.

The gun *I* now had complete control of.

"Wh-what are you doing?" I asked shakily. My instinct was to drop the gun, but my mind wouldn't let me do it. "It's not loaded, right?" I asked—no, *demanded*.

"It's loaded," he calmly replied. "Take your finger off the trigger and pull back just a little on the front of the gun. You'll see the bullet in the chamber. There's also a chamber indicator on the gun..."

I didn't listen to the rest of what he said because I was too focused on the weapon in my hand. I knew in my gut he was telling the truth... that the weapon was loaded. I shouldn't have believed him, but I did.

How many times had I dreamed of a moment like this? Of having something at my disposal that would let me fight back against my captors and *win*? Or at least cause them some of the same pain they'd caused me? When I'd been sucking guys off in alleys or some trick had decided to take more than what he'd paid for, how many times had I fantasized about being able to pull out a gun like this and point it at them? I'd carried a little knife with me when I'd started working for Les because the pimp hadn't wanted to pay for handlers for his merchandise, but the thing hadn't done me much good. And Les hadn't given a shit if his "property" ended up raped or beaten or lying in a pool of our own blood in some back alley somewhere. I'd never had the funds to buy a gun, though. And I doubted I would have had the courage to use one.

But now?

Now I wasn't sure what I felt.

Powerful?

Definitely.

Safe?

Not really.

"Why are you doing this?" I whispered. I still had the gun aimed at him, but it was almost like I'd forgotten about it. I was so fucking angry at him for doing this to me... for confusing me like this. If it was a mind game, he'd bested me by a million percent. I reached up to pick at the nonexistent scabs on my head. The soft, clean hair that greeted me still felt foreign, even after two years.

"So you can tell me why you do things like that," Luca said softly.

When his eyes shifted to the fingers that were still scratching at my scalp, I stilled my hand.

"The *truth* about *why* you do them," he added. "How many times have you wanted this moment, Remy? This moment where you get to tell me anything and everything that happened to you... because of me? Because I didn't come back for you?"

He was provoking me. I knew that.

And it was working.

I shook my head. "You don't care," I murmured. "You don't—"

"Hurt?" Luca interrupted. "Feel?"

I nodded.

"You're right," he said coolly. He held out his hands and said, "I don't." He said it so easily... *too* easily. "Why do you touch your hair so much?"

I dropped my hand but didn't answer him. "Why were you in that house that day?" I blurted. I'd had no intention of revisiting the past, but the question was out before I could stop it.

"I was looking for someone."

I waited, but he didn't continue. His calm manner angered me. I felt like I was going to implode from the way my body was violently reacting to him, the situation, the weight of the gun in my hand and what it meant... but *he*...

It was like he said... he didn't feel.

"Why do you touch your hair so much?" he asked again.

"Who were you looking for?"

He didn't answer. The rules of the game hit me then. I told myself not to play because it was exactly what he wanted and I couldn't believe anything he might say, but he'd said he wanted the truth. So fuck if that wasn't what he was going to get.

"I'm not used to it long. Who were you looking for?"

"My son."

He said it without hesitation, without emotion. I nearly stumbled back, and I had to tighten my grip on the gun so I wouldn't drop it. "You're lying," I said angrily. "Game's over."

I kept the gun pointed at him and lowered my free hand to search out the doorknob. I'd go back to Violet's room and call for Ronan. He'd end this and no matter what it cost me, I'd beg the man to help me with figuring out how to keep Violet safe.

I closed my fingers around the knob at the exact moment that Luca reached into his pocket. The move startled me so badly I nearly pulled the trigger by accident. "Don't!" I shouted. Luca hesitated, but continued to pull something from his pocket at an almost glacial rate.

His phone.

Not another gun.

I felt like a fool.

And I could barely breathe.

I lowered the gun so I wouldn't risk accidentally shooting it. I hated Luca, but the gun wasn't who I was. I'd only ever wanted to protect myself, not seek vengeance for what had been done to me.

Luca hit something on his phone, then put it on speaker.

"Where are you?" was the first thing the voice on the other end said.

"I'm safe," Luca said. "Vaughn, put Aleks on the phone."

There was a beat of silence, then I heard some muffled voices on the other end of the phone.

"Luca? It's Aleks," I heard Aleks say. I could tell he was still on speaker on his end. "Are you all right? Vaughn and I have been trying to reach you for a week... you switched hotels—"

My friend sounded almost frantic. I wanted to tell him that he should save his concern for someone who deserved it, but my eyes were fixated on Luca.

Who was watching me just as intently.

"I'm sorry, Aleks. I didn't mean to worry you. I just needed some time to myself."

Had Luca's voice really gone a little softer just then?

"Aleks, I need you to tell Remy about Gio," Luca continued.

"What? Remy? Are you... are you with Remy?" Aleks asked, his voice full of confusion.

"I am. He's okay, Aleks," Luca said. "Will you tell him about Gio for me, please?"

There was a definite tremor in Luca's voice this time and I felt my heart begin to pound even harder in my chest.

"Remy?" Aleks said softly.

I needed to yell at Aleks to call Ronan or the cops or something. I needed to tell him that Luca was... what?

What was he doing exactly?

The gun was in my hands. I could easily call out for Ronan. Hell, there was a landline half a dozen feet from me on a small table. I could call the cops myself.

"I'm here," I said.

I heard what sounded like a half sob followed by a beat of silence. "Gio, um, he got taken, Remy. Like you and me."

I shook my head in disbelief because I knew Aleks would never lie to me. It wasn't in his DNA. And if he was telling me the truth, that meant what Luca had said was true.

My pounding heart suddenly seemed to seize in my chest and I felt lightheaded. I leaned heavily against the door in the hopes of staying upright, but my knees wouldn't support me. I let my back slide clumsily down the door but before my ass hit the floor, Luca was there. He caught me under the elbow with one hand while his other hand took the gun from my grip. In my confusion, I'd slung the thing across my own midsection as I'd tried to keep myself upright. Luca supported some of my weight as I sat down on the floor.

"Gio was eight," Aleks continued, oblivious to what was happening. Luca had left his phone on the back of the couch. "He was with his mom when they took him, so they... they shot her."

I felt sick to my stomach. I didn't want to hear this. I didn't want to be here.

"Luca and Vaughn and their brothers have been searching for Gio for years—"

"Stop!" I called. "Aleks, please stop." My head hurt so bad I was sure it was going to pop right off my fucking body. "Please," I croaked.

I didn't realize I was hanging on to one of Luca's hands until he loudly said, "Vaughn."

"I'm here," Vaughn said. I was sure I heard crying in the background. I wanted to apologize to Aleks for snapping at him, but I couldn't think, couldn't breathe.

"I'll call you later," Luca said.

A beat of silence followed, then Vaughn said, "You'd better, brother." Then the call disconnected.

"Remy," Luca began, but the second he touched my cheek, I jerked away from him. I ended up hitting my head on the door in the process. And then the damn tears returned with a vengeance and I knew I was fucked.

There was no game.

There were no winners.

Or losers.

Just the truth.

And that was one thing I'd never truly figured out how to fight back against.

CHAPTER EIGHT

LUCA

†4

My plan had been to give Remy what he wanted.

Me as a punching bag... both literally and figuratively.

But all I'd done was fuck things up. I'd broken him even more.

Maybe it hadn't all been about giving him the chance to lay into me... a part of me really did need to know everything he'd been through. Yeah, he'd told me what had happened to him, but his goal had been to shock me, to stun me, to knock me off my axis that night in his apartment. And he'd done all that. But I doubted he understood that it was the little things that weighed just as heavily on me.

Like how he'd talked about the kid in the warehouse who I'd given money to. He'd said the kid could only save himself, but how many times had the same thing happened to Remy? How many times had assholes like me come along and promised to give him the safety and protection he craved? How many times had he needed someone to stand in front of him and take on his battles, even if just for a little while? He'd already had to fight so many in his young life...

It gutted me every time the "nothing can touch me anymore" mask he wore slipped just a little bit.

His fear of dogs, the little nervous gestures he seemed to uncon-sciously engage in, his instinctive jerking away from any kind of phys-ical contact... they were like little knives being slid directly into my heart each time I saw them.

And that brief look of betrayal when I'd told him I was leaving the bathroom and he'd misunderstood me and believed I was leaving him again. He'd said he didn't care, but the words were clearly his only self-defense mechanism. I'd also known he didn't believe a word I said.

Hence my brilliant plan to let him confront me with everything. I'd thought lancing those wounds might be the start to healing them, but all I'd done was draw more blood.

"Remy—"

"What do you want, Luca?" he whispered. His face was pressed against his drawn-up knees and he had his arms wrapped around his legs. "You did it, okay? You won."

"This wasn't some game, Remy," I snapped and then immediately regretted it when Remy's whole body seemed to flinch. "Remy—"

"I kept it short because I kept getting lice, okay?" Remy yelled in frustration.

I realized he was answering my earlier question about his hair. His eyes pinned mine.

"After getting high, I'd wake up in these god-awful places and I'd be covered in fleas and roaches and shit. And my fucking head would itch so bad that I'd pick at my scalp until it bled. My skin too. I couldn't do anything about my skin, but it was easy enough to shave my head. So there. How does that help? Am I supposed to be magi-cally cured? Do you feel better now? Is this some come-to-Jesus moment that's supposed to fix me?"

I didn't have an answer for him. I didn't have any answers at all. I'd tried to steel myself for revelations like the one he'd just told me, but there was no preparing for them. I'd forced him into opening old wounds, and I hadn't even thought to have some fucking way to bandage them back up.

I collapsed onto my ass so I was sitting across from him because I simply didn't have the energy to get back on my feet. My legs ended up on each side of him, but I made sure not to touch him in any kind of way. I clasped my fingers at the back of my neck and stared at the floor because I didn't know what to do next.

So I took a page out of his book and went with brutal honesty.

"I'm terrified of what will happen to you and Violet if I let you out of my sight."

He didn't respond right away, and I wasn't sure if that was a good or bad thing.

"We're not your responsibility."

"You feel like it," I said. I didn't add that there was something else there too. Something that went beyond guilt and obligation or righting the wrong I'd done to him. I wasn't prepared to deal with those unexpected emotions myself, so I wasn't about to share them with him. I was physically attracted to Remy, but lust wasn't what made it impossible for me to walk away.

"Isn't it enough that you helped me find Violet?" Remy asked. His voice sounded a bit more even, but I couldn't bring myself to raise my eyes to look at him. I wasn't ready for him to see what was there. I needed more time to get my mask back in place.

"Is it enough for you that she's safe?" I asked. I pulled in a few breaths to internally calm myself, then lifted my head. As expected, he was watching me. But gone was the emotionless young man who'd told me not to waste time trying to save kids who weren't ready to be saved. There was no hint of the manipulative Remy who'd tried to shock me into walking away that night in his apartment when he'd told me what life after his abduction had been like. Unlike me, he didn't seem to be trying to slip any of his masks back into place.

He slowly shook his head.

"We want the same thing, Remy. To make sure Violet ends up someplace where she'll never face that kind of danger again. Can't that be enough for now?"

"Ronan can help me—"

"I couldn't save you," I interrupted angrily. "I couldn't save my son. I know you think I'm a heartless son of a bitch, but seeing that little girl in that room with that fucking needle in her hand—"

My voice dropped off because even the memory of it was making my heart race. How many kids at this very moment were in the exact same circumstances? How many wouldn't make it out of a room like that? Or if they did, it wouldn't be until after they'd been used and discarded like the garbage around them? How many would end up like Gio? Brainwashed until they didn't know who they were or that they were loved by the very families they'd been taken from?

I dropped my eyes again. My inner voice shouted at me not to expose my throat to Remy, but my stomach was knotted with fear for what would happen to him and Violet if I wasn't there to protect them. I heard myself whispering, "You owe me nothing, Remy, but I'm beg—"

"Okay," Remy cut in.

I was so caught off guard that I snapped my head up. Before I could express my disbelief, he added, "But Violet and I get to leave whenever I say."

I began nodding, but he put his hand up. "That day in the house never happened, do you understand me?"

I did, but he and I both knew there was no way to just pack that day away. But I merely nodded. He didn't need to hear about how none of this would change the fact that I wouldn't sleep tonight or tomorrow night or the next. He didn't need to know that every time I closed my eyes, I still heard his whispered pleas to come back for him. Or that my nightmares almost always had the defining moment where I had to choose between him and my son.

And no matter how often I vowed to save them both in the dream, I always failed.

Always.

"Luca?"

It wasn't until he spoke that I realized I'd dropped my gaze again. I couldn't remember a time I'd ever had so much trouble looking someone in the eye.

"Did you ever find your son?" Remy asked hesitantly.

I nodded. I knew what Remy would ask me next, so I automatically added, "He's alive."

He looked so relieved that it hurt to look at him. He must have seen something in my expression because the tension returned to his features. He started reaching for his hair, then seemed to remember himself.

"I'm sorry," he murmured. He might not have known the circumstances of Gio's situation, but he got it. If anyone understood that finding an abducted child alive and safe wasn't the same thing as alive and well, it was Remy.

"Do you know what Violet's mother's last name was? Or any information about her?" I asked. I wasn't trying to be dismissive of Remy's sympathy for Gio, but it wasn't something I could talk about.

"She never told me her last name, but I remember her talking about summers in the South. She had a Southern accent. And I think she named Violet after a relative... it was her aunt's middle name, I think. I'm sorry, I don't know anything else about her. I guess she just wanted to get lost and start over."

"Is that why you came here?" I asked.

I hadn't expected him to answer, but he surprised me when he said, "The getting lost part, yeah. I had help with the starting over part."

I wanted to ask him if it was Ronan who'd helped him, but Remy must have anticipated the question because he stopped me with one of his own.

"Do you think you can find Jackie's family?"

"If they reported her missing, then it should be pretty easy. If not, it will take a little more time."

"What happens to Violet if Jackie's family doesn't want her?"

I knew it was a possibility, but I couldn't picture any parent being willing to lose the last link to their child by abandoning their grandchild. With all the kids we'd reunited with their families after getting them out of the child sex trafficking trade, we'd never once run into a case where family members hadn't been overjoyed to get their loved one back. But if Jackie's family had kicked her out or abandoned her even after knowing she was pregnant, it wouldn't be good news for Violet.

"We'll find her a loving family, Remy," I said. It was a promise I knew I could keep. Even if I had to set up a trust fund for the toddler that would guarantee her future, I'd do it in a heartbeat.

Remy nodded and dropped his eyes. I swore I saw him wipe at them. I wanted to reach out and tip his head up so I could be sure, but it was really just an excuse to touch him.

"What? What is it?" I asked.

He let out a harsh laugh. He swiped at his face again. "I guess they're harder to stop once you start," he muttered.

Was he talking about the tears?

He didn't continue, so I just watched him for a moment. "Do you want her, Remy?" I asked after a moment. "Do you want to raise Violet yourself?"

He sat perfectly still for a moment, then let out a choked sob. "No," he whispered. I barely heard him, but he shook his head almost frantically. "I... I know that makes me a terrible person, but I'm not what she needs. I love her, Luca, I really do—"

"Hey," I said as I scooted forward enough so I could put my hand on his knee. He was working himself up with his explanation, like he owed me one. I was glad when he didn't pull away from me. "Take a few deep breaths, okay?" I urged gently.

He nodded and dragged in one breath after another. I gripped his knee every time he pulled a breath in. It took me a second to realize he'd started matching his breaths to the little squeezes I was giving him.

"She's such an amazing little girl and I'd be so lucky to be able to call her mine, but I'm not ready for that kind of responsibility. And she deserves someone who is... someone who can and will put her first. I... I'm still figuring out how to put one foot in front of the other."

His face went red with color, and when I saw him reach for his forearm, I knew instantly what he was afraid of. And I was so fucking proud of him for his strength that I just wanted to grab him and tell him how amazing he was. He was an addict who was still working through his own recovery and he was smart enough to know that trying to care for a child, and one with special needs at that, would put his own health at risk. And putting his sobriety on the line meant nothing but bad things for Violet.

"It doesn't make you selfish," I said. "You are doing exactly what Violet needs... you *are* putting her first. You saved her life, Remy."

He shook his head and climbed unsteadily to his feet. He seemed like he was on the verge of running. "I didn't do enough. I should have called CPS or something. Maybe if I had, Jackie would still be alive—"

"Don't," I said firmly as I rose. I took a chance and grabbed both his upper arms. His hands came up to grab my wrists, which still had smatterings of blood on them from where he'd scratched me, but he didn't do anything but hang on to me. "That little girl is so lucky to have someone like you in her corner. You could have just looked the other way entirely. But she's out of that hellhole because of you. If you're going to blame yourself for one event, you need to give yourself credit for the other."

He didn't respond, but he didn't look away from me, either. It felt like the smallest of wins. Several seconds passed before he did look down, but just to look at where his hands were holding on to my wrists. Awareness sizzled through my nerve endings as something shifted between us. I doubted he even noticed it, but it was impossible for me to miss. He began rubbing the thumb of one hand along one of the bigger scratches on my right wrist. He soon did the same with the other hand. His touch ignited a fire in my blood that had been dormant for a really, really long time.

For good reason.

"I'm sorry, Luca. I—"

"Remy," I nearly growled because I was trying to keep my rioting body under control. Remy stilled his fingers and looked up at me. His eyes widened slightly and his nostrils flared. He was like a prey animal that was trying to pick up the scent of danger in the slightest of breezes.

He was so very right to be wary.

"Don't ever apologize to me. Do you understand me?" I asked, forcing myself to keep my voice calm and even so I wouldn't scare him even more.

His breathing ticked up, but he didn't release me. In fact, his fingers began moving over my skin again, but even more softly this time. And his eyes were trained on mine.

Like he was trying to read my reaction.

If I just pushed my hips forward a little, he'd *feel* my reaction.

I told myself to release him, but it wasn't until he parted his full lips just a tiny bit and I saw his tongue dart out to wet them that I jerked back. I turned on my heel and fisted my hands. My body was screaming, but fortunately, I had an outlet to keep my hands busy. I snatched my phone off the back of the couch and sent a message to King with the details that Remy had shared about Jackie. I got a response almost instantly that my brother was on it. When I turned around, Remy was gone and the door was standing wide open.

So was the door to the room Violet was still in.

I pulled myself together as best I could. I tucked my gun back in my pants before heading across the hall. I stopped in the doorway of the yellow bedroom when I saw Ronan sitting on the bed with Violet in his lap. The toddler was holding a tablet, completely entranced by whatever she was looking at. I could hear music and sounds coming from the tablet—the annoying kind that usually accompanied kids' games. Remy was standing a few feet from the bed, clearly surprised at the sight of a quiet Violet on Ronan's lap.

Ronan's eyes shifted from Remy to me, then he leaned down and said something to Violet that I couldn't hear. The toddler ignored him. She didn't make a sound when he set her on the bed and left the tablet with her. His next stop was at Remy's side and I felt the same rage I'd experienced earlier in the day when he'd put his hand on Remy's shoulder. He didn't touch Remy this time, but he might as well have because seeing the big man whispering into Remy's ear had me seeing only red. It was all I could do not to yell at him to back the fuck off.

I was almost happy when the grim-faced surgeon strode toward me. He stopped directly in front of me and said, "If he tells me anything about you laying a hand on him in there"—his chin jerked in the direction of the room across the hall—"you're going to wish some of my men were on the grounds because they'd be the only thing to keep me from killing you."

I believed him. "If you thought me capable of hurting him, you never would have left me alone with him for so long."

"Who says I did?" Ronan asked. He lifted his phone to show a video feed of the room across the hall.

The fucker had been watching the whole time.

"You're lucky you gave him that gun when you did, you son of a bitch," he said softly as he leaned in so only I could hear him. His voice had changed from the cool, calm guy he'd been earlier when we'd been talking on the balcony to deadly and ice cold. "It's the only thing that kept you breathing."

"You know what happened in there," I said, undeterred. "He chose to stay with me."

"And if that's what he still wants, he'll cover for you. But if he's changed his mind…"

He let the threat hang there. Maybe if I hadn't already lost the most important thing in my life, I might have been a little frightened. Or maybe I was just itching for someone, anyone to get payback against me on Remy's behalf.

"What did you say to him?" I asked even as Ronan started to close the door to the room, leaving me outside it. I didn't like the idea of Remy being by himself with the other man, but it wasn't because I thought Ronan would hurt him. No, it was pure, old-fashioned jealousy.

"I told him he was family now," was all Ronan said right before he shut the door in my face.

Despite the fact that I didn't believe in that high and mighty family shit Ronan had spewed at me earlier, I couldn't help but also be a tiny bit grateful.

Because like Violet, Remy needed a lot of strong, good people in his corner. And while Ronan still annoyed the fuck out of me, I knew that he and the men and women who worked for him—fine, the men and women in his *family*—would be able to offer Remy more than I ever could.

But that didn't mean I was ready to let Remy go… yet.

CHAPTER NINE

REMY

+4

O nce unleashed, the man didn't do anything in simple measures.

And it wasn't just the fancy hotel room.

As soon as I'd finished my very long conversation with Ronan, I'd stepped out of the bedroom to find Luca nervously waiting. It would have been almost cute if the whole thing wasn't so fucked up. But as soon as I'd told him Violet and I were ready to go, he'd launched into action.

Starting with handing me a big plastic bag full of over a dozen new outfits meant for Violet. They'd been in various sizes and had included pants, skirts, dresses, onesies, pajamas, socks, shoes, tights, and underwear. There'd also been a few different sizes of diapers. Since Luca wouldn't have had the time to go shopping while I'd been in the room with Ronan, I could only assume he'd sent one of his men to pick up some stuff.

If I'd thought the clothes, in terms of just sheer volume alone, were a little over the top, as soon as I'd stepped outside of Ronan's house with Violet in my arms, I'd realized the man was just getting started.

Where there'd once been one car and two bodyguards, there'd been three cars and six men. Big, scary, clearly armed men.

Violet and I had been escorted by Luca to a large SUV which had had a brand-new child safety seat in it. In the back of the SUV, there'd been at least half a dozen plastic bags full of more clothes and toys for Violet. Luca had let Violet pick a toy out of one of the bags as he'd gotten her strapped into her car seat, since I hadn't had a clue how to do it. Violet had picked a doll, but when I'd tried to take the keychain from her so I could return it to Luca, she'd started throwing the mother of all temper tantrums. Luca had been the one to calm her by saying she could keep the keychain.

The hotel we'd gone to had been one of those fancy high rises and there'd been a couple more bodyguards waiting for us.

Along with some of my own possessions from my apartment.

I hadn't had time to be pissed at Luca for the invasion of my privacy because he'd insisted that Violet and I relax while he made us some dinner.

Yeah, the man cooked.

So he was gorgeous, rich, *and* he cooked.

While he'd made dinner, Violet and I had played in the spacious living room which had an amazing view of downtown Seattle, the waters of Elliot Bay, and the Olympic mountain range. Violet and I had watched the ferries go back and forth on the water for a bit before we'd settled down and started going through her new toys. I'd never seen her more excited. Dinner had been an informal affair. There'd been stir fry for me and Luca and some mac 'n' cheese for Violet. Within minutes of eating, Violet had started to nod off, and I'd taken her to the bedroom I was sharing with her and put her down for the night. I'd tried to go to sleep myself, but I'd been tossing and turning for the past few hours.

Hence the wandering around in the fancy hotel suite that was more like a luxury apartment.

I made my way to the full-length windows and stared at the twinkling lights of the city below. I still couldn't believe I was there... that I'd gone with Luca instead of staying with Ronan.

Ronan was, by far, the safer, smarter choice. That'd become even more clear after he and I had talked in his daughter's bedroom as Violet had played a game on his tablet. I didn't believe his claim that I was family now, but I hadn't argued with him about it. I'd already known Ronan would help me simply because Aleks was my friend. It was the same reason one of his men, Memphis, had helped me two years earlier after I'd left Chicago. Getting out of the city had been my only goal at that time. Aleks's brother, Dante, had made it happen after I'd told him where to find Aleks.

When I'd gotten off the bus in Seattle, Memphis had been waiting for me. He'd taken me straight to a methadone clinic, then an NA meeting. When I'd left the meeting an hour later, there'd been an apartment waiting for me, as well as the promise of an entry-level job at a security firm. I'd taken those opportunities and run with them.

I'd done everything right, yet fate had led me here.

I shook my head because as hard as I'd tried over the past several hours, I still couldn't process any of it... or what was to come.

The idea of being reliant on Luca scared the hell out of me and I was having a case of extreme buyer's remorse that I'd decided to go with him. But the thing that had led me to say yes to him earlier when he'd started to beg me to let him help me was the same thing that was keeping me from packing Violet up and going back to Ronan's or reaching out to Aleks for help.

He'd lost his son... and found him again.

I was desperately curious to know what all that meant, but the part that was keeping me rooted in this place that I had no business being in was a cold, hard truth that was forcing me to change my perspective about the day I'd first met Luca.

He'd been looking for his child that day.

And he'd found me instead.

I had a million questions that I wasn't sure I wanted the answers to. What I wanted was to have that day back. I wanted it to have been some other man who'd walked into that dirty room. Someone who would have done to me what all the others had. Another nameless, faceless pervert who took what little hope I'd had left inside of me.

Not a man who'd made me hold on to that little scrap of possibility with everything I was.

The sound of a sliding door jarred me from my thoughts. I turned to see a figure on the balcony. We were too high up for it to be an intruder, and the sight of the individual flicking a cigarette butt over the railing was proof that it wasn't someone with nefarious intent. I'd noticed the faint smell of cigarettes on Luca when we'd been in the den at Ronan's house, but I hadn't actually seen him smoking. But the tall outline of the figure and the way he moved left no doubt as to who it was.

Surprisingly, Luca didn't notice me at first when he came back into the suite. I remained silent as he moved to the small bar on the opposite side of the room. A little light above the bar came on when he opened one of the cabinet doors to retrieve a glass. He poured himself a shot of something and downed it, then filled the thick crystal glass with the same liquid, only more this time. He added a few ice cubes, but instead of taking another drink of it, he leaned against the bar. His shoulders rolled forward as he hung his head. His hands gripped the side of the bar. There was no mistaking the way his long fingers curled around the burnished wood.

I felt like an intruder on his private moment. But I couldn't make my feet move silently across the carpet to go back to my room. I should have cleared my throat or something, but truthfully, I was too caught up in the things I was feeling to even consider alerting him to my presence.

He made no sense to me.

No, scratch that.

I didn't *want* him to make sense to me. Whether I wanted to admit it or not, Luca had been playing a role in my life for much longer than I'd realized. There was still this part of me trying to hang on to the hate I'd felt for so long, but every time I tried to let it rise up so I could make decisions that made more sense, like choosing to stay with Ronan over Luca, I remembered the cracks in his voice as he spoke, the tremor in his hands when he touched me, the exquisite sensation of his lips briefly skimming the spot where my neck met my shoulder as he'd rested his head against me.

And then there were moments like this where his body spoke in ways that belied his wealth, power, and strength.

He frightened me.

But for the wrong reasons... or maybe the right ones. I didn't really know.

Luca hung in the same position for a moment, then grabbed his drink off the bar. He turned in my direction and instantly stopped. The only light in the room was coming from the bar.

We both just stood there for several beats. It should have been awkward enough to have me moving, but I stayed where I was.

"Do you want me to go somewhere else?" Luca asked quietly.

It was the last thing I expected him to say. This was his place, after all.

I shook my head but realized he might not be able to see me. "No," I managed to say. "I should... I should go back to bed."

He didn't respond. There was no confirmation that I should go, no argument that I should stay. He merely went to one of the leather chairs in the spacious living room and sat down. He held the glass in his hand and took a long sip before settling his hand on the armrest and just rolling the glass so the ice clinked against the crystal.

He was still wearing the same clothes he'd changed into when we'd gotten to the hotel room. His outfit had been a replica of what he'd been wearing earlier in the day. He'd even kept the gun on his person, though he'd untucked his shirt so it would cover the weapon when he was around Violet. But it looked like since we'd gone to bed, he'd tucked the shirt back into place. It made me wonder where his gun was.

It also made me wonder what kind of life he led that he needed so many men to watch his back and had to be armed at all times.

I remembered the way he'd put the gun to Taz's head that morning and demanded information on where Carla was. The move had been second nature to him. I'd fully believed he'd shoot the pimp to get what he wanted from him.

Luca took another sip of his drink. He never looked my way or acknowledged my presence. I moved to the couch and gingerly sat down on it, fully expecting him to tell me to leave the room.

But he remained silent.

"What happens tomorrow?" I asked softly, since that was one of the biggest reasons I was having so much trouble sleeping. I wasn't used to not being in charge of myself. I ignored the voice in my head that insisted that maybe, for once, it wasn't such a bad thing.

"Ronan gave me the name of the specialist he wants Violet to go see. He would have texted you the information, but you don't seem to be carrying your phone anymore."

"I was afraid Aleks could have Vaughn track me if I had it with me," I murmured. "So I left it at my apartment. I'm not really used to having a phone anyway... Aleks is the only one who ever calls me," I added absently. My heart was in my throat as I said, "But Ronan already examined Violet. He said she was okay."

I saw Luca glance at me, though I couldn't see his expression. But his voice was noticeably softer when he murmured, "She probably is, Remy. The therapist will be able to ask her things in a way we can't. If she's suffering from any kind of emotional trauma, we need to know so we can deal with it."

"Right," I said softly as I clasped my hands together and looked at the floor. I wouldn't have even thought to take Violet to someone like that. It was just further proof that I wasn't equipped to take care of the child. Guilt slammed into me all over again. The same guilt that'd had me seeking escape this afternoon when I'd admitted to Luca that I didn't want to try and raise Violet. I'd never felt like more of a failure in my entire life.

I felt the cushion next to mine dip, but I didn't look up.

"Talk to me, Remy. Tell me what you need."

I needed him to not be so damn observant... or I needed to get back to being better at pretending at things.

What I really needed was a fix.

Then none of this shit would matter.

I waited for the instinctive need to fight back against my own body's needs to kick in, but it wasn't there. I reached for my left forearm to run my fingers along the many, many track mark scars in the hopes of reminding myself why I needed to make sure I never stuck another needle into my veins ever again. But the agitation grew and grew and soon I was picking at my skin, then reaching for my hair.

My hand never made it there.

I jumped when Luca's fingers closed around mine.

"Tell me what you need," he whispered. My hand was cradled between both of his. One of his thumbs was rubbing against mine. Goosebumps exploded along what had to be my entire body. His touch was definitely a distraction, but it seemed to only fuel the hunger that was making my blood burn beneath my skin.

"Distract me," I choked out. "Tell me... tell me about the ocean and the dolphins."

It was the absolute worst topic I could have chosen, but with how quickly I was falling down the rabbit hole, I knew I needed something big to hang on to. I'd tried so many times *not* to remember the things Luca had told me about himself the night he'd pretended to assault me for the benefit of the people watching us via hidden video cameras, but when things got really bad and I needed something worth fighting for, my mind inevitably went back to the sound of his voice and the promise of someday seeing his beach, those dolphins... to the knowledge that I was finally safe... and free... and *wanted*.

"I remember the first time I saw them. It was shortly after we moved into the house. Vaughn and I were mad because it meant we had to switch schools, leave our friends. Vaughn and I were in the backyard pouting... and planning. Our mother didn't buy into any of that nonsense, so she just left us out there. We missed dinner and everything. But we were determined to get our way, so we didn't go back into the house. It was summer so it stayed lighter longer. Vaughn and I were both starving, but we'd agreed that we couldn't back down. We were sure that if we just held out long enough, our mother would give in to our silent protest and take us back to the city."

"How old were you?" I asked.

"I was seven, Vaughn was nine."

"And did your hunger strike work?" I asked.

I swore I heard Luca chuckle. He was still holding on to my hand. My racing heart finally felt like it wasn't going to jump right out of my chest anymore, but I was still on edge. I focused on Luca's voice and touch and tried to match my breathing to the rhythm of his finger stroking mine.

"Not even a little bit. Vaughn decided we should go for a walk on the beach to keep our minds off of food. I was whining like a baby and reciting all the foods I wanted to eat at that very moment. I was pissing Vaughn off. We started arguing, but then I saw this flash of something out in the ocean. We thought it was a shark at first, but Vaughn said the fin wasn't right. And there were too many of them."

"Dolphins," I said softly. Despite having lived in Seattle for the past two years, I'd only seen the Sound and not the actual ocean. And I'd yet to see anything like the orcas or other mammals that called the beautiful blue waters home.

"Vaughn and I didn't even have to say anything. We just looked at each other and then ripped our shirts and shoes off. The water was cold and rough, but we both knew how to swim and only had one goal in mind. But by the time we swam out to the spot where the dolphins had been, they were gone. We were so damn disappointed."

I found myself leaning in toward Luca because the adrenaline that had been trying to make up for my body's need to get high was starting to crash and I felt cold.

"We treaded water while we tried to figure out which direction they'd gone, but the waves were too big. But just as we were about to swim back, this fin came up out of the water right between us. I freaked out," Luca murmured. "Not sure how I managed not to shit myself."

I heard myself laughing. Luca's body radiated heat, so I tried to subtly shift closer so I could absorb some of it.

"Vaughn was so fucking excited because one fin after another began appearing around us. The whole damn group had come back. I thought they were going to eat us or something."

"Why'd you go into the water, then?" I asked.

Luca shrugged. It took me a second to realize I'd *felt* the shrug rather than just witnessing it. How the hell had I ended up practically pressed up against the man? And was his arm actually around my shoulders?

"I would have followed Vaughn anywhere he went... except up trees. I'm not a fan of heights."

"Luca, we're in the penthouse. You were just outside on the balcony," I reminded him.

Another chuckle. Luca shifted a little and then suddenly he was leaning back against the couch cushion, taking me with him in the process. The move was so fluid and relaxed that I wondered if he even realized he'd done it.

"You didn't see me out there. I was pretty much hanging on to the door handle, and I smoked that cigarette so fucking fast it almost wasn't even worth it."

Luca was still holding my hand, but the free one he had around my shoulders wasn't just sitting idle. No, he was gently gripping my shoulder and releasing it, much like he'd done with my knee that afternoon when I'd been having a similar episode.

"So the dolphins?" I reminded him.

"Right. Vaughn pretty much told me to stop acting like such a baby and then he started stroking the fin of this one dolphin that kept coming close to him. None of the rest of the dolphins stuck around long, but that one did. It was the coolest thing I'd ever seen."

"Was it enough to make you end your hunger strike?" I asked.

"You could say that. Our mother found me and Vaughn the next morning asleep on the beach surrounded by bags of chips and boxes of cookies. Our plan had been to watch for the dolphins to come back. We ended up being grounded for a week. The day our punishment ended, we were back in the water with the dolphins."

"Did *you* get to touch one?"

"No, I chickened out," Luca murmured.

"Do you... do you still go to the water?"

Luca didn't answer right away, and I automatically tensed up

99

because I thought maybe I'd overstepped my bounds. I started to sit up, but his fingers subtly gripped my shoulder to keep me from moving. I could have easily moved away from him, but for reasons I didn't want to explore, I didn't.

"Vaughn and I still own the house we grew up in. I don't go there much anymore, not after Gio…"

His voice dropped off for several long seconds. I thought he wasn't going to continue, but he pulled in a breath and said, "The few times I've been there, I still see them. I know they're not the same ones, but sometimes I wonder…"

This time when he fell silent, he stayed that way. I couldn't be sure what he would have said next, but I figured it probably had something to do with swimming with the beautiful animals again. I'd only ever seen them in movies and on TV, but it was easy enough to imagine what it was like to watch them in the wild, to be envious of the freedom they had.

Neither of us spoke again for a while. I was surprised that Luca still had his arm around me, but I was just as surprised that I was allowing it. I had no idea what Luca's sexual orientation was, but at the moment, I didn't really care. If he'd wanted to hurt me, he would have done it in the den at Ronan's house or during any of the many opportunities today when it'd been just me and him. There'd been a few times when he'd been touching me that I'd been sure he was into men, but he also had a son, so for all I knew he could be just curious and his preference was mostly for women.

Whatever it was, I was just glad to be able to take advantage of his strength and warmth for the moment. The tempting taste of heroin on the back of my tongue was finally starting to fade and I felt like I could breathe again. I wasn't proud of the fact that I'd had to rely on Luca to pull me out of the episode, but it was what it was. There'd be plenty of time tomorrow to beat myself up over it. Admittedly, I'd been hanging on by a string all week as I'd had to enter my old world to search for Carla and Violet. Under normal circumstances, I might have had enough fight in me to deal with all of that, but Luca's reappearance in my life earlier in the week had fucked with my head a lot more than I wanted to admit. Searching for Violet had given me something to keep me moving, but now that things had quieted again, the old demons were trying to take advantage.

"Better?" Luca asked quietly. He didn't sound triumphant or gloating. In fact, he sounded calmer himself. He'd left his glass by the chair he'd been sitting in. At some point he'd put his feet up on the ottoman in front of the couch. His one hand was still holding mine, but his thumb wasn't stroking mine in a consistent pattern anymore. I wondered if that was because he knew I no longer needed that rhythm to focus on... or *he* didn't need it.

To an outsider, we probably would have looked like a couple having a sweet, domestic moment.

I nodded in response because I was starting to feel my eyes getting heavy. My cheek met with a little bit of resistance while I was moving my head. Good lord, when had I started resting my head on his shoulder? I jerked my head up and mumbled, "Sorry."

The hand he had on my shoulder came up to brush the side of my head and then to my utter shock, he was urging my head back down. "S'okay," he said. Did he sound a little tired himself? Maybe he'd just had too much to drink? I'd only seen him have the one shot, but he certainly could have had more before his cigarette.

But he didn't smell heavily of alcohol.

"Do you have a dolphin story?" Luca asked. He was still toying with my hair and the sheer pleasure of it had me leaning more heavily into him. Warning bells were going off in my head, but I couldn't make my legs and arms follow the silent order to get up and go back to bed.

"I've never seen any," I said.

I felt Luca shift a little and when he next spoke, I swore I felt his mouth against my temple.

"Is there something from when you were a kid that you'll remember forever... before you were..."

Taken.

He didn't need to say the word. I was glad he hadn't.

"My grandmother taking me to a movie set when I was around eight." The second I allowed the memory to take root in my mind, my eyes began to burn.

"Your grandmother was an actress?" Luca asked in surprise.

I shook my head. "She was a caterer. The movie was only in town for a week or so—they were filming a couple of scenes at this old farm. It was a horror movie... like with vampires and zombies." I forced back the emotion that was threatening to close off my throat. "She told me to stay with her by the catering tent, but I was fascinated by all the people in costume. These zombies would come over in full makeup and start chatting with her like a regular person and I was just completely entranced. I was sure I'd never seen anything cooler. I started wandering around the set and asking everybody questions about their jobs. The director took notice and put me to work. I ran errands for him and everyone else... taking scripts to people or getting an actor a snack or something to drink. When the film finished wrapping and left town, I was so disappointed."

"Did you want to get into the business after that?"

I shrugged.

"Because you do the voices—" Luca began, but then stopped abruptly. "I'm sorry," he murmured.

And I knew why.

He was remembering the reason I'd started mimicking voices in the first place... to entertain the kids who'd been abducted just like me.

"I try not to think about it too much anymore," I admitted. I closed my eyes as I let Luca's strong fingers massage away the tension that had started building in my head as I'd remembered those days. Memories like that had kept me going for a long time after I'd been taken. Sometimes too long. "I should go to bed," I said drowsily, even as I folded my arms and shifted closer to Luca so I could steal more of his heat for myself.

"Just stay a little longer," I thought I heard Luca say, but I couldn't be sure. All I knew was that one minute I was listening to the sound of his heart beating beneath my ear and thinking it meant I was probably pressed up a bit *too* close to him, and the next minute I was slipping into the darkness where there was nothing to greet me but blissful silence.

CHAPTER TEN

LUCA

+4

I'd expected him to be gone by morning.

Not *gone* gone. Just not sprawled across my chest anymore.

But Remy was pretty much in the same exact position he'd fallen asleep in hours earlier, as was I. I wasn't sure which was more miraculous... that Remy had let me hold him or that I'd slept for more than a couple of hours at a time.

Okay, so it'd only been like four hours, but sleep was sleep. I'd gone without it for so long that four hours felt like four days in my book.

As good as the rest felt, though, I wasn't sure there was anything that could match the feel of Remy's light weight on top of mine or the way his fingers kept reflexively curling into my chest. I still had my hand in his hair and the other was covering the one he had just above my heart. I wished I could see his face from our positions, but it was impossible, and I didn't dare move him for fear of waking him up. I'd seen enough of the strain in his features yesterday to know he was just as behind on sleep as me. So the only thing I could really study was his hair. It was thick and soft, and I couldn't even imagine him with no hair and bloody scabs all over his body. He smelled of the hotel shampoo and his skin finally had a little color, though he was still pretty pale. I wasn't sure if that was just his natural skin tone or something a good percentage of the residents of Seattle had in common... the sun did seem to neglect this part of the country quite a bit.

But not today.

The sun was just rising and though our view from the room was of the west, the sun's rays were casting a unique symphony of light and dark colors across the sky. It would probably be a perfect day to spend outside.

A perfect day for soccer with my kid.

The warmth I'd been feeling evaporated almost instantly at the thought of Gio lying practically comatose in his bed.

He was alive, but he was as out of reach today as he'd been over the past eight years.

More so, actually.

Remy stirred against my chest and I held my breath. I wasn't ready for him to wake up yet. I didn't want to see the regret in his eyes when he saw where he was... and I sure as hell didn't want to see the hate or disappointment. Because despite him knowing about Gio, I hadn't expected things to really change between us. How could they? I'd still left him. He'd still suffered terribly because I hadn't kept my promise to him. It didn't matter that I'd tried to find him. I'd been too late, and I'd known that was a very real possibility when I'd chosen to leave him to follow the lead on Gio.

And, of course, because fate didn't think any of that was enough to contend with, I now had to battle a growing attraction to the young man in my arms that I hadn't been prepared for. I'd been with a decent amount of men since I'd accepted my sexuality in college, but they'd mostly been anonymous hookups in shitty clubs.

The closest I'd come to having a relationship was with a young man who'd come on to me shamelessly at work after he'd been hired in the mail room. He'd been an insatiable fuck who hadn't wanted anything more than someone to set him up in a nice place that a mailroom clerk would never be able to afford. There'd been no pretending that he was anything more than the gigolo he'd always wanted to be. He'd never sworn his undying devotion to me and I'd never had to pretend I had any personal feelings for him. I'd needed an exclusive fuck toy and he'd wanted to be just that. In exchange, he'd gotten a healthy bank account, a credit card with a generous limit, and an apartment in a swanky neighborhood. When things had ended right after Gio had been taken, I'd made sure the guy was taken care of long enough for him to move on to his next sugar daddy.

I hadn't been with anyone since I'd lost my son. Sex hadn't even been anywhere on my radar. I'd been consumed with finding my child and as the days had changed to months, then years, I'd added on to my obsession by getting as many kids as I could back to their families. In between all that, I'd had to keep up the persona I'd spent a lifetime building. No one besides my brothers had known that Luca Covello, the former-mobster-wannabe's-son-who'd-gone-legit, had lost the only thing in his life that'd really mattered. I had been and still was a shell of a man on the inside, but to the outside world, I was the domineering, ruthless businessman who walked that fine line between legal and shady. Even having Gio back, no matter what his condition was, I still couldn't claim him like I'd always wanted. My father had made sure of that. I'd inherited too many of his enemies to risk exposing my son to.

My vibrating phone on the small table next to the chair I'd been sitting in the night before had Remy stirring against me. I moved my hand down to his back and ran my fingers up and down his spine in the hopes that he'd settle again, but it only lasted as long as it took my phone to start vibrating again, about thirty seconds after it stopped the first time.

Remy sighed and shifted his body until his face, more specifically, his *lips*, were pressed against the column of my throat. My dick, which was already half-hard, started to throb, and it was all I could do to keep my lower half under control. I knew I needed to wake Remy up because *this* wasn't exactly what I'd been expecting.

"Remy," I said softly.

What I could only classify as a sexy little whimper escaped his throat and then he was moving again. His nose nuzzled me, then it was like he was inhaling, like he was trying to breathe me in.

"Remy," I repeated, this time through gritted teeth because Remy had tugged his hand free of mine and was sliding it across my chest. His palm landed on my nipple, which tightened beneath my shirt. My phone began vibrating again, but I couldn't have moved even if I wanted to.

And I definitely didn't want to.

I was caught in this weird, semi-frozen state. I knew I couldn't touch him and I knew I couldn't let him touch me anymore, but I also couldn't make my body respond to any of my commands to release him. Remy's lips were on my Adam's apple. My swallowing must have registered with him, even in his sleep, because his mouth opened just a little over the bump. His hand applied pressure to my nipple at the same time his warm breath skittered over my throat. The pressure in my balls became too much.

"Remy, baby, please, you have to wake up," I pleaded as I moved the hand I had on his back to his head. I tried to grab his wayward hand with mine, but he moved it up to my throat. I covered his slim fingers at the exact moment that he placed them behind my ear. I tilted my head so I could look down at him on the off chance he was awake and wanted this, because that was really all the permission I needed.

I was *that* far gone.

I saw his beautiful blue eyes staring back at mine, but I could tell he wasn't completely awake. That was probably why his hold on me tightened. His intent was clear as he held me in place while he started to scoot up my body enough so our mouths would be in line.

"Remy, you need to wake up," I repeated. I put my arm around his waist to keep him from moving up my body anymore. "It can't be like this," I whispered, more to myself than him. His mouth landed on my jaw, but before he could tip my head so the next caress of his gorgeous lips would land on mine, there was a soft knock at my door.

"Mr. Covello?"

The sound made Remy pause, but it wasn't until the next knock that his eyes cleared. I expected him to yank himself away from me, but he didn't. I wasn't sure why he hung there for another beat, but I could still feel his breath on my face. He was panting like he'd run a marathon. His body tensed against mine and I found myself holding him tighter rather than releasing him.

"Luca?"

He said my name as a question. Like he truly didn't understand what was happening. His eyes dropped to my mouth and then lifted again, and the question became a different kind.

Or at least, that was what I was imagining.

It was less about confusion and more about permission.

"It's okay, Remy," I murmured as I began to dip my head. I justified to myself that he was fully awake now. Nothing else in that moment mattered.

Or so I thought.

Because Violet and whatever dick of a bodyguard was knocking on my door chose that moment to demand our attention. The little girl started shrieking from the bedroom she and Remy were sharing and the knocking on the front door turned into heavy pounding. Remy and I quickly separated and right before he took off, the regret I'd been hoping I wouldn't see filled his eyes to brimming.

"Remy!" I called because I just didn't want him to completely freak out.

"I'm fine," he responded. He sounded like the Remy from yesterday morning… the angry, bitter one who thought I was a fool for trying to save some random kid turning tricks in a warehouse full of addicts.

I got up and stormed over to the side table to grab my phone, then went to the front door and practically ripped the thing off its hinges. "What?" I snarled.

The bodyguard had the decency to look apologetic, but I still wanted to rip his hand off.

"I'm sorry, sir, we're having difficulty keeping him downstairs. Should we call the police?"

"Who?" I asked. Wasn't I paying these guys a small fortune to deal with the exact shit that was causing this asshole to pound on my door at the crack of dawn?

"Your brother, sir."

"Which one?" I asked, since it could have been pretty much any one of them except Lex. Lex would have just hacked my phone so he could turn the ringer back on to get my attention.

My phone chose that moment to vibrate in my hand. I glanced at it and nearly growled when I saw Vaughn's name and the message he'd sent.

Fuck it, I'm coming up.

I swiped my phone to unlock it, then hit my brother's name. Before the call connected, I saw a second message that read, *Get down here, asshole. We're in the lobby.*

Vaughn picked up on the first ring.

"I'm coming down," I snapped impatiently and then hung up. I was sure I heard a muffled sound on the other side that sounded a lot like groaning, but I doubted it was Vaughn making the sound.

"If Mr. Valentino asks, tell him I'll be right back," I said to the bodyguard. I untucked my shirt as I moved to the elevator so I could cover the gun at my back. The hotel was understanding about my security detail, but I couldn't exactly walk around with an exposed gun and I wasn't about to leave the thing behind. Maybe if it'd been all of King's men protecting me, I would have. But aside from Terrence and Stan, the men I'd brought with me from New York, I'd hired these particular guards from a firm in Seattle... and not even the best security firm.

Because it just so happened that Remy worked for the best security firm in Seattle. Or at least he had. He hadn't been to work at Barretti Security Group in the past week as he'd searched for Violet, so I had no clue what his employment status was. But I hadn't wanted to risk any of his co-workers somehow finding out what was going on with him, so I'd settled for the second-best firm in the city.

So it was no surprise when I reached the lobby of the hotel and saw one of the bodyguards sitting on a decorative bench near the elevator. He had his hand at his bruised throat and one of his teammates was holding a bottle of water.

I scowled at both men.

"Where's my brother?" I asked. The man whose ass Vaughn had clearly kicked actually blushed and stared at the floor.

"We put them in a conference room," the other bodyguard said. "The hotel guests were getting nervous."

"Them?" I asked, not caring about the other guests. I should have just rented out the whole damn hotel. At least Vaughn had had someone with him to take down the bodyguard. That was remotely comforting.

"A young man," the bodyguard said. "They appeared to be... *together*."

Aleks.

I shook my head at the bodyguard and nearly fired them both on the spot but managed to hold my tongue. Since Aleks didn't have a violent bone in his body, I knew it was back to just Vaughn kicking ass by himself.

"I'll escort you, sir," the bodyguard said.

"Don't bother," I snapped.

"It's the Olympic conference room," the man called sheepishly. I waved him off and went in the direction of the conference rooms. I had already memorized the layout of the hotel, so I knew how to get there.

When I opened the door, I saw Vaughn standing in front of a visibly upset Aleks. He was caressing his face and whispering something to him. Aleks was holding on to Vaughn's wrists.

I'd gotten used to such intimate scenes in the six weeks I'd been around my brother and his young lover, but it still got me in the gut every time. I was both envious and overjoyed that my brother had found his other half. No one deserved to be together more than Vaughn and Aleks. But I also knew what it meant for me.

Vaughn wouldn't be coming back home with me.

Aleks had a huge family here in Seattle. Along with his older brother, Dante, and Dante's husband, Magnus, Aleks was a part of Ronan's weirdly close group. And, of course, there was the added caveat that some of the very men who worked for Ronan were in relationships with men related to the Barretti family.

The same Barretti family Remy worked for.

I considered myself a smart man, but it was impossible to keep track of who was who and what side of the family tree they fell on. But it didn't really matter because all those branches meant one thing.

Vaughn would be staying here with Aleks when the time came for me to take Gio home. It was a heartbreaking thing to have to accept, but I wouldn't have had it any other way. Vaughn had loved Aleks for years and he'd given up so much already to help in the search for Gio. And Vaughn had saved countless lives with the work he'd done. It was his turn to have the family he'd always deserved.

Vaughn and Aleks both looked at me when I entered the room. My brother looked pissed and Aleks was a mess. He'd clearly been crying. Vaughn took Aleks's hand as they both approached me. I fully expected Vaughn to take a swing at me. We'd resolved a lot of things with our fists, especially in recent weeks when Vaughn and Aleks had been reunited. But my brother merely dropped his lover's hand so he could wrap both his arms around me.

"Thank fuck," he murmured.

I was surprised at the show of emotion, but even more surprised when I felt tears sting the backs of my eyes. Vaughn and I had said some shitty things to each other recently, and while we'd come together in a last-ditch effort to find Gio and keep Aleks safe, I wasn't sure our relationship was going to survive the betrayals we'd inflicted upon one another.

I found myself clinging to Vaughn for several long seconds, much like I'd done when I'd come out to him as a terrified nineteen-year-old gay college freshman who'd just learned that one drunken encounter with a woman had resulted in a very unexpected pregnancy.

I felt my brother's big hand settle at the back of my head, like he knew what I was feeling at the moment and was giving me that extra bit of reassurance I needed that everything was going to be okay.

With Remy.

With Gio.

When he released me, Aleks practically pushed into my arms. The show of emotion wasn't unusual for Aleks, but it *was* unusual that he'd show it with me. I hadn't exactly been his favorite person.

"Remy's okay," I said to Aleks as I embraced him.

"I know," Aleks said.

"Did he call you?" I asked in surprise.

Aleks shook his head. "He's with you, so I know he's safe," was all Aleks said. I looked at Vaughn in surprise, but he just smiled like Aleks's confident statement was the most natural thing in the world for him to say.

"What are you doing with him?" Vaughn asked once Aleks released me. I didn't miss how the younger man immediately returned to my brother's side.

I sighed and motioned to the chairs surrounding the conference table. Once we were seated, I said, "I was worried about him after what happened at the wedding."

"He was with his sponsor, Joe," Aleks said. "I talked to him. He said Remy was okay. Remy said that too."

I wasn't about to divulge Remy's secret that he'd been pretending to be Joe when he talked to Aleks, so I simply said, "A lot has happened since then." I gave my brother and Aleks a quick rundown about Remy's search for Violet. If either man thought it strange that I'd been following Remy, neither said it. I also left out the details of just how tense things had been between me and Remy.

"So they're both with you?" Vaughn asked in surprise. "Remy and the child?"

I nodded.

"And you got Ronan involved?"

I nodded again. I knew what my brother wasn't asking. It was the same question I was still asking myself. Why was Remy with me instead of Ronan?

"I've got King working on trying to find Violet's family."

"Then what?" Aleks asked. "If you find her family, what happens to Remy?"

I shifted my eyes to the younger man. A month ago, he'd been afraid to talk to me directly. He'd been terrified of angering me and being punished like he had been for so many years by the men who'd used him like he was nothing more than a piece of property. I couldn't help but glance at the scar on his neck. His previous captor had caused the mark when he'd had the links of a collar welded together while it was on Aleks's neck.

"You said Remy saved your life," I murmured as I considered the many differences between Aleks and Remy. When Aleks had told me about Remy, I hadn't known at the time that the young man was the boy I'd left behind. I'd been lost in my own grief about Gio at the time, so I couldn't remember the details of what he'd told me. But there was one thing he'd said that I hadn't forgotten. "You said he was a fighter."

Never would there be a truer statement about Remy.

Aleks nodded.

"I'm sorry, I don't remember the rest of what you told me that night we talked," I said.

Aleks dropped his eyes, a move that was something that had been ingrained in him for a long time. But he lifted them again almost just as quickly, and I felt so proud of him. I knew it was something he was working on to build up his self-confidence around people.

"I thought the first time we met was in this bathroom at one of the auctions. Someone had hurt him pretty bad," Aleks said softly and I saw his eyes tear up. He moved closer to Vaughn, and not surprisingly, my brother put his arm around him and kissed his temple. "Remy wasn't there to be auctioned off, but I guess he was supposed to be... *entertainment* for some of the customers while they waited for the auction to start. He, um... we don't talk about the stuff that happened that night," Aleks explained. "Dante told me that last part. Anyway, when I saw him in the bathroom that night, he was really upset. I wasn't supposed to talk to anyone else, but I just wanted to make him feel better. There was this flower arrangement in the bathroom. It had some really nice blue irises in it, so I gave him one and told him what it meant... hope. Flowers... they always made me feel a little better, so I thought..." Aleks dropped his eyes again and said, "It was stupid. After what that man did to him, a flower—"

"Hey," I said before my brother could respond to his lover's comment. "Aleks, look at me," I urged. I was glad when he did. "I don't need to ask Remy to know it meant something to him... you were probably the first person in a long while to offer the very hope that none of you were allowed to have."

Aleks considered my words for a moment, then nodded. "Dante told me that Remy and I had met before. We were both in the same house after I was taken. Remy recognized my birthmark." Aleks pointed to a spot on his collarbone. "That's how he knew it was me in the bathroom. But I don't remember meeting him before that." Aleks paused and added, "Remy and I don't talk about those times. I've tried a few times, but he... he just wants to forget."

Aleks looked so heartbroken that I said, "He said he used to act out certain voices for kids in those houses, Aleks. Do you remember someone doing that?"

Aleks stared at me a moment, then his whole body went stiff. He nodded almost frantically, but he couldn't seem to find his voice. He turned to Vaughn. "I do," he finally managed to get out. "Oh my God, I do," he repeated. "I, um, didn't understand English, but when the men took the TV away and told us to go to sleep, I couldn't stop crying. This boy, he was three or four years older than me, started talking in this funny voice. I couldn't understand the words, but it was that cartoon duck... the one who's hard to understand and is friends with the mouse."

"Donald Duck," I said. "Gio always liked him." Vaughn glanced at me with concern, but I didn't hold his gaze.

"Yeah, him," Aleks said. He slumped against Vaughn. "I can't believe that was Remy. He never told me his name and he was gone the next morning." Aleks fell silent for a moment. My brother was soothingly stroking his upper arm. Aleks dashed at a few stray tears, then looked directly at me. "Can I see him, Luca? Please?"

Even if I'd wanted to say no, I couldn't. I wasn't sure if Remy would be okay with seeing Aleks, but I owed Aleks everything. I couldn't deny him this. And even if Remy didn't agree, he needed it too.

I nodded. "He's upstairs," I said. Aleks seemed nervous as he and Vaughn followed me to the elevator. The worthless bodyguard

Vaughn had kicked the crap out of was back at his station but when Vaughn passed, the man pretended not to notice him.

I really did need to hire better security.

The bodyguard waiting outside the room opened the door for me. I entered and saw a fully dressed Remy sitting on the floor in the living room with Violet. She was working on a bottle of milk at the same time that she was playing with her toys. My body reacted to the sight of Remy when his eyes met mine. He was clearly tense because he climbed to his feet and wrapped his arms around himself.

Then he saw that I wasn't alone.

Neither Aleks nor Remy spoke when they saw each other. Not surprisingly, Aleks broke first. He moved past me and hurried across the room. I heard a choked sob leave his throat right before he reached Remy. Relief went through me when Remy opened his arms for Aleks. Remy enfolded Aleks into a tight embrace. While Aleks might have been the more vocal of the pair in terms of expressing his emotions, Remy wasn't completely unaffected. He closed his eyes as he held on to Aleks and at some point during the exchange, it seemed like the roles reversed and Remy became the one who was being held. Remy's eyes met mine over Aleks's shoulder, but I couldn't tell if he was pissed or not. I would have liked a few minutes to talk to him about what had happened earlier when he'd woken up in my arms, but even if I could have convinced my brother and Aleks to give us a few minutes, Violet clearly wouldn't have been as receptive to letting Remy out of her sight because she began calling his name and holding out her arms when she realized we had visitors.

"Make me some breakfast, brother," Vaughn said as he gave my shoulder a light punch. I knew it wasn't the food he was interested in, but the privacy that came with me cooking. He'd be able to lay into me while well out of hearing distance from Aleks and Remy, who were both preoccupied with Violet. The little girl seemed wary of Aleks, but I doubted it would take her long to accept him. The way he was cooing at her and marveling over the cute little dress Remy had put her in was sure to earn him bonus points with the shy toddler.

I forced myself to turn away and go to the kitchen. I still had a view of the living room, but there was no way I could hear anything Remy and Aleks were saying.

"What the fuck are you doing?" Vaughn asked as he leaned against the counter and folded his arms.

How was I supposed to explain something to him that I didn't understand myself? I'd told him what I'd done to Remy when he'd been a kid, but Vaughn hadn't been there. Yes, he'd lived in that world for a long time as he'd searched for Gio, but he'd never put his hands on a kid... he'd never left one behind...

Even as I considered the thought, I knew it was bullshit.

He might not have left Aleks behind, but he'd been forced to allow things to happen to Aleks so he wouldn't break his own cover. He'd "worked" for the man who'd held Aleks captive for years. He'd finally broken his cover when he'd had no choice, but how many times had he had to watch the young man he'd started to care for suffer at the hands of his abuser and been able to do nothing about it because Aleks's captor was the only lead we'd had on Gio at the time?

"I couldn't do it again," I muttered.

"Do what?"

"Walk away," I bit out as I took my frustrations out on a couple of tomatoes.

"So what's the plan? You help him find the kid's family, and then what?"

"I don't know," I admitted.

"Luca—"

"I don't know, Vaughn," I snapped. I realized my voice had carried when I looked up and saw Aleks, Remy, and even Violet looking at us. The trio slowly went back to whatever they were doing on the carpet in the living room. Vaughn watched me with pity.

I diced some scallions so I didn't have to look at him. "I'll make sure he's okay before I leave. Is that what you want to hear?"

"It's not him I'm worried about," Vaughn murmured.

That got my attention. I stopped cutting and looked up.

"What are you talking about?"

"It won't change what you feel, Luca. I don't think you get that," my brother said. There was no doubt about him pitying me now... it was clear as day in the way he sadly said my name.

"If you want to say something to me, brother, then just fucking say it," I muttered. "I'm just righting a wrong, nothing more." My internal bullshit meter was off the chart, but I wasn't about to tell him that.

"Hey," Vaughn said angrily as he straightened and stepped into my space. He kept his voice low. "You did the best you could with the circumstances you were given. If you'd gotten Remy out when he was a kid, you still would have had to live with the guilt of missing out on the chance to find Gio. You were in a lose-lose situation."

Rage flowed through me, but only because Vaughn was saying everything I already knew to be true. I was seeking absolution but there was none to be had. Even if Remy somehow miraculously forgave me, I would never be able to rid myself of the guilt.

But it wasn't about me.

"So what, Vaughn? I'm just supposed to apologize and move on? Leave him to figure things out with Violet on his own?" I huffed. I pushed past my brother, but predictably, he grabbed my arm.

"That's not what I'm saying, and you know it. Don't put fucking words in my mouth. But he's"—Vaughn motioned in the direction of the living room—"not alone. He has me, Aleks, Ronan—"

"Remy chose me," I blasted back because I was sick of hearing Ronan's name when it came to Remy.

Vaughn stilled and his expression went from frustration to confusion. "Luca, tell me you didn't bring him here because you—"

"Don't," I snarled as I got into my brother's face. "It isn't like that, and fuck you for thinking so little of me... *brother*," I bit out.

"Can you blame me?" Vaughn responded, unfazed by my fury. "After what you tried to do to Aleks?"

He might as well have shoved a knife in my gut. I'd regretted the plan I'd had for Aleks, but I'd been desperate to find Gio. I'd apologized to Vaughn and Aleks both, but to have Vaughn throw it back in my face... it was proof that I hadn't earned back his trust.

Maybe I never could.

But for him to think I'd brought Remy here just so I could take advantage of him?

"James," Aleks interrupted, his voice quiet and mixed with what sounded a little bit like disappointment. I'd only heard him call my brother by his first name on a few occasions, but it never failed to catch me off guard.

Until now.

Now I was just too fucking pissed to care.

Aleks was standing on the other side of the counter with Remy right behind him. Remy was holding a quiet Violet. I had no idea how much the younger men had heard, but it didn't matter. I just needed to get the hell away from Vaughn before we once again came to blows.

I shoved past my brother and bit out, "Make your own damn breakfast and then get the fuck out." I carefully moved past Aleks who reached out to touch my arm. I heard him say my name with regret, but I just shook my head. I needed to lick my wounds in private. I didn't dare look at Remy as I walked past him too, even though I knew it would likely be the last time I saw him.

As I headed toward my bedroom, I told myself it was better this way... that Remy would get the help he needed, and he'd get it from people who cared about him and would be there for him beyond whatever happened with the little girl he cared so much about.

That's what I told myself, but fuck if there wasn't another louder, more insistent voice in my head that kept repeating one word over and over... a word that proved that maybe my brother wasn't as far off the mark as I would have liked.

Mine.

CHAPTER ELEVEN

REMY

†4

I didn't feel as bad about entering his room when I found him on the balcony once again smoking. I chose to believe he hadn't heard my soft knocks rather than ignoring them altogether.

Violet was quiet in my arms, as she had been since Vaughn and Luca's blow-up in the kitchen. She was toying with Luca's keychain.

Unlike the night before, Luca was standing close to the railing of the balcony. In fact, he was leaning against it and was staring down at the traffic below. He looked tense, of course, but I wasn't sure how much of that was from his aversion to heights versus his argument with his brother.

I hadn't heard Vaughn and Luca's entire conversation, but what I had heard was still disturbing as hell, especially the part about Vaughn's accusation that Luca had done something to Aleks.

When Luca came back into the bedroom, he looked pale.

And surprised to see me.

But his expression quickly hardened as he said, "You're still here" and then went to the closet on the far side of the room. He removed his gun from the back of his waistband and set it on one of the closet shelves before he began stripping off his shirt. It was all I could do not to stare at his muscled back. His moves were quick and efficient as he tugged on another crisp white shirt. I wondered if he even owned any other colors or any clothes that weren't dressy.

"Vaughn and Aleks are waiting downstairs," I said, carefully watching his reaction. I swore I saw him pause in the act of buttoning up his shirt sleeves. "I asked them to wait ten minutes for me."

"You can ask Terrence to help you pack Violet's things and get them downstairs. Terrence is the guard by the front door."

The indifferent dismissal was answer enough, but instead of sending me for the door, it had me stepping closer to him.

"What is this, Luca?" I bit out impatiently. I covered one of Violet's ears as I gently pressed her head to my chest. "Yesterday you practically begged me to let you help us and today you're telling us to fuck off?"

"You're better off with Vaughn and—"

"I didn't put my trust in Vaughn," I snapped. "I put it in *you*. Because that was what you asked!"

He didn't respond. Hurt lanced through me. "You know what, forget it," I said. I turned to go, but he suddenly grabbed my arm and gently pulled me back.

"Wait," he murmured. "Just wait."

Where his expression had been dull and lifeless before, his eyes were full of emotion now.

I shifted Violet in my arms because despite her smaller than average size, she was still heavy in my arms. Luca must have noticed because a second later he was steering me to the bed. "Here, sit," he urged.

I sat down on the edge of the mattress and turned Violet so she could sit on my lap. But she extended her arms to Luca and said, "Ca."

I wasn't sure who was more surprised, Luca or me. But Violet wasn't in any mood to be patient and so she called for Luca again. Luca actually looked at me questioningly. I nodded and picked Violet up so she was standing on my lap. Luca carefully took her. The way he expertly cradled her against his chest tugged at something deep in my chest. How many times had he held his son like that?

"What did you do to Aleks?" I asked as Luca dutifully admired the keychain Violet was showing him... *his* keychain.

Luca stilled and looked at me. I wasn't one for beating around the bush, so I didn't really feel bad about the bluntness of my question. And truth was, I really needed to know what he'd say that he'd done to my friend because it would be the driving factor behind my next decision.

The shame in Luca's expression helped more than he probably realized.

Luca sat down on the bed next to me and shifted Violet until she was in a more comfortable position.

"I sent men to kidnap him," Luca said quietly. His eyes were on the floor. "Six weeks ago. There was a man from his past who wanted Aleks for himself and I wanted to find that man because I thought he knew where Gio was. I wanted to use Aleks to lure the guy out of hiding."

"The Stylianos guy, right?" I asked.

Luca looked at me in surprise. "You know?"

I nodded. "Aleks gave me the abbreviated version a few minutes ago. I just wanted to make sure you told me the same thing."

Luca let out a long sigh. He studied Violet who was watching him with big eyes. "Vaughn said it wouldn't change how I feel," Luca said softly. "He was talking about you, but I think he was trying to prepare me for Gio too, you know?"

I considered his words along with his behavior over the past twenty-four hours. Actually, it'd been more than that, since he'd been following me for a week.

"Guilt," I said quietly when it hit me all at once. "Your brother was trying to tell you the guilt wouldn't go away."

Luca nodded. "He's right. He always is."

There was a trace of amusement mixed in with the sadness in his voice. My own chest tightened in response. This man confounded me and I had so many mixed feelings about him, even more so since I'd woken up this morning practically lying on top of him with his mouth mere inches from mine. But all that aside, I wasn't a vindictive person. I didn't want to add to his suffering.

"Luca, I—"

"Don't, Remy," he murmured right before he turned his head so he could look at me. "I have to learn to live with what I did to you. There's no forgiving it. Just like I have to learn to live with not being able to save my own child when he needed me most. I justified the things I did to you, to Aleks, by saying nothing was more important than bringing Gio home. There's no undoing that. There's only living with it."

Luca gave Violet a quick kiss on the top of her head, then handed her over to me. "I'll have Terrence help you with Violet's stuff."

I knew I should just let him go. Going with Aleks and Vaughn was the safer bet. But in my heart, I knew the safer bet wouldn't make me feel safe. It was the same reason I hadn't stayed with Ronan when he'd offered. Nerves rattled my insides as I grabbed Luca's hand the second he stood. I couldn't bring myself to look at him.

"Do you want us to go?" I asked. It was a cowardly move, putting the question on him so I could use his response as an excuse, but I didn't care. I didn't understand what the fuck was going on at the moment, so yeah, I wanted *him* to decide.

I was looking at Violet, so when Luca dropped my hand, I wanted to die, to slink away and lick my wounds.

But then his fingers were tipping my chin up so I had no choice but to look at him. His thumb slid up my cheek. God, the man was beautiful.

He stroked my skin for a moment, then shook his head. "No. No, I don't want you to go."

A wave of heat went through me, but I wasn't sure if it was his touch or his response. I nodded and said, "Can I use your phone to call Aleks?" I really wanted Luca and his brother to talk, to patch things up, but I figured they probably both needed some down time to process the things they'd said to each other.

Luca handed me his unlocked phone, then took Violet. The move was so natural, like we'd been sharing responsibility for the toddler our whole lives. "How about some pancakes for breakfast, princess?" Luca asked.

Violet babbled some incoherent response, then showed the keychain to Luca. As he carried her from the room, I heard him admiring the little trinket like he'd never seen it before. I swore I also heard him say something about how she'd probably be a great soccer player someday, but I wasn't sure. The mere fact that Luca talked to her the way he did, like she was a regular little girl and not one who had endless obstacles to overcome, possibly for the rest of her life, made my throat feel thick with emotion. I took a couple minutes to collect myself before calling Aleks. I kept my explanation that I would be staying with Luca simple, and my friend seemed unsurprised. There was a lot I needed to talk to Aleks about, starting with the admission I owed him that I'd lied to him a week earlier about Joe, but it wasn't something I could do with a brief phone call.

After hanging up with Aleks, I went to find Luca and Violet and discovered them having breakfast. Only, Violet was on Luca's lap as he fed her tiny pieces of pancake he'd cut up. I knew Violet didn't understand the concept of using any kind of utensils, even when someone was feeding her, so Luca was handing her the sticky food with his fingers. Both man and child were covered in syrup but neither seemed to notice.

And Violet was clearly in love.

With both the man and the pancakes.

I went to sit across from the pair at the small table. Luca glanced up at me and I felt my heart start slamming even harder in my chest when he smiled at me.

"I'll clean her up, I promise," he said.

I had no doubt that he would. As rough as the man's edges were, he clearly knew what he was doing when it came to Violet. I looked around the kitchen to confirm what I'd already suspected—he'd cooked the pancakes himself instead of ordering them from room service.

"You're a natural at this," I said as I watched Violet start reaching for the food on the plate on her own. Her moves were awkward and clumsy as she grabbed the next piece of pancake but when she got it to her mouth on her own, Luca praised her like she'd just painted the Sistine Chapel.

"I wasn't always," Luca responded after a moment. "Did you ever see that *Three Men and a Baby* movie?"

I laughed because I had seen it once. I nodded.

"Well, add another man to the mix, and that was us. I'm pretty sure there were times V wasn't convinced she'd get our son back in one piece."

"V?" I asked.

Luca stiffened just a little, like he hadn't really even realized what he'd said. "Gio's mom. Genevieve. I started calling her V about five seconds after she introduced herself to me in freshman economics."

"How long were you guys together before you had your son?" I asked. I told myself I wasn't fishing for confirmation that Luca was, at the least, bisexual, but my mind didn't hesitate to call me a liar.

"We weren't together... not really," Luca said. "I... I never had those kinds of feelings for her. I loved her, but just as a best friend. We, um..."

I actually felt myself smiling when Luca began struggling to find his next words. The man was blushing... actually blushing.

"You..." I prodded.

Luca chuckled and shook his head. The sound went straight to my groin.

"Let's just say midterms were particularly stressful, and V and I celebrated passing our econ exam with some really bad scotch I'd stolen from my dad's liquor cabinet one weekend. She and I pretty much pretended the whole thing hadn't happened until two months later when two little lines instead of one on the first of many pregnancy tests proved it had."

Luca's easy smile faded. "I thought it would be the worst thing to ever happen to me, but it turned out to be the best."

"Did you guys get married?" I asked.

Luca shook his head. "When V told me she was pregnant, I told her

I didn't want the baby... that I couldn't be a father. Even if I'd come from a normal family..."

Luca's voice dropped off for a second before he finished with, "I couldn't be a father. I couldn't risk turning out like..." He shook his head and focused on Violet once again.

I knew he wanted to drop the subject. It was written in the way he held himself, in how quiet he'd gone as he cuddled Violet and watched her eat. I should have let it go, but I'd never seen him so vulnerable. From the day he'd strode into that room when I'd been a kid, I'd felt his power, confidence and control. He'd been back in my life for such a short time, but all those things were still there. But he'd let me have little glimpses of something else too... something just under the surface. It was the *something* I'd latched on to as a child. In that room in that awful house eight years earlier, he'd been strong and in charge, but he'd been scared too. I'd heard it in the crack of his voice as he'd whispered to me that everything would be okay, even as he'd put on a show for the cameras.

He'd fought despite his fear.

So after he'd left, I'd done the same. No matter what my captors had done to me after that, I'd fought.

And not just because I'd believed Luca was coming back for me.

But because I'd wanted him to be proud of me for surviving when he did find me again.

I'd had moments like the one he was having too, though. Moments where I'd felt so tired that my resolve had started to fade.

"Like?" I prodded carefully. At worst, Luca could shut the conversation down. It was a risk I was willing to take. My need to know the answer was greater than my need to not churn up the calm waters between us.

Instead of answering, Luca looked directly at me and I just knew. No idea how, I just did. It bordered on scary, how certain I was.

"Your father," I said. He didn't confirm it, but he didn't need to. "What changed?" I asked.

"Vaughn," Luca returned.

"He convinced you that you wouldn't be like your father?"

Luca shook his head. "He convinced me that it was okay not to be."

"I don't understand," I admitted.

Luca looked thoughtful for a moment, then said, "Our father had big dreams for himself. Not us... just himself. You know those gangsters like Al Capone and Bugsy Siegel? Well, Vidone Covello pictured his name would be in the history books alongside the likes of them. He wanted to be respected... feared. The funny thing is, he was a great businessman and he could have had all those things if he'd just focused on making a name for himself that way. But given the choice to earn a legitimate buck or a questionable one, he'd go for the questionable one every time. He built businesses based on intimidation and fear... crooked deals were more satisfying than negotiating good ones. Swindling people was a rush. When our mom paid for it with her life, it just became more of an obsession with him. He was convinced it was a professional hit meant to send him into hiding when it was really nothing more than a broken man getting revenge against our father for cheating him and causing him to lose everything."

Luca fell silent for a moment. "Vaughn and I bought into what he was selling for a long time, but I think all we really wanted to do was please him. Which meant I couldn't have a kid at nineteen years old. My father had a lot of plans and none of them included his son having his own child... or being a fag."

I barely managed to stifle the sound that tried to burst free at Luca's admission about his sexuality. The crude word he'd used was telling. I doubted it was his word, but rather his father's.

"You said Vaughn changed things for you."

Luca nodded. "Vaughn and I had been acting for so long, I think we both got caught up in it. We'd let our father put us in these roles he'd created after our mother died. Vaughn was the brawn and I was the brains. I was the face of the business, Vaughn was the muscle behind it. But we were never those people. The first thing Vaughn said about me becoming a father was how much our mother would have loved that... after lecturing me on safe sex practices, of course." Luca smiled again and I instantly felt the rubber band that had been stretched tight within my chest start to relax. "We spent hours just talking about our mom and I started to realize that maybe I'd end up being a great parent like she was. V had already decided to keep the baby, no matter what, but I'm ashamed to say it took me a little longer to get on board."

"What did your father say about the whole thing?" I asked.

"By the time I told him, I'd gotten smart enough to realize he didn't get a say."

I must have looked confused because Luca continued without prompting.

"Even though my father was just a wannabe gangster, he'd managed to make a lot of enemies and the cops were constantly investigating him for things like fraud, racketeering, tax evasion, and money laundering. I couldn't risk what had happened to my mother happening to Gio or V, so I kept their existence a secret. I didn't get to be in Gio's life full time and I had to take a lot of steps to cover up my connection to him. It meant secret meetings, no going to his school to watch him in recitals and stuff, no giving him my last name... nothing that would tell the world he was a Covello. But when he was five, I finally decided to tell my father about him. I guess deep down I was hoping Gio would change him like he'd changed me."

Luca shook his head. "The old man looked at my son like he was a prize bull who'd bring in big money at an auction." Luca was toying with the keychain as he spoke. Violet had finished eating and was nodding off in his gentle hold. Her eyes were fixated on the little soccer ball.

"It was so fucking easy," Luca whispered. He sounded almost confused. "I'd spent years trying to find the guts to walk away, but the second the bastard gave my son the last name I'd been too afraid to for all those years, it was like I just woke up and took this deep breath. I took everything from him after that. The money, the businesses... he'd already put things in my name to protect them from the government investigations. He'd been *that* confident I'd always be under his thumb. I could have just liquidated it all, but maybe a little part of me *was* like him, because I wanted to make him pay for all those years he'd made us, Vaughn in particular, suffer. I made him watch me take his businesses legit and make more money with them than he ever could have. And I never once had to break the law to do it."

Luca's tone wasn't one of arrogance, but rather, satisfaction. Like he hadn't realized until that very moment that he'd managed to pull the whole thing off.

"And Gio and V?" I asked.

"I still couldn't claim Gio," Luca murmured. "I wanted to, more than anything... but my father had made way too many enemies and I couldn't be sure how deep he'd managed to get his fingers into the organized crime world before I'd put a stop to all of it. I couldn't risk my son. I did everything I could think of to protect him. And none of it made a fucking bit of difference," Luca finished bitterly.

I still had a million questions, but when Luca gave Violet a little squeeze and said, "Let's go get you cleaned up, honey," I knew he was done talking. To me he said, "Our appointment is at ten and it will take about an hour to get to the therapist's office."

Right, Violet's session with the counselor.

Reality was a cold slap in the face. "I'll be ready," I managed to say. I felt Luca's eyes on me, but I kept mine downcast.

"I made you some pancakes. They're in the microwave."

I wasn't sure if I told him thank you or not. By the time my mind cleared enough from all the newfound revelations I was having about the man, it didn't matter if I thanked him or not because he'd already left the room.

Which, I needed to remind myself, was probably a good thing.

CHAPTER TWELVE

LUCA

†4

"Sir, we're being followed."

The words tore me from the act of watching Remy without making it look like I was watching him from where he was sitting on the other side of Violet's car seat. Violet had nodded off after her session with the psychologist, so Remy was staring out the window. He had it open like he usually did, but only a few inches.

I swung around in the SUV's seat. "Which car?" I asked. The second set of bodyguards who were driving the SUV behind us were still there.

"Dark blue Impala," Terrence responded. I glanced at the man as Stan, who was in the front passenger seat, checked his gun.

"We're being followed?" Remy said, his voice tinged with fear.

"It's probably nothing," I said. "Evasive maneuvers," I murmured to Terrence, since my only goal was to get us back to the hotel where we'd have more guys to cover us. Not to mention I didn't want to risk any kind of gun play with Remy and Violet in the car. If we'd been in New York, I'd have directed my men to lead the tail we'd picked up on a bit of a chase before maneuvering them into a position where they'd become the hunted and I would have been able to find out who they were. But it wasn't the same game out here. Especially with a child in the car... and Remy.

My gut churned familiarly as I tried to put a label on what Remy was. I'd been trying to do that for the better part of a week as we'd lived in this strange little bubble that was both comfortably domestic and weirdly strained at the same time. If we had Violet between us as a buffer, Remy and I could usually chat aimlessly about some kind of safe topic or just play with the toddler. But when it was just the two of us because Violet was sleeping or lost in some TV show or educational game she was playing on my tablet, things like eye contact and speaking became strained. I'd thought the perfect solution would be to just move to another room and do some work, but the second Remy was out of my sight, I obsessed over him even more. Even when I knew he was perfectly safe, I couldn't stop worrying about him. I'd even taken to watching him sleep the past couple of nights because it was the only thing that calmed my frayed nerves.

The SUV began making several turns on various side streets as we approached downtown Seattle. I glanced behind us again and saw that the bodyguards in the other vehicle didn't even look fazed. In fact, the driver had fallen several cars behind us and it looked like he and the other bodyguard were casually chatting.

"Get those assholes on the phone," I snapped at Stan. Stan looked over his shoulder at me, saw the direction I was looking in and frowned. He snagged his phone from his pocket but before he could even dial, there were several horns sounding. My stomach fell out when I saw that an older model van had veered into the SUV, causing it to sideswipe a couple of parked cars. The van, which was missing its front plate, took off, leaving the disabled SUV in its wake.

"Fuck," I bit out. "Go! Get us back to the hotel," I called as I saw a dark blue Impala swerve around the SUV and speed up.

Terrence took another turn, then another as he sped up. But after the third turn, he was slamming on the brakes. I automatically reached a hand out to grab Violet's car seat. Remy did the same. We hadn't been going particularly fast since Terrence had just turned the corner, so Violet only woke up enough to scrunch her face around and yawn before she dropped her head against the side of the seat again.

"We're pinned," Terrence called out. Sure enough, behind us was the Impala. And in front of us in the narrow alley was the van that had taken out the second set of bodyguards.

"Get down, sir," Stan said.

I ignored him and reached for my own gun. To Remy I said, "Get her out of the car seat and lie flat on the floor between the seats."

"Luca," Remy whispered fearfully, even as he began following my order.

Stan was in the process of dialing 911 when Terrence reached out to stop him. "Wait," he murmured. "Um, sir," Terrence said questioningly. "Look."

I was still focused on helping Remy get a now grumpy Violet from her car seat when I looked up and saw a familiar figure standing at the van's back doors.

"Son of a bitch," I snapped as I put my gun away. "I'm going to fucking kill him," I bit out as I grabbed Remy's arm to keep him from moving to the floor between the seats like I'd told him to.

His gaze followed mine and I heard him exhale sharply. "Is that your brother?" he asked.

"Yes," I growled as I reached for the door handle.

"He's with Dante," Remy murmured.

I glanced at the man standing next to my brother and realized that Remy was right. Aleks's older brother, Dante, stood next to Vaughn, his arms crossed. But while my brother looked forbidding and cold, Dante had a shit-eating grin on his face. I wanted to strangle them both.

I climbed out of the SUV and quickly closed the distance between us. I was taking a swing at Vaughn the second I entered his personal space. "You fucking son of a bitch!"

Though he was a smaller man, Dante managed to catch my fist before it could make contact. Vaughn, for his part, barely reacted. In fact, he hadn't even tried to defend himself.

"Take it down a notch, hotshot," Dante said, that stupid grin still on his face. "That little demonstration was my idea."

"I have a fucking kid in the car," I snapped at him.

"Oh yeah, I've heard all about that little cutie," Dante said as he motioned to something behind me.

Not something, *someone*.

Remy.

He was holding a very cranky Violet. Dante pushed past me and went to stand in front of Remy. I shot my brother an angry glare, then went to join them. It was all I could do not to put my arm around Remy to claim him in front of Dante. Dante's eyes slid to mine. They were full of humor. "You gonna pee on him, hotshot?" he asked as he eyed the way I was standing just a bit too close to Remy.

I was actually reaching for the slightly smaller man when Remy's fingers closed around mine. "What are you doing here, Dante?" he asked. "You're supposed to be on your honeymoon."

Dante's grin slipped. "*Supposed to* being the operative words."

"Did something happen?" Remy asked.

"Yeah," Dante responded. "These two ass—" Dante paused as he looked at Violet and then continued with, "*ass-trological* idiots decided to have another one of their be-all and end-all fights." He cast a glance at Vaughn who was standing behind him. My brother was still expressionless.

"The husband and I were enjoying all the *comforts* our room had to offer when I get a call from my little brother who explains to me in tears that the man he plans to spend the rest of his life with has had a terrible fight with his brother. This one," he jerked his finger at Vaughn, "tells me everything is fine and not to worry myself about it."

I practically rolled my eyes at the insinuation that a fight between Vaughn and myself had forced Dante and his new husband to cut their honeymoon short.

"Sounds like you guys were just looking for an excuse," I said.

Dante eyed me. "Yeah, Ronan said you wouldn't get it."

I had no clue what he was talking about, but before I could question him, Dante continued with, "If it wasn't bad enough to learn that my baby brother felt responsible for the big guy here and hotshot not making up and playing nice, then I have to go and learn that you hired a bunch of idiots playing bodyguard to protect our Remy and his little sweetheart."

By that point, Violet had calmed considerably and seemed fascinated with Dante. When he reached out to tweak her chin as he spoke, she actually smiled.

"That's one area MawMaw and I agree on," Vaughn inserted. Dante's expression stiffened at the strange nickname, but all he did was shoot my brother an annoyed glance.

"As of this moment, you're under the protection of Remy's family," Dante explained. "When he's wised up and decided to get away from your *ass-trological* backside, then you can go back to hiring the mercenary wannabes."

I opened my mouth to argue the point, but then realized it was pointless. As much as I wanted to kick Dante's ass for his little demonstration, he was right. If this had been a real attack, Remy and Violet would've been in serious danger. That just wasn't an option.

"Fine," I snapped. "But you guys answer to me."

I cut Dante off before he could respond because I was just fucking done. "Get something straight here, MawMaw," I cut in. "You and your little family might have gotten the drop on us in New York, but I guarantee you, that's not going to ever happen again. Ronan may think that money can't buy the best protection, but it sure as hell will buy me a lot of bodies to put between us and you." I stepped closer to him and lowered my voice so only he and Vaughn would be able to hear me. "And the next time you put those two in danger, my fondness for your brother won't make a bit of difference."

Remy still had a hold of my hand, and that was the only thing that kept me from fisting it hard like my left one. I wanted nothing more than to slam it into Dante's face, but as pissed as I was, I knew he'd done me a favor by showing me how completely worthless my hired help had been. I hadn't liked how he'd gone about it, but it was all about Remy and Violet. "Follow us back to the hotel," I bit out. "I'll give you your orders there."

Dante grinned again, and I knew it wasn't a fake smile. He was truly enjoying the byplay between us.

As I turned to leave, Dante said, "Aw, does that mean we're not going to be besties? What about you and your brother? Are you two going to kiss and make up?"

It was on the tip of my tongue to tell him to fuck off, but then I remembered that little ears were listening. I kept my mouth shut as Remy and I returned to the SUV. I was about to take Violet from him so he could get into the car first and then put her in her seat, but he surprised me when he pulled me aside so we were out of earshot of Terrence and Stan.

"We're fine, Luca," Remy said softly, and then he gave my fingers a little squeeze. His gorgeous eyes were full of understanding as they held mine. "We're fine," he repeated.

I pulled in the breath I hadn't really known how badly I needed and nodded. The fact that he knew that most of my anger was really just my adrenaline crashing as my mind tried to make sense of the fact that the young man and little girl were no longer in danger was a reminder of how fucked up things were between me and Remy.

We stood there for several beats as I tried to calm down. "Better?" Remy asked softly, making sure to keep his voice low enough that no one around us would hear. I nodded. I should've been ashamed for my display of emotion, but strangely enough, I wasn't. I was surprised when Remy handed me the baby.

"Let's go home," he said with a small smile, then he moved past me, his hip brushing mine. I found myself turning and watching him climb into the SUV. Our eyes met briefly before he disappeared inside. As I moved to the door, I glanced at Dante who was talking to my brother. Vaughn looked at me at the same time, his eyes hard like they usually were, unless he was around Aleks. But I swore I saw the briefest softening in them as we watched one another. Then it was gone and I remembered all the things he'd accused me of and all the things I'd done... the unforgivable things.

To him.

To Aleks.

And most of all, to Remy.

By the time I climbed into the SUV and handed Violet to Remy so he could get her settled in her car seat, all the tension had returned. When I felt Remy's confused eyes on me, instead of trying to explain myself, I pulled out my phone and texted King to see if he'd made any progress on finding Violet's family.

Because the sooner I got out of Seattle and away from Remy, the better.

Even if that wasn't something I was sure I even wanted anymore.

CHAPTER THIRTEEN

REMY

+4

If I'd thought Luca an overprotective, sometimes domineering man before Ronan's men took over our protection detail, he pretty much became a tyrant after Dante and the other men started shadowing us. We hadn't seen Vaughn, but from Luca's behavior, I suspected his brother was around. I hated that the two men weren't talking and that the last time we'd seen Vaughn, Luca had gone instantly on the attack.

Because of us... me and Violet.

The fact that he was so protective of us should have been something that made me feel a level of comfort I wasn't used to, but all I felt was guilt. Luca had been so insistent on keeping an eye on the two of us, but now that he was doing it, it seemed like it was doing him more damage than good. I'd known the whole thing had been about him finding some kind of absolution for what had happened between us when I was a kid, but if anything, us being around was only driving him deeper and deeper into himself.

He rarely spoke to me, unless it was to tell me something about the day he had planned. He no longer cooked for me or Violet; in fact, we usually didn't see him at all. Even when he was with us, he wasn't really with us. Not even little Violet could draw him out of the shroud of silence he'd wrapped himself in. When he did speak, it was to bark orders at the men who were entrusted to watch over me and Violet. On the one hand, I'd never felt safer or more protected, but on the other, I'd never felt more rejected.

Which was a ridiculous thing, because to feel rejected you had to feel wanted in the first place. Those were emotions I'd felt in the first few days Luca and I had been together taking care of Violet, but now I just felt like a burden and nothing more. There'd been several occasions where I'd almost called Aleks to ask if I could come stay with him, but something had held me back.

I knew what the something was, but I was afraid to acknowledge it. I no longer trusted my own instincts. As Luca ignored me day after day, I would tell myself it was time to walk away, but then there would be these brief moments where he looked at me and I could see something there in his eyes, something... *more*. It was that little look keeping me in the too-big penthouse suite.

The visits with Violet's counselor had been a daily thing and we were starting to see results. Thankfully, the therapist hadn't seen any signs that Violet had been abused in any kind of way by Carla or any of her johns. There was still no news on locating the toddler's family, or if she even had any, but she was making good progress with things like her hand-eye coordination, language skills, and balance. Violet had a lot of therapy in her future, but the steps she'd made in just a handful of days was proof that she would be able to live a normal life. We just had to find the person who could give that to her.

As much as I wished I could be that person for the little girl, I knew in my heart that I couldn't. The fact that the need to get high continued to plague me, especially in response to Luca's indifference, was proof that I wasn't in a place that I could guarantee my sobriety. I hated to admit to that weakness, but I wasn't foolish enough to pretend it was something I could just get past. Once all this was over, I'd get back to normal, to the way things had been. I was certain that the balance I'd managed to find in my life would return.

It had to.

As we made our way back to the city, I sent Luca a sidelong glance.

He was working on a laptop computer on the bench seat next to me. Violet was between us in her car seat, but he hadn't paid the child much attention. She'd finally nodded off a few minutes earlier. I used the opportunity to study Luca and didn't like what I saw. His jaw was set like it usually was and his fingers flew over the keyboard. His eyes stayed on the computer screen in front of him. It was like we weren't even there.

I told myself to just leave it all alone, that the sooner this ended, the better. But then I remembered waking up pressed against him on the couch, his fingers trailing up and down my spine. The image of his mouth descending toward mine after I'd all but begged him without words to kiss me was etched into my brain, and I relived that moment over and over in my mind every single night. I'd even gone to the living room a few times in the hopes of finding him again just so we could pick up where we'd left off. I was desperate to know what his touch would feel like. I wanted to hear the gruffness in his voice as he said my name with that mix of need and denial.

"Luca," I said softly. I assumed he wouldn't hear me the first time I said his name, but I saw his fingers pause and his already stiff jaw got even stiffer. But he didn't take his eyes off the computer.

It was pretty much a slap in the face.

I turned to look out the window again, but then that little part of my brain that had always urged me not to remain silent began to ping. I reminded myself that Luca had insisted that Violet and I stay with him. If he didn't want us anymore, he'd have to come right out and tell us. The silent treatment just wasn't going to work for me anymore.

"I'd like to take Violet to the park," I said firmly. I could feel a little bit of the old me returning as I considered how much fun Violet would have playing outside. The penthouse at the hotel was gorgeous, but it couldn't replace the feel of soft grass beneath one's feet or offer the coolest of breezes washing over skin.

"It's too dangerous."

That was his only response. He didn't even look up when he said it.

I kept my voice soft so I wouldn't wake Violet up. "It's been two weeks. What danger are we actually in?"

Not surprisingly, he didn't answer me.

I leaned forward and stuck my hand between the front seats. "Stan, may I use your phone?"

Before Stan could even hand me the phone or look to Luca to get his permission, Luca was saying, "Who are you calling?"

"Information," I sniped. Something in his tone bit at the last little reserves of patience I had left. "To ask them why you're being such a dick."

The silence in the car was deafening. But I kept my hand opened expectantly and saw Stan's eyes dart back and forth between me and Luca. Normally, I would've taken pity on the man, considering how temperamental Luca was these days, especially with the men he paid to protect him, but I was fed up.

"If you want to call someone, you can use my phone," Luca muttered. I looked over at the confounding man.

"I want to use Stan's phone. I like Stan's phone," I responded just to needle him. "Stan's phone is comfortable and fits me perfectly."

If I hadn't had Luca's attention before, I certainly did now. His flinty eyes met mine and then he was looking at Stan. I was definitely going to owe Stan an apology after all this.

Luca's eyes returned to mine and we stared at one another, each waiting for the other to back down. But now that my blood was finally boiling with something besides the need to get high, I wasn't going anywhere. Luca controlled everything about my life at the moment, but I'd be damned if he controlled something as frivolous as this. I told myself that the excitement that was firing beneath my skin had absolutely nothing to do with the way Luca was watching me. And I definitely, absolutely did not want more than anything in the world to be alone with the man at the moment.

I. Did. Not.

Even as I lied to myself, the image of Luca pushing me down on the seat as his heavy body came down over mine had my dick straining against the zipper of my jeans.

I had no clue how long we stared each other down for, but surprisingly, there was no sense of victory when Luca merely nodded his head at Stan and Stan handed me his phone. I began dialing Aleks's number with the intent of asking him to meet me at the hotel because I wasn't quite brave enough to be in Luca's presence when I told Aleks I thought I'd made a mistake staying with Luca, but before I could hit dial, Luca slammed his laptop shut. I ended up flinching at the sound and when I looked over at him, I saw that he was staring out the window.

Whatever, it wasn't my problem. He'd had his chance... he'd had lots of chances.

This time it was his phone ringing that interrupted my own call. I let my finger hover over the green button on the phone as I watched Luca from my peripheral vision. He pulled his own phone from his pocket and glanced at it. His expression changed instantly, and he practically fumbled to answer the thing.

"Luca Covello," he said. "Dr. Taylor?"

Where Luca's eyes had been dead before, now they were filled with a host of emotions. "Is he all right?"

What I wouldn't have given to hear the voice on the other end of the phone. But all I could do was watch and listen as I watched the man before me transform from an angry, cold, distant person into a scared yet hopeful human being. In my gut, I knew what the subject of the call was.

His son.

"Yes, I understand. I'm on my way." Luca hung up the phone. I was shocked to see that his hand was trembling as he gripped the device. "Terrence, stop the car."

"Luca," I began, but it was like I wasn't even there. Terrence pulled the SUV over to the shoulder.

"Take Mr. Valentino and Violet back to the hotel." That was all he said before he reached for the door handle. I expected Terrence or Stan to say something, but they remained silent. I reached across Violet's car seat and grabbed Luca's arm before he could open the door.

"Where you going?" I asked. "What's happening?"

"Stay with Terrence and Stan. They'll keep you safe. I'm going to grab a ride with the other car."

I knew he was talking about the SUV trailing us with another set of Ronan's men. His voice was shaky, much like it'd been the day in Ronan's den when he'd begged me to stay with him, to let him watch over me and Violet.

I dug my fingers into his arm when he began to climb out of the car. "No, Luca, don't go." He looked down at my hand where I was holding on to him, but he didn't try to pull free, though he easily could have. "Is it about your son? Is it about Gio?"

I expected him to blow me off with the denial or just more silence, but he surprised me when he hesitated, then jerked his head in a quick nod.

"I have to get to him. He's awake."

I had no clue what that meant, but I didn't need to know. The terror and hope in Luca's expression told me enough. I gave him a gentle tug and felt my heart nearly explode when he gave in to the silent request and sat back down in his seat. I was dimly aware of the fact that we had an audience in Terrence and Stan, but I didn't care. I let my hand drift down Luca's arm until our hands were touching. When I laced my fingers through his, he didn't protest. His hand was damp, but his skin felt chilled. I didn't speak as I continued to hold on to him. I was glad when he slowly shut the door.

"Take us to Luca's son," I said to Terrence, not looking at the man. I only had eyes for Luca. Luca's fingers tightened on mine just a little bit when I mentioned his son. I was glad Terrence didn't ask me any questions, specifically about where Gio was. But I also hated the fact that the bodyguard seemed to know about the boy while I didn't. I heard Stan's quiet voice as he spoke into the phone, presumably to tell the bodyguards behind us about the change in plans, but I didn't really listen to his words. I kept my eyes on Luca, even as he turned his head to watch out the window. But he didn't release my hand.

With the heavy traffic we encountered, it ended up taking a couple of hours to get to our new destination which was on the eastern outskirts of the city. Violet woke up several times, but fortunately I had packed enough toys and snacks to keep her occupied. Luca had bought the child her own tablet and had filled it with educational games for her, so she spent quite a bit of time with that. I tried a million times to ask Luca where we were going and what had happened to his son, but I couldn't get the words out. I was afraid that speaking would somehow change the fact that he'd let me come with him.

The stately building we arrived at was clearly a hospital, but not a typical one. The sprawling grounds were beautiful and lush with trees and flowers. There were multiple paved walking paths and I saw numerous patients in white robes being escorted by staff members. The entire facility was surrounded by a tall black iron fence. In my heart, I knew what kind of hospital it was. I just didn't want to believe that Luca's son was in that kind of place, beautiful as it was.

I stuck close to Luca's side as he, Violet, and I were escorted by a nurse to the third floor of the hospital. I was glad to see that it was clean and bright, but there was no denying the state of the few patients we saw. Some were completely silent, almost dead in the eyes, while others were talking to themselves with words and phrases that made sense only to them. I wanted to demand that Luca tell me exactly what had happened to his son to make him end up in a place like this, but the reality was that I already knew. There were lots of different kinds of survivors who managed to get away from the men who'd owned them. I'd just assumed that wherever Gio was, he was like me, just trying to get by every day. Or he was like Aleks and had learned to adapt and was in the process of trying to become who he'd been before he'd been taken. But clearly, he hadn't been so fortunate. My heart broke for Luca, and despite not knowing exactly the state Gio was in, it still broke for him too.

I cuddled a very quiet Violet to my chest as we followed the nurse to a waiting room. There was a man waiting for Luca. He extended his hand and the two men stepped to the far side of the room to talk. I sat down in one of the chairs to give them their privacy. Luca had agreed to let me come with him, but that didn't mean he wanted me listening in on his conversations. I assumed the man was one of Gio's doctors, but I couldn't hear anything that they were talking about. Whatever the doctor was saying, it had Luca remaining silent.

Stan had accompanied us into the hospital and had taken up position near the entryway. When Luca told him to stay with us, the man nodded. Luca's eyes met mine, but he didn't say anything. I gave him a nod of encouragement since there was literally nothing else I could do. I had no clue what he was about to face. I wished I could face it with him, but I knew he wouldn't let me.

Luca followed the man from the room, leaving me and Violet alone with Stan. Not long after Luca left, I could smell the telltale signs that Violet needed a diaper change. "I have to take her to the bathroom," I said to Stan. He nodded and then motioned to the entryway. Violet continued to play on the tablet even as I carried her. We followed Stan to the bathroom, and he made sure it was empty before letting me go in. I was glad the men's room had a changing table. I made quick use of it, taking Violet's tablet away and replacing it with the keychain to keep her attention while I changed her.

As we followed Stan back to the waiting room, I heard yelling coming from a small room a little farther up the hall. Stan automatically stopped us and urged us closer to the wall so he could stand between us and any potential danger. There were more raised voices from within the room and a moment later, the door flew open. I could hear banging and clicking sounds, but it was difficult to see anything around Stan. By the time I'd moved a little to get a better view, I saw a young man sitting in a wheelchair trying to get the thing through the doorway of the room where the yelling had been happening. He was wearing the same gown that the other patients in the hospital had, but I didn't see an orderly or anyone else pushing the chair. The kid was trying to get out of the room on his own.

"No! I want to go back to my room. Stay away from me!" the kid screamed. He finally managed to clear the doorframe with the bulky chair.

"Gio!" I heard Luca call from within the room and my whole body stiffened.

My eyes flew back to the doorway. Luca was standing there with

143

the doctor and I could see that the smaller man was holding on to Luca's arm, probably so he couldn't chase after his son. A young woman squeezed between the two men and hurried after Gio, but when she tried to push him in the wheelchair, he jerked away as best he could and said, "I've got it."

Gio was nothing like what I'd pictured. He had bright blond hair and was small framed. I guessed him to be around fifteen or sixteen at the most. His skin was pale and sallow and he was frighteningly skinny. His eyes were focused on the ground in front of him, so he didn't appear to notice me or Stan or anyone else for that matter. I glanced back at the room where Luca had been, but the door was shut, so I assumed the doctor had taken him back inside to talk to him. I couldn't even begin to process why Gio would have no interest in being around his father. From everything Aleks had said to me, Luca had been searching for Gio for years. The boy undoubtedly had emotional and physical scars that would take a lifetime to heal, and even that might not be enough time, but why wouldn't he be happy to see his father?

Violet chose that moment to point at the wheelchair and say some unrecognizable word that was her version of asking what she was looking at. It was enough to get Gio's attention as he rolled by us. The mix of anger and despair in his gaze was all too familiar. I wanted to say something to Gio but found myself tongue-tied. After all, what could I say?

I get it?

So many of us had all suffered the same fate, but being abducted and violated was never the same experience. I could understand some of the things that Gio had been through, but I would never truly get all of it. So it wasn't right for me to say anything at all, to presume that just because I'd been through similar things that telling him so would somehow make him feel better.

"Gio," I heard the nurse say softly to the young man from behind him.

"Nick!" he snapped. "My name is Nick! I don't belong here. That man is not my father! You can't keep me here!"

Surprise went through me when I heard Gio call himself by another name. Maybe I had misunderstood something? It would certainly explain the boy's anger if he weren't actually Luca's son but was being treated like he was. And if he was being held here against his will because they thought he was someone else...

The young man, Gio or Nick or whatever his name was, shot a glance in Violet's and my direction when Violet let out a little cry. His raised voice and demeanor had clearly upset her. Tears began streaming down the toddler's face as she clung to me. I did my best to comfort her by stroking her back and whispering in her ear that everything was okay. The squeaking of the chair caught my attention as the teenager rolled by. I saw what looked like regret in his gaze as he looked at Violet.

"Sorry," he murmured. I realized he was apologizing for having frightened the child.

"She's okay," I reassured him. Violet chose that moment to turn her head so she could look at the young man. She kept her cheek tucked against my neck.

The teen sent her a small smile and then softly repeated his apology. Violet didn't respond verbally, but she did hold up her little keychain as if to show it off to the young man. I was about to make a comment about all being forgiven when I saw that the kid's eyes were homed in on the keychain. He looked like he had seen a ghost because his pale skin went even whiter. He stopped rolling his wheelchair so suddenly that the nurse behind him almost ran into him.

I felt my heart skip a beat as I realized why he was looking at it the way he was.

He remembers it.

I glanced down at the little soccer ball and saw Gio's name on it. I knew in that instant that no matter what he believed, the young man *was* Luca's son. There was just no other explanation for the way he was staring at the keychain.

Longingly.

But also with stark, absolute fear.

I opened my mouth to ask him about the keychain, but he yanked his eyes away.

"Take me back to my room," he demanded of the nurse. He jerked his head away and didn't spare me, Violet, or the keychain another glance.

"We should get back," Stan reminded me softly. I'd forgotten all about the man's presence. I was tempted to ask him what was going on but realized it wouldn't be fair to expect him to tell me about his employer's situation, even if he did happen to know it. But there was one person who could tell me, who *would* tell me.

So as we made our way back to the waiting room, I once again asked Stan for his phone and he gave it to me without hesitation. Aleks picked up on the third ring.

"It's me," I said softly.

Aleks let out a little breath of air and then gently asked, "Are you okay?"

I really wasn't.

I was confused as hell.

About everything.

But I sidestepped the question and simply asked what I needed to know most at the moment. "Tell me about Gio."

CHAPTER FOURTEEN

LUCA

14

I sensed him before I saw him but kept my head down as I tried to focus on the words in front of me. But none of the letters made sense to me even though I'd been looking at them for hours now. It wasn't because the subject matter of the contract was complicated. In fact, I'd gone through contracts like this a hundred times over and never had an issue, even when things had been at their worst while I'd been looking for my son. But it might as well have been written in a foreign language because I couldn't make sense of anything that I was reading. And since I hadn't turned the page, I supposed I wasn't technically even reading.

I'd been too busy thinking about how badly I'd fucked things up again with Gio.

My son's angry words rang in my ears, and it was all I could do not to slap my hands over them in an effort to stem his accusations.

"Violet's asleep," Remy said softly from the doorway of my office, or rather, the hotel suite's office. We'd arrived back from the hospital a couple hours earlier, but I'd pretty much ditched Remy and Violet the second we'd walked through the door. And if I were being honest, I'd ditched them long before that because we hadn't spoken at all on the trip home. Remy had tried a few times to engage in conversation with me, but I'd merely stared out the window and he'd eventually stopped asking questions.

I didn't respond to Remy purely for the selfish hope that he'd leave me be. I began flipping pages on the contract to make it look like I was actually reviewing the thing, but when there was movement from the doorway, it wasn't the kind of movement I wanted because moments later, the guest chair on the opposite side of the desk scraped softly over the hardwood floor.

I ached to look up at Remy, but I also wanted to escape him, to hide somewhere and lick my wounds in private. I knew I probably at least owed him an explanation about what had happened at the hospital, but I was too raw to even consider it.

"I never talk about it," Remy said quietly. I found myself looking up at him because I'd been expecting him to bombard me with questions about Gio. I'd been preparing myself for his voice to drip with pity as he offered up platitudes about how Gio would be okay, that we'd both be okay.

But when I looked at him, his eyes were on the ground and he had his hands pressed together. His right leg was tapping incessantly but there was no sound, so I figured he was barefoot. He'd changed his clothes and was now wearing thin pajama pants and a plain white T-shirt. His hair was damp, so I figured he'd just gotten out of the shower.

I didn't prod him to go on because I already knew what the "it" was.

A good minute passed before he continued on his own with, "Aleks has been saying we should talk about things, that it would help." Remy shook his head. "You think that's true?" he asked. "Do you think talking about things somehow makes them easier to deal with... or to forget, I guess?"

Pain spread throughout my chest. "I don't know," I admitted.

"Ask me any question you want, Luca," Remy choked out.

I didn't understand where he was going with all this and it pained me to see him struggling the way he was, but the selfish part of me didn't want to miss out on the chance to learn more about him.

"Why didn't you go home, Remy?" I asked. "After you escaped?"

Remy's foot tapping increased even more and he began rubbing his palms up and down his thighs. I also noticed him swallowing over and over again, like he was trying to rid himself of a bad taste in his mouth.

"I did," he responded after several beats. "What happened in that room today with Gio?"

Remy looked up at me as he asked the question. His expression was soft and understanding, like he already knew my answer, or at least wouldn't judge me for what I was about to tell him. But even so, I could feel heat enveloping me as the self-hatred threatened to consume me.

"I fucked it up again," I whispered. "He said it was too soon, but I didn't listen."

"Who said that?"

"Gio's doctor. I insisted on seeing Gio, but Dr. Taylor told me it was too soon. I thought..." I heard my own voice crack as I tried to continue.

"My family lives in Nebraska," Remy said. My stomach dropped out as I finally realized what we were doing. He wanted me to tell him things he knew were hard for me, but he was giving the same back to me as well. There was absolutely no reason that he had to tell me things from his past, but he was willing to do it.

I found myself getting up from my chair and going around the desk. I couldn't explain the need to touch him, I just did. I stopped by his chair and reached out my hand. A small half sob escaped his throat. He reached up and took my hand. When he stood, his body was nearly pressed to mine. But his head was still hung and I didn't try to force it up, even though I really wanted to see his eyes. We held there like that for a moment before I led him over to the small couch. If we were going to do this, I needed to be able to touch him, feel him, hear him.

I sat and then eased him down next to me. He was stiff beside me at first, but when I put my arm around his shoulders and encouraged him to lean against me, he did so without hesitation. His body felt

149

unyielding and cold and there was no denying how hard he was shaking. I found myself running my fingers through his hair and then pressing my lips against his temple. I wanted to give him more; I wanted to give him some kind of verbal reassurance that I was there and that what we were about to do meant more to me than he would ever know, but I couldn't find the words.

"I went to see them after I got to Seattle. I was struggling with the methadone program I was in. I had my new job, the apartment, but it..."

"It wasn't enough," I finished for him.

Remy nodded against my shoulder. I kept stroking the back of his neck and along his spine in the hopes of calming him.

When he didn't continue, I said, "I thought if Gio saw me, he'd remember me. I thought maybe this time it would be different."

"This time?"

"I saw him about a week after he was admitted into Dr. Taylor's care. When I went into his room, I was just so relieved to see him, I didn't think about what I was doing. I grabbed him, hugged him, told him I loved him. He just... he lost it. He didn't remember me, didn't know me, didn't know himself. Kept saying his name was Nick and that we'd killed the man he loved."

I felt sick at the reminder of what had been done to my son, of the brainwashing he'd endured. "All these years I thought that all I had to do was get him back and everything would be okay."

"I thought that too," Remy murmured. "I thought the second my family saw me..." He shook his head.

"What happened when you went to see them?"

Remy was silent for a while. He was leaning against my chest, his ear pressed over my heart. At some point while I'd been talking, he'd put his arm around my waist. He smelled of shampoo and soap.

"My mom answered the door. They were still living in the same house I grew up in. I remember thinking that maybe they'd stayed there all those years so I could find them. All these little scenarios kept playing out in my head as I waited for the door to open. It couldn't have been more than fifteen seconds until she answered, but I must've lived through a hundred ways of being welcomed home. When I saw my mom, I just started to cry." Remy's voice became strangled as he added, "I thought she'd know me. Even after all those years, I was so sure she'd see me and she'd just *know*."

I wrapped my arms around Remy's thin body. His pain was a palpable thing and I wished I could take it from him. It was clear from the story that his mother hadn't recognized him like he'd thought. I hated the woman for that fact alone. I would've known Gio anywhere. It wouldn't have mattered what he looked like or what the circumstances of our reunion would have been, I would've known him. I *had* known him. Long before the DNA results had come back proving he was my son, I'd known it was him. Parents just knew these things.

But obviously not all parents.

"I got angry with Gio," I somehow managed to get out. "The more he denied knowing me, remembering me, the more he said he loved the man who'd been hurting him for all those years, the more upset I became, and I demanded that he tell the truth. All the kids my brothers and I tried to help over the years, but I never really understood what they went through... what their minds were put through, you know? Gio just started shutting down. It was like losing him all over again. It was like he was being stolen away in front of my very eyes, but there was nothing I could do to stop it. The doctor said it was some kind of break from reality... that his mind was trying to protect itself. He stopped talking, stopped moving, stopped eating, drinking. He was there, but he wasn't."

The agitation and helplessness inside me began to build and build upon itself. I wanted to get up and hit something. I wanted to inflict pain on something just so I could feel that I could inflict it on myself too. I knew the restlessness would just get worse, so I loosened my grip on Remy in order to escape him.

"Don't," Remy whispered. He ended up tightening his arms around me to keep me from moving.

"Remy," I began, but he cut me off.

"You have to fight it, Luca," he whispered. He kept one arm around my lower back as he shifted back enough so that he could look at me.

"I know it hurts, but running won't help. Not feeling won't help. There's no drug or drink strong enough to make us forget. There's no place far enough away for us to hide."

I hated that he was right.

"She didn't recognize me. When I stopped crying long enough to tell her who I was, she just stood there. Then she asked me what I was doing there. She thought I wanted money. She said they didn't have any," Remy explained. He dropped his eyes again and when I pulled him back against my chest, I stroked my fingers over the shell of his ear as he continued on his own.

"They never even looked for me, Luca," Remy choked out. I felt moisture seeping through my dress shirt and knew exactly what it was. "They told people I ran away. But I didn't. Things were bad at home when I was a kid, but I still loved them. I never would've run away. I had my little brothers and sisters to watch out for. I never would've done that to them... left them like that." Remy's sobs began to consume him as he added, "They never even looked for me. All those years I waited, and they weren't even looking for me."

My eyes stung and my throat felt tight as I dropped kisses to the top of his head and murmured incoherent words to him in the hopes that I could somehow offer comfort. I wanted to kill the people he called his parents. They weren't that. They'd lost that right the moment they'd turned their back on him.

"They didn't deserve you, baby," I whispered to him as he cried.

His agonized, harsh sobs racked his body for what seemed like hours. When he finally quieted, the front of my shirt was soaked through and I felt physically exhausted, as if I'd been the one enduring the emotional onslaught. I expected him to release his hold on me when he calmed down, but I was glad that his grip remained as tight as ever and that he made no move to distance himself from me. My insides felt stretched thin as a war raged within my brain. The idea of exposing myself any more to this man went against everything I understood about myself, but it was like he'd said—there was no place left to run.

"I love him so much, Remy," I breathed. "I just want him back."

I waited for the standard line about how I *would* get my son back, but when Remy did respond, he did so without any words. He leaned back enough that he could look at me. His face was wet with tears and his skin was flushed. Both of his hands came up to cradle my cheeks and I was surprised when I felt his fingertips swipe across my own damp skin. His eyes held mine as he stroked my face with the gentlest of touches.

The need to run, to escape, eased, and when he used his hands to tip my head forward just a little, I went without hesitation. His soft lips pressed against my forehead and held there for the longest time. The gentle kiss had a shudder running through me and when I let out the breath I'd been holding, the jumbled knot of sensation in my belly started to ease. He hadn't spoken any words, but he'd still managed to say exactly what I needed to hear.

That everything would be okay. That *I* would be okay.

When Remy ended the soft caress and began to pull back, I found myself reluctant to release him. His cheek was pressed to mine, and I could feel and hear his soft exhale of breath when he realized I wasn't letting him go. But he didn't fight me. In fact, when I began to move my mouth along the line of his jaw, the only movement he made was to curl his fingers into my hair. I knew I needed to stop because there would be no interruption this time. There would be no bodyguard knocking on the door or toddler screaming for attention. But I silenced all the warnings in my brain saying this was a phenomenally bad idea and did exactly what Remy had told me to.

I *felt*.

CHAPTER FIFTEEN

REMY

✝4

He gave me every chance to pull away before his lips met mine. There was absolutely nothing holding me to him beyond his loose grip on my waist. In fact, if anything, *I* was the one holding on to *him* because I still had my hands on his face. And when there were just a few millimeters separating our mouths, it was me who lifted up just a little in order to close the small distance that kept us apart.

I expected him to do what all the other guys who'd kissed me had done—plunge his tongue roughly into my mouth. The few men who had paid for the boyfriend experience had always plied me with soft words of love and adoration before sex, but they'd always fucked me as mercilessly as the rest of my tricks. And I couldn't imagine any boyfriend wanting to hear the ugly words that had been said to me while I was being pounded into a mattress or against a wall.

So I had no clue why I was allowing any of this to happen. And worse, why I *wanted* it to happen.

My intent had been to offer Luca someone to talk to about the day's events, especially since he and his brother still weren't on speaking terms. Aleks had provided me with enough information about Gio to understand why the young man had reacted so strongly to his father's presence. My heart was breaking for Luca because there was no doubt in my mind that all he wanted was his child back. I couldn't even imagine what it must've been like for him to search endlessly for his son only to find him alive but unwilling to acknowledge him and their relationship.

Luca had made it pretty clear from his silence that he'd just wanted to be left alone, but I'd been worried about what that would do to him. No, he wasn't a drug user like me, but I'd known his first instinct would be to try and escape or ignore the pain.

A week earlier I would've told him that he needed to just let things go, forget about the past... In fact, I *had* told him that when it came to what had happened between the two of us. But seeing how Luca behaved with others versus how he behaved when it was just him and me and Violet, at least in the days right after we'd found Violet, had been an eye-opener. With others, including his brother, he always had this mask on. He'd played all the roles he was supposed to with them.

Tough.

Cold.

Distant.

But those few instances when it had been just me and him and Violet doing something simple, like having breakfast or playing a game on the living room floor with Violet, had shown a side of the man that I was beginning to believe was who he really was. It was *that* man I'd suspected was trying to deal with the fallout from his encounter with his son earlier in the day.

I'd known when I'd entered the office that he wouldn't just tell me what had happened, and telling him I already knew from Aleks wouldn't have accomplished anything either, so I'd given him a piece of myself that no one else had. It had hurt like a son of a bitch and I couldn't say that I somehow felt better, but I'd gotten the words out and I was still there. It seemed like such a small victory, but that's what it was.

My heart had felt like it had been cleaved in two when Luca had whispered about how much he loved his son and just wanted him back. In that moment, I'd never wanted to give anyone anything more.

155

I'd been at a loss for the right words to say to make him feel better, but then I'd realized that there was no feeling better. Just like there was no feeling better about my parents abandoning me to my fate not once, but twice. First when I'd been taken, and then again when I'd returned.

So in that moment, I'd let my heart take over from my brain and then my lips had been on his skin and he'd been gripping me tightly while his rough breaths had washed over my throat.

And now his mouth was on mine. It was nothing more than his lips briefly brushing my own, and I should've been grateful for that. But when he pulled back, I felt deprived, and I was the one who ended up following him so I stayed within the circle of his arms. I kissed him like he'd kissed me, but there was still no crashing of his mouth down on mine, no bruising of my lips, no tongue being thrust into my mouth, gagging me.

To the outside world it would've looked like the simplest of kisses, but I'd never felt anything more intense in my entire life. I was nearly as afraid of his gentle touch as I'd been of the cruelest men who'd used me when I'd been a kid.

Every time our mouths separated, the loss was overwhelming and I found myself seeking out another kiss. My brain kept screaming at me that the contact was enough, that it was *too much*, but I kept going back for more.

Luca kissed me back each and every time but he never asked for more, never demanded it. His mouth was firm but soft at the same time. I could taste the salt of his tears on his lips. It should've been enough to remind me that I hadn't come here for any of this, but I couldn't make myself stop. I'd never wanted to physically be with a man, even the few I'd been attracted to in the past couple of years. But I understood *want* because I wanted other things. Freedom, family, drugs... the want I was experiencing now was the same, yet different. And that was the problem.

It was all too confusing and new and exciting. It was something that would be beyond my control, and my entire life for the last two years had been about control, about fighting my desires and needs, ignoring them.

The idea of losing control was enough to have me pulling back. I wasn't sure if I was glad or disappointed that Luca's mouth didn't follow mine. I pressed my forehead against his and tried to catch my breath. The fact that I even was out of breath because of a few chaste kisses was mind-blowing. At some point, my fingers had threaded through Luca's hair and I was actually hanging on to him that way. My muscles felt like they were at war with one another as I fought the urge to pull him closer and cover his mouth with mine again.

"Luca," was all I managed to get out. How was that one word, his name, supposed to explain to him why I'd stopped? And why I hadn't wanted to.

"It's okay, Remy," was his response. His nose nuzzled mine and the gentle move almost threatened to have me in tears again. "Why don't you go to bed?" he offered. If he was irritated by my reversal, he didn't show it.

"What about you? Are you coming?" As soon as I heard my own words, I felt the heat in my cheeks. "Coming to bed... I mean, *going* to bed," I quickly amended. "Are you going to bed?" I swore I heard him chuckle softly right before his lips skimmed my temple.

"Yeah," he said softly. "I'll be right behind you."

Even though I'd been the one to make the clarification about separate beds, I found myself wishing that maybe I hadn't made the distinction. Maybe by some miracle, we could've shared a bed and I would have gotten to feel his arms around me all night.

Even if there was no way I was ready for that.

I mentally shook my head at myself because I couldn't seem to get my thoughts straight. There was absolutely no reason to be jittery or nervous. I'd been around Luca long enough to know that he wouldn't do anything without my permission.

But maybe that was the problem. I wanted to give him that permission. I didn't care if it meant I'd have to pretend to like what he was doing to me or I'd be forced to go to that place in my mind where nothing was happening at all.

If it meant I could get to that part afterwards that I'd seen in movies and on television where the worst was over and there were just those few moments of gentle contact, I could probably go through with it. Except that was the new problem, the one I hadn't expected. I was starting to like these moments where it was just Luca and me. I liked the feel of his arms around me and I liked the way he looked at me and spoke to me.

Like I was *somebody*.

Like I meant something to him.

Yes, it was all about guilt on his part, but was it so wrong to reap the benefit of that?

I knew the answer to that, of course. It was how I managed to remove my fingers from Luca's hair. He rose with me when I stood. His hands remained on my hips for a moment before he dropped them, and I felt the loss with more awareness than I would've liked. We hadn't really finished talking, but I hoped that I'd done enough, said enough, to at least get him through the night. He would feel the loss of his son in the days to come and for however long it took to get Gio back. I knew that better than anyone. Maybe I couldn't help him deal with the pain, but maybe he felt a little less alone now.

"Good night," I managed to get out. My body felt thwarted, even though I had no one but myself to blame. I wanted him to ask me to stay. I wanted him to take my hand and lead me to his bed and lie down next to me so for once I wouldn't have to be afraid while I slept. But becoming dependent on him was as dangerous as becoming dependent on heroin. I'd already gone through needing him once when I'd been a kid and I couldn't do it again.

"Night," he returned. His hands dropped to his sides, but I still couldn't make my body move. It took everything in me to finally turn on my heel and walk away from him. My lips tingled and my body ached, and they both stayed that way long after I returned to my own bed. Hours later when my eyes finally did begin to drift shut, it wasn't thoughts of my past or getting high that followed me into the darkness.

It was Luca.

Only Luca.

14

"Remy, I need you to wake up, sweetheart."
I couldn't help but jerk awake because I simply wasn't used to being woken up in the middle of the night by a strange voice... Or *any* voice, for that matter. My heart rate instantly went through the roof and I fisted my hands in preparation to fight off whatever man thought it was his right to hurt me.

"Shhh, it's okay, it's just me, Luca." A gentle hand on my shoulder accompanied the voice. "Violet is still sleeping."

The reminder of Violet helped me focus on where I was, and more importantly, *when* I was. My eyes adjusted to the dimness of the room. It helped that I always left a light on for Violet so she wouldn't be scared if she woke up in the middle of the night. Luca was sitting on the edge of my bed, his hip brushing mine through the thin blanket.

As I fought to catch my breath, Luca's hand came up to cup my cheek. "Sorry, but I thought you'd want to know as soon as I found something out."

"About what? Is it Gio? Is he okay?" I began asking, my fear for Luca causing my heart to jump in my chest again.

"It's not about Gio. It's about Violet."

I automatically looked at the crib the hotel staff had brought us when we'd first checked in. I could still see Violet's sleeping form. "She's okay?" I asked anyway.

"She's fine," Luca responded. His hand was still on my cheek, and that had me turning my attention to him. I realized he was dressed in a pair of sweats and nothing more. I couldn't help but feel strangely glad that he'd gone to bed at some point after our late-night kiss.

"Then what is it?" I asked.

Luca seemed to hesitate and that was when I knew. My heart fell and it suddenly became hard to breathe. "You found them, didn't you? You found her family."

"Let's go to my room to talk," he said softly.

I didn't want to. Not because it was his room, but because I didn't want to hear what he had to say. The pity was clear in his voice. No matter what he was about to tell me, it meant I was going to lose Violet sooner rather than later. If he'd found her family, she would have a place to go, but if he hadn't, then Violet faced life in foster care.

"Just tell me, please, Luca," I begged. I kept my voice low so Violet wouldn't wake up. Somehow, I needed to keep my eyes on her while I took in whatever it was he was about to tell me.

He sighed and dropped his hand, but only so he could place it over mine. I had my hand on my lap, so technically his was precariously close to my groin, but I didn't even care. There was nothing sexual about the contact. He was merely trying to comfort me.

"My brother, King, found Jackie's family. Her parents divorced about a year ago. Her father died in a car accident and her mother is in jail for drug possession. The only other relative is an aunt... the one Violet was named after. King checked her out, both on paper and in person. She's a retired schoolteacher. She has no criminal history and it looks like she's been looking for Jackie ever since she disappeared."

It was good news. It was. But I still felt sick to my stomach.

"Did you talk to her?" I asked.

"Not yet," he said. "I wanted to make sure that you hadn't changed your mind about wanting Violet."

I dropped my eyes and automatically shifted them to Violet's crib. My head hurt and my chest felt tight. Pain radiated up and down my spine, though I didn't really know why. In that moment I wanted to tell him that I *had* changed my mind. I wanted to tell him that I loved the little girl and I would give anything for the chance to be her father. But before I could open my mouth, a familiar sweetness washed over my tongue. The fact that heroin was choosing that exact moment to remind me that I was far from its grip made me feel like more of a failure than I ever had in my entire life.

All I could do was jerk my head back and forth because my mouth couldn't form the words. My body started to shake, and the dreaded hot and cold sensations began to hit my body in violent waves. I shook my head harder in the hopes that Luca would get the message and leave me be. But when he rubbed his fingers over mine and whispered, "Remy," it was too much. I choked back a sob as I pushed him away and climbed out of the bed.

I bypassed the attached bathroom and hurried to the one that was part of the third guestroom, since I didn't want to chance waking Violet. I stumbled a few times as I made my way into the bathroom and got the water going. My blood was racing through my veins so fast it actually hurt. I felt betrayed by my body. All these weeks I'd managed to keep the urge at bay, but here it was, stronger than ever. It felt like I was going through withdrawals all over again.

When the water was as cold as it could be, I didn't bother trying to take my clothes off because the tips of my fingers actually hurt. I was in the process of stepping into the shower when a hand closed over my wrist.

"Remy, wait," Luca said and then he was drawing me back.

"No!" I shouted. "Please, I need to..." I began, but the rest of the words wouldn't come. The humiliation was as painful as the physical symptoms I was experiencing. I tried to tell myself that I was the one in control, but that had never been further from the truth. All the strength I'd somehow managed to find in the past to fight this thing had deserted me in a big way.

I expected Luca to try to calm me down or argue with me in some kind of way, especially once he reached out to touch the water. But his eyes settled on me for only a moment and then he was taking my arm and helping me into the frigid spray of the shower. I cried out when the water hit my skin but there was also an instantaneous feel of relief... temporary as it might be. Shame crawled through me as I relished the feel of the icy water stinging my skin and drenching my clothes. I hated that Luca was seeing me like this, but I didn't have the energy to ask him to leave. I turned my head so I wouldn't be tempted to look at him.

But within seconds of me getting into the shower, there was movement behind me and to my surprise, a moment later, Luca was at my back.

"Luca, what are you—" was all I got out before he wrapped his arms around me from behind and drew me back against his chest. The move stunned me into silence. But only for as long as it took me to accept that the still-dressed man had just stepped into an icy cold shower with me just so he could offer comfort. There was no recrimination or judgment.

Just him.

All the emotions I'd been trying to hold in check came flooding back and I began to sob uncontrollably. I could feel Luca's mouth by my ear, and I knew he was whispering words into it, but the roaring in my head was too loud for me to actually hear anything. It didn't matter, though, because he was there.

I allowed him to turn me in his arms and draw me forward until I was enveloped in his grip. I wasn't sure how long we stayed like that— him holding me as I cried for everything I'd lost. But at some point, the water temperature changed. I hadn't even felt Luca move, but somehow, he'd managed to turn the water to warm.

"Is it okay?" Luca asked, his lips skimming my neck. I was wrapped around him like a vine. The muscles of his back flexed beneath my fingers. I knew he was talking about the fact that he'd turned the water to a warmer setting. He was clearly concerned that I was still fighting the onslaught of need for heroin. The fact that he'd figured out why I'd gotten into the cold shower fully dressed should have been embarrassing, but maybe I was just too tired to care.

I nodded. While the water was warm, it wasn't really warming me up. Luca must've realized that because he kept slowly turning the water temperature higher and higher, letting my body adjust a little each time as I continued to hold on to him. It took a few minutes for the heat to finally penetrate my chilled skin, but when it did a wave of exhaustion slid over me and instead of just clinging to Luca for comfort, I was holding on to him to stay upright. His arm around my waist felt strong and solid.

"Can I take this off?" Luca asked as he gave a little tug on my T-shirt. I nodded because the clothes felt heavy and uncomfortable.

Luca eased the shirt up over my head. I heard the wet fabric slap against the tile floor outside the shower. The now hot water felt good along my back. It was easier to breathe, and I ended up dropping my head to Luca's chest. With the shower as loud as it was, I couldn't hear the strong, steady beat of Luca's heart, but imagining it was enough.

Luca's fingers skimmed the waistband of my sweatpants, but this time he didn't ask me for permission to remove them. He didn't really need to, either. For the first time in a very long time, probably since the time he'd strode into that dark room my captors had put me in, pulled me up off the floor, and told me everything would be okay, I felt safe. I felt like I didn't need to fight. I felt… *trust*.

Luca pushed the sweatpants down and shifted his own body long enough to work them off my legs. Once the heavy material was gone, he straightened and pulled me against him again. There'd been nothing sexual in the way he'd touched me as he'd undressed me, and I was glad for that. I wasn't in any position to deal with those particular emotions.

I wasn't sure how long we stayed in the shower, but when Luca turned it off and then reached for a towel and began gently drying my body, I didn't protest. I felt warm and tired and, for the moment, strangely sated. I knew I still had to deal with the news about Violet, but I pushed it to the back of my mind. When Luca was finished drying me, he wrapped a fresh towel around my waist and then took my hand. But we didn't go back to my room.

And truthfully, I was glad about that.

I probably should have been concerned when he led me to his room, then his bed, but I was relieved. It was what I wanted.

Luca got me settled under his covers, but he didn't join me. I was about to tell him it was okay when he suddenly turned his back to me and lowered his soaked sweats. The sight of his naked backside had me clapping my mouth shut. The man was absolutely beautiful. I'd never actually fucked a guy because none of my tricks had ever wanted that, but I couldn't deny the thoughts that went through my brain as I wondered what it would be like to push myself into Luca's gorgeous body. I felt my skin heat as I imagined the sounds he'd make as I took him.

Luca seemed oblivious to my perusal of him as he moved to the dresser and found a fresh pair of sweats. I got a brief glimpse of his half-hard cock as he pulled the material up. My mouth, which had been watering just minutes before for a hit of heroin, began to fill for a whole other reason. I'd never particularly liked blowing a guy, but I had a feeling I wouldn't have that same problem with Luca.

Luca returned to the bed and sat down on the edge of it. "How are you feeling?" he asked. His concern for me made me feel like an idiot. While I'd been drooling over him, he'd been worried about my mental well-being. I couldn't really blame him, considering how I'd behaved.

I nodded because somehow saying the word "better" seemed too simplistic.

He reached out to touch my face, much like he had when I'd been in my own bed. I didn't know what to make of his expression as he studied me. But I did know that my lips started to tingle in anticipation. The feeling apparently wasn't mutual because he dropped his hand a moment later and said, "I'll be right over there if you need me." He pointed to a chair in the corner of the room.

The thought that he had no plans to sleep with me caused a streak of self-doubt a mile wide to go through me. Maybe that kiss tonight hadn't been what I thought it had. Maybe he'd only been indulging me. Or if he hadn't, maybe now that he'd seen me in full-on mental breakdown mode, his interest in me just wasn't there. I tried to remind myself that was a good thing, but when Luca stood, I grabbed his hand before he could walk away.

My throat felt too tight to actually speak, so I willed him to understand like he had so many times in the past. I didn't want to be alone. It was as simple as that. And him being on the other side of the room would make it feel like there was a crater between us.

I held on to him, even though I couldn't look him in the eye. I held my breath for the many long seconds it took for him to move. And it was all I could do not to let out a cry of relief when he pulled the covers back and began to climb into the bed with me. I shifted to give him enough room but put my back to him. It was ridiculous because I was the one who'd wanted him to stay with me, but now that he was there, I didn't know what to do.

Thankfully, Luca made the decision for me and pressed himself up against my back. His body felt hot and I loved how his warm skin slid over mine. I was still wearing the towel, but we were both naked from the waist up. His left arm wrapped around my waist while his right one snaked beneath my head so I was lying on it rather than the pillow.

"Go to sleep, Remy. We'll talk in the morning."

I wanted to tell him that the last thing I wanted was to sleep. But I also wanted everything to be figured out so I wouldn't have to think about it anymore, wouldn't have to worry about it or fight it or obsess over it. I just wanted things to be easy for once. My thoughts drifted to Gio and I instantly felt shame. The teenager didn't have it easy and probably never would. And neither would his father. And there were thousands of other kids out there who hadn't made it home and never would. Compared to them, I *did* have it easy.

I could feel the anxiety starting to build again as I considered all the ways I'd failed to live my life in the past two years. That same feeling of not deserving the things I'd been given, like my job and my apartment, started to consume me. "Luca," I whispered brokenly. I loved that he knew something was wrong. He might not have understood the details, but he knew just by the way I said his name that I wasn't okay yet.

"Tell me what you need, sweetheart," Luca murmured from behind me. His fingers began rubbing circles into my skin.

"Tell me something about you that no one else knows," I croaked.

I swore I felt his lips skim the back of my neck right before he said, "I used to write Harry Potter fanfic."

"Liar," I automatically said. I couldn't help but be a little disappointed.

"I swear on all things Muggle," Luca responded, his voice light and soft and holding a hint of amusement. His lips pressed a kiss to the soft spot right behind my ear and I promptly forgot what we were even talking about.

"I had a thing for Harry," Luca continued. Between his hand rubbing my abdomen and his mouth moving over my neck, I was having a hard time coming up with any kind of response. But when he said, "and Draco Malfoy," I forced myself back to the task at hand.

"Fine," I breathed as I tried to will my body not to react to his sensual touch. I absolutely would not survive the embarrassment if he realized what the contact was doing to me. As someone who'd been with plenty of guys, I should've known how to guard my reactions better. But Luca wasn't just some guy. He was only trying to comfort me, and I needed to remember that. "Tell me some of it," I challenged.

"Harry's body quaked with excitement as Draco moved closer, his huge wand in hand. God, how he wanted to feel Draco's wand for himself."

I turned around in Luca's arms so quickly, I ended up hitting him in the chin in the process. He had to be messing with me. "You wrote *gay* Harry Potter fanfic?" I asked in disbelief.

Luca rubbed his chin, but I barely noticed because my eyes were caught on the faint smile on his face. "I was seventeen and horny for guys," he murmured. His hand skidded over my hip and I could feel him toying with the edge of the towel. "And I had a thing for nerds."

"Oh my God, you're serious," I said.

"I had quite the following," Luca added with a grin. "I wasn't the only one who wanted to see Harry end up with the bad boy instead of that annoying Weasley chick. Hell, Harry and *Ron* would've been a hotter couple."

I shook my head because he'd left me completely and utterly speechless. Never in a million years would I have guessed he had a lighter side like this. Or that he'd use it to make me feel better. The reminder of why we were there in the first place was a punch to the gut, but I set it aside and wrapped my arms around Luca, no longer caring that there was so much skin touching. How had I ever thought this man was cold and aloof and unfeeling?

I opened my mouth to apologize for something he probably hadn't even realized I'd thought about him, but it was at that moment that his fingers brushed over the raised skin just above my left hip. The mere act of him pausing to examine the scar had my mouth going dry and my throat closing up. I willed him to move on, which he did, but only to seek out the next scar, the one on my shoulder. Then came the one on the back of my arm.

"Tell me about them," Luca whispered softly.

I wanted to tell him no. I wanted to talk more about him and all the little things that made him so different from the man I'd pegged him to be. But before I knew what I was doing, I was opening my mouth and letting slip free the things that I knew would end anything between us before it had even really begun.

I told him the truth.

CHAPTER SIXTEEN

LUCA

ᛏ4

Knife.
Boot.
Cigarette.
Hit by a car.
Dog.

All his responses were equally horrific and they kept coming for every scar I put my fingers on. "Dog?" I asked as I rubbed the old puncture wound on his lower arm.

Remy had gone still and stiff in my arms, but surprisingly, he was still talking. Part of me was sorry I'd ruined the light moment between us, but the other part of me had to know the truth. I hadn't really noticed the scars in the shower because I'd been too focused on getting Remy warm and comfortable. But now, I felt them everywhere. They were various shapes and sizes, and I couldn't help but think of them as a roadmap of the life he'd been forced to face alone.

"They'd use them to track me when I tried to escape. By that time I was already just a sample, so it didn't matter if the dogs marked me up a little."

As I remembered his fear of Ronan's dog, I wanted to find the men who'd hurt him and tear them limb from limb.

"Sample?" I asked in confusion.

"That's what they called the kids that weren't worth enough money to sell. I guess it was their way of letting buyers sample the quality of their products before any money changed hands."

I felt bile crawl up the back of my throat and it was all I could do to keep my grip on him soft. I'd known that was what Remy was when I'd been taken to the room he'd been in, but I hadn't known there was an actual term for it... or that Remy himself had known that was what he was.

"Most of them are from Les or johns," Remy continued, his voice flat and empty.

I forced myself to focus on what Remy needed from me here and now rather than trying to force back the regret that burned at my insides like acid.

I knew what Remy meant by johns, of course. "Les?"

"My pimp. The people who took me sold me to Les when I was too old to be useful to them anymore. Five minutes after they handed me over to him, he shot me up and that was it. I was a junkie from that moment on. My only goal in life was to get high and Les was the only way I could do it."

I made a mental note of the name. How hard could it be to find a pimp in Chicago named Les? Hell, if there were more than one, I'd make sure they all paid.

"How did you get away?" I asked.

"Aleks's brother, Dante," Remy responded.

I remembered the story Aleks had told me about how Remy had saved him. "Dante went looking for Aleks a few years back, right? You and Aleks met when you were kids. He had a unique birthmark on his collarbone and when you saw him again, you told Dante."

Remy nodded. "Dante helped me get out of Chicago."

"Is that when you went home to see your family?"

Remy shook his head. His hair brushed my chest. I hated that I wasn't able to look him in the eyes as he spoke, but I suspected he felt more comfortable with the positions we were in.

"No, um, I didn't want them to see me like that. All strung out. I was part of this methadone program that helped with some of the withdrawal symptoms, but it was still rough. I waited until I had a job, my own place, that sort of thing. I guess I wanted them to be proud of me or something." Remy let out a harsh laugh. "I had this whole speech planned for when I showed up at their door... I was gonna tell them all the good stuff first. Tell them I was okay and that they didn't need to worry. But I just kind of ended up blurting it all out."

I ran my fingers through Remy's hair as he spoke. He seemed calm. Too calm. Whatever had switched on inside of him when he'd learned that we'd found Violet's great-aunt, it seemed to have switched off entirely as he talked about the circumstances that had taken him home.

"What happened after that?"

Remy shook his head. "Nothing, really. After my mom told me they didn't have any money to give me, she asked me to leave. Then my dad was there. They wouldn't even let me inside the house. I didn't really understand what they were saying. I guess I was kind of desperate because I begged them to let me come home. They said they couldn't do that, that they had to protect my brothers and sisters from what I'd done. What *I'd* done. That's when I knew they didn't believe me, not the part about me being kidnapped, anyway. All they saw was that I was a junkie and a whore. I turned and never looked back."

"Did you ever talk to anyone about it? Aleks?"

Another shake of his head. "I couldn't. If I said it out loud, it would be true. It would mean my family didn't really want me. It was some-thing else I would have had to fight. Like the drugs, the people who'd taken me, Les, all the guys I'd sold myself to..."

"Me," I reminded him because I belonged at the top of his list.

Remy was quiet for a long time, but then he pulled back a little so our eyes could meet. He reached out to run his thumb up over my cheekbone. "You're the reason I *kept* fighting, Luca. That day in that house when you walked into the room, I was done. I was ready to die. I was ready to beg you to kill me. You gave me a reason to keep going. And yes, I hated you for not coming back for me and maybe that drove me to fight even more, but I think that was what I needed."

170

"Remy—" I began to say but suddenly he leaned in and kissed me softly, cutting off the argument I'd been about to make that I wasn't deserving of any kind of forgiveness or understanding.

The kiss was light and quick, though the impact was anything but.

"He was your son, Luca. You had to find him. You wouldn't have been able to live with yourself if you'd chosen me over him. I wouldn't have been able to live with it, either." Remy's words were gentle but firm at the same time.

"I swear to God, Remy, I *did* look for you. Even when I had to stop, I didn't. Every picture that came across my desk of the kids my brothers and I were able to help, I looked for your face. I wished for it with everything I was," I admitted. My voice sounded tight and desperate. I'd meant to comfort him, but somehow he'd turned the tables on me and he was the one doing the reassuring.

"I know you did," he whispered and then he kissed me again. I told myself to be satisfied with the simple kisses, but this time when he made a move to pull back, I found myself following. I closed my mouth over his and heard him let out what I chose to believe was a sigh of relief. I ran my tongue over the seam of his lips and when he opened his mouth in surprise, I dipped my tongue inside.

Remy jerked, but didn't pull away. He held perfectly still in my arms as I tentatively explored his lush mouth. When my tongue came into contact with his, he let out a little whimper. I forced myself to pull back, to give him the space he needed and to try to get my raging body under control. I tried to remind myself that I shouldn't have been kissing him in the first place, but then he was following and it was *his* mouth on *mine*, *his* tongue seeking entry. I groaned under the onslaught and opened eagerly for him. I had no clue if he'd been kissed like that before, but there was a certain level of hesitation in his touch that told me even if he had, he hadn't necessarily liked it.

Our tongues began to slide along each other's as we found our rhythm. I struggled to keep my desire in check as I let him set the pace, but when he pulled back enough to whisper my name desperately, I lost it and grabbed the back of his head so I could draw him back down to my mouth. I slanted my lips over his and hungrily consumed him. Then I was moving us so I was pressing him back into the mattress and my upper body was covering his. He let out a sexy moan and put his arms around me. I kissed him until I was dizzy with it, and even then, I only stopped long enough to let him catch his breath. I used the unwanted reprieve to explore his jawline and the column of his throat with my lips and tongue until he was the one gripping my hair so he could pull me back up to his mouth for more.

I loved the feel of Remy's fingers running down the length of my spine as our mouths mated. He stopped short of touching my ass, but I was much too greedy for his mouth to stop long enough to tell him that he could touch me wherever he wanted. I let my hand roam down his side with the intent of divesting him of his towel, but when my fingers grazed the scar on his hip, the one he'd said had been caused by a car, I hesitated.

While Remy was one of the strongest people I'd ever met, he was also one of the most vulnerable. And all the things he'd said about it having been okay that I'd chosen my son over him didn't absolve me of my sins. The last thing on this earth I should be doing was taking advantage of the young man who'd given me so much.

I removed my hand from the scar and reached out to capture his face as I eased back from the kiss. His mouth once again tried to follow mine, but I gently gripped his chin to keep him where he was. "We should try to get some sleep," I said softly as I stroked his skin.

He had a tiny bit of stubble on his jaw. It made my unruly cock even more difficult to try to control, especially as I imagined what that stubble and his gorgeous lips would feel like around my shaft. I quickly dropped my hand and added, "We have a lot that we need to talk about tomorrow concerning Violet."

Remy's eyes were glazed over and he was breathing hard. It seemed to take him several long seconds to catch up, but when he did, he nodded his head and then pulled away from me. I lifted my body so I was no longer pinning his to the bed. But when Remy made a move to get up, I grabbed his arm. "Sleep here tonight," I insisted. "Just sleep."

He hesitated for so long that I was sure he would insist on going back to his room, but then he settled back down on the bed. He didn't say anything as he put his back to me and when I pulled him against my chest, he remained stiff. It felt like I'd lost him all over again and I knew it was because I'd pushed him too far with my physical advances. I cursed myself for not being able to control my reactions to him.

"Remy," I began to say, but then he was sitting up in bed.

"I should, um, go check on Violet. She might get scared if she wakes up alone." He sounded nervous and uncertain, so this time I let him go when he moved away from me. I might have said something along the lines of agreeing with him, but I couldn't be sure.

The only thing I was sure of as he practically ran from my room was that I'd fucked things up.

Again.

CHAPTER SEVENTEEN

REMY

+4

"You sure you're okay?" Luca asked from the other side of the bench in the back of the car for what had to be the tenth time that morning.

This time I only nodded my head instead of saying the words, "I'm fine." What was I supposed to say? That I *wasn't* fine, that I was a complete and utter coward? Or that I was so fucking selfish that I was putting everything on Luca that morning when it came to making decisions?

It was all I could do not to look at Violet in her car seat as I considered that, at that very moment, Luca was waiting for a call back from the child's great-aunt.

By the time I'd gotten up that morning and found the courage to face him after the disaster that had been the short encounter in his bed, he'd already had extensive background checks done on Marilyn Landry. He'd also gotten Violet out of her crib and had taken care of her morning routine, including cleaning her up and feeding her breakfast. I'd walked in on the pair sitting on the living room floor playing a game that clearly Luca had made up but that'd had Violet giggling in delight. I'd felt a brief moment of complete and utter peace as I'd watched the pair and then I'd remembered that I was losing not one but both of them.

In truth, I'd already lost Luca, even though I supposed it was hard to lose someone you'd never really had. The memory of his touch and the way he'd quickly ended our kisses made my heart hurt even now, and I found myself reaching up to touch the middle of my chest. I'd been a fool to think that Luca might want me. Especially after all the things I'd told him. Even if he could have gotten past my too skinny, scar-riddled body, he clearly wasn't able to overlook how I'd gotten the scars... the things I'd done to deserve them.

When he'd seen me enter the living room, he'd invited me to come and join him and Violet, and there'd been nothing more I'd wanted to do in that moment. But I'd already determined that living in a domestic bubble with him, even if it was only for a few more days at most, wouldn't work. It would only make it harder to walk away from the both of them. Or let them walk away, rather.

"I can still have the other car take you back," Luca offered.

"No, it's all right. I'd like to go with you, if that's okay." I didn't look at him as I spoke. It was true that I *did* want to go with him to the hospital to see his son.

Well, he wasn't actually going to see his son. Rather, he was just going to talk to the doctor again about the plan going forward to treat Gio. Luca had accepted that it might be a while before his son was ready to talk to him. He'd told me that as he'd watched me move around the food he'd made me for breakfast that morning. While I'd wanted to ignore him just so I could spare myself the pain of conversing with him, there was no way I could've let him go by himself.

I wasn't looking at Luca, but I saw movement in my peripheral vision. I couldn't be sure, but it looked like his right hand was reaching for me. I tensed as I waited for his fingers to make contact with my shoulder, but then he appeared to pull back at the last minute. The disappointment was like a living, breathing thing beneath my skin. The night before had been a jumble of emotions for me, but when Luca had kissed me and settled his weight on my body, every-thing else had disappeared.

I'd wanted him.

In every way I could've wanted another man.

And while that was confusing to me now, it hadn't been then. But then he'd stopped and suggested we go to sleep. Even *I'd* known what that meant.

He'd been trying to let me down easy. He'd kissed me out of pity but when it had come down to it, he hadn't been able to make himself touch my disgusting body. The men who'd paid to fuck me hadn't ever given a shit what my body looked like, not that I'd ever cared what they'd thought.

But Luca's rejection hurt.

The rest of the trip to the hospital was made in silence. Violet slept for most of the way. When we reached the spacious grounds, Luca was the one to get Violet out of her car seat. He came around the car with her in his arms, but then put her on the ground so she was standing on her feet.

"Let's try something," he said to me. He put Violet's hand in mine so she could hang on to me and then he took her other hand. The little girl seemed confused by the fact that she was standing between us, but when Luca encouraged her to take a step using the two of us for balance, she did it, and all the pain and doubt I'd been feeling went by the wayside as Luca and I praised her. Violet smiled a big toothy grin and took another step. It was slow going to the entrance of the hospital, but it didn't matter. Violet was walking.

I wanted to kiss Luca because my joy was just so profound at that moment. But I settled for the hug he gave me after he picked Violet up and told her what an amazing little girl she was.

As we made our way to the floor where Gio's room was, Luca's lightness receded, and his body became tense and stiff. I found myself moving closer to him, but I didn't touch him or say anything, even though all I really wanted to do was hold his hand and tell him everything would be okay. The reality was I just didn't know what was going to happen. Not to mention I wouldn't be around for any of it. Even if Violet's great-aunt didn't check out, the time had come to make some choices about Violet's future. It was a future I wouldn't be a part of. And coward that I was, I didn't want to be around when those decisions were made, either. I wanted to escape back to my boring little apartment and lick my wounds. I trusted Luca to make sure that no matter what happened, the little girl would be okay.

I was lost in my own thoughts when I sensed Luca come to a stop next to me. I looked up and was surprised to see Vaughn and Aleks standing by the entrance to the waiting room. There were two other men with them. I didn't recognize them as bodyguards, and with the way they were looking at Luca, I suspected they weren't that anyway.

Luca silently handed me Violet, and the child, sensing the tension in the room, remained quiet and clung to me. I stayed where I was as I watched Luca approach the men. One of the men was taller than the others and had dirty-blond hair that was cut short along with a thick five-o'clock shadow. He had a big, heavy body that looked like it could do some damage and there were tattoos on the backs of his hands and across his knuckles. He was the kind of guy I would definitely avoid on the street, or anywhere else for that matter. The other guy was somewhat shorter and had a rangier body, but he was no less muscular. His black hair was pulled back into a ponytail.

I watched Luca approach the men and couldn't help but feel a little tense, especially given the way Vaughn and Luca had ended things the last time they'd talked. Vaughn looked as forbidding as ever, but when Luca approached him, something shifted and then the two men were embracing. I found myself hugging Violet tighter as I watched Luca being held by his older brother. I couldn't hear what Vaughn said to him, but Luca nodded fiercely and, in my heart, I knew it was something about Gio. I remembered Luca saying how he and his brothers had tried to help kids like me and his son and realized that was probably who these men were.

Luca went on to embrace the other two men who also spoke to him in low voices. The idea that they'd come here from wherever it was they lived to be with Luca made me both grateful and envious. I glanced in Aleks's direction and saw him watching me. I couldn't help but think he understood where my head was.

I watched my friend step forward into the group of men and once again felt those same emotions, this time for how easily Aleks was accepted into the fold. Luca even put his arm around Aleks's shoulders for a moment to give him a side hug.

Aleks said something to Vaughn, which had all the men turning and looking in my direction. Vaughn nodded and said something back, then gave Aleks a quick kiss. Aleks hurried toward me, but my eyes were still on Luca who was watching me with an expression I couldn't name. He cast a quick glance at Stan and motioned toward me. Stan had basically become my shadow, so I figured that's what the silent order was... for the bodyguard to stay with me.

When Aleks reached me, I didn't resist the embrace he gave me. We'd never really been the kind of friends who had a lot of physical contact, but I'd always figured that wasn't unusual, considering our backgrounds. I tried to hold myself stiffly in his arms, but when he didn't say anything, it made the embrace all the more stronger and I ended up gripping him tightly. It was like he knew what I was going through without me having to say it.

"There's a little playground out back. You want to take her there?" Aleks asked.

I nodded emphatically because I was having trouble forming words. Much as I would've liked to have been embraced in Luca's little circle of family, I knew I wouldn't be. I was just an obligation to him, a way for him to ease some of the guilt he felt for what had happened when I'd been younger.

Aleks and I didn't talk as we made our way outside and found the little playground he'd been talking about. Violet pointed at the sandbox right away, so I sat her down in it and then settled on a nearby bench in case she needed me. Aleks sat close to me, but he didn't say anything. I should have been happy about that, but the reality was that I needed someone to talk to.

"Are they his brothers? The other two men?" I asked.

"Yes and no," Aleks responded. "King and Con grew up with

Vaughn and Luca. They're as close as brothers can be, but they don't share any blood. There's another brother, a younger one named Lex. But he hasn't been around for a while. I've never met him."

I nodded in response. I had a million more questions, but I didn't really know where to start and they were questions I should be asking Luca.

"King called us last night. I guess Luca had told him Gio was awake," Aleks explained.

The idea that all the brothers had come together to support Luca, even Vaughn, made me glad for Luca and strangely envious again. What would it be like to have people like that come running when you needed them? Even as I asked myself the question, the answer hit me. I *did* have someone like that, and he was sitting right next to me.

"I lied to you, Aleks," I admitted as I kept my eyes on Violet so I wouldn't have to look at him. "The night you talked to Joe. That was me. Joe died six months ago. I knew if you thought I was alone, you'd come looking for me that night after the wedding. And I didn't want you to see me like that."

"Like what?" Aleks asked gently.

"Weak," I practically spit out.

"Is that how you see yourself?" my friend asked.

I glanced at him. "It's too hard to fight all the time." I was ashamed to say those words, but they were the truth, and I owed Aleks the truth.

"It's hard for me to make decisions," he responded. "Ever since I came home, I've had to make all these decisions that I was never allowed to before." Aleks's fingers reached out to touch the scar on his neck.

"I didn't want Dante to know that I wasn't okay, so I made all those decisions, but I was always so scared of making the wrong one... the one that would end up in me being punished. The one that would make Dante send me away. It was very tiring."

I knew exactly what he was talking about. "Is it better now?" I asked.

Aleks paused, then said, "I still don't like making them, but Vaughn is showing me that even if I make the wrong one, it's okay." The younger man had a little smile as he added, "He reminds me that I'm not broken."

When he looked at me, the light in Aleks's eyes had me smiling too.

"I'm glad, Aleks. I'm so glad you found him."

"Me too," he said. He actually seemed to blush a little, but I assumed that meant he was thinking something about his lover that probably wasn't any of my business.

"Are you all right, Remy? With Luca?" Aleks asked.

I automatically started nodding but stopped. I held my breath as I shook my head instead.

"Has he upset you?" was Aleks's next question. He'd asked it cautiously and I knew why. Not only was Luca basically a brother to him now, but we were in new territory when it came to our friendship. Aleks and I had certain things we talked about and certain ones we didn't. This particular conversation fell under the *didn't* category.

"He hasn't hurt me," I responded because I knew that was what Aleks really wanted to know.

"He's a good man," Aleks murmured. "But he does things that..."

I heard the uncertainty in the other man's voice. I had no doubt he was thinking about Luca's role in the abduction attempt on Aleks just a couple months earlier, as well as the knowledge that Luca and I had our own past. Whatever relationship Aleks and Luca had, it was undoubtedly as complicated as the one Luca and I had.

"He's only ever wanted his son back," I said. "I don't think it's something I ever really would've understood until her," I murmured as I motioned with my chin toward Violet. "She's not even mine, but I would do anything to protect her. *Anything.*"

"I would do the same for my family," Aleks responded. We both fell silent after that because we'd said a great deal without needing to say much at all. He and I were on the same page about Luca's actions in the past. We both had to find ways to forgive the man for decisions he'd made in the quest for his son, but like me, I knew Aleks understood it now.

When Violet started asking for food, Aleks and I took her back into the building and searched out the cafeteria. I was eager to get back to Luca, if only to find out how the meeting with Gio's doctor had gone.

As Aleks and I walked Violet back to the third floor on our way back from the cafeteria, a familiar sight greeted us when we got off the elevator. Aleks and I both exchanged glances as Gio was wheeled past us. The sullen teen glanced our way. If his expression hadn't shifted upon seeing us, I would've left the whole thing alone. But when I saw that little flash in his expression, the same one I'd seen the day before when Gio had recognized the keychain, I knew what I needed to do.

"I'll catch up," I said to Aleks softly once Gio was out of earshot. My friend nodded and then made his way back toward the waiting room while I went the opposite direction, a sleepy Violet still in my arms.

"Remy," Stan began to say but I shook my head at him.

"I just need a minute, Stan," I said. The bodyguard clearly wasn't happy about the deviation, but he stayed several steps behind, and I was glad that he didn't go for his phone to notify Luca of what I was up to.

It took just a minute for the nurse to get Gio to his room and settled. I watched from around the corner until she was gone, then made my way to the open door. The area we were in didn't have a lot of foot traffic, so no one intervened when I approached Gio's room. The teenager was lying in bed and staring out the window.

I cleared my throat a little so as not to startle him, but when he turned his head to look at me, he barely reacted.

"Hi, Nick," I said carefully. I managed to change the name to his preferred one at the last second as I remembered his near violent reaction the day before when he'd been called Gio. "Do you remember me?"

"You're with them," he muttered. "What do you want?"

"I just wanted to introduce myself. And say I was sorry for what my friend is putting you through," I lied. "I'm Remy, by the way. And this is Violet."

"You should get new friends, Remy," he said coldly. "Yours are murderers."

I was able to quell my instinctive response to deny his claim, since I already knew what had happened to Gio when he'd been found. Aleks had filled me in. It had been Ronan's men who'd found the teenager living in Texas. No one knew for sure exactly what had happened to Gio after he'd been abducted, but he'd ultimately ended up being traded or sold to a man who'd managed to brainwash the teen into believing he was someone else. Gio had believed himself to be in a loving relationship with the pedophile who'd hurt him. When Ronan's men had stormed the house where Gio was being kept, that man had killed himself rather than face the consequences of his actions. Gio, in turn, had tried to take his own life as well because he hadn't seen his rescue as a rescue at all.

I couldn't even fathom the mental torture the young man had been through to be so far gone that he believed that he loved the man who'd held him captive, and that the men who'd rescued him were his true abductors.

So no matter what I said, I needed to tread carefully.

"Someone died?" I asked.

"Like you don't already know," Gio whispered.

I ignored his jab and said, "It's hard trying to figure out your new normal, isn't it?"

Gio had turned his back to me, but I figured since he wasn't telling me to leave, it was still a victory of sorts. "Even when things aren't good, it's still hard to let them go and try to start over. Whoever you lost—"

"I didn't lose him!" Gio snapped. "He was *taken* from me. They murdered him! The things they said about him—" Gio's outburst ended as quickly as it had begun.

"I'm sorry," I repeated. "He obviously meant a lot to you."

"He was all I had. I loved him," the young man responded vehemently. "And he loved me."

"What was his name?" I asked.

"Kurt."

"Kurt," I murmured with a nod. Part of me just wanted to tell Gio that Kurt was a sick son of a bitch and that I hoped he was rotting in hell, but I tempered my words and instead said, "I'm sorry, Nick. I know how scary all this must be to deal with. Is there someone I can contact for you? Your family? Or maybe someone from Kurt's family?"

Gio didn't respond, so I figured my attempt to keep him talking had failed, but just as I was about to stand, he whispered, "There's no one."

"How about a friend? Someone who knew you and Kurt and who can tell everyone you're not this Gio person they've been searching for?"

I watched Gio's body as I spoke and saw him stiffen slightly when I said his name.

"It was just me and Kurt. We were each other's family."

Gio's despondent voice broke my heart. "I don't have any family either," I returned.

My heart just about leapt out of my chest when Gio looked over his shoulder at me. "You're with them," he accused.

I shook my head slowly. "I'm alone," was all I said. I'd intended to come in here to see if I could get anything out of Gio, but somehow it was me who was having to face the harsh truth.

Gio didn't respond to me, but I figured it was a win that he hadn't asked me to leave his room.

And when Stan told me it was time to go a good hour later, Gio and I hadn't said a single word to one another, but when I bid the young man farewell, I was certain I heard him murmur "bye" under his breath.

It wasn't much, but it was something.

CHAPTER EIGHTEEN

LUCA

†4

"How do you think he's going to take all this?" Vaughn asked.

I kept my eyes on Remy as I murmured, "Not good. He's gotten attached to her."

"Is he the only one?" was my brother's response.

I didn't answer him because there was no point in trying to lie or brush off the question. While there'd been a considerable amount of tension between myself and Remy that I couldn't understand the cause of, Violet had become the focus of our attention as we'd each counted down the days until her aunt took her home. I'd tried several times to talk to Remy about Marilyn, Violet's great-aunt, but beyond wanting confirmation that she would be a good parent to Violet, he'd had no interest in knowing anything about the woman or the place Violet would be calling home.

King and I had done extensive checks on the woman and my brother had even gone so far as to tail her for the better part of the week to make sure she wasn't hiding anything, but there'd been nothing to cause concern. If anything, it was the opposite. The woman had worked with children most of her life, she volunteered regularly at her church as well as the local hospital, and her husband had left her a considerable amount of money, so not only would she be able to afford to raise a child, but she had enough resources to give Violet the extra attention the child would need. She had a small, clean house in a good neighborhood and more importantly, when I'd called her to tell her about Violet, she'd cried for a good five minutes and then had insisted on catching the very next plane out. That had been this morning.

My brother and I watched Remy and Aleks play with Violet in the backyard for a few more minutes. The younger men were helping Violet walk back and forth between them. The child had made great progress with some of the physical challenges she faced. She still had years of therapy ahead of her, but we were confident that she'd be able to live a normal life.

"I shouldn't have said what I did," my brother suddenly said without any kind of provocation. When he, King, and Con had been waiting at the hospital for me, all the anger and hurt I'd been feeling had gone by the wayside. I'd had my brothers back and that was all I cared about.

"It doesn't—"

"Yes it does," Vaughn interrupted. I felt his gaze on me, but I continued to watch Remy. "It *does* matter."

"You were just trying to look out for your friend," I said.

"I was trying to look out for *you*," Vaughn responded. That had me looking at him in surprise. "I just wasn't doing a very good job of it."

I sighed and returned my attention to the window. "I'm tired of fighting with you, brother," I said softly. "I keep thinking we can get back to when we were kids. Before Mom..."

"Me too," Vaughn said.

"Just tell me if it's too late for that. If I fucked up too badly—"

"No," my brother cut in, his voice low and harsh. His fingers curled around my upper arm, forcing me to turn and face him. "No, do you hear me?" Vaughn practically snapped. "We've been through way too much shit together, Luca, to even consider throwing in the towel."

"I need more than that," I admitted. My gut rolled around uncontrollably as I considered what life would be like without my big brother. Vaughn's dark eyes held mine. "I need you to—"

"You have it. You have it all, Luca. My trust, my forgiveness, my loyalty... those things may have been tested, but you've always had them. Nothing will ever change that," my brother said firmly and without hesitation.

"It's more than I deserve," I said. "What I did to Aleks was unforgivable—"

"I think he forgave you about five minutes after you told him why you did what you did. And even if you hadn't, he still would've forgiven you because that's who he is."

I glanced at my brother's boyfriend and saw him cheering Violet on as she took a few tentative steps by herself. My eyes shifted to Remy and, even through the window, I could see the mix of joy and sorrow. The young man had been quiet all week. I'd tried to talk to him several times not only about Violet's aunt, but about what had happened between us in bed the night I'd told him we'd found the woman. He'd shot down the discussion by walking away from it, and I hadn't wanted to push. But the topic hadn't mattered because when I'd asked him things about his job and his future, he wouldn't answer me about those either. I couldn't say that he'd gone back to being the angry, distant Remy I'd first met a few weeks earlier, but I couldn't really put my finger on who he was now. There was a spark missing and I wanted it back.

For me.

For Violet.

For himself.

"You were right," I said to Vaughn. "My reasons for bringing Remy here were selfish."

"No, I wasn't, and no they weren't. He's a beautiful young man, but I know in my heart you would never take advantage of him. I also know that your priority has been keeping him safe. Him and the little girl," Vaughn responded.

"I thought maybe the guilt... maybe it would be less. But things are just more fucked up now." I considered what I was admitting to. As much as I was going to miss Violet, my thoughts always ended up back on Remy. The idea of not seeing him every day, of not talking to him, tore at something inside me. Which was ridiculous because Remy and I barely talked as it was. I had no clue how my life had become so intertwined with his. "I don't want him to go back to that apartment. It's all a sham. The smiles he puts on for people, the neat, tidy apartment, even that job of his..."

"He quit his job."

"What?" I said in disbelief as I looked at my brother in shock. While Remy's job had still been relatively entry-level, he'd already received two promotions in the years since he'd begun as a data entry clerk.

"Ronan told me. He's friends with Dom, the man who owns Barretti Security Group. I guess when all this stuff started happening with the little girl, Remy took some vacation time. But when that ran out, he just up and quit. Dom's been wanting to talk to him about it, but Ronan's convinced him to wait until things are settled with Violet."

I wasn't sure if I was more hurt or angry that Remy hadn't told me any of this himself.

"Maybe his boss was giving him a hard time about taking the time off?" I asked.

"No," Vaughn said softly. "The Barrettis don't work that way. They consider Remy family."

My phone rang before I could question Vaughn further. When I answered, my brother King said, "We'll be there in fifteen."

"Thanks," I said and then I nodded to Vaughn. I made a move to step past him so I could go tell Remy that Violet's aunt was almost here, but Vaughn surprised me by stepping in to hug me. My brother and I had never been super touchy-feely, but I had to admit it felt good to have his arms around me. It had been a lonely couple of months without him, and truthfully, he'd been working undercover for so long that it felt like I'd lost him years ago.

I hugged Vaughn back, then moved around him and headed for the door leading to the backyard. I'd ended up renting a large house near the hospital where Gio was staying. Now that my son was awake, I had plans to go to the hospital regularly, even if all I could do was sit in the waiting room. If it took every day for the rest of my life, Gio would know I was there. That I'd always been there and always would be. His doctor had recommended that I not have any encounters with Gio for a little while, but he was fully on board with me visiting the hospital every day.

Since waking, Gio hadn't spoken to his doctor other than to continue to insist that he wasn't my son and that he wanted to leave. It was a frustrating experience because I just wanted to take Gio home and be his father. I felt almost as helpless now as I had while he'd been missing. To know that my son had been brainwashed so convincingly by the man who'd hurt him in the most inconceivable ways made me violently ill. But Dr. Taylor had warned me that undoing the damage Kurt had inflicted would not be an easy thing. It would take months, even years before Gio accepted he was safe enough to face what the sick son of a bitch had done to him.

As I approached Remy, Aleks, and Violet, the little girl spied me and began clapping her hands together excitedly. Remy looked decidedly less happy to see me. Aleks got up from the little group and made his way back to the house, grabbing my hand in a simple embrace as he walked by me. I was grateful that he seemed to know I needed some privacy with Remy.

"Hey, princess," I said to Violet as I took Aleks's spot on the grass. Violet immediately began pumping her arms up and down like she was going to take flight. Remy had a hold of her, but he knew what she wanted and gently released her once she was steady on her feet. The child was off and running, though technically, she was walking. She wobbled as she moved, but her balance was good enough to keep her upright. I put out my arms and enfolded her within them when she reached me. I showered her with words of praise.

"I always regretted not seeing Gio do this," I murmured.

"You didn't see him walking?"

I shook my head. "Not his first steps," I admitted. "I was doing a deal somewhere... I don't even remember where. How sad is that?" I asked. "It was a deal I thought worth missing so many of my son's firsts, but obviously it wasn't even important enough for me to remember where it took place. I don't even recall if the deal got made. All I remember is that I saw my son take his first steps on video."

I eased my hold on Violet when she seemed ready to take off again. Her little legs stomped across the grass as she tried to walk more quickly to Remy. His face lit up with joy when she practically threw herself into his arms. But it was short-lived.

"King and Con will be here in a few minutes," I said. My brothers had each volunteered to go and pick up Marilyn from the airport. Rather than choosing between them, I'd asked them to go together. Since they still weren't on speaking terms, they hadn't exactly been excited at the prospect, but I knew they'd work it out between them. They always did. King still hadn't told any of us what was up with Lex, but at Con's insistence, he'd once again reassured everyone that our youngest brother was safe.

"Your brothers are... interesting," Remy said softly.

I laughed at his observation. "My brothers are kind of nuts," I said. I saw Remy smile briefly but then it was gone just as quickly.

"How did you and Vaughn meet them?" Remy asked. "Aleks said King, Con, and Lex grew up in foster care."

I opened my arms so Violet would have a target as she began walking back to me. "We met on the basketball court. Our mom used to volunteer for this group home. King, Con, and Lex had all ended up there at one point or another. A lot of the families that took in foster kids were just in it for the money, so when the kids became too much to handle and were no longer worth the money they were getting, the parents would just bring them back to the group home. King practically lived there for the first few years. Lex too, but mostly because he had so many medical issues. Con was more in and out because he had a more laid-back temperament. But even he would get pushed too far on occasion. They were all together playing ball one day when my brother and I asked if we could play with them. King and Vaughn actually ended up in a fistfight because King knew who we were. He was never fond of rich kids. Con played peacemaker, and Lex... he just stood by the sidelines and waited until the drama was over. All he ever wanted to do was play ball because he was usually too sick to do even that."

"But he's all right now?" Remy asked.

I shook my head. "Not sure. He's been kind of MIA for a while now. King knows where he is and says he's okay, but..."

"But?" Remy prodded.

"It has to be pretty bad if it's keeping him from seeing his nephew. All of my brothers helped in the search for Gio because they all felt like they helped raise him. So for Lex to not show up when we found him..." I didn't finish the statement because I didn't want to consider all the possibilities that were keeping my youngest brother in hiding.

"I'm sorry, Luca," Remy said.

"He's strong, like you," I found myself saying.

Remy dropped his head and I swore I saw something in his eyes before he did. If I hadn't known better, it seemed like the remark had angered him in some way. But I couldn't, for the life of me, figure out why it would, so I convinced myself I was mistaken.

"Remy, we haven't really talked about Violet—"

"I know you'll make sure her great-aunt is the right person to take care of her," Remy interjected.

"I will, but that isn't what I meant—"

Remy began shifting his body before I even finished getting the words out, and he interrupted me yet again by saying, "Can you watch her while I go get cleaned up?"

Violet had made it to my arms and was keenly intent on returning to Remy's when he suddenly stood up, not even waiting to hear my reply. He wiped at his pants nervously and then turned and headed back for the house.

"Me-me," Violet called. I could sense her confusion.

"He'll be back in a bit, sweetheart," I said to her as I turned her to face me. It was then that I noticed she had my keychain attached to one of her little belt loops on the pink denim pants she was wearing.

But Remy didn't return and when I asked Aleks to check on him after Marilyn arrived and he still didn't make an appearance, a bad

190

feeling washed over me. It was confirmed a few minutes later when Aleks returned to the living room with Stan in tow. The looks on their faces were enough to tell me what I'd already started to suspect...

That once again, Remy had run.

CHAPTER NINETEEN

REMY

⊹4

My fingers were shaking badly as I flipped the cheap lock on the motel room's door. I didn't take a complete breath until the deadbolt slid into place. While that familiar taste tickled the back of my throat like it always did, for once, it wasn't the need for heroin that had me so on edge.

It was the fear of being found.

Namely by Luca.

Although it was probably ridiculous to think the man would be searching for me at that point. It had been over a week since I'd left the house he'd been renting. I'd taken the coward's way out, literally. Of all the things I'd done in my past, none seemed to compare to the guilt and shame I felt for abandoning Violet like I had. And knowing just how much Luca likely detested me for being such a coward made me sick to my stomach.

Maybe if it hadn't been so easy to walk out, I would've felt just a little less ashamed. At that point, though, there'd been no reason for Stan or any of the other bodyguards to keep close tabs on me. Ronan's men had stopped watching the house several days before I'd left, and Stan had only accompanied me whenever I'd left the stately home. So gathering my few things after lying to Luca about wanting to get cleaned up the day Violet's great-aunt had come to get her had been easy, logistically, anyway. There hadn't been much to gather up, since I'd left behind the majority of the things Luca had bought me over the several weeks I'd spent with him and Violet. I'd taken only what had belonged to me. Then I'd simply walked down the stairs and out the side door and that had been it. After that, it'd been easy to hitch a ride to wherever I'd wanted to go.

But for whatever reason, I'd ended up being far closer to Luca than I would've liked. I'd known better than to go back to my apartment in the city and I'd left behind the phone that Luca had bought me. However, I had gone out of my way to get what little cash I had left in my bank account out. I'd taken a bus all the way down to the Washington-Oregon state border to withdraw the last of my savings and had then closed the account. It should have been so easy to continue south or any other direction except back north, but north was exactly where my mind had decided to take me, apparently because it didn't believe in doing things the easy way.

As jittery as I was, I automatically reached for the hem of my shirt as I began walking toward the small, dirty bathroom. The place I'd chosen to stay was a dump, but with limited financial means, I hadn't wanted to waste my money on a nicer hotel room.

I made it about ten steps into the room when I saw the dark figure sitting in the tattered armchair across from the bed. I jumped backward and let out a harsh breath. In my gut, I knew who it was. The scene was all too familiar, considering the man had broken into my apartment and had been sitting in a similar position the night after I'd slugged him at the wedding.

This time he didn't speak.

And this time, I was too terrified to move.

I stood with my back against the door as Luca slowly rose. There wasn't any light in the room except for the little bit that filtered in from the parking lot through the curtains. It most certainly wasn't enough to see his expression, at least not from where I was standing. But I didn't need to see his face to know he was pissed. I tried to remind myself that he wasn't someone who would ever hurt me, but admittedly, it was difficult. In all our previous situations, I hadn't gone out of my way to deceive him and avoid him. And I hadn't run out on the little girl who'd needed me.

The reminder of what a selfish bastard I was made my knees feel weak and I found myself leaning heavily against the door for support. I deserved whatever he would do to me. There was nothing he could say that would make me feel any worse anyway.

I forced myself not to move as he closed the distance between us, his gait almost predatory in nature.

I wanted to ask how Violet was, how *he* was, but I didn't have that right. I tried to tell myself that I didn't care, but there was no way I could sell myself on *that* particular bullshit. Not to mention the fact that I'd spent the last week obsessing over that very thing. There'd been so many times I'd wanted to go back. That had been proof enough that I'd been in Luca's company too long, that I'd gotten too comfortable.

Luca kept coming until he was practically pressed up against me. There was enough light now to see his face, though I kind of wished there wasn't. So much for the days when his expression had been unreadable. There was no mistaking his anger this time. I thought back to the first night when he'd shown up in my apartment and I'd been strong enough to play mind games with him. But I'd had my hatred to hang on to then. The things I'd started to feel for him since then had absolutely nothing to do with hatred.

I waited for the barrage of questions, the anger, the disappointment. Since I just wanted it over with, the longer he remained silent, the more agitated I became. I absolutely would not humiliate myself further in front of this man by having to seek out another cold shower... one in a long line of many over the past week as I fought the urge to lose myself in an artificial high.

"What?" I finally snapped when he didn't say anything. I had my eyes straight ahead, which meant I was looking at the column of his throat. There was enough light filtering in from outside to see a small amount of dark chest hair against the whiteness of his dress shirt. The need to reach out and touch him made my fingers shake even more badly than they already were.

Luca didn't respond to my outburst. I wasn't really surprised by that. The man was much better at masking his emotions than I was. "What do you want?" I asked again, but this time my voice shook so badly I could hear it myself. I just wanted him to go. I wanted him to say whatever he was going to say and then leave me be.

I could feel wisps of his breath fluttering over my temple. Heat came off his body in waves and I imagined what it would be like to lean into him and absorb it for myself.

"I want to know if you're all right," he said.

I would've laughed if I weren't so close to tears. "I didn't use," I bit out. "I wanted to… I always want to, but I didn't." I berated myself for having said too much. That was what got me into trouble with this man. All the things I should've told him were on the tip of my tongue… like how I was an adult and he had no say in what I did or where I went, or how Violet was in better hands now and we both knew that, or that I had a life I needed to get back to.

That last part was definitely a lie, but he didn't need to know that. I needed to sever all ties with him. Knowing him, he'd want to offer me something, probably money, to help me. But the last thing I wanted was for him to continue to feel guilty about what had happened between us when I'd been a kid. And I certainly didn't want to be anyone's charity case.

I expected Luca to step back, or maybe even to say something along the lines of he was glad I hadn't used drugs, assuming he even believed me, but when his fingers dipped beneath my chin and lifted my head so I was forced to look at him, I didn't know what to say or do.

"I want to know you're all right," he said, his voice taking on a raspy quality. "*You,* Remy. I'm not asking about drugs or anything else you might have done after you left, because those things aren't you, they aren't who you are. I've been going out of my mind with worry that you were lying hurt somewhere needing me. I've barely eaten or slept or said a kind word to any one of my brothers because all I could fucking do was think about you and wonder what the hell I did or said to make you leave."

I opened my mouth in disbelief, but before I could say anything, Luca leaned down and captured my lips with his. Whereas all our other kisses had been relatively tame and exploratory, this one was the opposite. It was hungry and angry and desperate. I groaned under the onslaught of sensation that roared through me as his tongue licked over mine in greeting. I couldn't stop the little sounds that kept bubbling up from my throat as he kissed me over and over, stealing a little bit more from me each time. When I went to wrap my arms around his neck, he grabbed my wrists and pinned them to the door. But there was nothing rough or harsh in the way he was holding me. All I could do was hang on to him as he consumed me. My body went from hot to a full-on inferno in a matter of seconds and then I was kissing him back.

The few times I'd taken control of our kisses, I'd been hesitant because I hadn't wanted to screw it up. But *this*... this was different. This was my body reacting to his. There was no second guessing or self-doubt involved. My body knew exactly what to do, my mouth knew exactly how to bring pleasure to his the same way he was bringing it to mine.

Luca's body pressed mine against the door. I could feel his erection through his clothes. It should have scared me, but it didn't. I welcomed it, though I wasn't sure why. All I knew was that I didn't want him to ever stop touching me, kissing me, owning me.

But he ended the kiss way too soon. I was panting for breath when he pulled back and pressed his forehead against mine. At least he was breathing hard too.

"Are you all right?" he asked me again.

I probably should've told him yes, just so I could keep things easy. But the last thing I wanted to do was lie to him. I shook my head and whispered, "I miss you so much. You and Violet."

I was certain I heard him sigh in relief, but I didn't know why. Surely, he realized he was better off without me. He'd done what he'd set out to do... he'd protected me and found Violet's family. What else was there?

"Luca, if this is the guilt—"

"It's not the fucking guilt, Remy!" he practically shouted. "I want you! I've wanted you since the moment I saw you again."

I stared at him in shock and then shook my head. "No," I began. "No, you stopped. The last time we kissed, you stopped when you touched me. You felt my scars and you knew all the things I'd done to put them there. I'm a junkie and a who—"

That was all I got out before his mouth slammed down on mine once again. I groaned as he kissed me even harder than he had before. He jutted his hips forward until his dick was rubbing mine through our clothing. I cried out at the contact because it was so foreign to me. I'd never once gotten hard while being with another guy, so everything Luca was doing to me was a first. I kissed him back, feeling clumsy and inexperienced, but if it bothered Luca, he didn't show it. I didn't understand any of what was happening, but I didn't want him to stop either.

Luca's hands moved up my wrists, then over my palms. He twined our fingers together but kept my hands above my head and against the wood. He broke the kiss once again and this time I could barely catch my breath. His mouth was mere inches from mine, and I could see that he was in the same state.

"You don't ever call yourself those things again, do you hear me?" he growled at me. "You are none of those things." He gave my hands a little bit of a shake and repeated, "You. Are. None. Of. Those. Things."

I was too caught up in a haze of desire to do anything but agree with him. I still had no clue what was happening. The idea that he could actually want me wasn't something my brain knew how to process. The guys who'd paid to have sex with me hadn't exactly been picky. Luca could have any man or woman he wanted. Even if I hadn't come with the shit ton of baggage that I did, I was skinny and pale and practically had more scars on my body than not. Luca was built and beautiful. But on top of that, he was brave and kind and he had a softness about him when it came to Violet, to his son... to me.

"I stopped before because I didn't want to overwhelm you. I didn't want you thinking that I only wanted you physically. You were in a vulnerable state with everything that had happened that night. If I'd taken advantage of that..." He didn't continue, choosing instead just to shake his head. How had I ever thought this man was selfish and had only used me when I'd been a kid? How had I thought him unfeeling?

Luca released one of my hands and trailed his fingers down my arm, over my cheek, and along my neck. His hand kept going south until he reached my hip... the hip with the scar on it. "You're so beautiful, Remy," he whispered and then his mouth brushed a featherlight kiss over mine. "Every time I look at you, it's all I can do *not* to touch you." His hand moved back up my side and then settled in the middle of my chest. "And your heart, Remy. You have the most giving heart I've ever known. To survive what you have and to then offer forgiveness to someone like me..."

I covered his hand with mine. "Why won't you believe me?" I asked. "Why won't you believe that there's nothing to forgive? You didn't do anything wrong."

"Sweetheart," Luca said gently. "I think that's just going to be one of those things that we'll have to agree to disagree on."

I didn't like the idea of him having that guilt hanging over his head for the rest of his days, but when I opened my mouth to say as much, he silenced me with a kiss... another gentle, sweet one. It was mind-blowing to know that it didn't matter if his kisses were chaste or all-consuming—they slayed me either way.

"Tell me why you left," Luca said. His body was still pressed to mine, but he put some inches between our faces, presumably so he could look me in the eye.

"Because I'm a coward," I admitted. I could see he was about to protest, so I quickly continued. "I couldn't do it. I couldn't watch that woman fall in love with Violet, even though it's what I wanted. What kind of an asshole does that? I don't want her for myself, but I didn't want that woman to have her? And you... the sooner Violet leaves, the sooner you leave too. If we're being honest, there was really no reason for me to stay with you as long as I did. Playing house with you was too easy." I knew my words sounded pathetic even as I said them, so I added, "Besides, I had a life I needed to get back to. A job, friends."

"You mean the job you quit?" Luca asked. I felt my cheeks heat at the question. How the hell had he found that out?

"I—" I began to say, but then lost the words. I had no explanation, at least not one I wanted to share with him.

"And as far as I know, Aleks is your only friend, and even he didn't know where you were."

This time the accusation in Luca's voice was unmistakable. I didn't blame him. It was one thing to run away, it was another thing entirely to lie to his face. Since I didn't know what else to say, I kept quiet. I certainly couldn't tell him that I'd made the decision that it was time for me to move on from Seattle altogether.

"Fine," Luca said. He still had ahold of me with one hand and had moved his other so it was caressing my hip. "Let's table that particular conversation for now."

Thank God, I thought to myself. But that only lasted as long as it took for him to ask his next question.

"Would you like to explain to me why you've been going to the hospital every night for the past week so you could visit my son?"

ᵼ4

Even as my raging body demanded I take Remy's mouth again, I managed to ignore the command. But I didn't release Remy from my hold and I didn't ease up with how I was pressed against him. Bottom line was that it just felt too good, especially after a week of going crazy with worry for the young man.

I'd spent endless hours scouring downtown Seattle in an effort to find Remy. I'd even gone back to that terrible warehouse known as The Palace. There'd been no Remy, but I'd seen the kid I'd given the money to when Remy and I had been looking for Violet. The teenager hadn't recognized me, probably because he'd been high as a kite and in the midst of being fucked by two guys at once. I'd intervened in the hopes that stopping the degrading encounter would somehow wake the kid up, but he'd merely offered to let me join in for what he'd called a reasonable price.

It'd been like Remy had said. I couldn't save that kid because he wasn't ready to be saved. Even if I'd offered him a house, enough money to live off of for the next ten years, and a host of other amenities to make his life easier, he still would've chosen the drugs. I'd once again left him my business card in the hopes that maybe someday he'd call me and say he was ready. Then I'd continued my search for Remy.

But he'd been nowhere, and the pimp named Taz, who hadn't exactly been thrilled to see me, had said he hadn't seen Remy since the day we'd gone looking for Violet.

After that, I'd spent most of my days sitting outside Remy's apartment, but there'd been no sign of him. My brothers had helped in the search, but with no digital footprint to track after Remy had withdrawn his money from a bank near the state border, we'd all been at a standstill. I'd tried to accept the possibility that he'd left the state and that I might never see him again, but every time I'd considered it, I'd dismissed it just as quickly. I hadn't been ready to admit that I'd lost the young man a second time.

My search for Remy meant I hadn't been around while Marilyn had been getting to know her great-niece. Aleks had been the one left to introduce the little girl to the woman who was willing and able to give her a new life. But it still should have been me and Remy participating in that transition.

Together.

Admittedly, I'd been hurt and angry after he'd fled, but I'd understood what had driven him to it. I was struggling with the idea of losing Violet myself. She'd only been in my life for a few weeks, but between her and Remy, they'd changed something inside of me. Maybe not changed it, so much as brought it back. Those same emotions I'd felt after being handed my newborn son for the first time had been buried for so long after I'd lost Gio that I'd forgotten what they felt like. Remy and Violet had given me a glimpse. They'd been a reminder that *that* version of Luca was a pretty good one.

"How-how did you know?" Remy asked, stumbling over his own words.

"King saw you last night at the hospital as you were leaving the room. He asked the nurse about you and she said you had identified yourself as Aleks and that you'd been visiting Gio every night for the past week. King followed you back to this motel." I glanced around the dirty, musty room with disgust.

My Remy didn't belong in a place like this.

"I'm sorry," Remy began nervously. His palm felt sweaty and cold beneath my hand. "I only said I was Aleks because I knew he was allowed to visit Gio."

"I don't care about that," I said. "I just want to know why you were visiting him."

Remy swallowed hard but didn't answer. I huffed in frustration. Hadn't we gotten past all this? Hadn't we gotten past his mistrust of me?

Clearly not, or we wouldn't currently be standing in the piece-of-shit room.

"Just talk to me, Remy," I whispered. "Not because you feel like you owe it to me or any of that shit. Talk to me because you want to, because you need to, because it's me."

I saw the indecision flicker in his eyes, and it felt like some kind of death knell. If I hadn't managed to earn his trust by now, I doubted I ever would. That fact felt like a dagger was being plunged through my heart.

I released Remy and stepped back. Up until that very moment, I'd believed there was something between us. I'd spent a lot of the last week as I'd searched for Remy trying to sort out my feelings for the younger man. I'd been worried that all of my actions had been based solely on the guilt I'd felt for leaving him behind so many years ago. And yes, that was what had started this whole thing between us, but it wasn't what had driven me to seek him out again.

Remy leaving like he had meant I could have had a clean break. With Violet leaving too, I would've been at a point where I could go back to my old life while I waited for my son to return to me.

I'd known within an hour of Remy leaving that I didn't want my old life back.

I'd only wanted Remy.

I had no idea how he'd become such an important part of my life in the past few weeks, but he had. Every up-and-down moment I'd had in the past seven days, I'd wanted to share that with him.

But clearly, he didn't want the same things.

I ignored the stabbing pain in my chest as I reached past his hip for the doorknob. I expected him to move when I turned it, but to my surprise, he dropped his hand and closed it over my wrist. "Don't," he whispered so quietly that I barely heard him. "Please don't go, Luca."

I didn't move or respond for fear that I'd somehow shut him down again. He had his eyes closed, making me wonder what kind of internal battle he was waging with himself.

"I was going to leave. For real... everything." He shook his head. I wanted to ask him what he meant because I had no clue what he was talking about, but I held my tongue. He was still gripping my wrist, his fingers flexing occasionally.

He sucked in a breath and said, "I quit my job because I was going to leave Seattle. Just pack a bag and go. Somewhere, anywhere. I did that... I packed a bag, I went to the bus station. When the guy asked me where I wanted to go, this was the place I told him. I don't know why. I got this room and then I went to the hospital and told them I was Aleks and they let me see your son. I started saying goodbye to him... I don't know, maybe it was my way of saying goodbye to you." Remy laughed, but it was harsh and ugly sounding. "I don't know what's happening to me," he added, his voice desperate and confused. He chose that moment to look at me, and the pain in his eyes made it hard to breathe.

I used my free arm to reach for him and when I pulled him against my chest, he went without hesitation. His hold on me was tight. I kissed the top of his head, but then that wasn't enough. I understood his confusion because I'd been there myself. I still was. I tipped his head back so I could kiss him. His arms crawled around my neck instantly. He kissed me back with hunger and without reservation. At least this part of us made sense.

I forced myself to break the kiss and then I took his hand and led him to the bed. I didn't miss his hesitation as I sat down on it. I was about to reassure him that nothing was going to happen, but instead, I used the moment to figure out something else I needed to know. I drew him forward until his knees bumped mine. Remy was clearly nervous, but he didn't try to pull away or say anything. I dropped his hands so I could reach for his legs. I gently urged him to step on each side of mine and then I was drawing him down so he was straddling my lap. The fact that Remy did so without hesitation made my heart soar.

So there was some trust after all.

I rested my hands on his back and gave him a quick kiss. "If anything happens between us, sweetheart, it's going to be your choice and it sure as hell isn't going to be in a dump like this."

I saw a ghost of a smile on his lips. He seemed a little more relaxed. I kept my arms wrapped around his lower waist and was surprised when he lifted his fingers to sift through my hair.

"Why did you leave?" I asked.

Remy's fingers slid down the side of my face as his eyes met mine. His touch was gentle and sweet, and I could have sat like that forever with him just loving on me a little.

"I knew I wouldn't be strong enough to watch her take Violet away. When she did, there would've been no reason for you to…"

"To what?" I asked.

"To keep me around. I didn't want it to be like…" he began to say, then he dropped his eyes. I quickly tipped his chin back up so he had to look at me.

"Like what?" I prodded.

"Like when I went home." He shook his head and I saw his eyes fill with moisture. "I didn't want it to be like that. Not with you."

He didn't need to say anything else because I got it. He hadn't wanted to experience the pain of me turning him away like his parents had. The idea that maybe his feelings for me rivaled mine for him was overwhelming and exciting, but I didn't want to screw this up and scare him away again. I racked my brain for something smart to say, something that would reassure him that it wouldn't be like that. But all that came out was, "Then stay."

"What?" Remy choked out.

"Stay," I repeated. As soon as I'd said that word the first time, it was like a valve inside of me had been loosened and all the pain, guilt, and helplessness I'd been feeling for the past eight years started to ease a bit. "Just stay, Remy."

"I…" was all he got out.

I could see the idea was too overwhelming for him and since I was afraid of spooking him, I added, "Just for a while. We can see where things go... we can go out."

"What, you mean like on... *a date*?" Remy asked, his expression twisted with confusion and disbelief.

I found myself smiling as I realized that was exactly what I meant. "Yeah, a date," I said. "Preferably a lot of dates."

"You want me to stay with you... in your house. So you can *date* me?"

His confusion and disbelief were adorable. But then I realized how the concept might sound to someone with his past, so I quickly amended, "Just date. We go out to dinner, watch movies, whatever it is people do on dates. I've never really been on one, so we'll have to play it by ear. But just dates, Remy." I hoped that he'd get I wasn't trying to buy him for sex or something.

Remy didn't respond at first. I forced myself to remain silent so he could process my words. What I was asking was a pretty big deal. But I was more certain than ever that it was exactly what we needed. We'd been together for several weeks now, but our relationship had been anything but easy. It was like we'd started in reverse and we'd shared all the heavy stuff and been through all these traumatic things, but we needed to get to know each other outside of all that.

A voice in my head tried to remind me that I couldn't have a relationship, but I silenced it and focused on Remy instead. When it came down to a choice between a possible future with Remy and one without him, it was an easy decision. I'd learned from what had happened with Gio and I wasn't about to go through that again.

I'd tried to protect my son from my enemies, but I'd lost him anyway. And in trying to protect him as a child, I'd missed the most important parts of his life. I wanted to laugh because Ronan had tried to explain that very thing to me.

I considered the surgeon and his mysterious group of men and women. I didn't know their backgrounds, but it was like he said, there was always that potential of someone coming out of the woodwork to hurt me or someone I loved. The solution wasn't to push my loved ones away, it was to hold them closer and cherish every moment. And God knew I had the resources to protect my family like Ronan did his. It was something I'd have to talk to Remy about if I was lucky enough to get a future with him, but that particular conversation would definitely have to wait. At this point, I just needed him to agree to give me a chance to prove I was worthy of him.

"A date," Remy said softly, reverently. "I've never been on one either."

His fingers were caressing my face and his eyes never left mine. He shifted his body closer so our lips were just inches apart. That valve inside of me loosened another notch because I knew in that moment that he was going to give me this. It seemed silly, but I was beyond thrilled at the idea that we could share this first together.

"So you'll stay?" I asked, just to be sure. I ran my hands up and down his back.

He nodded. "I'll stay," he murmured and then his mouth closed over mine. The kiss was deep and hungry, but slow and thorough too. When we separated, it was all I could do not to grab his ass and pull him forward so we could grind our dicks together. I reminded myself that sex was off the table for a while. Remy wasn't a sex-on-the-first-date kind of guy. Neither was I, for that matter.

Remy continued to hold my face as his eyes studied me. "I talk, Luca. That's all I do when I'm with Gio. Talk. He doesn't respond to me or ask questions or tell me anything about himself, but I just thought that if he knew I was there and that I would be there night after night, maybe... I don't know, I guess I'm kind of winging it. I'm sorry, I should've asked you—"

I kissed him to silence him and when he was dizzy with pleasure, I pulled back. "Thank you, Remy," I breathed. "Thank you."

"I'm not really doing anything," he began to say.

"Yes, you are. You're letting him know he's not alone. Dr. Taylor said Gio is actually answering a few questions during their sessions. He wasn't doing that before. Whatever you're doing, it *is* helping. I don't know how to ever thank you for that. My son hasn't had anyone he could rely on for so long," I said, but then my words got stuck in my throat as I considered how afraid and lonely my child would have been for all those years. Tears stung the backs of my eyes like they usually did when I allowed myself to think of the mental and physical torture my son had endured.

Remy wrapped his arms around my neck and hugged me hard. He held me for the longest time. I loved how his fingers stroked the back of my neck in a soothing manner.

"Let's go home, Luca," was all Remy said. They were the perfect words because I wanted to do nothing more than get him out of there and back to my place.

Where he belonged.

CHAPTER TWENTY-ONE

REMY

╪4

As with every time I walked into Gio's hospital room, I was nervous. I had this terrible fear that I'd say the wrong thing to him that would shut him down again. I'd had the opportunity to talk to Dr. Taylor about my visits and he'd assured me that I was doing everything right, but it was probably even more intimidating now to chat with the teenager. It was like I'd told Luca, I'd gone to see Gio because he'd been my last link to Luca. Gio hadn't shown any interest in talking to me, so I'd been the one to talk.

I'd started off by talking about nothing in particular, but as the days had gone by, I'd found myself telling Gio things about my life that I'd never intended to share. Maybe because he hadn't been interested in conversing with me, it had been easier. And it wasn't like I had a lot of other things happening in my life that were worth discussing. I hadn't gone into the details of being abducted and what my life had been like before I'd been sold to Les, but I hadn't held back about the fact that I was a drug addict and that I'd sold my body to get the money I needed both to survive Les and to get the drugs I'd craved.

Dr. Taylor had encouraged me to continue to be open and honest with Gio. I still called the teenager Nick because it was what he wanted. Or at least, I suspected it was what he preferred. I doubted he was anywhere near believing he was, in fact, Gio. I didn't avoid talking about Luca during our chats, but I hadn't pressed the issue about him being Gio's father. I'd usually only referenced things like how Luca had helped me rescue Violet.

Luca and I didn't talk about the conversations I had with Gio. It was something we'd both agreed on. Luca wanted his son to have that bit of privacy, so he'd never once pressured me to tell him anything about what Gio and I talked about… or rather, what *I* talked to *Gio* about.

While Gio never spoke to me during our chats, he never asked me to leave, and every once in a while, I'd catch him looking my way as I talked about something particularly painful or humiliating. I wasn't as confident as Dr. Taylor and Luca that my conversations with Gio had changed his behavior in any way, but the fact that he was interacting a bit more with Dr. Taylor, even if it was just to talk about his medications or how he was feeling that day, made me more than happy to continue seeing the teen.

Admittedly, today I was more distracted than I would've liked. When I walked into the room, Gio looked my way briefly. His eyes quickly slid to Violet, who was walking next to me, holding my hand. It made for slow going, but just seeing Violet walk with such little assistance was a very big deal and if it had taken all day to walk from the parking lot to the room, I would've been fine with that.

"Hi, Nick," I said. "I hope you don't mind that I brought her with me. Luca and Marilyn are going over some legal and financial stuff with Violet's lawyer."

Since Marilyn's arrival and her interest in officially adopting Violet, we'd had to go through official channels. That meant reaching out to Child Protective Services. Violet had been declared a ward of the state and had been given her own attorney to advocate for her best interests. That man also happened to be a close family friend to both my old boss, Dom Barretti, as well as Ronan. The lawyer, Zane, had made sure that Violet could stay with Luca and me until custody was officially granted to Marilyn.

I'd wanted to dislike Marilyn when I'd met her, but it had been pretty much impossible. When I'd returned to Luca's, Violet had been happy to see me and while *she* hadn't been particularly clingy, *I* hadn't been able to put her down, even when she'd wanted to go to her great-aunt. But Marilyn hadn't pressed the issue and after several days of getting the chance to see her interacting with Violet, I'd found myself imagining the life Violet would have with her. The woman was kind, patient, and clearly loved the great-niece she'd only known for a week. She was also well versed in how to work with a child with developmental challenges. She'd even shown me and Luca several techniques we could use to help Violet learn different skills. The woman could have easily come in and demanded custody of her niece, but she'd treated Luca and me as members of Violet's family. She'd already extended several invitations to us to come to Louisiana to visit Violet, and she'd been promising to learn how to use her smart phone better so she could send pictures and videos of the child.

My heart still ached at the prospect of losing Violet, but it was tempered with the knowledge that it was what was best for the little girl. It was also what her mother would have wanted.

Gio didn't say anything, but I saw him shake his head a little. I wasn't sure if that meant he did mind or he didn't, but I chose to believe it was the latter. If he didn't want either of us there, he'd just have to say so.

I led Violet to the chair next to Gio's hospital bed. The teen was still confined to using a wheelchair to move around, but Dr. Taylor had indicated that was only because the young man was refusing to do his physical therapy. His muscles were still weak from being in bed for so long.

Gio turned his head so he could stare out the window again.

I glanced at the window myself and then made a decision that I knew could bite me in the ass. I sat Violet down in the chair next to the bed and said, "Honey, can you sit here for just a minute?"

The little girl nodded slowly. Things like seeing her sit up in a chair were such huge victories. It was a sign that her balance was improving and the things that most parents took for granted with their children were things that Luca, Marilyn, and I celebrated as big wins.

I went around the bed and grabbed Gio's wheelchair. I pushed it to the side of the bed and said, "Get in. We're going for a ride."

The teenager shot me a dark look, but I didn't care. I put on my best stern expression and said, "Get in the chair, Nick." When he didn't move, I added, "It's a beautiful day outside. Violet's going to be leaving soon and I want every moment I spend with her to be one she'll remember, so we're going outside to the playground so she can play in the sandbox because it's one of her favorite things to do." I kept my expression firm even as I wondered if I was allowed to take Gio outside. It wasn't like he could run away, since his legs weren't strong enough yet.

It became a standoff and I instinctively knew it was one of those things that if I backed down, I'd lose any progress I'd made with Gio. I reminded myself he was still just a child and needed rules and boundaries. I crossed my arms in what I hoped was an "I can do this for as long as you can" look.

I had no idea how long he held out for, but when he let out a huff and then began swinging his legs over the side of the bed, I wanted to do a victory dance. But I acted like it was no big deal and did my best to help him get into the chair. I pushed him around the bed and stopped next to the chair Violet was sitting in. I scooped her up and then deposited her on Gio's lap. I wasn't sure who was more surprised, Gio or Violet. I silently begged Violet not to freak out. Her wide eyes stared at Gio as he stared at her. I gave the wheelchair a tiny push and found myself hiding my smile when Gio's hands automatically came up to hold the little girl so she wouldn't fall off the chair.

By the time we reached the hallway, Violet was babbling about nothing in particular and was trying to show Gio the doll Marilyn had brought for her. Gio didn't speak, but he did nod his head as the toddler showed him the doll's movable limbs.

Fortunately, none of the nurses tried to stop us when we left the building. Gio actually squinted when we went out into the sunlight, but I also sensed him relaxing a bit. Maybe I was imagining that last part, but maybe not. I was just going to keep going with the flow to see what happened.

Violet began to wiggle with excitement when she saw the sandbox. Gio managed to hold on to her and he even told her a couple times that we were almost there. I quickened my stride and got us to the sandbox and put Violet down so she could play. Then I maneuvered the wheelchair to the bench and locked the brakes. I sat down next to Gio and just enjoyed watching Violet do her thing.

"Where is she going?" Gio asked out of the blue. I was so surprised that I actually stared at him for a moment. I gave myself a mental kick so I could answer him.

"Her great-aunt has come to get her. I can't remember if I told you, but Luca found her a few weeks ago. She's the only relative left, but luckily she wants to take care of Violet."

When Gio didn't respond, I was certain the question was just a one-time thing, but after another minute he said, "You don't want her?"

"I do," I said. "But it's not about what I want. It's about what's best for Violet. And I'm not what's best for her."

"Why not?"

"I'm not ready to be a parent," I admitted. "When you have kids, you're committing to something that's so much bigger than yourself. Your entire life becomes about them and that's the way it should be. I'm still trying to figure things out and it wouldn't be fair to Violet. She deserves someone who's going to be there for her one hundred percent."

There was another long round of silence, but I didn't pressure Gio to speak. As far as I was concerned, we'd had our little miracle for the day. More than one, actually. I couldn't wait to tell Luca that Gio had not only agreed to go outside, but that he'd spoken as well. I wouldn't tell Luca what Gio and I had actually talked about, but he'd be beyond elated to know that his son had taken those tiny steps.

"Kurt wanted kids," Gio murmured softly. I hadn't expected him to bring up his abuser. I reminded myself that he still saw the man as his husband, as the love of his life.

"Was that something you wanted?" I asked casually.

"I wanted whatever Kurt did," was the response. His answer didn't surprise me at all. He'd been brainwashed into being subservient to the man who'd owned him. It didn't matter that the relationship had been wrapped up in the package of supposed marriage. There'd been nothing equal in the relationship.

I wasn't really sure how to respond, so I didn't. But to my surprise, Gio continued on his own.

"He wanted to adopt an older kid. Said he'd found the perfect one."

I felt sick to my stomach because I knew what that statement really meant. The idea that Kurt had been on the verge of buying another child made me want to throw up and then run to Ronan and thank him for having found the man and getting Gio away from him.

"How did you feel about that?" I asked, then cringed when I realized I probably sounded like Dr. Taylor.

Gio shrugged his shoulders. But after a moment he said, "I didn't know how to share Kurt. So I guess I was kind of jealous."

His admission broke my heart. It was further proof of how ingrained Gio had become in pleasing Kurt and how Kurt had literally become Gio's entire world. The fact that Gio had tried to take his own life not once but twice after Kurt had killed himself had been frightening proof that severing the hold Kurt had had on Gio wouldn't be an easy process.

Gio closed his eyes and tipped his head back a little, like he was enjoying the sun on his skin. There was a slight breeze in the air, so it made for an almost perfect day. Gio didn't speak again and I didn't pressure him to. After about an hour, I settled Violet back on his lap and this time when the child spoke to him, he engaged with her with questions about her doll, like what her name was and if she had any others.

Unlike my earlier visits, since no sneaking around was required, I was able to visit Gio during the day. There was no rush to return to the house, so once I had Gio back in his bed, I said, "I'm going to run down to the cafeteria to get Violet a snack. Do you mind watching her for a minute?"

I was holding Violet in my arms and while it would have been easy enough to take her with me, I had an ulterior motive. I didn't really give Gio a chance to say no, instead I just plopped Violet down on his lap and handed her the remote for the television. "Thanks so much," I said as I began to walk out of the room. "Can I bring you anything?" I asked, but I didn't actually give him time to answer that question either. I figured I'd make up for it by bringing in several things from the cafeteria.

Fifteen minutes and an armful of goodies later, I nearly dropped all my purchases when I returned to Gio's room and saw Violet curled up against Gio's chest. Not only was the child passed out, but so was Gio. His arms were wrapped protectively around the little girl.

I carefully put the snacks down and pulled out the phone Luca had insisted I carry around on me at all times. I snapped a picture of the pair and then went and sat down in the chair next to the bed. For the first time in a very long time, I felt at peace. Things had been busy at the house ever since Luca had taken me back there, so Luca and I hadn't really had a chance to talk, or to go on our first date. The delay had made me doubt the encounter he and I had had in the motel room, but I'd managed to quell the need to run. I was giving Luca the one thing he truly wanted from me... my trust.

He didn't know it, but I was also giving him something I hadn't been willing to give anyone a piece of ever.

My heart.

And if I were being honest, it was a lot more than just a piece. I was well on the way to handing him the entire thing, and that was truly terrifying.

I just hoped I wouldn't get it back in pieces.

CHAPTER TWENTY-TWO

LUCA

+4

"I say the salmon," I heard someone say from behind me. It was Con, of course. Even if I hadn't known his voice, only he would call a shirt salmon. My brother was extremely fashion forward. The bigger question was, why did I even own a salmon-colored shirt? I didn't really care either way because I couldn't take my eyes off the picture I was looking at.

"Jesus, Con, what did you do, go out and buy that for him today?" King asked.

"Why? Is it so hard to believe our brother might actually have a little bit of fashion sense?" Con asked.

"Yes," Vaughn and King responded at exactly the same time.

Vaughn added, "The closest thing to Luca owning a pink shirt is the single *blue* shirt he has. Which, by the way, is the one he should wear tonight. That way Remy can see that Luca knows how to change it up."

I had no doubt my brothers were trying to provoke me into participating in the ridiculous conversation, but I just wanted to focus on the picture of my son.

My son.

Remy had shown me the picture on his phone when he'd gotten

home about an hour earlier, and then he'd sent it to me so I'd have a copy for myself. He'd seemed extremely positive about the visit he'd had with Gio today and while I hadn't asked for specifics, seeing my son with his arms wrapped protectively around Violet as the pair slept gave me hope like I hadn't known in a really long time.

"You think Remy sent him a dick pic or something?" Con asked.

That got my attention. "Hey," I snapped. "That's my guy you're talking about—" I began to say as I looked over my shoulder. All three of my brothers were staring at me with grins on their faces. I silently cursed myself for taking the bait.

"Well, *your guy* is going to end up waiting for you downstairs if you don't get a move on," Con said.

He was holding the pink shirt up along with what I assumed was supposed to be a matching tie.

"The blue one," I said, more to watch his expression fall than anything else.

Which it did.

"I give up, you guys are beyond help." Con tossed the shirt on the bed. "Show us what you've been staring at for the past twenty minutes."

I handed the phone over to my brothers and then began to change into the blue shirt. My thoughts drifted to my upcoming date with Remy. As excited as I was, I was strangely nervous too. I'd never been particularly good at charming people unless it was in a boardroom. If I wanted something, I pretty much took it.

"Oh wow," Vaughn said as he, King, and Con huddled in close so they could look at the screen.

"Is Gio actually talking?" Con asked in surprise.

The question, while innocent, brought about a mix of feelings. I was beyond happy that my son had seemingly come out of his shell a little bit with Remy. But it was bittersweet because I hadn't been able to see my son at all since the day I'd visited the hospital shortly after he'd woken up. I still went to the hospital every day to talk to his doctor and get updates, but Dr. Taylor didn't think it was a good idea for me to try to talk to Gio again. At that point, only Remy seemed to be making any kind of headway with my angry son. Based on the picture he'd taken that afternoon, he'd made a lot of progress.

I felt a hand on my shoulder as I was in the process of buttoning up my shirt. Vaughn was at my side, his expression one of understanding. "He'll get there, little brother. You're going to get him back."

I nodded because my throat felt thick with emotion. I was so glad to have my brothers back with me, though Lex's absence was noticeable. For once, King and Con weren't at each other's throats about Lex and whatever was keeping him away from us, so I figured that meant they'd had a chance to talk about it when they'd gone to pick up Marilyn on the day Remy had taken off.

My thoughts shifted to Remy as I continued to get dressed and my brothers talked amongst themselves. Although Remy had been back home for the past few days, there'd still been a level of awkwardness between us. I'd tried many times to draw him into conversation about unimportant things, but he'd seemed nervous in my presence and all we ever really talked about was Gio and Violet. Not to mention with the presence of my brothers and Marilyn, it meant that we were rarely alone. I was hoping our date would change all that.

As I slid my jacket on and checked my tie, my brothers gave me all sorts of what they probably considered useful advice, ranging from just being myself to remembering to open the door for Remy to whether or not I should order for him and on and on and on. I tuned most of it out because besides Con, none of my brothers were particularly good at romance. Vaughn had only had eyes for Aleks the past couple of years and I doubted King stopped working long enough to meet anyone. And if he did, it wasn't likely that he was in search of a relationship that would last more than the time it would take him to get off. The man wasn't exactly a people person. While Con did better in the romance department, he wasn't an expert at the long-term stuff either.

And that was what I wanted with Remy, the long-term stuff. It was a surprising revelation, but I wasn't going to try to write it off as anything other than what it was. I didn't understand what fate had had in mind when she'd decided that the young boy I'd left behind would become the man I couldn't be without, but I'd accepted it. Remy was mine. Now I just needed to show him that I was his. We needed to be more than just two people with an ugly past. I was also on a mission to change the way Remy saw himself. The idea that he thought I couldn't have feelings for him because of his past made me crazy. It was so easy for me to see how strong and kind and amazing he was, but me just saying so wouldn't be enough. I'd have to show him, and I'd start with this date.

I went to my brothers and grabbed my phone. All three asked similar versions of, "Will you send the picture to me?"

I quickly created the text and sent the picture so I wouldn't forget and found myself smiling when all three of my brothers snatched their phones out of their pockets so they could continue to look at the picture. While Vaughn and Con hadn't seen Gio in person, King had. It hadn't surprised me that, like Remy, he'd been going at night to visit Gio. But unlike Remy, I doubted that King spoke to my son. If anything, my son probably hadn't even been aware he was there because King was going so late in the evening.

King was the least patient of all of us when it came to fixing things. Like me, I knew it frustrated him that he couldn't just fix all this for me or for Gio. As with the rest of us, he'd suffered with the knowledge of how long it had taken to find my son. He'd driven his team ruthlessly to search for Gio at the same time that he'd had his men getting so many other kids out of that same world. He'd saved countless children, but I had no doubt that he saw it as a personal failure that he hadn't been able to find my son.

"We won't wait up," Con called, even as he continued to look at the picture on his phone. I flipped all of my brothers the bird, but doubted they'd even noticed. I was hopeful that they were, in fact, preoccupied because I really wanted them to miss me grabbing the little bouquet of flowers off my nightstand as I left the room. Remy was on the same floor as me, just a few doors down. But when I got to his room, it was empty. I couldn't help but feel a little nervous that he'd taken off again, but the sight of several sets of shirts and pants strewn across his bed gave me hope.

I hurried downstairs and went straight to Violet's room. Sure enough, I heard his voice, or rather, Scooby's voice, as I got closer. I entered the room quietly so I could watch him interact with Violet. While I understood that he wasn't ready to be a father, I knew that one day he would be. He was a natural at it. His giving nature and soft heart practically demanded it.

Remy and Violet were sitting in the big armchair by the window. Violet was freshly bathed and in her pajamas. She was sitting on Remy's lap, her head against his chest, as he told her a Scooby-Scrappy story. I could see that she was practically out cold. Remy's eyes lifted to meet mine, but he didn't miss a beat with his story or his impersonation of Scooby. My heart practically stopped in my chest when he smiled at me. It was the first time in a very long time, maybe ever, that I'd seen him looking so content. He was wearing a button-up shirt and a pair of khakis and his hair was curling just a bit at the ends where it was still damp.

I leaned against the doorjamb as I waited for him to finish. When he did, he leaned forward and gave Violet a little kiss on her forehead. I could have let him pick her up and put her to bed himself, but something had me moving forward to do it myself. I cuddled the little girl against my chest and when Remy stood, he was practically pressed against us. The scene was so domestic that it left me aching. I still had a hold of the flowers, so I handed them to him so I wouldn't damage them when I put Violet in her crib. Remy's eyes lit up at the sight of the flowers. I saw him sneaking a sniff as I carried Violet to her crib and settled her into it. The little girl didn't wake. I covered her with a small blanket and then Remy was at my side.

Yeah, this would definitely be us someday if I had my way. The only difference would be that Gio would also be there, saying good night to his little sister or brother.

Remy and I watched Violet for a moment, then I took his hand and led him from the room.

"Thank you," Remy said softly as he held up the flowers. I knew first-date protocol should have had me saying "you're welcome" or something a little more benign, but I couldn't stop myself from just leaning down and covering his mouth with mine. Remy automatically opened for me and let out a little whimper, but I managed to keep the kiss short.

We were still holding hands so when the kiss ended, Remy, looking a little dazed, was the one to lead me. I followed him to the kitchen where Marilyn and Aleks were sitting at the kitchen island having what I assumed was coffee or tea.

"She's asleep," Remy said.

"Oh good," Marilyn said, and then she was rising and hurrying to Remy. "My, you look handsome," the older woman declared as she admired him and then reached out to pat his cheek. While Marilyn was an extremely demonstrative and affectionate woman, I loved how she saved just a little bit more for Remy. I wondered if she somehow sensed that he'd gone for so long without any kind of maternal affection. Remy had seemed hesitant at first to accept the attention, but every day that went by, he basked in it more and more. Even now, his cheeks colored as Marilyn continued to gush over him.

"I had help with my outfit," Remy said as he shyly looked at me, then motioned to Aleks who was watching us with undisguised glee.

"I didn't," I said at the same time that my brothers walked into the room. Con grumbled something about salmon being all the rage right now, but I ignored him and asked Remy, "Are you ready to go?"

More color tinged his cheeks and if we'd been alone, I would've played around with how red I could get them.

Remy nodded and let me take his hand again so I could lead him from the room. There were lots of well wishes and comments telling us to have fun, but at that point I only had eyes for Remy. His hand was damp in mine, so I knew he was nervous. I was too, for that matter.

"I made reservations for us at this place by the water. They supposedly have the best oysters around. Is that okay?" I asked.

Remy nodded quickly. I had a feeling that no matter what I asked him, he'd agree.

While I'd become comfortable enough to reduce the amount of bodyguards keeping watch over us, Terrence and Stan continued to act as my primary security detail. I wasn't sure if Ronan was having any of his men shadowing us anymore, but even if they were, I certainly wouldn't have an issue with it. My only hope was that whenever Remy and I weren't together, every single person was focused on Remy. I remembered what Ronan had told me about all the men and women who kept an eye on his family. He'd said they did it because his family was their family. I'd scoffed at that notion just a few weeks ago, but admittedly, I was envious of that fact now. I liked the idea of Remy being surrounded by people who had a much greater reason than money to protect him from any danger.

Since it was just me and Remy and the two bodyguards, I'd arranged for a car that would allow me to put up a partition between ourselves and Stan and Terrence. I hadn't wanted Remy to feel like this was just any other day. This date was about him and me spending time together, getting to know each other, away from prying eyes and ears.

Once we were in the car, I told Terrence where we were going and then put the partition up. Remy shifted nervously in his seat.

"You look beautiful, Remy," I said. I risked taking his hand and holding it in mine between us on the seat.

"You too… handsome, I mean. Or beautiful. Both, I guess… I mean both, for sure. Not I guess. I mean I don't need to guess that you look good because you do. You look good. Really good."

I smiled as his cheeks went from pink to bright red. He seemed startled by his own inability to get his thoughts out. He shut his eyes and groaned. "Oh God, this is going to be so bad," he said. But then he laughed, and I knew right then that it would be anything but.

I pulled his hand up to my mouth and kissed his knuckles. "It's going to be perfect," I said. Despite the awkwardness of it all, it still felt like the easiest thing in the world just to be with him.

We found ourselves talking about the help we had getting ready for our evening, and Remy couldn't stop laughing when I mentioned the pink shirt. By the time we reached the restaurant, Remy had made me promise that I would model the shirt for him someday.

The restaurant was everything I'd expected it to be. Classy, intimate, and very expensive. We were shown to a quiet table in the corner of the restaurant but as soon as we sat down, I knew it wasn't going to work. Remy had gone from relaxed and chatty in the car to full-on terrified. He looked at all the silverware on each side of the plate in front of him and then began frantically searching the room. I realized he was trying to watch some of the other patrons to figure out which silverware to use.

I tried to draw him into conversation in the hopes that he would relax, but as soon as the waitress came and began talking about the different specials and which wine was recommended to go with them, I knew I'd fucked up. I asked the waitress to give us a moment, then looked at Remy who was now focused on the multiple glasses that made up the place setting.

"Baby, talk to me," I said as I reached for his hand. The one that couldn't stop touching all the silverware.

He looked up at me as if finally remembering my presence. Instead of taking my hand, he tucked both of his in his lap and shook his head. "I'm so sorry, Luca. I didn't mean to embarrass you."

The table we were at was one with a circular bench around it to give it more of an intimate feel. I shifted so I was sitting next to Remy, our bodies touching. I didn't care who was watching as I tipped his face up so he was forced to look at me. "You could never embarrass me, sweetheart."

I dropped a soft kiss to his mouth. He kissed me back, but there was no denying the nerves that continued to plague him. I felt like a fool for not considering that he might not want to go to such a fancy place. I was so used to impressing people with my money that I'd just naturally drifted to selecting a restaurant that was a reflection of that.

"How about we get out of here?" I asked as I sought out Remy's hand beneath the table.

"Oh no, Luca no, please, I can do better. I really want to have this date with you."

I squeezed his hand and said, "Remy, you couldn't get rid of me right now if you tried. We are most definitely having this date." I dropped my mouth so only he could hear me. "Truth?" I asked softly and then I let my lips skim the shell of his ear.

He sucked in a breath and nodded.

I toyed with his fingers as I whispered, "The second I saw you holding that little girl and talking all Scooby to her, it became the best date in the history of the world."

I sensed Remy relax slightly next to me and I instantly wanted to kill every single person who'd ever made him feel like he wasn't good enough for a place like this or someone like me.

"What do you say we get out of here? There's a fish and chips place down the street that Vaughn swears by," I said.

Another nod. I climbed out of the booth and eased Remy up behind me. I left enough cash on the table to cover the bill as if we'd actually eaten there and then led Remy to the door. Once outside, I put my arm around his shoulders, but I didn't fully relax until several moments later when he leaned against me and put his arm around my waist.

I let out a huge sigh of relief that he had to have felt.

It had been a near miss, but we were anything but down for the count.

"Epic first date, take two," I said softly and was rewarded with the best response I could've hoped for.

Remy's laughter.

♀4

"**S**o basically, you buy and sell companies, right?" I asked.

"Yep, that's it," Luca said with a grin. I knew that was far from "it" considering all the detail he'd gone into in the past few minutes as he'd explained what he did for a living, but admittedly, I'd had trouble understanding the complexities of it all, not to mention I'd found myself focused more on Luca's mouth than the words coming out of it. It had been like that most of the night as we'd talked—the part about me noticing different things about his body.

Like the way he talked with his hands and the way his forehead creased just a little bit when he was thinking about something. But up until that moment, I'd been able to listen to his words as well as admire his physique. And while the subject of his business had been hard to follow, I *had* been able to keep up with our earlier conversations, even as my body had insisted on noticing all the little gestures and movements he made as he spoke.

Admittedly, the change in the location of our date had made it possible for me to actually participate in it. I hadn't even considered the prospect of not being able to adapt to the fancy restaurant we'd first gone to. Yes, I'd been nervous, but I'd also been excited and very ready to get to know Luca in a different way. But as soon as I'd spied all that silverware and all the fancily dressed people, I'd known I was out of my league. And I'd been terrified of embarrassing Luca in any kind of way. It had also been a brutal reminder that he and I lived in very different worlds and while he could easily adjust to mine, there was no way I could learn to live in his. Even if I wore the right clothes and somehow managed to say some of the right things, I'd still always feel like a fraud. I'd expected Luca to take me home after he'd realized how badly I was freaking out. So his suggestion that we go to a different place to eat had been both a surprise and relief.

The little seafood place we'd ended up at had still been fancier than any restaurant I'd ever eaten at, but it had a more relaxed atmosphere and I'd actually recognized most of the food items on the menu. I hadn't known what to expect in terms of how a date between two men worked when they were among so many straight couples, but from the moment we'd sat down, Luca hadn't hesitated to hold my hand or speak to me in a way that made it clear to everyone around us that we were together.

Luca had spent the first few minutes telling me about his brothers and their complete and utter uselessness when it'd come to helping him get ready for our date. When he'd admitted to how nervous he was, it was like this calm had settled over me and all the things that were different about us had slipped away. From the outside, Luca was gorgeous, strong, and confident. But to know that he was plagued with some of the same insecurities I had reminded me that we weren't as different on the inside.

Much of our dinner conversation had revolved around little things like what kinds of movies we liked and what our favorite foods were. We talked about Violet and Gio too, but they hadn't dominated our conversation.

"What about you? What do you want to be when you grow up?" Luca asked with a smile.

I supposed it should have been an easy-to-answer question, but not for me. I didn't want to bring the conversation down, so I merely shrugged and said, "Not sure yet."

Truth was, I *was* sure about my career in that I didn't really have one... My goal in life at that point was to just find a new job and figure out how to move forward after I said my goodbyes first to Violet, then Gio, and ultimately, Luca. As much as I would've liked to believe that this was the beginning of something with him, I couldn't trick my brain into accepting it. Luca had an entire life on the East Coast, and those things that made us different weren't things we could just overcome. He was still the wealthy, successful businessman and I was the former junkie whore just trying to get through one day at a time.

"I got a call from Ronan this morning. Dom Barretti wants to talk to you about returning to your job," Luca said.

I looked at him in surprise. "What?" It was the last thing I expected to hear, especially considering how I'd left Barretti Security Group so abruptly. Not to mention the fact that Dom himself, the head of the company along with his brother, had no reason to be reaching out to someone who was so much lower than him on the corporate ladder. Hell, I probably wasn't even on the actual ladder.

"He's pretty adamant about coming to see you," Luca added.

"I guess Dom just feels guilty because—" I began, but Luca cut me off.

"I spoke to Dom this afternoon. The man cares about you. Guilt has nothing to do with it. He threatened to rip off a certain part of my anatomy that I happen to be quite fond of if I hurt you in any kind of way."

Luca said the words so casually that I almost couldn't process the meaning. When I let them sink in, I couldn't help but laugh. And then my stomach dropped out as I realized he was being serious.

"He really said that?" The idea that someone like Dom would be protective of me even though he didn't know me that well was both scary and overwhelming. Probably because the idea of someone else in my corner just seemed too good to be true. Ronan had told me that I was part of his family, but I hadn't really believed it.

Because who would let someone like me be a part of their family?

"He did," Luca said. "Between him and Ronan, I'm starting to fear for my health." Luca winked at me so I knew he wasn't being serious about that part, but I still couldn't help the rush of joy that went through me. Not the part where the other two men were threatening him with bodily harm, of course.

"So?" Luca asked after a moment.

My mind was still toying with the idea that maybe I had more friends than I'd realized, so it took me a moment to say, "I'll call him tomorrow. Ronan too."

Luca took a bite of the dessert we'd decided to share. He suddenly looked peeved and I wondered what I'd done wrong.

"Do you think I shouldn't call them?" I asked.

"You should definitely call Dom. But maybe just send Ronan a text."

The comment was so odd that I didn't understand it at first. But the more Luca stabbed at the dessert, the more an idea took hold.

Surely he couldn't be jealous of Ronan?

No, the thought was just ridiculous.

"You think Ronan wants to hear from me?" I asked.

Luca grunted in response and I felt something inside of me light up.

"Maybe I should go see him—" I began to say, but Luca started shaking his head long before I even finished the thought.

"A text is fine," was all he said, dropping his fork to the plate so that it clattered noisily.

He was definitely jealous.

In that moment, I lost the last few pieces of my heart I'd been trying to hold back from him. The idea that Luca would think that a) I'd choose Ronan over him and b) that Ronan even had eyes for anyone but his husband was ludicrous, but it meant Luca was doing exactly what I'd been doing all night.

Doubting himself.

Doubting us.

"I think I'll just text him," I murmured as I reached out my finger to swipe some of the chocolate from the dessert. Luca's eyes caught on my finger and I felt my body grow tight as he hungrily watched me lick the chocolate off. I hadn't meant the move to be seductive, but now more than anything, I wanted to grab the chocolate and my date and get the hell out of that restaurant. The thought that I might be ready for something more physical with Luca was daunting, but I also wanted to know if I could have that kind of relationship with him.

I'd always just assumed that if I decided to give myself to Luca, it would be to satisfy his needs and it would be something I would just have to get through. But nothing about how he'd touched me in the past was living up to that expectation. I was most definitely physically attracted to him and I'd already reached the conclusion that I was well beyond emotionally invested in whatever it was that we had between us. The question was, would I be able to go through with it if and when the time came?

"So do you think you want to go back to working for Dom?" Luca asked. His voice sounded strained and he was focused on my mouth. Clearly, I wasn't the only one affected by the rush of desire.

I pulled in a breath in the hopes of calming my raging body, especially my cock, which had gone from interested to yes-please-and-thank-you in a matter of seconds. "It's a good job," I said. "There's a lot of room for growth. The benefits are great and I like the people I work with."

Luca nodded in agreement, so it was a surprise when he said, "What is it that you really want to do?"

"I don't know," I admitted. "I guess I never really had time to think about things long term, you know?"

"Have you ever thought about doing something with your voice?"

"What do you mean?" I asked.

"You told me that you really enjoyed that movie set that your grandmother took you on when you were little. With the way you can copy a voice and do all those different accents that I've heard you do around Violet, maybe you could do something in the entertainment industry. Acting or something. If you don't want to be in front of the camera, you could always do something like voiceover work or maybe something behind the scenes, like production."

His remark left me speechless, not only because of his compliments, but because it wasn't something I'd ever even considered before. I'd always enjoyed doing the voices and I'd been curious about how things like television shows and movies were made, but never in a million years had I thought I could have a career in something like that.

"No, I couldn't," I said, but when I tried to find a reason why, there weren't any. I'd said the same thing when Ronan's guy had told me he'd found me a job working in an office. I'd never believed I could do something like that either, yet I had.

I looked at Luca, who was smiling. It was like he knew he didn't need to say anything because I was having the argument in my head.

He reached for his fork and took another bite of the dessert. "Just something to think about," he murmured knowingly. The bastard knew he'd planted a seed that I'd unlikely be able to get rid of now. Just to get even, I grabbed my own fork and took a bite of the dessert, though I put on quite the show while I was doing it. By the time the treat was gone between us, my insides were so hot and there was so much pressure in my groin that I actually had trouble sitting still. Luca's hungry eyes never left mine as he called for the check.

The few minutes it took for the waitress to bring the bill seemed like pure and absolute torture. While I understood the logistics of what was happening to my body, it was still a foreign experience. I remembered Luca's comments about how he'd been a horny seventeen-year-old, and I realized that was probably the only way to classify what I was feeling.

I'm horny.

I actually laughed out loud when I said the word in my head.

"What?" Luca asked. He was signing the credit card receipt for the meal.

"Nothing," I quickly responded. There was no way I was going to tell him what my dilemma was.

Of course, the man only took that as a challenge of sorts. When we got up, he took my hand to help me stand. I expected him to lead me forward, but instead, he stepped into my body and his hand slipped to the curve of my waist. His long fingers teasingly caressed the top of my ass as he moved his hand to my back. I forgot all about the fact that we were in a public place and tried to rub my groin against his in the hopes that it would offer some kind of relief.

"What?" Luca repeated, his voice all growly and sexy. He might as well have had his finger on a little button that controlled the ability to mute myself.

"I was just thinking that I could really use some Harry Potter porn-fic right now," I breathed. I didn't even recognize my own voice as I spoke.

"It was *fan*-fic," Luca reminded me right before his hand slipped briefly over my ass and gripped it. "And if you ask me nicely, maybe I'll read you something someday."

With that, he took my hand in his and led me from the restaurant. I expected him to take me back to the car, but instead he led me down to the waterfront. It was a weeknight, so the streets weren't overly busy. We ended up on a beach that had only a few couples here and there taking advantage of the cool, dry night.

Luca and I didn't really talk as we walked, and that was fine with me because there was something incredibly peaceful about just holding his hand and listening to the sounds of the waves gently breaking on the shore.

Several minutes passed before I realized that Luca kept reaching up for his shirt pocket. It took me a moment to realize what he was looking for. "If you want one, it's okay with me," I said. I'd smoked cigarettes myself a few years earlier, so I knew what the urge was like, especially after eating.

"I quit," Luca responded. "Force of habit," he said as he pointed to his shirt pocket where he'd always kept his cigarettes.

"You did?" I asked in surprise. "Just like that?"

"Just like that." Luca came to a stop and turned so he was facing me. He pulled me forward and reached up to run his fingers through my hair. "I've got a pretty good incentive to keep me from lighting one of those nasty little sticks up ever again," he added and then his mouth was on mine. Unlike the relatively tame kiss he'd given me in the first restaurant, this one was all in. I moaned as he took control of my mouth. Despite the fact that we were on a public beach, his hands roamed down to my ass and stayed there as he began grinding his lower body against mine. I cried out into his mouth as our dicks came into contact with one another through our clothes. Just like that, I lost all control of myself and I practically climbed up his body as I kissed him back. I was panting by the time Luca forced some space between us.

"Not here," he growled, though I knew he wasn't angry. He gripped my hand hard and we pretty much ran back to the car. Terrance and Stan were waiting outside the vehicle, but Luca barely paid them any mind other than to snap, "Take the long way home" and then he was helping me into the privacy of the car.

I had no clue how long the long way home would take, but I didn't care. I didn't care about anything but getting Luca's mouth back on mine where it belonged.

CHAPTER TWENTY-FOUR

LUCA

24

Not in the car.

Not in the car.

Those were the words I kept saying to myself as Remy and I fought for control of the kiss. I had him pressed back against the seat with one hand planted on the back of his thigh and the other tangled in his hair, but somehow it was his mouth that was driving our encounter. The second I'd slid into the back seat of the car, he'd been all over me. Not that I was complaining, of course. But with his fingers tearing at my tie and mine itching to feel his skin, the sweet little make-out session I'd planned was turning into something much, much more.

"Remy—" I tried to say, but his mouth stole over mine again.

I shifted my body off of his so I could at least get some much-needed oxygen to my head in the hopes that I could get control of my other head, but as soon as I leaned back against the seat, Remy followed, and I let out a loud moan when he climbed onto my lap. I could hear music playing somewhere, and I had to assume that my bodyguards were trying to give me and Remy a little bit of privacy by turning up the music in the front of the car.

The fact that we were just getting started and were already losing ourselves so completely in one another was both amazing and a bad sign. There was no way we could continue like this in the car with two of my men sitting just half a dozen feet away.

I tangled my fingers in Remy's hair and gently eased his head back so he was eventually forced to release my mouth. Despite my good intentions, I found myself still peppering his mouth with sensual kisses as I tried to bring us both down. Remy's pupils were blown and he was breathing erratically. His hands were on my neck and shoulders, unable to stay still. He'd somehow managed to get my shirt halfway unbuttoned, so when his fingers ran over my upper chest, my cock responded in an almost violent manner.

"We can't do this here," I was able to get out. I felt almost lightheaded from the need that was swimming throughout my entire body.

Remy's gorgeous eyes flooded with confusion, then despair. He began grinding his cock against my abdomen. My own dick seemed to have a mind of its own as it tried to bust out of my pants to get to the gorgeous man on my lap.

"Luca?" Remy practically cried. I realized then that he was too far gone already. The idea that I'd taken him to that level of need with just a handful of kisses and caresses only ratcheted up my own desire.

We hung there, me in fascination and him in desperation. When he whispered my name once again, I pulled his head down to mine and kissed him softly. "I've got you, sweetheart," I whispered. I couldn't help but wonder if this was another first for him. Not the making-out-in-the-car part, but just being with another guy and having it be about him. He obviously wasn't a virgin, but somewhere in the recesses of my mind, I did consider him that. I wanted—no, *needed*—to give him this moment where it was only about him.

Car and bodyguards be damned.

I kissed Remy and let my hands slide all over his body, but when he tried to touch me, I took his hands and moved them down to the zipper of his pants instead. "Take yourself out for me," I commanded softly as I dotted his mouth with soft kisses. His breathing was still uneven, but he seemed to be in a better state of mind to process my request.

I loved that he didn't hesitate to flip the button and pull down the zipper. Remy's fingers were trembling when he reached into his pants and carefully pulled out his very hard, very wet dick. My mouth watered at the sight of the pre-cum that was leaking out of his tip. If the car had been bigger, I definitely would've had him rising up on his knees so I could taste him. But I doubted Remy was in any position to even hold out that long. His body had started to shake violently and he was once again rocking his hips back and forth. The skin of his cock looked angry and he actually seemed on the verge of tears when he began to stroke himself. One of his hands came up to rest on my shoulder as he tipped his head back.

"Luca," he breathed desperately.

I lowered my hand and carefully pushed his away from his own flesh. He was hot and hard. He cried out my name the second my fingers closed around his shaft. He wasn't particularly thick, but his dick was long and the skin was soft. I tested his sensitivity level with a few strokes so I would know what was enough and what was too much. The sounds Remy made as I pleasured him made my own cock swell in my pants. But I didn't dare take myself out because I wanted this to be about Remy.

Only Remy.

I reached my free hand up and wrapped it around the back of Remy's neck. I drew his head down so our faces were aligned and then I began stroking him a little harder. Remy gasped and then began pumping his dick into my hand.

"That's it, baby," I said. "Fuck me with this gorgeous cock."

Remy's eyes were luminous when they opened and he stared at me. I knew in that moment exactly what he was thinking. He was wondering what it would feel like to push himself deep inside me. I was wondering about it too. It wasn't something I'd ever done with another man, but the idea of Remy and I joined together like that sounded like heaven personified.

I let Remy fuck my hand a few times and then I took over. I changed up the way I gripped him and used my thumb to toy with the sensitive areas on his shaft and crown. His pre-cum became a natural lubricant and within minutes, my fist was easily sliding up and down his length. Remy began to whimper as he tried to pump into my hand. He pressed his forehead against mine and whispered my name over and over. I knew that meant his orgasm wasn't far off. I pulled his mouth down to mine and kissed him as I increased the pressure. His hands were on my shoulders, then my neck. He kissed me back and pressed his entire body against mine so my hand was trapped between us. His thigh rode the length of my own cock and I felt the telltale signs of pleasure skating up my spine.

I lost the ability to speak after that. I doubted Remy even realized it, but he was pleasuring me in so many ways besides the obvious one of giving my dick the friction it needed. I'd never had a lover as responsive as him, as open. As Remy became more and more desperate to find his release, I increased the pace and the pressure. His fingers bit into the skin of my shoulders. I was excited at the prospect that I might have bruises there in the morning. Remy began to cry out desperately, signaling how close he was. I pulled his mouth down to mine and kissed him deeply. He kissed me back for as long as he could, but when the orgasm claimed him, he cried out into my mouth. I drank down the sounds of his pleasure as his release shot from his dick and hit my abdomen. The sticky, hot fluid seeped through my dress shirt and dampened my skin, then slid down my hand as I continued to stroke Remy.

His body jerked and thrashed against mine and his cries of relief spilled down my throat, triggering my own orgasm. I clamped my arm around his body and held him against me as my confined dick gave up the fight. I ripped my mouth from Remy's and buried it against his shoulder as the brutal climax washed over me in violent waves of sensation. I had enough sense to loosen my hold on Remy's cock, but I could still feel the heat of his flesh as more of his semen slipped over my fingers.

I had no clue how long we hung there for as we each rode out the pleasure, but when Remy slumped against me and whispered my name, I became aware enough to release my hold on his cock so I could put my other arm around him.

I wiped my wet hand on the inside of my jacket before reaching for the button that would allow me to communicate with the driver. "Take us home," was all I said before I cut the sound again. I wished I had a blanket to put over Remy, but the best I could do was turn up the heat in the back of the car. He hadn't said anything in a while, but with the way he was sprawled out against me, I was okay with that. Yeah, he was probably going to start thinking about what we'd done, but at least he had these moments of perfect contentment.

It was probably about five minutes later when Remy started to come back to me from the little daze he'd slipped into. I braced myself for him to freak out, but he surprised me when the fingers of one hand stroked my cheek and he pressed a kiss to my other cheek. "Thank you," was all he said, and then his arms went around my neck and he just held me like that.

Once we reached the house, I heard the driver and passenger doors open and close, but I was glad my men were smart enough not to disturb me and Remy. Remy had actually drifted off, so I had to give him a little bit of a shake to wake him up. He grinned like a Cheshire cat and stretched against me. Then his hand went to cover his eyes. The smile was still there though. "Oh my God, I'm never going to be able to look Stan or Terrence in the eyes again."

"Me neither," I admitted. "I sense a raise in their very near future."

"Haven't you ever..." Remy began and then snapped his mouth shut. The blush on his cheeks was adorable. He looked so happy and sated that I couldn't help but lean in and kiss him gently.

"Haven't I ever what? Had myself a little fun in the back seat?" I asked.

He nodded. I loved how shy he'd become, considering it hadn't been more than fifteen minutes since he'd been riding me like I was his favorite mount.

"I never mixed business with pleasure. And even if I had, I haven't..." I caught myself as I realized what I was about to admit to. "I haven't been with anyone since I lost my son," I said quietly.

Remy's eyes held mine as he stroked my face. "I've never... you know," he said as he looked down between us. His flaccid cock was

236

resting between us and was still covered with his juices. Whereas he'd been pink in the cheeks before, he was full-on flaming red now. "I mean, I did sometimes when I used my own hand," he began to say, then he covered his eyes with his hand and said, "Oh God, kill me now." The fact that we were talking, joking even, about me being the first guy who'd ever made him come was surreal.

I laughed at his embarrassment and then pointed to myself and reminded him, "Harry Potter gay fanfic writer here."

We both started laughing and then Remy hugged me again. "*Porn fic*," he corrected.

"Hey. Some of those stories had a lot of substance to them," I insisted.

Remy chuckled and responded, "Either way, I think Harry Potter is going to end up being my new favorite character."

I sighed because I just couldn't believe any of this was happening. He really was here in my arms and he was… happy. *I* was happy.

I eased him off my body because there was no way of getting around the fact that we were still sitting in a car with quickly cooling cum covering parts of our bodies. I climbed out of the car first and then took my jacket off. I helped Remy out, then draped my jacket over his shoulders. I hoped like hell my brothers hadn't decided to wait up so they could rip on us about our date. Despite their ages, they were still my brothers. I wouldn't have put it past them to be sitting around watching for me and my date to return home. They put teenage girls to shame.

I took Remy's hand in mine and led him to the house, which was mostly dark.

As we entered the dimly lit foyer, I realized our date was almost over and I had no idea what to do next. The very last thing I wanted to do was leave him, but I didn't know where things were at. I wanted to take things slow with Remy so I wouldn't risk scaring him off, but I hadn't anticipated that it would be this difficult to be away from him, even just for the night. And what if he had regrets after I left him and he ran again? The thought of losing him made my skin feel cold and my insides hollow. All the pleasure I'd just felt evaporated.

When had I gotten in this deep with him? We were supposed to be taking things slow and seeing what it would be like to do just the normal dating stuff without all the drama from our pasts. While I wanted to shower Remy with all the things that came with dating, it made my heart physically hurt to have to say goodbye to him, even if it was just for a matter of hours.

I led Remy to his room. "I had a good time," I said.

Good time? I'd had a *fucking amazing* time. Why hadn't I told him that?

"Me too," Remy said awkwardly. "Thank you for dinner. And that walk was great."

I hated that it felt like we were suddenly strangers again. But I supposed that was how first dates worked.

I bent and gave him a quick kiss because I figured it was part of the protocol. "See you in the morning."

"Yeah, see you," Remy said. He opened his door and disappeared into his room. It felt like I was carrying a thousand pounds of dead-weight behind me as I made my way down the hall to my own room. I half expected to find my brothers sitting there waiting for me so they could ride me about what had happened, but fortunately, the room was empty.

Empty except for a short note sitting on my bed. I recognized Con's handwriting.

See you at breakfast. Enjoy your reprieve until then. –C

Busybodies.

Each and every one of them.

I smiled and put the note on my nightstand. I knew I needed to shower because I could smell Remy's cum all over me. Not to mention my own. But I was reluctant to wash his scent away.

I was in the process of taking my shirt off when there was a knock at my door.

"Are you fucking serious—" I began to say when I yanked the door open, fully expecting one or more of my brothers to be there. Remy's startled expression greeted me.

"Sorry, I just wanted to," he began as he held out my jacket. His face was red and he quickly turned on his heel. "Sorry."

I grabbed him before he could even make it five steps. "No way. I thought you were one of—" I started to say and then realized I didn't care. He was there.

He was there.

I captured his mouth with mine, swallowing the sound he made as I wrapped my arms around him. His arms went around my neck and when I lifted him a little, he actually slung his legs around my lower half as best he could. I pressed him back against the wall and kissed him deeply. By the time we both came up for air, we were panting.

"That was what I should've done a few minutes ago," I said.

"I didn't really come here to give you your jacket," Remy said. He brushed a kiss over my mouth. Whatever tension had been between us before seemed to have completely disappeared because he added, "Thank you for the perfect night, Luca."

"Stay with me tonight, Remy," was my response. "Just to sleep," I quickly added.

To my surprise, he didn't even hesitate to nod his head. I kissed him again and then awkwardly stumbled into my room with him still wrapped around me. I managed to shut the door without releasing him and then pressed him to it so I could make out with him a little more. As much as I wanted him, I knew he wasn't ready for more. And in a way, I wasn't either. The idea that I would be the first man Remy had ever been with that he *wanted* to be with was daunting. No, he wasn't a virgin, but he might as well have been. He'd only ever been exposed to the ugliness of sex. And I didn't want to just have sex with Remy... I wanted more, and that was part of the problem too.

"I was just going to shower," I said against his mouth. "Do you want to shower first? Or... we could conserve water and shower together," I offered with a grin.

Remy was clearly aroused again because he nodded quickly and said, "That. We should do our part to save the planet." Since his hands were all over me and he was trying to grind our groins together, I had a feeling the planet was the last thing on his mind.

And I was just fine with that.

239

CHAPTER TWENTY-FIVE

REMY

╪4

"Armani, Luca? Really?" I heard someone say as the door to Luca's room opened. I probably wouldn't have even heard the man's voice if I hadn't already been awake. I'd actually been awake for hours just reveling in the feeling of Luca's arms around me. Oh, yeah, and replaying every moment of the night before over and over in my head.

Some I couldn't believe I'd done. Like let Luca make me come in the car like that. Or how I'd gone to his room with the excuse of returning his jacket because I hadn't been ready to say good night to him yet.

Some, I couldn't believe *he'd* done. Like worshiping my body from the moment we'd stepped in the shower until the moment I'd fallen asleep in his arms. He'd touched every part of me, every scar, every track mark. He'd done it with his fingers as well as his mouth. With his words, he'd told me how beautiful everything about me was. It had been highly intimate, of course, but it hadn't led to sex. It had just been him exploring my body like I was some piece of treasured art.

I'd loved our first date, but the night spent in his bed would go down as the best night of my entire life.

Hands down.

And watching him sleep these past couple of hours would probably be the second-best experience of my life.

Because I'd gotten to see the real Luca, the one who didn't have to worry about always taking care of others or wondering if his child would ever come back to him or needing to behave like the cold, distant man he was expected to be. For those few hours, he'd been mine.

Only mine.

I'd gotten to explore him too, though he'd slept through all of it. I'd fully expected him to want to fuck me after we'd gotten out of the shower, and I'd been ready to let him, but like with everything else, the man was determined to keep surprising me. With every touch, every caress of his mouth, and every softly spoken word, I was falling harder and harder for him. There was no doubt in my mind that he had every piece of my heart now and that no matter what condition I got it back in, it would never be mine again. But I refused to dwell on any of the pain that I knew was undoubtedly coming my way. Last night had been about what my life with Luca could have looked like if it'd been possible for us to be together. I would use those hours to sustain me going forward. When the time came that I would be on my own again, I would remember those moments with him and somehow they'd still be there within me, fighting beside me, fighting *for* me.

"I know you're practically made of money, man, but leaving a jacket this beautiful on the floor?"

I recognized the voice. It was Luca's younger brother, Con. Luca began to stir next to me.

"And why the hell does it smell like—" Con began to say and then his voice dropped off. Luca and I were tucked beneath the covers, so I wasn't sure if Con had seen me yet. Luca sighed next to me and I saw that his eyes had opened. But when they landed on me, they softened and his gorgeous lips pulled into a small smile.

Morning, he mouthed silently and then he leaned in and kissed me gently. I forgot all about Con and just focused on Luca. But the moment didn't last because Luca pushed the covers off and sat up enough that he could eye his brother.

"MMA or not, Con, if you don't get the fuck out of this room, I'm going to kick your ass," Luca growled. I'd never actually seen Con in one of his professional fights, but my bet was on Luca.

I sat up as well and added, "I'll hold him down for you."

Con's eyes were wide as he stared at the both of us. But then he grinned and said, "My kind of first date."

Luca threw a pillow at him, which Con easily caught and threw back. He looked at me and said "Do you like grits, Remy? Because I can guarantee that my grits are better than Luca's."

I had no clue what the man was talking about, but Luca clearly did because he climbed out of the bed and started for his brother. Luca was completely naked, but he didn't seem to notice or care. I certainly had no problem with the show as Luca manhandled his brother and forced him out the door.

"Ask him what he likes on his grits!" Con called through the door.

"Me!" Luca yelled back. "He likes *me* on his grits!"

When he returned to the bed, I nearly swallowed my tongue at the sight of his erect dick.

"Meddling asshole," Luca growled as he snatched his jacket off the floor. When he looked up at me, he stilled. Probably because he was realizing that I was completely entranced at the sight of him. He made no move to cover himself up, thank God.

"Like something you see?" Luca asked, his voice deep and rumbly. He moved closer to my side of the bed.

I finally forced my eyes up and saw the mirth in his. It was yet another perfect moment. The idea of being able to wake up like this every morning with him, being able to joke with him, being able to touch him whenever and however I wanted…

I told myself that I was just setting myself up for heartbreak when I thought about things like that, so I focused on the moment.

"Actually, I was just wondering what grits are," I lied. I managed to keep a straight face as I kept my eyes on his.

"All you need to know about grits," Luca said as he tossed the jacket back on the floor, "Is that mine are the only ones you'll be having."

He didn't hesitate to climb on top of me and cover my mouth with his. The blanket was still between us, but I opened my legs as best I could so he could fit between them. I wrapped my arms around him as he kissed me deeply. I probably should've been worrying about things like morning breath, but it wasn't even a factor. By the time Luca pulled his mouth free of mine, I was ready to pull the covers from between us. I'd been so certain that I wasn't ready to have sex with the man, but every time he touched me, it was like I momentarily forgot who I was and what I'd been. I was a new Remy, a better one. But I wasn't foolish enough to think that my body wouldn't betray me when it came down to it. So far with everything we'd done, I'd still been in control, or at least there'd been the illusion of that. But when it came to the idea of Luca holding me down as he entered me or pushing me face-first against a wall—it was hard to find arousal in that. No, I didn't think Luca would hurt me, but I couldn't figure out how he would make the act feel good, either.

So yeah, sometimes it felt like I was ready, but deep down I knew I wasn't. I wondered if I ever would be. And if I wouldn't be, would I be able to let Luca have what he wanted and pretend it was as perfect as all the other moments with him?

"Tell me what you're thinking," Luca said.

It wasn't until he'd spoken that I realized he'd lifted part of his weight off me and was studying me.

"Nothing, I'm fine."

"Remy—" he began.

"I swear, Luca, I'm fine." It wasn't exactly a lie. I was okay at the moment; I was just overthinking things like I usually did. I was so used to having to fight things in my life that I had a habit of preparing for them—preparing for the worst.

Luca was resting his head on his hand. He used his other hand to push the hair off my temple. I definitely liked having longer hair, even if it was just so he'd have an excuse to play with it.

"Okay," he responded. "But I need you to understand something."

I opened my mouth to interrupt him again because I didn't want to ruin this moment with talk about how things would be my choice and all that, but he covered my mouth with two of his fingers.

"All this is new to me," he said. "I want things from you that I've never wanted from anyone else."

I couldn't help the nerves that built in my belly. I already knew he wanted to fuck me. But for some reason, I didn't want to hear him say it. I didn't know why.

"I just need to know that when we get to that point that we can talk about it first. I know some guys like to stick to certain roles, but I'm not one of them... not with you, anyway. So if and when we get to the point that you might be interested in fucking me, I just want to know that we can take things slow because I've never let a guy do that to me."

I shook my head in disbelief because I had to have heard him wrong.

"You want me to..." I began, then I sat up, jostling him a bit. My eyes shifted to his gorgeous shaft, but I was too preoccupied with what he'd said to admire it. "You want me to..."

Why in the hell could I not get the words out?

Oh right, because it was too unbelievable. He was actually saying *he* wanted *me* to fuck *him*. Me—skinny, scarred, weak Remy—making love to gorgeous, strong, experienced Luca.

"Oh God, I'm still asleep," I blurted. That was the only way to explain why I was sitting in bed with the most beautiful man in the world and we were talking about me putting my unimpressive dick into his mouthwatering body. "I'm dreaming about all of this. You letting me fuck you, grits—whatever the hell they are—and your strangely sweet but kind of pushy brother."

Luca sidled up next to me. He rested his back against the headboard and put his arm around my shoulders. "I absolutely want you to fuck me, the grits thing is an inside story that Vaughn and Aleks started, and saying Con has boundary issues is like saying the Queen

244

of England is a bit stiff." He kissed my cheek and said, "How about we go get some breakfast and eat it in here, in bed? We can hide away from my brothers for a bit longer."

Whether I was dreaming or not, the answer to *that* question was an easy one. Any question that involved me spending more time with this man required no thought whatsoever. But instead of using words to tell him I thought his plan was an excellent one, I used my mouth instead.

44

The dream world I'd convinced myself I was living in continued throughout the rest of the morning and well into the afternoon. Although breakfast was supposed to have been in the privacy of Luca's room, Con had used the mother of all weapons against me and Luca a mere fifteen minutes after he'd left the room.

Violet.

When there'd been a knock at the door (which had been fortunate because Luca and I had once again been in a heavy make-out session), Luca had pulled on a pair of sweatpants before answering it. While the knock had been heavy enough to prove it had been an adult, the only one standing in front of the door when he'd opened it had been Violet.

Since there'd been no way the child could have gotten upstairs by herself, let alone knocked, we'd figured she'd had help, and Luca had spied his brother dashing down the stairs just moments after Luca had picked the toddler up. It had been a strange thing to be sitting against the headboard of the bed, my lower half covered by the blanket, as Luca had carried Violet into the room and set her on my lap. He'd then gotten in bed next to me and we'd played with the little girl for several minutes until Marilyn had made an appearance.

It had been a stark reminder that Violet's future with us was winding down, but there'd been no denying how attached the little girl already was to Marilyn when the woman had plucked her from the bed. If Marilyn had been concerned about seeing us in bed together, she hadn't said anything or even looked at us strangely. She'd merely smiled and invited me and Luca to join the rest of the family for the big breakfast she and Con were making. Violet had clapped her little hands together and called both our names, and there'd been no mistaking the way she'd then said, "Breakfast."

Luca and I'd been had, but we hadn't cared.

Breakfast had been loud and chaotic and perfect. All of Luca's brothers had been there, minus Lex of course, and Aleks had been there too. He'd given me the sweetest of hugs and a look that had said he'd have his own share of questions for me later. Surprisingly, I was excited at the prospect of talking to Aleks about Luca and our date, minus the more intimate details. It was the strangest concept to me, to have a friend to talk to about the man I was seeing.

The voice that reminded me that I wasn't actually seeing Luca because all of this was a temporary thing wasn't as insistent as it usually was. I wasn't sure if that was because of me or Luca. The man had pretty much been at my side all morning, and now as we walked through the hospital hallways, he was once again holding my hand. Guys who were temporary didn't do that.

Right?

That was another one of those questions I'd have to ask Aleks. I nearly laughed because Aleks was so innocent and sweet, and yet he'd somehow become the more experienced of the two of us when it came to relationships.

As perfect as our morning had been, I couldn't help but notice that Luca lost some of his fire as we made our way deeper into the hospital. I couldn't really blame him, considering the fact that *I* was about to go into his son's room while *he* would have to continue to the waiting room alone. I wished there was something I could do to convince Gio to give Luca a chance, but I knew if I pushed the young man too hard, he'd break again. As it was, he and I had barely made any progress anyway. A few spoken words on his part at the last visit didn't count for much. Hopefully today, he would still be in a talkative mood, but I had no way of knowing.

As we got closer to Gio's room, Luca's grip on my hand tightened a little and then he dropped it. The plan was for him to veer off to the right where the waiting room was, but just before he did so, there was a loud crashing sound.

Coming from Gio's room.

CHAPTER TWENTY-SIX

LUCA

☩4

The scene before me was reminiscent of the first time I'd pushed Gio too far. Only this time the object of his fury wasn't just me.

The room was trashed when Remy and I rushed into it. Gio was in the far corner of the room on the floor, his overturned wheelchair next to him. I could see that he was holding what looked like a piece of broken glass. Blood trickled down his fingers. His other hand was fisted. He was surrounded by two orderlies and a frightened-looking nurse.

My heart fell at the sight and I immediately looked down at my son's wrists. Thankfully, there was no blood pouring from the veins and arteries there. I hadn't witnessed either of his suicide attempts, but I felt like I was on the verge now. I didn't recognize the young man in front of me as my child. His normally pale skin was flushed with color and sweat and there were drops of blood on his white shirt. His face was pulled into a mask of fury and he was waving the piece of glass in front of his body. I was so stunned by what I was witnessing that I didn't register the security guard who rushed past me. But when I saw him pull what I knew to be a Taser, I reacted on pure instinct.

I lunged at the man and slammed his body up against the wall.

"Stay away from my kid!" I snarled. I didn't care if I'd hurt the man or not, I was only interested in getting to my son. One of the orderlies tried to stop me, but one punch and he was down too. The other orderly backed off and the nurse scrambled to the far corner of the room, leaving me to face Gio's wrath.

"You did this!" he screamed at me.

I didn't know what he was talking about, of course, or what had set off this particular episode, but I had eyes only for the piece of glass in his hand. I had no clue where he'd gotten it from, nor did I care. One swipe across his wrists, or worse, his throat, and I'd lose him for good. In my gut, I knew this time he'd make sure he was successful in leaving me.

"Gio," I began, but knew my mistake the instant I said it.

"That's not my name! My name is Nick! Stop calling me that!"

"Nick," Remy called as he moved into the room. I could tell he was just as surprised as me at the turn of events.

"You did this," Gio snarled as he turned his upper body so he could face Remy. "You planned this with him! You pretended to be my friend so you could trick me! All of you are trying to trick me!"

From the way Gio was holding the glass, I could tell he was cutting his own hand because more and more blood dripped onto the floor. But he seemed not to even notice. As badly as I wanted to get that piece of glass out of his hand, I was terrified that if there was a struggle, he'd end up hurting himself even worse.

"Nick," Remy began. "I swear, I don't know what—"

"This!" my son screamed as he flung something at Remy. My keychain with the soccer ball bounced off Remy's chest and hit the floor at his feet. We both stared at it in silence for a moment. Remy looked horrified.

"Nick, I—" he started to say, but then Gio was yelling again.

"Shut up! I just want to leave here! You can't keep me here like this! You killed Kurt. You all killed Kurt!"

Remy carefully stooped down to pick up the keychain. I could see that he was tearing up.

"Nick—"

Gio cut Remy off again. "You left that here on purpose! You..."—
Gio looked at all of us in turn—"You all planned this! You did something to make me think I recognize that!"

"No," Remy called, his voice cracking. "It was an accident. I had this
clipped on to Violet's pants. It must've fallen off yesterday when we
were here. I wasn't trying to trick you, Gio... Nick. I swear, no one is
trying to trick you."

Seeing Remy so distraught was as equally devastating as watching
my son fall apart. It was one thing when my son hated only me and
blamed me for what he was going through, but to put that on Remy...

"Gio," I said, knowing the use of his real name would divert his
attention back to me, "Let's just talk. You and me. We can figure out
what to do next."

The move worked because Gio turned his attention back to me. He
looked like a broken doll as he dragged himself backward until his
back hit the wall behind him. The move scared the shit out of me
because it smacked of desperation, fear, and a level of rage that was so
all-consuming that he probably wasn't even aware of what he was
doing.

"I don't know you," Gio whispered, his voice now quiet and lost.
He cradled the piece of glass against his chest almost lovingly. The
jagged edge was just inches from his throat. I was so terrified that I
couldn't move or breathe.

"Luca," I heard Remy call. I couldn't take my eyes off my son. "Tell
me about when you got this keychain from your son." I hated how
Remy's voice wobbled. I had no doubt he was somehow blaming
himself for this moment, but there was nothing I could do to comfort
him.

I sensed movement behind us but ignored it.

"It was a few days after I took Gio to Central Park for his eighth
birthday. We'd spent the day playing soccer, just the two of us. We
used the ball my brothers and I had used when we were kids. I gave
the ball to Gio to keep and promised we'd play again at least once a
week going forward. He wanted King, Con, Lex, and Vaughn to join
us—so we could play teams. Me, him, and Lex against King, Con, and

Vaughn. The prize was going to be a trophy we called the Covello Cup but when it came time to find something to use as a trophy, we couldn't find anything. So we bought three keychains with these little soccer balls on it." I couldn't help but glance at the keychain in Remy's hand. I could feel the tears stinging the backs of my eyes. I risked looking at my son as I continued. He was staring at the floor, so I wasn't sure if he was even listening.

"We played the following weekend. It was an all-day tournament. Gio's mom was our referee." I let out a watery laugh as I added, "Vaughn, King, and Con weren't too happy about that." I paused as the memory of that day washed over me. It'd been the last time we'd all been together as a family.

"It was a perfect day," I murmured. "After we won, Gio wrote his name on his keychain. He... he gave it to me because he wanted to make sure I never forgot him or that day. I put my name on mine and gave it to him because I never wanted him to doubt how much I loved him and that he would always come first in my life, no matter what."

Through blurry eyes, I saw that Gio had wrapped his arms around his legs and started rocking back and forth and shaking his head. The glass was still in his hand, but I could only watch helplessly as blood dripped onto the floor.

I dared to take a step closer to him.

"It's not real, it's not real," I heard him whispering.

I kept my moves slow and exaggerated as I crouched down when I was just a couple of feet from him. My heart felt like it had been cleaved in two as I watched my son go through his private torment.

"I lost him two days later," I whispered. "It was the worst day of my life."

I swore I heard Gio let out a choked sob, but I didn't trust my own mind at that point.

"Did you look for him?" he asked so quietly, it was a miracle I heard him. This time, I was the one letting out a sob. I wiped at my wet eyes because it felt like the strangest of victories to have him respond to me in any kind of way.

I couldn't help but glance briefly at Remy who was standing perfectly still near the rumpled hospital bed.

"Every day," I croaked. I turned my attention back to Gio.

Gio began to rock back and forth even faster. He ran one hand through his white-blond hair, streaking it with blood in the process. "No, no, no," he kept muttering. His agony clawed at me and I wanted nothing more than to gather him in my arms. I would do anything to end his suffering.

"Nick," I said, even though it felt wrong to call him that. "Dr. Taylor is here." I shot a quick look at the man standing in the doorway. At some point, he or someone else had managed to clear the room. "I'll go so you can talk to him, all right? Can you just... can you give me the piece of glass in your hand first? Or just drop it on the floor. Please, just..."

I couldn't get any more words out because my throat was too thick with emotion. The last thing I wanted to do was leave my son, but I knew my presence was only hurting him more. When Gio didn't react to my request to drop the glass, I glanced at Dr. Taylor. He nodded and slowly made his way to my side.

"Nick, if it's all right with you, I'm just going to sit here with you for a few minutes so we can talk. Just you and me," the soft-spoken doctor said.

I knew the man was close enough that he'd be able to intervene if Gio tried to hurt himself with the glass, but every bone and muscle in my body resisted my command to move away from him. It seemed to take hours to climb to my feet. I forced myself to move back a few steps. I wanted to curl into a ball on the floor and mourn the loss of my son yet again. I knew in my heart that I might never get him back... that the pervert who'd stolen his innocence had also stolen this too. How had I ever thought that all it would take was to find my son and things would be all right?

The despair was soul-stealing, mind-numbing. If Remy hadn't chosen that moment to twine his fingers with mine, I surely would have lost my hold on reality just as my son had.

Remy's other hand came to cover our joined hands and his presence at my side was a balm of sorts. It made it possible for me to move, to turn away from my child because that was what he needed me to do.

"They took it," I heard from behind me just as I took my first step. I froze in place, certain I'd only imagined my son's voice. I prepared myself to take another step forward when Remy's fingers tightened on mine, stopping me.

He hadn't heard it too, had he?

But when I looked at Remy, his eyes held mine for a moment before he slowly turned his head toward Gio.

I was afraid to move.

Remy squeezed my hand again, so I focused on that as I made myself turn around. Gio sat in the same position, still rocking, broken glass still in hand.

"I begged them to let me keep it," my son choked out. He began to shake his head. "It was nothing to them... it was just... it was just a ball with my dad's name... name on it."

I felt my stomach drop out at his words. Oh God, was he... *remembering?*

Gio began to let out one guttural wail after another as he fisted his hands against his head. "No, please, please," he cried. I had no clue who he was talking to or what thing he was trying to deny, but I didn't care. I only saw my child being torn apart from the inside. In three long strides, I was in front of him and dropping to my knees. I grabbed his fists just as he began pounding them against his own head. I covered his head protectively with my hands and leaned down so I could rest my face against his hair.

"I've got you, Gio," I whispered against his temple. "Daddy's got you."

My words set off another round of terrible screams. I heard the distinct sound of glass hitting the floor and then my son was pressing his face against my chest as his fingers gripped my shirt. I held him close as I lowered myself fully to the floor. I let out a thousand silent screams as I comforted my child and promised him over and over that everything would be okay.

And when he finally fell silent what could have been minutes or hours later, I once again made my son the same promise I'd been making since the day he'd been taken from me.

That I would bring him home.

CHAPTER TWENTY-SEVEN

REMY

☩4

"**R**emy," Ronan said in genuine surprise when he opened the door. I figured it was probably pretty hard to surprise someone like Ronan, but I couldn't say that was something I'd been going for when I'd impulsively decided to have Stan drive me to the surgeon's house.

"I hope I'm not interrupting anything," I said. "Stan was just driving me to my apartment so I could get some more of my things since I'm still staying with Luca..." I let my words drop off as I realized how much information I'd shared with the man who probably couldn't care less about any of it.

"No, of course not, Seth and the kids are at the store. They like to make this big deal out of making my birthday cake every year. It's usually more about what theme they can surprise me with. Last year it was unicorns." The man stepped aside and motioned me into the house. I couldn't help but smile at the idea of the big, tough guy being presented with a cake covered in unicorns and rainbows.

"Unicorns, huh?" I said.

"Yep. There was even a little hat with a horn on it. Just for me," he added. I would've smiled at that too, if the family's huge German

SLOANE KENNEDY

shepherd hadn't chosen that moment to come trotting around the corner from the back of the house. The large animal came to a stop when it saw me, but the little dog with it let out a yip and raced in my direction.

"Bella," Ronan said and the little dog came to a sudden stop, dropped down to the floor and began wagging her tail and whining. All of my muscles were locked in place as Ronan moved past me and went to pick up the little dog. I saw him make some kind of signal with his hand and then the German shepherd also dropped down to the ground.

"Let me just put them outside," Ronan began to say.

"No!" I called, my voice sounding sharp. "No," I repeated, trying to keep my voice more even. "Are they... are they friendly?" I pretty much already knew the answer to that, but I needed a reason to stall so I could work up the nerve to move closer to the animals.

"They are," Ronan said gently. Since I doubted Luca had told him about my fear of dogs, it meant the man had probably picked up on it the last time I'd been there. It seemed like a lifetime ago when Luca and I had taken Violet to his house. The reminder of Violet had tears threatening the backs of my eyes. She was leaving in a couple of days and while I did my best not to think about what that meant, any little memory of her was enough to bring me to my knees. I had no idea how I was going to deal with the actual moment when she walked out of my life for good.

I took a few steps toward Ronan who was still holding the little white dog. "Her name is Bella?" I asked. The bundle of fur was wiggling happily in Ronan's arms.

"Yeah, short for Isabella. Nicole won the opportunity to name her when we got her, and she was and still is rather obsessed with a certain brooding vampire and the beautiful new girl in town who wins his heart."

"Hi, Bella," I said as I reached out to let the little dog sniff my hand. She immediately licked it and wriggled in her owner's arms. I cautiously petted her head and when she didn't snap at me, I gave her

256

a scratch behind the ears. "Um, you can put her down, if you want to, I mean."

Ronan eased the dog to the ground and while she happily rubbed herself against my legs, she didn't jump up or nip at me. I bent down to pet her some more and was rewarded with more doggy kisses. My eyes shifted to the German shepherd who was quietly watching us from the end of the hall. The animal thumped his tail when I looked at him, but it was still difficult to force myself to move toward him. "What's that one's name?"

"Bullet," Ronan said. "That name was all Seth." I could hear the softness in his voice as he said his husband's name.

Even with Ronan at my side as I reached the larger animal, I couldn't stifle my reaction to him. My blood ran cold at the memory of running through the woods with barking dogs quickly catching up to me, then latching onto me and dragging me to the ground.

"Do you want me to put them outside?" Ronan asked, probably because I hadn't moved in several minutes.

I shook my head. "Can we just talk right here so I can get used to him?" I asked. I knew I was being ridiculous, and the man probably thought I was the biggest coward on the planet, but I didn't want to give up on this. So many of the things in my past that I hadn't had the energy to fight were things that were easy enough to avoid, like encountering dogs and riding in the backs of cars.

Or trusting in people.

"Of course," Ronan said. "What can I do for you?"

"You already did it," I said. "But I never thanked you for any of it. Helping Violet, me... now *and* two years ago. The methadone program, the apartment, the job... I should have thanked you for all of that sooner, but I guess..."

"You guess what?" Ronan asked gently.

"I guess part of me wasn't actually grateful," I admitted. If I expected judgment, I didn't get it because Ronan continued to look at me in the same way... with understanding. It helped me to continue with my explanation. "I think there were times when I just wanted to have that excuse to go back to the way things were. Especially in those early days. Using was the only thing I really ever knew how to do. It was easy to say, '*if only*,' but then you and Dante actually gave me that *if only*. There were no more excuses for losing myself in drugs or selling my body. Or keeping people at a distance. Having all those things meant it wasn't okay to fail. Does that make sense?"

Ronan nodded. "I kept secrets from Seth when we first got together. I told myself it was better for him, but there was a part of me that wanted him to find out so he'd know I wasn't worth it. So that he'd be the one to walk away."

I looked around the hallway, specifically at all the family pictures that lined it. "Guess it didn't work," I said with a smile.

Ronan chuckled. "Not even a little bit." He glanced at the pictures himself and I could see the pure joy in his eyes. I couldn't imagine the man having ever *not* wanted what he was looking at. As his gaze settled on me again, he said, "And you're very welcome, Remy, for everything. I wish we could have made it so you never had to fight all those battles."

I felt the backs of my eyes stinging. "That's the other reason I came here," I said. "I spent a long time in that world. I know names, I know faces. I remember some of the places they took me. I was never very good in school, but I always had a pretty decent memory. If I tell you stuff, would it help? Would it help get some other kids out?"

"Yes," Ronan said without hesitation. "We may not find a kid today or tomorrow, but even just knowing a name or two will lead to another and another. Getting those people off the streets means saving all the kids they would've hurt. So yes, anything you tell us will help one way or the other."

I nodded, both nervous and relieved. I'd spent so many years dealing with the fallout of being abducted that I hadn't even considered that some good could come from it. I knew that not having shared what I knew hadn't necessarily made me a selfish person, but watching Gio struggle with everything he'd been through had been an eye-opener in a different way.

I thought about all the kids who were yet to be taken... all the families out there who were going about their lives not knowing what was coming. Maybe I couldn't bring kids home like Luca and his brothers had, but maybe there was another Gio out there who wouldn't lose his mother to an act of violence or have to fight his own mind to remember his father.

It had been over a week since Gio had admitted to remembering Luca, but it hadn't been some quick, joyous reunion. While Gio hadn't reverted to his near vegetative state, he had become very quiet and withdrawn again. There were days that Luca would go to the hospital and just sit in the room with his son, no words spoken between them. But every once in a while, there'd been a sliver of light as Gio would seem to remember some snippet of his childhood and would ask Luca if it were real or not.

They hadn't talked about Kurt or what had happened after Gio had been abducted, but unfortunately it was only a matter of time. That was something I was coming to understand as well. I'd spent so many years believing that not talking about my past would make it go away more quickly, but life with Luca had proven otherwise. I might have fought battles, but I was far from winning the war and I was tired of doing it by myself.

"When?" I asked. "When do you want me to tell you everything?"

"Have you talked to Luca about this?" Ronan asked.

I shook my head. "Luca and I... he's got his son back now and he needs to focus on him," I murmured awkwardly. "As he should," I added because I didn't want to make it sound like I was jealous. It was just my messed-up way of dancing around the truth—that I was losing Luca soon.

"Well, I don't know what's happening between you and your man—"

"He's not mine," I found myself interjecting, because it actually hurt to hear Ronan refer to Luca that way—in the way that I so badly wanted.

"Remy, that man has been yours from the moment he saw you again at that wedding. It's more a question of whether or not *you* want him to be yours."

I swallowed hard but didn't respond. What was I supposed to say? That I'd give anything to have a future with Luca and Gio? It was the same reason I couldn't be with Violet—I wasn't in a position to be the things Luca and his son needed.

The silence between Ronan and me stretched until Ronan said, "Why don't you start writing things down as you think of them? We can begin going through them and when we need more detail on something, we'll sit down together and talk about it. But Remy, I need you to promise me that you'll reach out to someone if it becomes too much to deal with by yourself. I know you don't think of us as your family, but that doesn't change the fact that we do. Me, Seth, Aleks, Dom, Dante... we may not have experienced the same things that you have, but we all understand that forgetting doesn't make things go away."

"Okay," I said. I was completely overwhelmed at the idea that this man truly did consider me a part of his family. There was no reason for him to lie about something like that. And he'd said as much the day he'd talked to me in his daughter's room after Luca had begged me to let him watch out for me and Violet. "I should go," I said. "Dom made me promise to stop by the office after I pick up a few things from my apartment."

"Just remind Dom that I won this round," Ronan murmured as he began walking me back toward the front door.

I looked at him questioningly.

"He and I may have had a little bet going about which one of us would make sure your rent was all taken care of so you wouldn't have to worry about it for a while."

"What?" I said in disbelief. "You paid my rent?" I'd assumed that when I went to my apartment I'd find at least one eviction notice on it, since I hadn't been back to the place in several weeks and rent hadn't been at the top of my list of things to worry about. I'd planned to pay what I owed with the little bit of savings I had left, but I wouldn't have had enough for next month. Even if Dom was kind enough to give me back my old job, it would've taken time to earn enough money to get caught up on all my bills. As it was, I was planning on selling my car just to make ends meet.

Ronan shrugged. "I suppose technically Luca won."

"Wait," I said. "I'm confused. All three of you paid my rent?"

"Well, Dom tried, but I beat him to the punch. You can ask your man how he managed to trump both of us." Ronan smiled and reached to open the door. I was still as confused as ever but decided some things just weren't worth arguing about.

"Thank you, Ronan," I said. I reached out to shake his hand, because hugging the man wasn't something I was ready for just yet. But I'd get there.

"You're welcome, Remy. Thank you for what you did for Aleks. I hope you'll consider what I said about needing someone to talk to."

I nodded. I turned to leave, then paused and glanced at Bullet who hadn't moved from his spot. "Can I call him?" I asked. I automatically began shaking again as I considered what I was about to do, but when Ronan gave me permission to say the dog's name, I did so. The animal trotted right up to me, and it was all I could do not to move.

I stood frozen in place expecting the animal to nip at my fingers, rub up against me, or something else that would show his power over me. But all he did was sit expectantly at my feet and wait. I put my hand out to let him sniff it, but even then, he didn't get pushy. I wondered if the animal had a sixth sense about these things. Like he knew I wasn't ready for more than a quick pat on his head. I did just that and then turned and left the house. It might not have been the most graceful of exits, but I was exceedingly proud of myself for having dealt with my fear head-on.

With Ronan and the dog.

My experience with Dom when I arrived at the office was strikingly similar to my encounter with Ronan. There was no judgment as I apologized profusely for having walked away from my responsibilities. I explained about Violet but made it clear that I understood it wasn't an excuse. I fully expected the man to reprimand me in some kind of way or to warn me that it couldn't happen again, but when I was finished talking, he simply handed me my employee badge and asked if I'd be able to start again on Monday. Then he promptly invited me to the family dinner and told me to bring my guy and the rest of my family with me.

Family dinners with the Barretti clan were an event in and of themselves and while I'd been to a couple of them, I'd always stayed on the outer edges and left as soon as I could. And while the idea of attending one of the busy gatherings was intimidating, I couldn't help but picture myself walking into the place with Luca at my side.

I was emotionally drained by the time I left the office. I conveyed Ronan's message to Dom about winning the rent thing they'd had going on, but Dom had merely shrugged it off and muttered something under his breath that I hadn't dared asked him to clarify. I was eager to get back to Luca, so I skipped the trip to my apartment and had Stan take me back to the house.

I expected the place to be swarming with Luca's family, but it was eerily quiet when I entered through the front door. I also hadn't seen any cars in the driveway, including Marilyn's rental car. I'd asked Stan if he knew where everyone had gone, but he hadn't.

I was on edge as I began searching the house. What if Marilyn and Violet had left without saying goodbye? Maybe the woman had thought it would be easier that way for me and for Violet.

What if Luca had left? He had everything he wanted, so maybe he'd decided to head back to the city so he could go back to his office. At some point he'd want to take Gio home to New York. Maybe this was his way of telling me. We'd spent every night together since our first date, and I'd even slept in his bed, but we hadn't gotten physical again beyond some kissing and touching here and there. Maybe he knew I wasn't ready for more and he was tired of waiting.

"Luca?" I called, even as I tried to convince myself that it was okay, that it was the way things needed to be. I was supposed to be able to let him go, so now was as good a time as any.

Except that it wasn't. I wasn't ready.

"Luca!" I practically screamed at the top of my lungs as I began searching each of the rooms. I dashed up the stairs, but just as I went to open the door to his room, I heard my name being called.

I turned and looked over the banister and saw Luca standing in the foyer watching me with concern. To see him there when I'd convinced myself that he was gone stole my breath.

"Remy? What's wrong?" Luca asked.

But I couldn't find the strength to respond. The relief that he wasn't gone was so overpowering that I had to grab onto the banister to stay upright. Even then, I felt my knees buckle and a harsh sob I hadn't been expecting burst from my throat.

He was next to me within a matter of seconds. His arms went around me as he worriedly asked me again what was wrong. I shook my head because I'd been momentarily robbed of the ability to speak. I wrapped my arms around him and was glad when he just hung onto me.

"Talk to me, baby," Luca said after I'd calmed down a bit.

"I thought you'd left," I admitted. "I thought I was ready, but I'm not. I'm not, Luca!"

He wiped my face, and I felt bad for being such a blubbering fool around him that he probably couldn't even understand what I was saying.

"Then don't be, Remy," he said softly.

"Don't be what?"

"Ready. Don't be ready to let me go. Because I sure as hell am not ready to let you go."

I stared at him in disbelief. I had to have heard him wrong. "Luca, I—"

"Stay here with me," Luca said, his voice almost harsh. His desperation mirrored what I'd been feeling just moments ago. "Stay with me and we'll figure the rest out."

"I can't," I automatically said. "You live in New York, I live here. You have a son you need to take care of and I... I'm such a fucking mess, Luca. I know you don't like hearing me say that I'm an addict, but I am. That's never going to change. I could never be someone that you could proudly show off to your friends or your family—"

I shook my head as I heard my own words. "Maybe that's not what you want anyway," I said as I looked down at my arms and the track

263

marks that still covered them. "Even if I was capable of having just a physical relationship with you, I don't want to. I think maybe I deserve better than that. I know that doesn't make sense, but I just—"

"I love you, Remy," Luca growled as he gave me a little shake. I lifted my eyes in shock.

"What?" I choked out. But he continued on as if I hadn't interrupted him.

"And you deserve *everything*. I want to *give* you everything. If there was a way I could undo that night we first met, I would. If there was a way I could go back and take you home like I should have, I would. There are a million things I would do differently, but I can't regret even for a moment that we found each other again. You're not some secret to be hidden away, Remy. I would be proud to call you my partner, my best friend, my lover... because you are all those things. But more than anything, I want to call you my husband. I love you. Sex or no sex, I love you. New York or here, I love you. Past or no past, I love you. I love you." His declaration was so fierce, so powerful, that there was no room in my soul to doubt him.

"Luca—" I began.

"Just say you'll stay," he cut in.

"Luca—"

"No, don't do this. Just say you'll stay and we can figure it out, baby. I promise. We'll be a family, you and me and Gio, and we'll make sure to see Violet as often as we can. Please, just don't give up on us—"

I ended up slapping my hand over his mouth to silence him. Tears were coasting down my cheeks. "I love you, Luca," I said quickly, just so he wouldn't get the opportunity to interrupt me again. His eyes went wide, almost comically so. The idea that this beautiful, amazing man actually thought it was possible that I didn't have the same feelings for him as he did for me was almost too much to comprehend. I dropped my hand and threw myself into his arms.

"Say it again," he demanded, his breath skimming over the spot where my neck met my shoulder.

"I love you." I would happily say it a thousand times over. Loving him was the easiest thing I'd ever done, and now I was wondering why I'd feared it in the first place.

His mouth sought out mine and I happily kissed him back. He couldn't seem to keep his mouth off me nor I him, and as the disbelief turned to acceptance that he was really mine, it felt like a million pounds being lifted off my shoulders all at once. I laughed for no other reason than I could. He did the same and then we were embracing again. I had no clue how long we stayed there like that, but as I ran my fingers over the back of his neck, I found myself telling him everything about my conversations with Ronan and Dom. He listened without interruption.

When I was finished, he pulled back enough so he could look me in the eye. "I'm so proud of you, baby," he whispered. His eyes roamed over my face and it was like he didn't want to ever stop touching me. I felt the same.

"Where is everybody?" I asked. As happy as I was, I couldn't help but have that little shadow of sadness inside of me. "Did Marilyn and Violet leave?"

Luca shook his head. "My brothers and Marilyn took Violet to the zoo. I was planning on jumping you when you came in the door and begging you not to leave me. I guess I kind of missed the jumping part because I was getting my cell phone out of the car in the garage, but at least I guess I got the begging part right." He winked at me and then kissed me lightly.

I chuckled and said, "I think I get to take the drama award for today considering I was screaming like a banshee when I thought you'd left me."

His expression grew serious and he shook his head. "Never. I could never leave you. You're stuck with me now."

"Happily stuck," I said.

He nodded and then we were climbing to our feet. "I need to tell you something," he said. "I hope I did the right thing."

"Tell me," I insisted softly. At that point, nothing he told me would change anything. "We're stuck with each other, remember?" I asked with a smile.

He chuckled. "I talked to Marilyn this morning. I asked her if she might consider staying in Seattle and raising Violet here. She would still be her primary caretaker, but I thought that we could be the extended family Violet needs. I know there are things that you're not ready for, but we could take it day by day and see how it goes. Vaughn is staying here with Aleks and Gio won't be ready to return to New York anytime soon, and you have family here—"

"What did she say?" I asked, barely able to contain myself. He was right about me not being ready to take on the full responsibility of parenting Violet, but the idea of getting to be in her life was something I'd been afraid to consider.

"She agreed," Luca said. "She thinks Violet needs all of us and that we need each other."

"She's right," I said. "And you were absolutely right to ask her. Thank you, Luca. I love that little girl so much, but it's such a big responsibility that I wasn't ready for by myself. But with you by my side, I know I can learn. Maybe someday, if it's something you want—"

"It is," Luca whispered. "It absolutely is."

When he pulled me into his arms again, I happily went. There was still so much to figure out, but the hardest part was behind us. We would start a life together. We would have a family that included Gio and Violet and Marilyn and all of Luca's crazy brothers as well as the huge family that I'd only just accepted that I had on my side. I'd continue to fight all the battles thrown my way, but I would no longer have to do it alone. Not only did I have Luca, but I had Aleks and Ronan and all the other men and women who cared about me. And I'd figure out how to help Luca give Gio what he needed so we could bring the young man home with us. He might never have a normal life, but like me, he'd figure out how to move forward and he'd find love and success and family.

And he'd do it with the thing Luca had given me so long ago the day we'd first met.

Hope.

The slamming of car doors and loud voices outside drew our

attention and we reluctantly parted. But Luca didn't let me get far because he grabbed my hand.

"I don't know who has the crazier family, you or me," he murmured as the front door opened to reveal Con and King doing what they did best.

Arguing.

Luca began to lead me down the stairs. I was both nervous and excited to see everyone, especially Violet and Marilyn.

"I don't know my family as well yet, but apparently when they argue, they place bets instead of threatening to beat the crap out of each other," I said. "That reminds me, did you pay my rent?"

Luca was decidedly quiet.

"Luca?" I prodded.

"Huh?"

"Did you pay my rent?" I asked again.

He started to pat his shirt pocket and then seemed to remember he'd quit smoking. "No," he finally said.

"Luca, Ronan told me about him and Dom betting about who'd pay my rent first. He said you trumped both of them."

"I can honestly say I did not pay your rent," Luca responded over his shoulder. His refusal to make eye contact had me tugging him to a stop. I ignored the fact that his brothers were still arguing downstairs and that Vaughn had gotten into the melee. Violet was happily chattering about something in the background, but I avoided looking her way so I wouldn't lose my train of thought. I gave Luca what I could only classify as my best version of the evil eye.

"I didn't," he insisted.

"Fine, what did you do?"

He leaned in and gave me a quick peck on the nose. "I love you," he said cheekily.

"What did you do?" I repeated, though I was quickly losing interest in ever finding out. At the moment, all I wanted to do was grab my gorgeous man and get him in a room somewhere so I could finally find out about the stuff couples did when they made up after fighting. I'd even heard Aleks and Vaughn passing jokes back and forth about the virtues of make-up sex. I might not be ready for all the sex stuff, but I would certainly be okay with a repeat of what had happened in the back seat of Luca's car on our first date.

He must have seen something in my expression because he grinned and suddenly—and very proudly—announced, "I bought your building. Sorry, honey." And with that, he trotted down the stairs, leaving me to gape after him in disbelief.

CHAPTER TWENTY-EIGHT

LUCA

†4

I was in the process of hanging up my phone when I heard the door open and close behind me. When Remy's slim arms slid around me from behind, some of the tension I'd been feeling eased a bit.

"What? What is it? Gio?" Remy automatically asked as he moved around so he could face me. The fact that he was already so in tune with me wasn't a surprise.

I held up my phone for a moment and then said, "It was Lex."

"You heard from him? Is he all right?" Remy asked, his hand reaching for mine. I welcomed the contact. It was yet another sign of how so many things had changed for me since Remy had come back into my life. A month ago, I'd avoided physical contact with anyone and everyone, because it'd always felt like I was too raw and that one touch would somehow ignite the fuse that had been simmering inside of me for years. But not Remy. He'd been different.

"He says he is," I murmured.

"You don't believe him."

I shook my head. "He was asking about Gio, but he didn't say anything about coming to see him. He and Gio were just as close as

Gio and all my other brothers. Gio's finally back, for real, but he still isn't coming to see him. It doesn't make any sense."

"Did he say where he is?" Remy asked.

"No. He's hiding something. King says he knows what it is…"

"Do you trust King?" Remy asked.

"With my life."

"What about with your brother's life?"

I didn't need to think about that answer either. "Yes."

"Then trust King to tell you if and when Lex needs you. He may not be ready to ask for help," Remy pointed out.

I nodded, but it wasn't an easy concept to swallow. Lex had always been sickly and weak and that'd made him a target for bullying. He'd grown into a capable, talented man, but he'd still always be the heart of us… the softness of us.

"You're right," I forced myself to say. The fact was that Lex was a grown man and if he wanted my help, he'd ask for it. At least he'd finally made contact, and from the way he'd spoken, he sounded okay. Quiet, but okay. And he'd been beyond happy to hear that Gio was finally making progress.

My thoughts turned to my son. Today had been a good day with Gio. We hadn't really talked about anything in particular, but we'd watched some sports on television, including several soccer games. At one point, Gio had made a comment about a referee's call, and that had been enough to get us talking about the different players. I knew it would be a long time before we got around to the subject of his abduction and what had happened, but he was no longer ignoring or avoiding me.

Remy took the phone from my hand and went to set it on the nightstand by my bed… or *our* bed, rather, since we'd been sleeping in it together ever since our first date. Things had been too crazy with Gio for either of us to consider moving forward with our physical relationship, but that hadn't mattered today as I'd left the hospital, eager to get home to Remy so I could talk to him about our future.

I stayed where I was as Remy came back around me and began working on the buttons of my dress shirt. I couldn't help but reach out and run my fingers over his face. He'd already changed into his pajamas.

Although he was focused on the buttons, his mind was definitely somewhere else when he said, "Did we get engaged today, Luca?"

He looked up at me as he spoke the last words. His expression was soft, almost dreamy. I still couldn't believe that he loved me. It felt like I'd finally done something right in my life.

"I think we did," I said. "Actually, I think I kind of asked you, but I'm not sure you answered me."

"Are you sure you want that? If it's because of what I said about feeling like I deserve—"

"I want it. I want it more than you'll ever know, Remy. I want to walk in a room with you on my arm. I want everyone to see that wedding ring and know that I was the one who was lucky enough to be worthy of you. I want to wake up with you every morning in our bed and I want you in my arms at night where you belong. I want to share all the ups and downs I'll be going through with Gio, and I want to watch you find yourself for real and live the life that you want, not the life you think you're supposed to have. And someday in the future, I want to have children with you because you're going to be the most amazing father. So yes, I want to be your husband," I said as I drew him closer to me. While my proposal this afternoon hadn't exactly been romantic, I'd meant every word of it.

Remy was tense in my embrace, but his fingertips were rubbing over the muscles of my chest.

"I want to try," he murmured, his eyes still downcast.

My heart sank. If he wasn't a hundred percent committed to marrying me, I didn't know what I'd do. "I love you, Remy, but I can't do some kind of trial relationship..."

Remy jerked his head up. "What?" he asked in surprise and then he began shaking his head vehemently. "No, no, that's not what I meant. I want to be your husband for real. But I..." His words hung for a moment and then he said, "I want to be your husband out there." He looked in the direction of our bedroom door. "But I also want to be your husband in here," he added firmly.

Understanding dawned and I felt like an idiot. "We will be, no matter what happens in this room," I said. "I love every moment I spend with you, Remy, but sex can play as much or as little of a part in our lives as we want. And there's no rush to figure that out."

"But if I can't… can't…" Remy said as he took a step back from me. "If I can't, then we need to talk about maybe you finding someone who can—"

I grabbed him by the arms and gave him a tiny jerk to get his attention. It was all I could do to keep my anger in check. "No way, not happening. We do this and I'm yours and you're mine and that's it. I'm not interested in any kind of open relationship or special arrangements. Our marriage will be what we make it. And if that means my hand and my dick need to become best friends, that's fine."

Remy stepped forward and began caressing my arms and chest like he was trying to soothe me. I supposed I had gotten a bit passionate about the issue.

"I still want to try," Remy murmured. His finger slipped down to the buttons at the bottom of my shirt. He began untucking it.

"Sweetheart, we don't have to do it this way now. I'm very ready to know what it's like to have you inside of me," I said softly as I leaned down so I could run my mouth along his jaw. He tipped his head back to give me access to his throat.

"Let's call that Plan B," he said. He managed to get my shirt loose and open. His warm hands slid over my sides and then over my back as he continued to move his head in different directions so I had easy access to all the parts of his throat. I let him push the shirt off my shoulders, but since he'd forgotten to undo the buttons at my wrists, the fabric didn't go very far. Not that I cared, because I had a plan of my own.

I dropped to my knees in front of Remy as I continued to caress his chest with my hands and mouth. Remy seemed lost in a sensual haze as I loved on his body. But when I went to open his pants, he snapped out of it and dropped his hands to mine to stop them. "What —what are you doing?" he asked.

"Did you want the play-by-play?" I teased as I tugged my hands free and ran my knuckles over the bulge behind the thin material. "Because I'm good with that," I said with a grin.

Remy laughed and said, "No, I just thought you would want me to… since you're going to be the one to…"

If he'd been any other man, his comments would've been adorable, but knowing what caused them only managed to hurt my heart. Remy had never known pleasure when it came to sex; he'd never been on the receiving end of it. He'd assumed that since I'd be the one taking him, *he'd* have to get *me* ready. It was a sign that he probably wasn't expecting to get much out of the encounter.

I climbed back to my feet and drew him against my body. I kissed him deeply until he was completely pliant in my arms. "Do you trust me, Remy?" I asked.

"Yes," he said without hesitation.

"Remember what you said about needing to feel? That's what I need you to do, Remy. Just feel."

Remy nodded and drew in a deep breath like he was gathering his courage. Then he was reaching for the back of my head and drawing me down for a kiss. A deep, dirty, consuming kiss. I let him control our mouths for several minutes until I once again felt his body relax and then I worked my way down to the floor again, exploring his body with my hands and mouth. I was glad he was wearing his pajamas because it made it easy to manipulate the fabric.

I pushed the shirt up enough that it was clear to Remy what I wanted, and he went ahead and removed it from his body. I hated to see how he discreetly tried to cover some of the larger scars on his body. While Remy was definitely on the skinny side and he had more scars than the average person, I still couldn't get past how beautiful he was. So that was what I told him. I said it with words, I said it with my mouth, and I said it with my fingers. I would happily spend the rest of my life showing and telling him he was perfect just as he was.

I left his pants on and nuzzled his belly button, as well as the thin line of hair that started there. My hands were roaming anywhere they could reach and while Remy was still tense, his fingers were on the move as well. He ran them through my hair, alongside my neck, and over my shoulders. He finally seemed to realize my shirt was still partially on, so as I followed his treasure trail with my tongue, he began working on the buttons at my wrists. But of course, as soon as I lowered my mouth and closed it over the outline of his cock, Remy forgot all about my shirt as he let out a loud groan. I mouthed him through the fabric of the pajama pants until I had dampened the length of his dick. Remy's fingers twisted in my hair and gripped hard as he tried to make it so that my mouth was focused on his crown.

I reached up to pull his pajama pants down and watched his ruddy cock slip free of the material. It looked painfully hard and red and was glistening with moisture. I forgot that I was supposed to be going slow and simply closed my mouth over the head and swallowed him to the back of my throat. Remy screamed in surprise but didn't try to pull away. As his taste slid over the back of my tongue, I began sucking hard so I could collect every last drop for myself.

While his dick wasn't huge, it was still difficult to work the length down my throat so I could rub my nose in the hair at his groin. Tears pricked my eyes as I tried not to gag. I pulled back until almost his entire shaft slipped free of my mouth and then I sucked him again. I let my tongue explore all the ridges, but I didn't count myself truly victorious until Remy grabbed ahold of my shoulders and began pumping himself into me. I held on to his hips for leverage as I let him fuck my mouth. He was moaning and grunting as he used me, and I loved every second of it.

"Luca, Luca, I—I can't—oh God!" was all he got out and then he was shouting in relief as his semen began to shoot down my throat. I swallowed eagerly, loving the salty bitterness that coated my tongue. The release seemed to go on forever and while I was able to consume most of Remy's essence, some of it dripped out the side of my mouth. I continued to suck on Remy's dick as his orgasm eased and used my hands to hold his body up because he was shaking so badly. I gently released his cock and then stood. His skin was flushed and sweating and his eyes were half closed. I could see he'd been crying at some point because there were the remnants of tears on his cheeks.

"Luca," he said drowsily, but I didn't miss the confusion in his voice. I assumed it was another first for him... getting a blow job. I covered his mouth with mine and kissed him gently so he could taste himself on my tongue and know that it had really happened. He was clearly tired as he kissed me back, then his arms went around me and he leaned heavily against me. I reveled in the feel of it.

"Do you want more?" I asked.

He nodded without hesitation. "I want it all," he whispered.

I settled my hands on his ass, then lowered them to the backs of his thighs. As soon as I lifted him, he stepped free of his pajamas and wrapped his legs around me. It was only a few short steps to the bed, and when I laid him down on it and covered his body with mine, he dragged my mouth down to his for a drugging kiss.

"Do you want me to...?" Remy asked as his eyes shifted down to my groin. The idea that he thought he had to reciprocate was just further proof that no one had ever taken the time to make this kind of encounter solely about him.

I was going to change that.

I shook my head and said, "If you get your mouth anywhere near me, I'm going to blow, and at my age, recovery isn't a sure thing." I winked at him, which had him smiling. He ran his hands down my sides and over my ass.

"I'll keep you young, old man." Remy grinned when he said the words and my heart felt lighter than it ever had. I knew in that moment that no matter what, we would be okay.

"I'd be satisfied if you'd just finish what you started," I said as I lifted my hands to point out that my shirt was still hanging off my body because he hadn't undone the buttons at my wrists. Remy grinned again and then, instead of reaching for the buttons, he grabbed the shirt and simply yanked it off my hands. He did the same with the other sleeve. But once his fingers went for my pants, I grabbed his hand.

"Not yet, my love. I need all the layers I can get between my dick and this gorgeous body of yours."

I was glad that Remy didn't seem overly nervous about the fact that he was now naked beneath me. He opened his legs to make room for me and we spent several minutes just exploring each other's mouths.

Then I was on to the rest of his body. Now that I had him flat on his back, it was easier to love every inch of him. I teased his cock with my mouth but didn't suck on him again. He was already growing hard, so I knew it would only be a matter of time before he was fully ready to go again.

I moved down his body until my knees were on the floor. I lifted his legs so his feet were flat on the mattress. I felt him tense up at being exposed and vulnerable like he was, but he didn't protest the move. I kissed his inner thighs and teased his cock with a few fluttering kisses and then mouthed his balls. I placed my arm around his hips to keep him in place as I sucked one of the tight orbs into my mouth. Remy's back arched and if I hadn't been holding him down, he most surely would've come off the bed entirely. As it was, he called my name and buried his hands in my hair. I gave the rest of his flesh the same treatment and then I was pulling him farther off the bed and folding his legs in on himself.

But I didn't give him time to wonder what I was doing.

Instead, I went in for the kill.

CHAPTER TWENTY-NINE

REMY

✝4

I wasn't exactly a religious person, but I spent the next several minutes begging the man above to both release me from the torment of Luca's incredible mouth and to make it so he never stopped. I hadn't really understood what Luca was planning until his tongue had swiped over my hole the first time. At that point, a spark of logic had returned to my overworked brain and I'd tried to say something about how what he was doing had to be wrong. But then that sinful tongue had moved over me again and again and with every intimate caress, I'd felt the muscles of my body grow tighter and tighter as fire had flicked up my spine and radiated out to every nerve ending.

Whatever was building inside of me bordered on painful, but there was this need there as well.

I'd always been clueless why guys had paid me money for something that'd seemed so disgusting as them putting their dicks in my mouth or up my ass. But after having Luca's mouth literally pulling out the most intense orgasm from my dick that I'd ever experienced, things were starting to make more sense. I'd never had someone put me first before, or even care about whether I experienced pleasure or not. I was suddenly glad that I hadn't because it made it possible to compartmentalize what other men had done to me versus what Luca was currently doing.

I couldn't make sense of any of the words or sounds that were coming out of my mouth, but I knew they probably had something to do with the mental begging I was doing. I wanted more, but I was also afraid of it. Luca's tongue practically worshipped the part of my body that had only ever experienced pain. Along with the overwhelming sensation came a mix of emotions that were hard to process.

Then I remembered Luca's words. I was supposed to feel.

So that's what I did.

I felt loved and wanted and cherished as Luca did the most plea-surable things to my body. When his tongue pushed inside of me, there was no time to be frightened of what was to come. I reached down to grab my dick because it was once again hard and I could feel my orgasm building in my balls. I started to stroke myself, but Luca's hand came up to cover mine. I thought he was going to help get me off, but instead he held my hand where it was, so I could do nothing but hold myself as he continued to fuck my ass with his tongue.

I felt thwarted, but it didn't matter because it wouldn't take much more of Luca's mouth on me to get me off.

But when Luca's lush tongue pulled free of my body, I cried out his name and tried to sit up. "No, Luca, please don't stop. Please, I'm so close."

Luca climbed up my body and covered my pleading mouth with his. He drank down my words and it was only when he rubbed his groin against mine that I realized he'd gotten rid of his pants at some point. His hot, hard, heavy cock pressed against mine. I hated that I instantly tensed up.

"No, please no! I'm not ready." I began crying, despite my intention not to.

"Shhh," Luca murmured in my ear as he kissed my cheek, jaw, and mouth with the softest of caresses. "Take a few deep breaths for me, baby," Luca said softly.

"I'm sorry, I'm so sorry." I kept repeating the words because I didn't know what else to say. We'd gotten to this moment that I'd feared, and I'd failed. Everything had been so beautiful and perfect, but the moment I'd felt his flesh on mine, the past had come hurtling back. The wall I'd put up to keep the men who'd hurt me out of this encounter had come crashing down.

Luca lifted his weight off of me a little bit, but not completely. His hands settled on my cheeks. "Hey," he said gently and then he kissed the tip of my nose. "Look at me, my love."

I didn't want to. I was way too humiliated. But his voice was so kind and gentle, and I owed him the respect to do what he asked. He'd done absolutely nothing wrong. This was all on me and my messed-up mind.

"I'm sorry," I croaked again when I opened my eyes and saw Luca watching me with concern. I loved him even more in that moment. But in my heart, I knew this was never going to work.

"Nuh-uh," Luca gently admonished as his eyes held mine. "You don't get to give up yet. You don't get to give up on us."

He was right. God knew I'd done this plenty of times; surely I could give him this.

"I'm okay," I insisted. "You can—"

"Don't you dare," Luca said, his voice tainted with anger. "Don't you dare pretend that you're okay and you want this."

At that point, I pretty much lost it. I began to sob uncontrollably and the beautiful moments I'd had with him went up in smoke. I expected him to get up and leave me there, but instead, he rolled to his side, pulling me with him. He held on to me but didn't speak. The tears seemed endless, but through it all, Luca stroked my back and my hair.

When the tears began to fade, my need to escape was all-consuming, but when I murmured something about wanting to get cleaned up, Luca refused to release me. He rolled me on my back again but kept his lower weight off of me. In typical Remy fashion, I went from scared and embarrassed to angry and quiet.

"I told you this wouldn't work," I bit out.

He didn't respond to the comment. Instead he just held me and while he didn't touch me intimately, his fingers were never still. I waited for him to argue his side, to tell me that everything would be fine and that we'd figure it out, but all Luca did was hold me and touch me. Every once in a while, he'd nuzzle my cheek or my neck.

I wasn't even aware I'd fallen asleep until the next morning when I woke up, still in his arms. We were both naked, but he'd moved us beneath the blanket. He looked so peaceful when he was sleeping. Regret for my behavior the night before was instant and painful. I'd taken what had started out as an amazing experience and tainted it. I couldn't understand why he was still there.

I probably should've gotten out of the bed, but I was reluctant to leave the warmth of his arms. I did to him what he'd done to me so many times and just explored his features with a soft touch. After a few minutes, I saw him smile. My heart swelled with love for the man. I couldn't stand the idea of losing him.

"I'm still here," he said drowsily. His eyes opened more fully and then he said, "You're still here."

I shook my head because I didn't understand what he was trying to say. Before I could open my mouth, he kissed me. "We're still here, Remy. Last night might not have worked out the way we'd hoped but look at us... we're still here. We are waking up in each other's arms exactly the way we wanted. I'm right where I want to be."

My throat felt tight with emotion. "Me too," I agreed. "Luca, I'm—"

He placed his fingers over my mouth to silence me. Then he was rolling us so he was on his back and I was lying on top of him.

"Morning," he said to me and then he pulled me down to kiss him. I accepted that he didn't want or need an apology. The kiss started off light and sweet, but quickly changed. Luca was already hard beneath me, probably because he'd been so all night, and my own dick was responding to the close contact. Luca tore his mouth from mine, presumably to end the kiss before it became too much to handle, but that was the last thing I wanted. I followed his mouth and grabbed his chin with my hand so I could control the kiss. Luca groaned as I explored his mouth and tangled my tongue with his. His hands slipped up and down my back, skimming the top of my ass but nothing more.

Despite feeling his cock against mine, the same fear I'd had the night before wasn't there. I only felt tense and needy and unsatisfied. I began rubbing my hips over his so our shafts were sliding together. It felt so good I cried out and then buried my face in Luca's shoulder. I could have easily made myself, and probably him, come just by grinding against him, but there was a strange sensation inside of me... this emptiness, this incompleteness.

And I knew why.

"Remy," Luca groaned as I began kissing his throat and then sucking on it so I could leave my mark on him. I shifted my body up his just enough so his hard dick slipped behind me. My eyes practically rolled back in my head when his damp shaft began sliding up and down my crease. I was torn between rubbing my cock against his muscled abdomen and trying to increase the pressure of his shaft against my crack. Luca's mouth searched out mine and as we made out, our bodies hung there, trying to ride one another and find relief from the building pressure inside. I knew we could eventually find it in the positions we were in, but it wasn't enough.

I knew that, just like I'd known the night before that I wasn't ready.

But I was ready now. The new position where I was the one in control, I was the one making decisions about how we found our pleasure, had unlocked that part of my brain that had been so closed off the night before. The man beneath me was the love of my life and anything we did together would be about pleasuring each other, about losing ourselves in one another's bodies. There would be no pain or humiliation, because that wasn't who we were. That wasn't what Luca wanted from me. He was the last man on the planet who would ever let me feel those things again. If I wanted him to stop, I'd only have to say so. Or move away. I knew I could easily take him the way he'd offered, but this was one of those moments where I wanted to fight my fear and I wanted to do it now.

"Condom, lube?" I breathed into his mouth between passionate kisses. The man was desperate beneath me, just like I had been last night when he'd been tonguing me.

"Nightstand," he managed to get out. His hands caressed my ass, splitting me open so his dick could ride my crease. I cried out at the sensation of his hot, firm skin sliding over my clenching hole. Sweat poured down my forehead as I continued to pump my cock against his abdomen and then rolled my hips so that he was fucking my crease. Luca's eyes had gone black with passion, but I saw more there.

I saw *him* there.

I fumbled in the nightstand for the condom and lube. Fortunately, I had plenty of experience with both and it took just seconds to get Luca ready. I heard him say my name in confusion and realized he'd probably thought, considering our positions, that I was going to fuck him.

I settled his lubed cock back in my crease and then leaned over him and kissed him hard. "Need this," I bit out against his lips. "Need you inside me."

I was glad when he didn't question me, but he did search my eyes for what felt like the longest time. Then he was reaching between our bodies and swiping his fingers over his lubed cock. I expected him to push his dick into me, but it was one of his fingers that began probing me. It felt so good to have him rubbing the sensitive skin with his rough finger. I was sweating and panting and so very ready, so when he started to push the digit into me, I bore down hard. He took his time prepping me, but when he withdrew his finger and asked, "Remy?" I knew he was still hesitant. I didn't blame him, considering how I'd acted the night before.

"I'm feeling," I whispered against his mouth and then I kissed him. I told him everything he needed to know with my mouth. He moaned and then he was reaching between us so he could position the head of his dick against my entrance.

There was pain as he began to push inside me, but the burn that followed was new and breathtaking. I tried to make sense of the warring sensations but gave up quickly. All that mattered was that I wanted more. I bore down on Luca so I could take more of him into me. Luca's hands rested on my thighs and he began massaging me as he urged me to relax. I took several deep breaths and then felt something within me give. Luca and I both groaned when his crown slipped past the outer muscle that had been trying to keep him out. The burn of his thickness stretching me had me gasping for air. I was half-leaning, half-sitting over him, but something inside of me had me straightening. I barely heard Luca warning me to take it slow, but I didn't want to. Now that he was fucking me, it wasn't a question of whether I wanted more or not. I *needed* more.

I carefully straightened my body so that I was able to take more of his length inside of me. Luca's fingers closed around mine so he could support me as I found the right angle that had him slipping all the way in. His balls brushed the skin of my ass. I cried out in relief, knowing we were finally one.

I wasn't sure how long I hung there for as my body stretched to accommodate him, but when I looked down at the man who'd changed everything about my life in the best way possible, I saw that he was watching me with a mix of need and reverence. If I'd ever doubted that he loved me, there was no question of it now. It was in his eyes as clear as day.

Instinct quickly took over and I began moving, using Luca's hands for leverage as I tried to figure out the right pace and rhythm. Luca and I both grunted and moaned and whispered things like "yes" and "there" and "harder" as I took him in and out of my body. The coil of need inside of me began to tighten with every stroke. I knew I wouldn't last because I could already feel the orgasm in my balls.

"Luca," I called out, not sure what I actually wanted.

Luca knew and as he sat up, his arms went around me. He held on to me hard as he began to pump his hips up and down, surging inside of me deeper and deeper and then pulling out just enough to have my body screaming for more. I wrapped my arms around his shoulders, not caring that my cock was squashed between our bodies. All I cared about was him being a part of me in a way that no man ever had been or ever would be again. Our bodies became primal in nature as we fucked. It was rough and fast but then Luca's hands were in my hair and he was pulling my head down so he could look me in the eye. We stared at each other, no words spoken, as we made our bodies one. I felt powerless and powerful at the same time. Lost and found, scared and joyful, and most importantly, no longer alone.

We came at nearly the exact same time and it was all I could do to keep my eyes open so I could see Luca's expression as his release found him. He was beautiful—perfect in his blissful agony.

I could only watch him for a few seconds because then it was my turn. Light and dark collided behind my eyelids as my body exploded. Pleasure detonated beneath my skin and I could feel jet after jet of hot cum covering me and Luca. Luca's cock throbbed inside my ass and I could feel the heat of him through the condom. Luca buried his face against my chest as he yelled, and I covered his head with my arms to hold him there.

We stayed like that for what felt like forever. Aftershocks riddled our bodies, but there finally came a point where we each found the strength to seek out each other's mouths. We said everything we needed to with our mouths and bodies.

When I managed to find enough oxygen to tell Luca I loved him, he said the words back.

"Luca," I said a little later after he pulled free of my body and disposed of the condom. We were lying in bed with my back to his front. His body was wrapped around mine and I'd never felt warmer or safer.

"Yeah?" my man said tiredly from behind me.

"I said yes, right?"

His fingers were joined with mine and pressed against my chest. I felt his thumb brush my skin.

"Yes to what?"

"Yes to being your husband," I said. All the foolish doubts I'd had were gone. Completely gone. And I knew in my heart it had nothing to do with the fact that I'd been able to let him make love to me. It had happened before that. It had happened when I'd woken up in his arms... when he'd still been there and so had I.

"Yeah, you did." Luca's lips were at the back of my neck and I was sure I could feel him smiling.

I snuggled closer to him and closed my eyes. "Good," I murmured tiredly. "Just making sure," I added before the peacefulness of sleep in the arms of the man I was going to spend the rest of my life with claimed me.

EPILOGUE

LUCA

+4

THREE MONTHS LATER

"What do you think?" I asked as I held Remy against my chest.

His back was to my front and he automatically reached up to put one of his hands over one of mine. The ocean breeze was gentle that day, so I had no trouble hearing him when he whispered, "Beautiful."

Coming back to the house in the Hamptons had been a spur-of-the-moment trip after Gio had remembered details about the place. Dr. Taylor had been the one to suggest that a trip to New York might be a good thing for my son to help him continue to remember things from his past.

"I was thinking we might get married here," I said to Remy. "Just you and me and a few people like Gio, my brothers, Aleks. We can do something bigger for our families back in Seattle."

Remy leaned back against me and turned his head so he could kiss me. "It's perfect," he said. He rested his head against me so he could just watch the water. We were standing near my mother's bench, the one she'd spent hours on every day as she'd watched the water. It made it feel like she was there with us.

"My mother would have loved you," I murmured.

Remy smiled and closed his eyes for a moment. "I want you to tell me everything about her," he responded.

That would be an easy thing to do because even though I hadn't had my mother for long, to this day, I remembered everything about her.

We stood there for a while, just taking in the vast ocean before us. We never really talked about the night I'd promised to bring Remy here to this place because that night no longer defined us. I still had moments that I had to work through where the guilt would become overwhelming, but I was starting to accept that maybe that was just the way things would be. Most days I wouldn't focus on the boy I'd been forced to leave behind but rather the man I'd been lucky enough to find again. On the rare days when I would wonder if there could have been a way I could have saved the young man I'd known only as Billy, it was Remy who was there to hold me and let me go through all those emotions.

To feel them.

Just like I was there for him when the urge for a hit would catch him out of the blue. While Remy had started going to NA meetings again and had found himself a new sponsor, it was still me he came to first when those urges became too much to handle. On the really bad days, we relied on the cold shower method and I held him as he let out tears of frustration and anger. On the days where the need wasn't as prominent, we'd try to work through it using the methods Remy's new therapist had provided.

It was difficult for Remy to rely on others to help him fight all the battles he'd been dealing with on his own for so long. But watching my son go through the same thing had made Remy want to be a role model for Gio. While my son continued to work through his own issues, his relationship with both me and Remy had continued to improve. He was still living at the hospital, but he was spending more and more time with us as he adjusted to what in his life had been real and what hadn't. He'd finally started to accept that Kurt hadn't been his husband, but he was still confused by his feelings for the man. Remy and Aleks were the ones he talked to the most when it came to things related to his abduction. I knew it was just a matter of time before he was ready to share those details with me, but for now, I was happy to take on the role of his father in any way that he let me. And I was beyond eager to have him come home.

Remy and I had ended up buying a home that was close to Aleks and Vaughn's in a quiet neighborhood. I was still adjusting to the idea of having people in my life that I would have to worry about on a near constant basis when it came to my enemies. But I was also learning that maybe there weren't as many enemies out there as there'd once been. And moving to Seattle had certainly helped ease my discomfort.

I still did what Ronan did and made sure my loved ones always had someone with them, but I made sure they were men and women who were part of our lives beyond just being hired guns. It wasn't something I'd ever admit to Ronan, but he'd been right about family and the value of having people around you could trust to watch your back and whose backs you could watch in return. It had been me and my brothers for so long that I'd forgotten what family really meant.

I'd also taken more of a backseat role at work. The mentality that I always needed to win and make money and own more had begun to change. Life was now about making sure my family was provided for, but more importantly, that *I* was there for my family. Literally.

Violet and her great-aunt were a regular part of our lives. We saw them nearly every day and Violet was thriving in Marilyn's care. They lived only a few miles from us, and we happily babysat several times a week with Violet sometimes even sleeping over at our house.

While Remy had gone back to work at Barretti Security Group, he'd also begun to sneak peeks at casting calls, specifically for voice-over actors. He hadn't wanted to commit to the idea of making something like that a full-time career, despite the fact that I could afford to support him while he pursued it. I suspected it was more that he was afraid to fail at something so soon after getting back on his feet. He'd also started taking acting lessons and while he didn't have any immediate plans to be in any kind of productions, he was enjoying learning the process behind and in front of the camera.

Remy had also been meeting with Ronan and several of his team members over the past few months to share information about the men and women who'd held him captive for so long. Ronan had already managed to shut down one of the cells outside of Chicago. His information had come directly from Remy, and at least half a dozen kids had been saved. My brother, King, had reluctantly agreed to work with Ronan and his men, though my brother still wasn't overly trusting of the group. Con had returned to Las Vegas for a few fights over the past several months, but in between he would travel to Seattle to visit us and spend time with Gio. My son had started to remember who his uncles were, so each of them, aside from Lex, spent as much time with him as they could.

I refused to let my thoughts drift to Lex because it would ruin this moment I'd been dreaming of for so long with Remy. My brother was okay, so I supposed that was all that really mattered.

"Luca," Remy said as he patted my hand. "What is that?" he asked as he pointed at the water. I looked back and forth to try to see what he was talking about, but nothing stood out.

"I don't—" I began, but then I saw it. A flash of gray in the water.

My heart leapt in my chest as I realized I was going to be able to give the man I loved *everything* I'd promised him so long ago.

"Is it—" Remy asked excitedly.

"Yes," I said. Just as I confirmed it, a second fin appeared and then a third.

"Oh my God," Remy whispered. We watched as the group of dolphins began growing and growing.

I kissed Remy's cheek and said, "I love you."

He lifted my hand to his mouth and kissed my palm and then repeated the words back to me. Then he turned to face me and started stripping off his clothes. I smiled and reached for the top button on my shirt.

"Are you sure?" I asked.

The smile on Remy's face lit up his entire expression. He nodded and then he was kicking off his shoes. I had to hurry to catch up to him. My pants had barely cleared my ankles when Remy grabbed my hand. We both began running toward the water's edge, dressed in only our underwear.

As we swam out to meet the group of dolphins, there were two things I knew for sure.

This time I *would* touch one of the beautiful animals.

And I'd do it with the love of my life at my side.

14

REMY

"You realize that it's going to be a lot harder to say no to getting a dog now that you've touched about a dozen dolphins," Luca said as we stepped out of the water. I was still riding the natural high of interacting with the beautiful animals. I practically threw myself into Luca's arms.

"Thank you," I said. Seeing the dolphins had been a dream in itself but to have actually been able to swim with them…

"You're welcome, baby," Luca said as he held me.

"And we're definitely getting a dog," I said. "But I claim naming rights."

Luca laughed in my ear and said, "Deal." He started to say something else, but a voice calling from the house caught our attention.

We saw Gio waving at us from near the pool. We quickly pulled our clothes on and then hurried to the young man.

"Is everything okay?" Luca asked worriedly.

While Gio looked physically better than he had a few months earlier, he was still struggling to get to his full health, both physically and mentally. Luca had been nervous about this trip to the Hamptons, but we had plenty of support in the form of Gio's uncles to help us watch out for the teenager.

We'd only just arrived that morning, but already Gio was starting to ask questions about the house and the area. His memories at that point were pretty simple, but we knew there would be a time when he might want to see the place where his mother had been killed or the house he'd grown up in before his abduction. Those were things we'd deal with when we needed to. Right now was all about Gio taking things at the pace that he needed.

"Um, yeah," Gio began. "Con—I mean, Uncle Con—said you should come to the house. There's someone here... Dad."

Luca and I both froze at the title. It was the first time Gio had actually called Luca that. I knew Luca was likely struggling to not completely lose it because he'd been dreaming of this moment. I reached for his hand just so I could give his fingers a squeeze.

"Um, yeah, okay, we're coming," Luca said. His voice sounded thick and uneven, and I suspected he was doing everything he could to keep his cool and not make a big deal out of things. Luca took a step forward, but I dropped his hand so he could walk to the house next to his son.

But instead of walking away, Gio held his ground, so Luca stopped. "Thanks for bringing me here, Dad. It's really cool."

Luca tried to say something but gave up and then reached out to put his arms around his son. I smiled at that because Luca was rarely a man who was at a loss for words. Gio, for his part, seemed a little uncomfortable at first, but then he was hugging his father back. As much as I loved swimming with the dolphins, this moment would be what I would always remember about being at this house for the first time.

Luca held his son for a moment, then kept his arm around his shoulders as they started to walk back toward the house. But he stopped after just a few steps and held out his free hand to me expectantly. I hurried to catch up to them and felt my heart turn to mush when he closed his fingers around mine.

It took just moments to get inside and to the front part of the house. We walked past the foyer, which was empty, and into the library next to it. I saw Vaughn, Aleks, Con, and King first. I immediately noticed how quiet they all were. Tension hung in the air and I steeled myself for whoever the visitor was. What if it was someone from Luca's past? What if it was a threat?

I turned to seek out the stranger and saw two men standing near the fireplace. I didn't recognize either of them, but when Luca breathed, "Lex," my breath caught in my lungs. Luca dropped my hand and hurried across the room to his youngest brother. I couldn't help but notice that all of the other brothers had remained silent and weren't moving to join in on the embrace.

I started to sidle up to Aleks to see if I could ask him what was going on when my eyes caught on Lex as he turned to face his brother. The fact that he was wearing sunglasses inside threw me at first, until I noticed what he was holding in his hand. I felt my heart drop as my mind connected the dots. I wanted to warn Luca, because I knew he was too excited to even notice what everyone else had.

Sure enough, Luca walked straight up to Lex and embraced him hard. "Lex, thank God. We've been so worried about you," Luca said. He pulled back and opened his mouth to say something else when his eyes caught on the sunglasses that his brother hadn't taken off, despite the room being quite dim. And then his gaze fell to the red and white stick in his brother's right hand.

"What—" was all Luca got out as his mind came to the same realization that the rest of us had already reached.

That Lex, the youngest of the brothers, was blind.

44

"Holy shit," I bit out upon walking into the bedroom I shared with Luca. Considering the events of the day, I hadn't been expecting to see my soon-to-be husband at all that night. After Lex's arrival, there'd been a wave of awkwardness that had lasted several tense minutes until the man with Lex had introduced himself to Luca and me.

In all honesty, at the moment I couldn't even remember the man's name because I was still in shock over the fact that Luca's youngest brother had lost his sight. Since there'd been no mention of that in all of the time I'd known any of the brothers, I'd figured that had been the reason none of them had heard from Lex for so long.

I'd only caught bits and pieces of the conversation that'd followed because I'd been helping Aleks get refreshments and move everyone to the living room where there was more seating. Whatever condition Lex was suffering from, he'd indicated it was permanent after all of the brothers except for King had insisted that Lex see all manner of specialists for more opinions. I'd felt sorry for Lex because I'd seen a hint of the treatment he'd probably received as a child from his older, more protective brothers. I had no idea what Lex was like regularly, but he'd definitely been quiet. When his brothers had finally finished talking *at* him, Lex had asked them all to sit down so that he could go through his condition once and only once. I'd admired the way he'd put his foot down with his brothers, but I hadn't missed the fact that while doing so, he'd seemed to lean heavily on the man with him.

Both literally and figuratively.

While Luca and the other brothers had tried to process the discovery about Lex, Lex had started talking to Gio and they'd begun to share memories of one another. Lex had told funny stories about all the trouble his brothers had gotten into when they'd been kids, and that had helped lighten the mood considerably. Dinner had been a much lighter affair and most of it had been spent reminiscing. Topics like Gio's abduction and Lex's condition had been carefully avoided. I'd excused myself around midnight, along with Aleks and Gio, so that we could leave the brothers to talk amongst themselves, but I'd figured they would spend most of the night together.

"Why aren't you with your brothers?" I asked. Luca was standing at the window that overlooked the ocean. It was night out, but he'd opened the window so we could hear the roll of the waves coming in. I went to stand behind him and held him like he'd held me on the beach earlier in the day.

"Lex was tired," he said softly.

"I'm sorry, Luca. I can't even imagine what you guys are going through right now."

Luca covered my hand where it was resting on his chest. "He

293

seems okay with it," Luca said. "I guess he's had time to accept it. He asked us to do the same."

I knew how difficult such a request would be for Luca. He would want to fix things for Lex. It explained why Lex had gone silent for so long. If his brothers had known about his condition, he likely would've been inundated with the same responses he'd gotten today about getting second opinions and surgical options and such.

"Let's go to bed, Luca," I offered.

Luca nodded, but then said, "I've got a surprise for you first."

I shook my head because the man had given me more than enough surprises. But when I went to argue with him, I saw what he hadn't said... that *he* needed this moment to distract himself from his brother. No one was more familiar with the need for distraction than me, so I quickly said, "What is it?"

Luca smiled and took my hand to lead me to the bed. In the three months since we'd had sex for the first time, we'd been on each other on a near constant basis. For someone who'd been so abhorrent of sex before, I'd done a complete one-eighty.

Because sex with Luca wasn't sex at all. It was an experience, a new beginning each time.

"I believe I promised you a taste of Harry and Draco," Luca said as he kicked off his shoes.

I opened my mouth in shock and said, "You're kidding, right?"

Luca pulled out a few sheets of paper from the inside of his jacket pocket.

"Where do you want to do this?" he asked. I practically jumped on the bed and sat cross-legged at the foot of it. I pointed at the head-board. Luca grinned and slipped off his jacket, then sat down on the bed with his back against the headboard. He extended his legs and then made a big production of reaching into his discarded jacket and pulling out a huge pair of glasses. I nearly laughed because there was actually no glass in them. But they sure did look a lot like the type of glasses a certain Quidditch-loving wizard wore.

Luca made a show of clearing his throat as he opened up the papers. It was all I could do not to laugh. He was so different from the man I'd met so many months ago, and yet he wasn't. I'd seen this side of him only a handful of times. But in the past few months I'd seen more and more of the real Luca come out, and only on the rarest of occasions did I see the man who'd been comfortable toting around a gun and kicking the asses of bad guys to get what he wanted.

"Harry and His Big Wand," Luca began. I couldn't help but laugh at the ridiculous title. Luca looked over his glasses at me in all seriousness, and I lifted my hand to my mouth and made the motion of zipping my lips.

"Harry peered around the corner, his heart racing. The last thing he wanted was another confrontation with Draco. He needed to find Hermione and Ron and maybe get some Quidditch practice in. Since there was no one around, he decided to make a run for it, but as soon as he rounded the building, a figure stepped out. It was Draco. Harry swallowed hard at the sight of Draco's wand. As much as he hated Draco, he'd always been impressed with how he handled his wand."

I was trying so hard not to laugh that I nearly bit my lip in two. Thank God the man was better at business than he was at writing.

I ended up tuning out the next little bit as I watched Luca get more comfortable. He crossed his legs as he read and scratched at his jaw. Just those little moves had me getting hot and bothered.

"Hey, are you even listening?" Luca asked with mock irritation. "We're getting to the good stuff."

"I'm listening," I assured him. "It's good," I managed to say, though he eyed me pretty hard.

"When Draco stepped forward, Harry had no choice but to go backwards. His back hit the tree behind him, but before he could move, Draco was in his face. Harry couldn't help but notice how good Draco smelled. And then he remembered that they were sworn enemies and he shouldn't be smelling Draco. 'What do you want, Draco?' Harry asked. He practically jumped out of his skin when Draco lifted his hand like he was going to cast a spell on him. Draco's wand brushed over Harry's and Harry felt sparks shoot up and down his arm. 'Isn't it obvious?' Draco asked. Why did his voice suddenly sound so much deeper? Why did Harry want to do whatever the boy said? And why was it no longer *just* Harry's actual wand that was hard?"

Luca looked up at me as if to make sure I was still paying attention. Maybe if it'd been any other man reading the ridiculous lines, I would've been on the floor in tears. Or I would've at least cared what Harry did with Draco's wand. But at the moment, I had only one man's wand on my mind.

"What do you think?" Luca asked. "Pretty good, right?"

"I think you should put the pages down," I said as I reached for the hem of my shirt and lifted it teasingly so he could see a strip of my belly. Luca froze in place as I revealed a little bit more of myself to him. When my hands stopped, his eyes jumped to my face. Then he was tossing the pages aside and crawling across the bed to reach me. I landed on my back with his big, heavy body covering mine.

"Note to self," he murmured. "Write more Harry Potter porn-fic," he said right before he kissed me.

"I thought it was *fan*-fic," I corrected between kisses.

He growled at me because he couldn't kiss me the way he wanted while I was trying to talk. I couldn't help but laugh, but when his hand settled on *my* wand, I was a goner. He nodded approvingly, then used his free hand to reach for the fake glasses.

"Leave them on," I murmured. "I'm about to get lucky with Harry Potter."

This time it was Luca's turn to laugh.

It was a sound I knew I'd never get tired of. Not five minutes from now, not five years from now, not even fifty years from now.

I'd never get tired of it.

And I'd never forget it.

THE END

ABOUT THE AUTHOR

Dear Reader,

I hope you enjoyed Luca and Remy's story. And yes, Lex will be getting his chance at love in the next book in the series!

As an independent author, I am always grateful for feedback so if you have the time and desire, please leave a review, good or bad, so I can continue to find out what my readers like and don't like. You can also send me feedback via email at sloane@sloanekennedy.com

Join my Facebook Fan Group: Sloane's Secret Sinners

Connect with me:
www.sloanekennedy.com
sloane@sloanekennedy.com

ALSO BY SLOANE KENNEDY

(Note: Not all titles will be available on all retail sites)

The Escort Series
Gabriel's Rule (M/F)

Shane's Fall (M/F)

Logan's Need (M/M)

Barretti Security Series
Loving Vin (M/F)

Redeeming Rafe (M/M)

Saving Ren (M/M/M)

Freeing Zane (M/M)

Finding Series
Finding Home (M/M/M)

Finding Trust (M/M)

Finding Peace (M/M)

Finding Forgiveness (M/M)

Finding Hope (M/M/M)

Love in Eden
Always Mine (M/M)

Pelican Bay Series
Locked in Silence (M/M)

Sanctuary Found (M/M)

The Truth Within (M/M)

The Protectors

Absolution (M/M/M)

Salvation (M/M)

Retribution (M/M)

Forsaken (M/M)

Vengeance (M/M/M)

A Protectors Family Christmas

Atonement (M/M)

Revelation (M/M)

Redemption (M/M)

Defiance (M/M)

Unexpected (M/M/M)

Shattered (M/M)

Unbroken (M/M)

Protecting Elliot: A Protectors Novella (M/M)

Discovering Daisy: A Protectors Novella (M/M/F)

Pretend You're Mine: A Protectors Short Story (M/M)

Non-Series

Four Ever (M/M/M/M)

Letting Go (M/F)

Short Stories

A Touch of Color

Catching Orion

Twist of Fate Series (co-writing with Lucy Lennox)

Lost and Found (M/M)

Safe and Sound (M/M)

Body and Soul (M/M)

Crossover Books with Lucy Lennox

Made Mine: A Protectors/Made Marian Crossover (M/M)

The following titles are available in audiobook format with more on the way:

Locked in Silence

Sanctuary Found

The Truth Within

Absolution

Salvation

Retribution

Logan's Need

Redeeming Rafe

Saving Ren

Freeing Zane

Forsaken

Vengeance

Finding Home

Finding Trust

Finding Peace

Four Ever

Lost and Found

Safe and Sound

Body and Soul

Made Mine